W(

By
Alex Martin

Book Five
The Katherine Wheel Series

ACKNOWLEDGMENTS

My heartfelt thanks go to Phil, as always.

Sincere thanks to the Semi-Colons; for their unswerving, honest but constructive criticism.

Thanks to Tom for giving up some of his holiday to edit the first draft with his incisive pen.

Thanks go to Jane Dixon-Smith of
http://www.jdsmith-design.com/
for her professional and skilful interpretation of my ideas for the cover.

Appreciative thanks to the Museum for the Auxiliary Transport Service, at The Maidenhead Heritage Centre https://atamuseum.org/ who were incredibly helpful and patient with my detailed enquiries. Likewise, the tourist office at Bayeux, France http://www.bayeux-bessin-tourisme.com/ and the Caen War Memorial Museum https://normandy.memorial-caen.com/ who gave me their time and expertise.

Spencer the Rover – Traditional folk song

This tune was composed by Spencer the Rover
As valiant a man as ever left home
And he had been much reduced
Which caused great confusion
And that was the reason he started to roam

In Yorkshire near Rotherham, he had been on the ramble
Weary of traveling, he sat down to rest
By the foot of yon' mountain
Lays a clear flowing fountain
With bread and cold water he himself did refresh
With the night fast approaching, to the woods he resorted
*With **woodbine and ivy** his bed for to make...*

Anon

CHAPTER ONE
CHEADLE MANOR
JULY 1939

The heat of the summer's day drove Charlotte Flintock-Smythe inside Cheadle Manor. The shade provided by the octagonal hall soothed the dazzle from her eyes and she welcomed the chill of the marble tiles through her thin summer sandals. She paused a moment at the foot of the grand staircase amongst the green potted palms, wondering what to do with herself.

Lottie was at a loose end now her school days were over. Her final term had been hectic with examinations, leaving rituals and the more public duties she had to perform as head girl of her private school. Now she had nothing to do but worry about her beloved grandmother, who lay upstairs on her sickbed waiting for the doctor to call and wonder whether she'd see Al Phipps from the Katherine Wheel Garage anytime soon. She hadn't seen him since the Easter holidays and longed to catch up, see how he was, discover how he felt about her. She'd not stopped thinking about him all through this last, busy term of school life. The whole summer stretched ahead and seeing Al was her top priority.

Since he'd been banished from the manor by her grandmother after that disastrous day by the river a few years ago, Lottie had had to find ways to see Al away from the estate and Granny's long tentacles. Her grandmother might be bedridden, but she knew every tiny thing that anyone got up to. Lottie suspected several spies among the staff, but none would admit to it. She knew why Granny had banned Al, she'd lost her temper in haste and wouldn't backtrack. Lottie had a temper herself and understood, but it had made things awkward. A lot depended on Granny getting a clean bill of health. Not only would it mean her grandmother wasn't as ill as everyone feared, but Lottie

1

would be free to gallivant with Al out of her reach instead of staying home to help her beleaguered mother look after the demanding patient.

Andrews, the butler, disturbed her reverie by answering the doctor's rap on the heavy oak front door but as soon as Dr Benson entered the large hall, her widowed mother, Cassandra, appeared from the study and whisked him upstairs to see Lady Smythe, leaving Andrews with nothing to do but retire behind the green baize door for servants.

A strange, unpleasant smell emanated from upstairs whenever her grandmother's bedroom door was left open to the galleried landing. She was glad when it finally shut. Lottie retreated to the drawing room to wait for the doctor's verdict.

With its owner absent, she took her grandmother's chair. The strategic position of Lady Smythe's 'throne', as everyone in the family (bar its owner) called it, guaranteed a commanding view of the large room and all the doors leading off the hall beyond, if the double doors were left open. Lottie made sure they were as wide as they could go and sat waiting, tense and expectant.

The sound of the front door opening unexpectedly made her jump. Her sister, Isobel, who, at sixteen, was almost three years younger than her, passed the drawing room door, looking prettier than ever.

"Hello, Lottie, any news? I saw Dr Benson's car on the drive." Isobel looked flushed and her flyaway blond hair stuck to her forehead. Anyone else would have looked a mess.

"Yes, he's with Granny now." Lottie jerked her much darker head up towards their grandmother's bedroom.

"Is he? Oh, I do hope she's better. I'll be down in a sec. Just got to change out of these shorts. I've been out on a bike ride and I need to freshen up - it's so hot!"

"Oh? Where did you go?"

"Only down to the garage to see Al."

Isobel trotted lightly up the grand staircase and disappeared into her room.

Lottie returned to sitting, waiting and fuming. How come Isobel had more freedom than her? She would make more use of the ancient pushbike herself from now on. It simply wasn't fair that their mother expected Lottie to help and not Isobel. It was true that she was closer to Lady Smythe than Isobel, or anyone else for that matter, but it still seemed unjust.

Every thirty seconds her eyes darted towards the upper floor. Even before she saw young Dr Benson, she heard the soft closure of Lady Smythe's bedroom door, followed by his footsteps along the wide, T-shaped landing.

By the time his brogues hit the last stair, Lottie stood at its base, one hand on the curved balustrade, braced for impact. "Well, doctor?"

Simon Benson smiled - the perfunctory professional smile of a medic about to break bad news. "It's not good, I'm afraid, Charlotte. Your grandmother is suffering from gangrene as a direct result of the diabetes mellitus."

Lottie's hand clenched on the carved wooden banister. "Gangrene? I thought that only happened to wounded soldiers."

Dr Benson shook his head. "Sadly, no."

Lottie lowered her voice. "Is that what's causing the awful stink?"

Dr Benson dispensed with his false smile. "That's right."

"But what can be done?"

"I'm not sure we should discuss this without your mother." Dr Benson looked anxiously behind him.

"Why?" Lottie's chin poked forwards.

Just then, her mother descended the stairs with an unusually heavy tread. Lottie loved her mother dearly, but she wished she'd break free of the perennial grief that enveloped her like the long, floaty cardigans she favoured.

Cassandra Flintock-Smythe never complained and she always had a smile for her girls, but she never looked truly happy. Tall, with her fair hair cropped fashionably short, her mother always looked elegant and poised. It was easy to see where Isobel's fine bone structure originated. If only those genes had been shared out equally with her. Lottie had neither her mother's height nor looks.

There was no denying it; she was the spitting image of her shorter grandmother and had inherited Lady Smythe's beaky nose and strong, dark features. Lottie tried every day of her life not to resent this and usually failed. Her only consolation was the sharp brain she'd also acquired from her.

"Let's go into the drawing room, shall we?" Cassandra ushered them into Lottie's earlier waiting room.

They all gravitated towards the sofas on either side of the massive fireplace which, though empty, provided a focal point around which they each sat, seeking comfort.

"Do you think I should find Isobel to hear the news?" Cassandra spoke as if to herself, as she often did, as if she was talking to her husband, who had died so long ago, Lottie struggled to remember him. She looked at her father's portrait on the grand piano. Douglas Flintock-Smythe smiled back at her, looking the same as always, his mouth drawn up in a carefree laugh, his head thrown back slightly, showing his chiselled cheekbones to advantage. He was wearing a white boiler suit, customary for racing drivers in the 'twenties and held a leather balaclava and goggles in his hand. His other hand rested against a low-slung racing car sporting the number five on its bonnet. Although black and white, the photograph revealed the sparkle in his eyes and Lottie had no trouble remembering how blue they had been. But, however charming, her father was no longer here, and only she could answer her mother's anxious question.

"No, Mother. Isobel is too young to hear this, but I'm not, so come on Dr Benson, spill the beans." Lottie smiled encouragement at the doctor and squared her shoulders in readiness.

"Right," Dr Benson took a deep breath, "it won't prevent the diabetes taking further hold but, in order to stop the gangrene taking your grandmother's life, we must amputate her toes."

"What?" Lottie gripped the arm of her seat.

Cassandra spoke for the doctor. "That's right, Lottie, I saw it all the time in the war. Once the feet go black, there's no other choice. It will be unpleasant but not as much as the alternative."

"But the risks! Will she have to go to hospital? Granny would hate that."

Simon Benson shook his head. "No, I can perform the operation here. I will ask my father to assist. He knows your grandmother well and his presence would calm her."

"Oh yes, that is a good idea. Mother thinks the world of him, and she would find that very reassuring." Cassandra nodded her agreement. "And, of course, Simon, please let us know what you will need in the room."

"Yes, I will. Here's a list of requirements." He began to scrawl on a notepad. "Scrupulous hygiene will, of course, be essential."

"I'll give it to the housekeeper and make sure Mrs Andrews cleans the room herself, with my personal supervision." Cassandra took the slip of paper Dr Benson had scribbled on. "That all looks very straightforward."

Lottie chipped in, now she had her breath back. "But, Dr Benson, forgive me, but you said this wouldn't help the diabetes - so what's the point of putting her through it?"

"That's a fair question, Charlotte. She would lose the toes anyway as they would die back for lack of circulation and the gangrene would spread further up her legs, if not arrested. It would lead to a very unpleasant death."

Lottie swallowed hard. "But...isn't she going to die anyway?"

Dr Benson nodded briskly. "Yes, she is, I'm sorry to say, but we can strive to make her situation as comfortable as possible. Regrettably, the new sulphur drugs I had prescribed have not had the desired effect, leaving us with no alternative."

"I see," Lottie said, the doubt she felt showing in her voice. "But there are risks with anaesthetic, aren't there?"

Cassandra intervened. "You must allow the doctor to make his medical decisions without questioning everything."

Dr Benson shook his head. "No, Charlotte's concern is completely understandable and it's best you both know all the implications. There *is* a real risk of a heart attack from the trauma of the procedure. Patients with diabetes are more vulnerable to a cardiac arrest at any time. Again, this is because their circulatory system is compromised by the disease."

"And what causes this dreadful diabetes?" Lottie had to know.

Dr Benson's face was grave. "We believe it is diet related, probably due to the intake of too much sugar."

Lady Smythe's consumption of sweets, cakes and puddings was legendary. Lottie met her mother's eyes as they both recognised how the patient could so easily have brought this fate upon herself. Before she had taken to her bed, Lady Smythe could barely squeeze into her beloved armchair and had taken to ensconcing herself on the sofa where Lottie now sat, usually with a fire roaring up the chimney. She'd overheard a couple of the servants muttering - out of Lady Smythe's hearing - that her ladyship might have renounced her 'throne' but she would never give up her constant demand for sweet temptations.

They all looked up when Isobel entered the drawing room, as quietly as she did everything. She'd put on an attractive flowered dress and looked both demure and effortlessly elegant.

"Hello, darling," Cassandra extended her hand to her youngest daughter who came and sat next to her on the sofa opposite Lottie's.

"Hello, Mummy. Is this about Granny?"

Lottie thought how extraordinary it was that Isobel always looked beautiful, whatever her mood. At this moment, the carefree smile she'd worn after her bike ride had been replaced by a serious demeanour, befitting the occasion. Isobel looked solemn and worried but the little frown on her forehead merely underlined the regularity of her delicate features, enhancing her perfect oval face. Lottie resisted the stab of jealousy that always smote her when she made unflattering comparisons between herself and her only sibling. Blonde like their mother and also blue-eyed like their father, Isobel's colouring couldn't have been more different to her sister's.

Lottie loved Isobel just as fiercely as she loved her grandmother. It was hard not being as pretty, that was all, especially when Al was around. His handsome face swam into her mind. Katy and Jem's son, Albert Phipps, had inherited his father's wavy chestnut hair and brown eyes. Al always had a ready quip on his smiling lips and Lottie wished he was here in this room right now.

Cassandra took Isobel's hand in hers. "Dr Benson has told us that Granny must have a little operation on her toes to make her more comfortable. The good news is that he can do it here, so she won't have to go to hospital. So, we'll have to be her nurses, won't we?"

"I'll help." Isobel looked from her mother to the doctor and back again.

"Of course, you will," Cassandra smiled at her and squeezed her hand and then looked quickly, no, guiltily, back at Lottie.

Hurt, Lottie did what she always did, covered her bruised feelings with a smile. "We'll all do our bit, Bella. We won't let Granny suffer. When do you expect to perform this gruesome deed, Dr Benson?" Lottie turned back to the only male amongst them, still sitting beside her.

"The sooner the better, I think. Would Wednesday suit you, Mrs Flintock-Smythe?"

Cassandra nodded. "Yes, best to get it over with, I suppose, and it'll give me today and tomorrow to have the bedroom scrubbed and get things organised. At least both my daughters are here. Isobel has her summer holidays and Lottie has finished school entirely, so I'll have their marvellous support."

Dr Benson stood up. "That's settled then. My father and I will be here at two o'clock on Wednesday afternoon, if that gives you enough time to prepare your mother?"

"Yes, that sounds ideal."

Cassandra got up and showed the doctor out through the hall.

Lottie looked at Bella, who had gone suspiciously quiet. "You do realise what Dr Benson is going to do, don't you?"

"Not entirely."

"Do you want to know?"

Isobel nodded.

"Chop Granny's toes off. They've gone black with gangrene and it will spread up her legs if it's not tackled."

Isobel's exquisite face blanched white and she put a hand to her mouth.

"God, Bella, you're not going to spew, are you?"

Isobel didn't answer but jumped up and ran from the room.

CHAPTER TWO
CHEADLE MANOR
JULY 1939

Lottie's mother popped her head round the drawing room door the next morning, while Lottie was taking a quiet moment to read the new book by Graham Green, a riveting thriller called 'The Confidential Agent' that she was finding hard to put down.

"Ah, there you are. You'd better come, Lottie, your grandmother's asking for you."

When Lottie entered her grandmother's sick room, the dreadful smell enveloped her, making her gag, despite the housekeeper's best efforts to clean it. She took a handkerchief from her pocket and clamped it over her mouth. How did her mother stand it? Sitting there in silent vigil, hugging her habitual cardigan around her thin frame for hours on end. Despite its generous proportions, Granny's bedchamber was crowded with dark walnut furniture carved in the fussy scrolls and embellishments so popular in her own Victorian era. No less than three wide wardrobes vied for space against the flock wallpaper and a similar number of tallboys were crammed between them. The overall effect was claustrophobic, especially so in the summer heat.

"Here, Lottie, put some drops of cologne on your hankie. It makes all the difference." Cassandra glanced at the bed and spoke very quietly. She lifted a dainty bottle from the side table next to her armchair and took off the lid.

Lottie seized it and sprinkled the delicate fragrance liberally on the small cotton square. She held it to her nose and inhaled the citrusy, herbal notes of Cassandra's favourite scent.

"Granny's dozing at the moment." Cassandra looked at the mountainous figure on the bed.

"Should we wake her, do you think?" Even Lottie, much as she adored her grandmother, quailed at incurring her wrath, however weak she might be.

As Cassandra hesitated, Lady Smythe stirred. "Cassandra, help me to sit up. Is that Charlotte I can hear? Good, I want a word with the dear girl."

Although she denied it vehemently, Lady Smythe's sight was failing. Lottie was unsure if her grandmother could see at all but there was nothing wrong with her voice. Her imperious tone was as strong as ever and made Lottie doubt she was dying. They went either side of the four-poster bed and got ready to heave the old woman up.

"On a count of three." Cassandra nodded to her daughter.

It took all of Lottie's strength to help shift her grandmother's bulk into an upright position. Already a heavy woman, her illness had made her a dead weight.

It took several hoists to get her sitting up before Lady Smythe was satisfied. "I suppose that will have to do. Cassandra, you may leave us."

"But..."

"I said, leave us, Cassandra. I want to speak to each of my granddaughters alone. In private. You may send Isobel up to me when Charlotte returns downstairs."

"Very well." Cassandra left her mother's bedside and slipped quietly out of the room.

"You may brush my hair, Charlotte. You have a way of doing it that no-one else appears to be able to master. I have to make do with Maisie these days. She's nowhere near as good as old Harrison. I blame using the servants' first names. Standards have slipped ever since the war. Maisie belongs below stairs, not above, but what can you do when no-one wants to fill a domestic vacancy anymore?"

Lottie was comforted by Lady Smythe's diatribe on the familiar subject of incompetent servants. She seemed much her old self - and this was before the operation. Maybe she'd make a full recovery once it was over. She tried not to shudder at the prospect of dealing with the dressings on amputated feet.

"What's the matter with you, child? You're getting as clumsy as Maisie. Pass me the mirror. Let me see if you've made a decent job of it."

Lottie laid down the brush with relief and exchanged it for the hand-mirror, holding it up so that her grandmother could study her appearance through squinted eyes.

"A little rouge, I think."

Obediently Lottie went to the ornate dressing table and picked up the enamelled rouge pot.

"You know, this pot is very valuable - Fabergé. Sir Robert bought it for me in Paris when your grandfather and I were on our honeymoon. Ah, Paris was glorious then. La belle époque, they called it and so it was, my dear child, so it was. You should visit your little French penfriend, now you have finished your schooling. She lives in Paris, doesn't she? What is her name?"

"Françoise."

"Oh, yes. Pretty name."

For a moment, Lady Smythe appeared to be lost in fond memories and Lottie did not feel she could intrude, so rarely did Lady Smythe reminisce in a joyful manner. Had there been a time when she was happy? She had never even hinted of it before.

"Paris was a beautiful city in my day. I wish you'd go and discover it for yourself. A little French couture would do wonders for your figure, Charlotte. Ah, when I was young, fashion was truly elegant, you know. None of this exposure of the legs that I find so vulgar. Our gowns even had small trains for quite minor occasions such as going to the theatre and supper parties. Oh, and the jewels! Which reminds me. Go back to my dressing table and open the small drawer on the left."

Lottie did as she was told.

"Have you done that?"

"Yes, Granny."

11

"Good. Take out the red jewellery box and bring it over here."

Lottie extracted the square velvet box, almost as wide as the drawer was deep and surprisingly heavy.

"Well, open it, child."

"It's locked."

"Oh, of course. The key is here, in my bedside cabinet. It is gold, pure gold, you cannot mistake it."

Lottie rummaged in the drawer amongst countless bottles of tablets, bags of sweets and lacy handkerchiefs. She found the shiny yellow key right at the back and lifted it out.

Carefully, she inserted the key into its matching gold lock. It fitted perfectly and opened the box with a smooth, precise click.

When she heard the little noise, Lady Smythe gave a sigh of satisfaction. "I want you to have my tiara. It is made of twenty-four carat gold and Indian diamonds. You will see that the diamonds are set between these small rubies. I hope the occasion will never arise for you to sell it but, if you ever are in dire straits, it would fetch a princely sum."

"I'm sure that won't be necessary."

"Don't be stupid, Charlotte, or contradict me. Lying here, I have nothing to do but listen to the wireless. I have heard about all this Fascist nonsense in Germany and I have grave misgivings. Winston Churchill is the only man who seems to understand what Hitler is doing with his Anschluss and taking over territories that don't belong to him, but everyone is calling him a warmonger. That ruddy Chamberlain is too weak to lead our country. All this talk of appeasement. It won't work, I tell you, the whole approach is naïve." Lady Smythe shook her head, making her jowls wobble. "You never knew your uncle Charles, my first-born and most beloved child, after whom you were named."

Lottie winced at this honesty. Her poor mother, always to have come second in her mother's affections, however lukewarm.

"Twenty-one. Dead at twenty-one. Your mother does her best, I know that, and I am very fond of her, but the estate is not as it once was. We used to have at least fifty servants in my day and not a speck of dust anywhere. You could write your name in the dust in here before I got Mrs Andrews to clean it more thoroughly."

Lottie opened her mouth to speak but her grandmother held up an imperious hand.

"Let me continue while I still have breath in my body. In the old days, your grandfather was master of the hunt and we had a full stable of hunters and hounds, as well as my black horses for the carriage. None of these raucous automobiles. I hated the car when Sir Robert bought one before the Great War and I still hate them now we have even more of the wretched things. Why, if it hadn't been for motor-racing, your father would still be alive."

Lady Smythe gazed out of the window, her eyes unfocussed but apparently seeing a different scene to the sweep of the driveway that Lottie could see. Lottie tried to picture her father but, as usual, could only visualise his photograph.

Lady Smythe's memories of him were obviously more vivid as she carried on her seamless narrative. "Driving at such a reckless speed; a family man too. Leaving your mother in the lurch. She's never got over it. I couldn't see what she saw in him in the first place, except some superficial American charm, but she was so happy. Now she goes around as if every week is a wet one."

Lottie had some sympathy with this view and said nothing in her father's defence. Life would have been so different with him around.

"Charlotte, you must consider your future. I trust you have no romantic associations in your life?"

Lottie was glad her grandmother's sight was failing. She could feel a flush spread from her neck to her eyebrows. "Um, no, not really." Lottie shook her head, blotted out the image of Al's handsome, smiling face.

Lady Smythe nodded. "I thought so. Charlotte, my dear, I am aware I have not got long to live. Now, lift the base of the jewel case. Go on. Lift it out."

Lottie prised the edge of the velvet inner casing with her fingernail and gingerly raised it. Underneath was a large envelope. Her name, written in fine copperplate writing, marched across its manila expanse.

"This is a letter for you, with some important papers. Take it out."

Lottie withdrew the envelope, which was bound with red ribbon and sealed with red wax of a darker hue.

Her grandmother's strident voice quivered with emotion. "It is imperative you read what's inside." Lady Smythe pointed a be-ringed finger at Lottie. "Before you do, know this, your mother finds the burden of running the estate very heavy. I'm doing what I know is best for you all. I want you to bear that in mind when you read my wishes. Do you understand?"

Lottie nodded.

"You may break the seal." Lady Smythe pointed her arthritic finger at the red wax.

The seal was strong. Lottie had to fetch the paperknife from Lady Smythe's dressing table. She slid it under the flap of the envelope, splaying the paper into a frayed edge. Her grandmother nodded encouragement as she slipped her hand inside and drew out a document. The stiff legal paper crackled as she spread it out. Lottie quickly scanned the words, stumbling over some of the stilted, old-fashioned language. Their meaning, however, was clear.

When she had finished, she turned it over, but the other side was blank. Like her mind.

"You cannot mean to do this, Granny."

"But I do, child."

"But why? What about Mummy...and Isobel?"

"It is your mother I was most concerned about when I made this arrangement, oh, over two years ago now. She is worn out by the burden of running the estate. It is too much for her. When I am gone, as I soon will be..." Lady Smythe raised her blue-veined hand. "Don't interrupt me. Your mother will have carried the heavy duty for long enough by the time you inherit, five years from now.

"In fact, Sir Robert did something very similar in his will. I have never forgotten it. Further, he made sure that the estate can be carried on down the female line – a most unusual amendment for a baronet – but a sound one, I'm sure you will agree."

Lottie, though desperate to interrupt this startling monologue, remained silent, despite all the questions whirling through her brain.

"You see, the document states that the estate will remain in trust to you, and only you, until your twenty fifth birthday; Mr Leadbetter, and his useless junior partner, Mr Brown, are the legal trustees, but I am the primary trustee. In that capacity, I took the decision to entrust it to you. By then, Charlotte, my dearest girl, you will be mature and strong enough to take up the reins. You are intelligent and resourceful, and I know I can leave Cheadle Manor solely in your capable hands."

Lottie, struck dumb at this announcement, closed her mouth, which had dropped wide open.

Lady Smythe continued her seamless narrative. "I cannot see your mother remarrying now. There was a chance, once, with Lord Finch, but he has not visited since your father died. He married some heiress, I believe. New money, of course. Sadly, there has been no one else to suit your mother. So many boys died in the war. Both the eldest Ponsonby boys never came home, just like Charles. Luckily for the family, there is a younger child, but he's too young for Cassandra, and a wastrel by all accounts. No, that ship has now sailed."

Lady Smythe pushed herself up on her many pillows. The effort was ineffectual. She flopped back in the same position, looking exhausted. "So, Charlotte, you will inherit the estate, in its entirety, on your twenty-fifth birthday. By gifting it to you now, no tax will go to the grasping Chancellor. As things stand, I understand there are none due upon my death, as I was married to Sir Robert, but this makes sure of it, should the law change. It gives me much satisfaction to cheat the government, I must say."

"But what of Isobel? Surely, she has some right to share in the inheritance?"

"You know I have always prided myself on speaking plainly and I will not change now. It may pain you to hear this but there is nothing else for it. Your sister is extremely beautiful, whereas you, dear girl, are not. I'm sorry to say this, but you resemble Sir Robert's rather stocky line, although you do share some of my strong facial features which does offset the overall effect."

Lottie smarted under this criticism; despite its truth or perhaps because of it, it hurt.

Her grandmother, seemingly unaware of her granddaughter's distress, carried on in her loud, gravelly voice. "Douglas may have been an American but even I must allow he was handsome and his mother, Selina, was a very attractive woman. Isobel has inherited these rather, shall we say, alien genes and she must use them to her advantage and marry into a fortune." Lady Smythe nodded, as if agreeing with her own summary. "Yes, she is capable of it. She is a biddable, sweet girl who will appeal to many men."

She looked Lottie full in the face, her puffy eyes screwed up into narrow slits. "You have other qualities, Charlotte, and will run this estate as well as any man. I could have done the same in my time, had I chosen to do so, but Sir Robert was very set in his ways.

"Do you know - I envy you the freedom I am bequeathing you? You will be independent and authorised

16

to make decisions in your own right. Further, the estate will remain one entire whole, and not be broken in half. I know you will acquit yourself well because, my dear, we are very alike in character, are we not?"

"Yes, but..."

"No buts, Charlotte."

Lottie closed her mouth again. She was too shocked to say very much.

"Good, now put the will back underneath the tiara. Keep it safe and tell no-one you have it. Mr Leadbetter has another copy. It's all legally binding and effective from the first of December 1936 when I signed it and had it witnessed, just before King Edward's abdication. What a wretched business that was. Another pushy American of course."

Lady Smythe pointed her finger at the paper on Lottie's lap.

"You see? There's the date there, in black and white. You're good at mathematics – how many years remain before your twenty-fifth birthday?"

"It's five and three-quarter years until 26th April 1945." Lottie mumbled.

"Yes, quite right. I have been waiting for the right moment to give my will to you, but I see no reason to tell either your sister or your mother until after my death. Promise me you will not do so. It is enough that it is done; I do not wish to *personally* witness any distress." Lady Smythe shut her eyes. "I am tired now. Tell Isobel to come up and see me in half-an-hour, after I have slept a little."

Lottie got up, screwed up her nose and her courage and kissed her grandmother on her wrinkled forehead. At her request she closed the heavy blue curtains and left the darkened room clutching the jewellery box and the sheets of paper dynamite lurking within its red velvet folds.

CHAPTER THREE
CHEADLE MANOR
JULY 1939

"Granny says you're to go up in half-an-hour. She's sleeping for a bit." Lottie found Isobel in their old nursery, sorting out her paint-box.

They both loved this big, scruffy room. In front of one of the casement windows stood an old rocking horse, tatty from frequent gallops across imaginary paddocks. Shelves of dog-eared books they had read and re-read bided their time, patiently waiting for a rainy afternoon. Dolls and teddy bears, old companions of picnics and tea parties, leant together in a tired slump next to spinning tops and atlases. It was a place to feel safe in, their mutual refuge. Lottie resisted the sneaking suspicion that she was now an adult, a traitor trespassing inside it.

Isobel looked up from her task. "So, what did Granny say?"

Lottie hesitated. Her mind was in such disorder she didn't know what to reveal and what to hide until she had some time alone to think. "Um, she gave me her tiara."

"Golly, the one with the little rubies and diamonds?" Isobel took a bunch of paintbrushes and arranged them in an old vase.

"Yes."

"It be worth a bit."

"Hmm, and she said the oddest thing." Lottie wandered over to the window seat and stared out at the orchard below, reflecting that the comment about the jewellery was the least of what Granny had said, but she had to say *something.*

"What was that?"

"She sort of hinted I could sell it if my life was in danger. She seems to think there's another war coming." She decided not to disclose the strange business of the hidden will. For all she knew, it wasn't valid, just the mad wanderings of a sick old woman. No one could be that unfair, surely? She must consult Mr Leadbetter, the family solicitor. The time for that would come later. She had made her promise to remain silent and must stick to it.

Isobel shivered. "Perhaps it's just her illness making her nervous."

"Perhaps, but she's a sharp old trout and she listens to the wireless all day long."

"Grown-ups are always fretting about politics, though, aren't they?" Isobel shut the wooden lid of her paint-box with a snap.

"And usually with good reason. I'm going out for a walk." Lottie banged the door shut behind her.

***

Isobel needed a moment to think too, but not about herself. She was busy calculating Al's age. They had both been born on Christmas Eve, but he was her elder by three years. Al had left school a year ago and was working for his parents at the Katherine Wheel Garage and its rubber factory next door. If there was a war, he would be old enough to fight. She couldn't bear the thought of it.

She always found it easier to resolve problems when her hands were busy, so she opened the big cupboard in the corner where they stored all their craft-making things and took out all the chaotic heaps of paper, spreading them out on the worn Persian rug, ready to sort into neat piles, according to their size and weight. After half an hour she was satisfied with the result and felt much calmer, and she needed to be calm before she faced the ordeal of an interview with Granny.

Isobel had always struggled to love her grandmother and often wondered what Lottie found in the old dame to admire so much. Of course, it was generally understood that Lottie greatly resembled Lady Smythe in her younger days, but Isobel could never see the likeness. Lady Smythe was grossly overweight, highly autocratic and exceptionally critical. She terrified Isobel. Lottie, however, never showed an atom of fear when in their grandmother's presence, but then, she wasn't afraid of anything. In her final year at school Lottie had made a seamless progression into the position of head girl. Everyone respected her authority, and Isobel supposed in that regard she did resemble their grandmother. Being head girl was not something Isobel would ever aspire to. Having to give speeches to the girls and even sometimes parents on Sports Days would be her idea of sheer hell. School was bad enough without that and she still had another year to go before she could matriculate. She hated being away from home.

She was startled out of her reverie by the distant sound of Lady Smythe's handbell in the quiet house. It's ring was a familiar call to action and had been kept by her grandmother's side all her life, whether ill or not. Responding to its command with the unbidden reflex of a Pavlovian dog, Isobel's heart began to thump. She went to the mirror and smoothed down her wavy blonde hair, which was always straying from its velvet band. Her mother's hair was the same, although hers was now streaked prematurely with grey. Poor Mummy. If only she could find another man to make her happy.

The bell rang again. She could hesitate no longer. She left the haven of the well-worn nursery with its comforting boxes of jigsaws and faded dolls and walked along the galleried landing to her grandmother's room.

Isobel took a deep breath and turned the door-handle. Her grandmother's bedroom was dimly lit, making the large space gloomy and full of shadows. With the royal blue curtains drawn against the summer sunshine, the room was also airless, its fustiness emphasised by the sickly smell coming from its only occupant. A huge four-poster bed dominated the over-stuffed room, hung with matching brocade drapes, and the vast form of her grandmother sat upright against its silken bed-head, her hand hovering over the bell ready to ring it again. Even in the darkened room she looked ghastly, her wrinkled face almost as pale as her lace cap. But the overwhelming sensation on entering the sick room was the disgusting stench of gangrene.

Despite herself, Isobel gagged, lifting her hand to her mouth to stop the acid rising up from her protesting stomach, instinctively gravitating towards the waft of welcome air by the window.

"Ah, is that you Isobel?"

Isobel couldn't speak for fear of throwing up and hoped her vigorous nodding would suffice.

"Come here, no, closer to the bed, so that I can see you properly. Why are you nodding your head like a jack-in-the-box, you silly girl? What on earth took you so long? Did you not hear my bell?" Lady Smythe squinted at her.

Why, oh why, couldn't she see her from the window, which thankfully, someone had left open.

"No, it's no good, I can't see you clearly. Draw the curtains, child, so I may look at you."

With more haste than grace, Isobel drew the weighty old curtains back, making dust motes dance in the bright light. Surreptitiously, she also opened each of the casement windows a little wider, drawing a deep breath of fresh air with all three of them. The room, now flooded with sunbeams, felt immediately less forbidding, unlike her grandmother. She could now see that her lined face, above its folds of chins, was greyish-white with two over-bright circles of red on each cheek. The rouge only served to make the rest of her skin more ashen by comparison. Granny's eyes had sunk deep into their sockets and bore black shadows beneath them.

"Yes, yes, that will do. Now come over here to my bed."

"Coming, Granny." Isobel returned, far less swiftly.

"I have bequeathed my tiara to your sister. I'm sure she has already informed you."

"Yes, Granny."

"You shall have my sapphires. Fetch the blue box from the chest of drawers by the furthest window. The smaller drawer on the right-hand side." As her sister had done before her, Isobel withdrew a jewellery box and duly opened it in front of her grandmother. Nestled against heart-shaped rich navy velvet lay a delicate necklace, and matching drop earrings, set with little deep blue sapphires amongst sparkling diamonds. Their multifaceted surfaces caught the light and dazzled her. They were quite beautiful.

"Your mother begged me to sell these during the Depression, but I refused. I always meant for you girls to have my jewellery and the time has come to pass them on. At least this way you won't have to pay tax on them after I'm gone. Hold the necklace against your chest, Isobel. I wish to see the effect."

Isobel lifted the necklace over her head with a reverent hand. She felt uncomfortable wearing the old-fashioned chain but straightened her back when Granny scowled at her.

"That's better. Tall girls should never slouch. Lower your shoulders and turn your face to me. Yes, I can glimpse your beauty now. That little bit of blue suits your eyes. You could turn heads with your looks, Isobel. I think it will fall to you to marry well and rescue the estate from poverty. You must promise me that you will make a prudent match, for I believe you could attract anyone, even those of the highest of ranks, but please, no new money. Be sure it is someone of good breeding. Blood always counts, you know, and a better title wouldn't hurt."

"Granny, I'm not thinking of marrying anyone yet!"

"Not yet, no, but soon, or the manor will not survive. How old are you now?"

"I'm only sixteen."

"Ah, I thought you were older. Well, you shall be seventeen soon enough and must be presented at Court at the earliest opportunity. We cannot have the estate going to rack and ruin by waiting another year and, with the world in the state it's in, I doubt anyone will make a fuss."

"But, Granny, I might not love a rich man!"

"My dear, I insist you fall in love with a man of means. You must bestow your favours in a circumspect way and choose amongst those of your own rank, or above. The future of the family depends upon it."

"Why me? Why not Lottie? She'll be twenty next year."

"Charlotte has many qualities, but she does not share your beauty and she is too strong willed to please many men, and anyway, I doubt she'd be willing. She is more suited to an independent life, one with responsibilities. No, my child, the marriage market is your fate."

Isobel was shocked. Surely the days of being trapped into a marriage of convenience had gone out with the ark? How could she tell her grandmother that she had already decided to marry Al? But even though the factory and the Katherine Wheel Garage were doing well, he would never have enough money, even of the new variety, to save the manor.

"You are silent, my dear, but this is my dying wish. Oh yes, I know I do not have long but you cannot deny me this. I *must* have your promise before I die." Granny's voice had risen alarmingly.

Isobel tried to calm the older woman. "You won't die - the operation is going to make you better."

"Stuff and nonsense. There are no guarantees at this stage of one's life. Promise me you will oblige the family by making a good marriage. *Promise* me!" Lady Smythe's voice was querulous as well as loud.

"Er, of course, Granny, I will do my best but..."

"Enough! You have said enough, and I know you will not break your word to a dying woman. Go now. Take the sapphires and keep them safe but be sure to wear them at your presentation at Court. If your mother won't take you, I know someone who will, for a fee."

Isobel removed the sparkling jewels from around her neck and felt relieved when they nestled back into their slumbering box.

"Thank you for the jewels, Granny, they are lovely. I will always think of you when I look at them."

"And wear them, child, don't forget that. There is nothing like the flash of a diamond to attract attention. Use them well."

Her grandmother closed her eyes. Taking that as a dismissal, Isobel slipped off the chair and quietly left the room.

CHAPTER FOUR
CHEADLE MANOR
JULY 1939

Lottie resembled her grandmother in more ways than one. She'd been told not to look at the will, so she didn't. Strong willed yet disciplined, Lottie could not break her word once she'd given it. So, the document stayed in its binder within its red ribbon, under the diamonds and rubies - and under her bed.

She struggled to get through the following day without talking of it to anyone, especially her mother. How could she be the one to betray her grandmother's strange request and yet how could she keep it to herself behind her mother's back? Sworn to secrecy but feeling like a spy, she avoided company except at mealtimes and then snatched some food, pretending she was too busy to stay. Dr Benson called in the morning and kept her occupied, preparing the room after Mrs Andrews had scrubbed it. Her mother had offered to help but Lottie said she'd be glad of something to do – at least she could be honest about that - and she concentrated single-mindedly on the task in hand until Andrews sounded the dinner gong.

That evening, Lady Smythe's health dominated the conversation over dinner, just as much as she would have done, had she been present and presiding over the dining room table as usual, with her interminable monologues.

Lottie made her excuses to leave before the dessert, on the unassailable pretext of sitting with the source of her anxiety. Once upstairs, she read aloud from her new book to the accompaniment of her grandmother's snores. Annoyingly, if she stopped, Lady Smythe woke up and commanded her to continue where she had left off. It seemed her grandmother didn't miss a trick, even when appearing to be asleep. When Maisie brought in the dessert Lottie had refused, Lady Smythe polished it off without hesitation.

Lottie watched her grandmother despatch the sweet delight in disbelief. "Not worried about tomorrow, Granny?"

"Not a bit of it. What will be, will be, my dear, and meringue has always been my favourite. Could you pour me some extra cream?"

The next day, the day of the dreaded operation, was no less hot than the days that had preceded it. Straight after lunch, Lottie meticulously checked Lady Smythe's bedroom to make sure everything was ready before the two doctors arrived, glad to focus on something practical, and even more glad that her grandmother slept – soundly this time - through her inspection.

Lottie had set up a trolley by the bed, and had personally scrubbed it, ready to receive the doctors' instruments. She checked the bandages and cleaning utensils on the washstand for the hundredth time.

The door opened quietly, slowly. Cassandra and Isobel tip-toed in and joined Lottie in Lady Smythe's spotless bedroom. They entered as if glued together, both pale, both subdued and nervous but their silent presence somehow woke the old lady. They did their best to allay Lady Smythe's fears, uttering soothing words and fussing over her until she told them, in unequivocal terms, that she had none. Lottie held back, biding her time.

When Dr Benson and his father were ushered in by a wide-eyed Maisie, Lady Smythe demanded that Cassandra and Isobel left the room. Only then did Lottie come forward to hold her grandmother's hand and look deep into her eyes. No words were exchanged and yet they communed, soul to soul.

Young Dr Benson set out his medical implements with great precision before turning to address them. "We need to begin the operation, Lady Smythe. You are ready? Charlotte, you are welcome to be present, should you wish."

Lady Smythe kept her gaze on her eldest grandchild and nodded.

"I'll stay," Lottie said, returning the look and squeezing her grandmother's wrinkled hand. The jewels of Lady Smythe's rings dug into her palm. She felt the flesh spilling over around the metal bands and wondered if it hurt.

The elder Dr Benson leaned over the opposite side of the bed and placed the mask of chloroform over her grandmother's mouth and nose, explaining the procedure to the patient as he did so. Lottie experienced a moment of vicarious suffocation before, to the doctor's steady count, Lady Smythe lost consciousness and her breathing deepened.

Dr Benson nodded his white-haired head to his son.

Simon Benson picked up his scalpel and, before applying it, looked at Lottie, who still sat next to the bed holding her Grandmother's hand. "You may want to leave the room now, Charlotte. Your grandmother is unaware of what is happening. She will not know you have gone."

"I'll stay." Lottie looked at both men briefly and then returned her gaze to her grandmother's grey face.

The stench was initially worse. Much worse. Lottie struggled to control her nausea. She remembered the perfumed handkerchief her mother had given her earlier that morning and clamped it to her nose, relieved when the overwhelming desire to gag passed. She heard the plop of the severed toes in the kidney-shaped basin as they fell, one by one, into its metal bowl. She kept her eyes firmly on her grandmother's face, watching for any sign of consciousness and therefore pain, but there was none.

The operation seemed to last a lifetime. The elder doctor renewed the chloroform from time to time over Lady Smythe's face and checked her pulse often. Every now and then he would nod and smile reassuringly at Lottie, who watched anxiously, torn between repressing her desire to vomit and her fascination with the process.

Eventually, it was over. The stinking bowl was covered up and the wounds dressed with the spotless

27

bandages Lottie had laid out on the trolley. Old Dr Benson opened the window wider and took the amputated toes away, shutting the door behind him.

Lottie longed to go to the window and inhale the fresh air, but she stayed at her grandmother's side, grateful when the room gradually became less fetid. She was aware of Simon Benson's movements as he finished stitching and bandaging the wounds and went to the wash hand basin, tipped the jug of water into the china bowl, picked up the carbolic soap and scrubbed his hands vigorously with the bristle brush put ready for the purpose. Hearing this, Lottie felt it safe to look more closely at his handiwork. Her grandmother's feet were hygienically bandaged up in white bands of cotton, clean and no longer malodorous.

Lottie let out her breath more easily. "Will she feel pain afterwards, Dr?"

"Yes, it will be more painful now because her nerve endings are exposed. Only healthy tissue is left, you see. She will need regular morphine injections when she comes round."

"Of course, and you will administer them?"

Simon Benson nodded.

"When will she regain consciousness?" Lottie looked at her grandmother's face, deep in repose and surprisingly peaceful.

"Oh, quite soon - about an hour or so. My father will stay until she does. I'll dispose of the, er, unhealthy tissue and go about my rounds. I'll pop in later this evening before I finish for the day and give the first injection of morphine. I will leave you some oral medicine as well, in case it needs topping up during the night."

"Thank you, Doctor. I'll stay here, with your father and Granny."

"Splendid. Ah, here's my father now. Well, I'll leave you then." He offered his hand to shake.

Lottie couldn't take it. "Sorry, I'll just say goodbye, if you don't mind!"

The young doctor laughed softly. "Quite understandable. Don't worry about your grandmother. She's made of strong stuff."

Lottie laughed back with relief. "She is, isn't she?"

CHAPTER FIVE
KATHERINE WHEEL GARAGE
and CHEADLE MANOR
JULY 1939

"No, Al, *not* like that, I've told you. Oh, for goodness sake, give it here." Katy wrenched the gauge from her son's hands and barged him out of the way with her shoulder. "You have to be quite exact with this job, you see, or the engine just wastes fuel."

Her voice was softer now, but Al wasn't convinced. If only his mother wasn't so impatient. It was a lot easier when his father, Jem, was teaching him.

"Get behind the wheel and rev the engine, there's a good lad." Katy waved him towards the cab of the lorry.

Now this was something he *was* good at. Even his mother acknowledged his driving skills and after the disappointment of his higher school certificate results it was a little bit of pride to hang on to. He never thought he'd pass anyway but Mum had insisted he continue his education, despite his struggles with examination papers. He'd always preferred to *do* stuff rather than write about it.

He pressed the accelerator pedal and the engine screamed in protest.

"Not quite that much, you idiot." His mother never did mince words and with the factory so busy, her temper was shorter than ever.

He eased back on the throttle.

"A bit more...that's it...and stop." There was a bit of fiddling under the bonnet before his mother shouted. "Okay, once more, please."

He revved the engine again. It sounded much better.

"That's it. The timing's perfect now. Shouldn't have any more hiccups along the road." Katy emerged from the front of the lorry and smiled at him through the driver's window. "Fancy taking her out for a spin? There's a load I want delivered to Southampton. Think you can manage it on your own?"

Al grinned. Southampton was further than he'd ever driven solo.

"Of course, if you trust me that far?"

"Wouldn't ask you if I didn't."

Al laughed. "That is certainly true! I'll drive over to the depot and collect the goods. Where's it going to?"

"Army stores, just outside the city. They've really upped their demand for rubber seals for windscreens and quite a few other things besides. I'd be pleased if I didn't think the powers that be are building up for another bloody war." Katy wiped her greasy hands on a rag.

"Do you really think it'll come to that, Mum?"

"I hope not but the army doesn't spend that kind of money without good reason. Not that I'm complaining about the increased business. We've done alright, but it's been a hard few years and we've got off lightly compared to a lot of other people."

"Maybe we need a war to get things moving again?"

"Only someone as young as you who has never lived through a war would say anything so crass." She shoved a piece of paper through the window. "Here's the order and the address."

Al felt humiliated all over again at his mother's uncompromising words. Had she forgotten where she learned to be a mechanic in the first place? If it hadn't been for the last war she wouldn't have a garage, or a factory come to that, but he knew better than to remind her. Instead he reversed the lorry out of the garage hangar carefully, did a perfect three-point-turn and drove it around the back to the rubber factory.

Once the lorry was loaded up by Len Bradbury, the factory foreman, and Al had checked the straps three times under his careful supervision, he went to the forecourt and filled up with petrol.

His dad, Jem Phipps, was inside the shop, sorting the change in the till and he stuck his head out of the door when he heard the lorry pull up.

His kid sister, Lily, was there too, playing with a new batch of kittens in the sunshine outside. "Where are you off to in the lorry, Al? Can I come?"

"No, it's too far for you, I'm going to Southampton."

Jem looked up at him. "That's nearly thirty miles. Going on your own?"

"Yes, Mum's orders."

"I'm not sure I like the sound of that." Jem paused in his counting of pennies with his one good hand. He'd devised a method of dropping them back into the till as he counted, and Al never ceased to admire his dexterity.

"I'll be fine." He was miffed that his dad had less confidence in him than his ever-critical mother.

"Are you sure you know the route without anyone to navigate for you?"

"Yes, I've been there before with Len. Army depot just outside town. It's dead easy. Don't fuss, Dad."

"I can read the map for you," Lily stood up eagerly, holding a kitten in each arm.

Jem grunted his disapproval. "You'll stay right here, young lady. Where is your mother, Al? I never know where to find her these days. She doesn't stay still long enough in one place."

"In the garage workshop. She wanted to do a stock-take of supplies, I think she said."

"Did she now? Hmm, you wait here while I have a word with her." Jem closed the till drawer with enough force to make the coins inside it rattle and walked out on to the forecourt.

His father disappeared into the back of the workshop and Al finished topping up the petrol tank and screwed the cap back on, whilst ignoring Lily's pleas to come with him.

"No, Lily, Dad said you had to stay here. And who would look after those kittens if you were out all day? I might not be back till dark." This was unlikely in the long, last days of July, but Lily had no idea how long he'd be.

Lily pouted but went silent. It made her look even more like her mother, even though she was only twelve. They both had black curly hair, like a gypsy's, and big dark blue eyes, brimming with intelligence. They shared similar natures too, impatient and quick-tempered; sometimes Al wished they were less alike.

Al checked the petrol cap was securely fastened and turned to his little sister. "If I were you, I'd get them off the forecourt before it gets busy with the afternoon rush. They could easily get crushed under someone's wheels."

"I know that. I was just going to transfer them to the empty hen house anyway."

"There you are then."

Lily scooped up the rug skilfully, managing somehow to keep all four kittens inside and strode purposefully off towards the bungalow garden where their father grew vast quantities of vegetables to sell in the garage shop.

Al watched her go while he waited for his father. When Jem didn't reappear for a full ten minutes, he decided to take matters into his own hands and climbed back into the cab, gave the map a quick glance and started up the engine. There was still no sign of either of his parents, though he could hear raised voices emanating from the workshop. He sighed. He hated it when they argued and they seemed to be doing that a lot these days. He could usually crack a joke and break it up with a laugh but today he didn't have the patience. He was just wasting time and would be late back if he didn't get going.

He pressed the starter button on the Bedford and the engine roared into life. He put the lorry into gear and let off the handbrake. As he paused before joining the main London Road, he looked in his rear mirror to see

Katy and Jem running towards him and waving like mad. Grinning, he depressed the accelerator and swung out towards Cheadle Manor, the opposite direction to Southampton. If they were worried about him going alone, he knew someone who'd love to come with him and, with Lady Smythe quarantined upstairs, he was determined to flaunt the ban and go and see Isobel at the manor for once. After their last meeting, he was longing to see her again. He simply could not wait another day to tell her about his feelings. He'd kept quiet long enough.

He parked around the back of the manor house, where the delivery vans always parked up, hoping his lorry would be mistaken for one. The gravelled parking area stood next to the kitchens, where his mother and father had worked when they were his age. He never could picture either of them as servants.

He found Isobel in the herb garden nearby, picking small branches of bay leaves from the tree in its centre. She already had an armful of roses in a basket by her feet.

"Al! How lovely to see you. These are for Granny. Smell them. The bay is as wonderful as the roses."

Al bent his head and dutifully inhaled. "Very nice. How is the old dragon?"

"Oh, Al, don't call her that. She's in a dreadful state." Isobel's eyes misted up. "She had to have her toes cut off yesterday."

"Bloody hell, that sounds drastic."

"Yes, she's had gangrene - they went black. It's too ghastly."

"That does sound bad. Listen, how about you pop those flowers inside and come for a spin in the lorry for a bit of light relief? I'm off to Southampton with a delivery of rubber seals for the army depot."

Isobel hesitated. She looked at Al and then at his lorry, just visible over the stone wall.

"Come on, Bella, I've got to get going or I'll not be back in time to do another delivery and Mum will give me merry hell, and so will yours, if she sees me here."

34

Isobel smiled, and her sweet face lit up. "I suppose I could get away for a little while. Alright then, I'll come, but I must tell Mummy, or she'll fret."

"As long as she doesn't stop you coming with me. Be quick!"

He watched Isobel run into the manor house through the servants' kitchen door. He kicked pebbles on the neat pathways running through the vegetable patch while he waited and wondered if his grandfather, George Phipps, had laid out the symmetrical grid years ago. As head gardener, George would have been the mastermind for some of the landscaping. He took in the tree-lined driveway that swept up the incline towards the graceful old stone building. Cassandra Flintock-Smythe kept sheep on the lawn these days to keep the grass down, saying it was cheaper than manpower. Funny how people who looked wealthy never had any cash in their pockets.

When Lottie appeared instead of her younger sister, Al knew his jaunt was doomed.

Lottie's face, always such a contrast to Isobel's, looked like thunder.

"Thought you weren't supposed to visit us at the manor, Al?"

"I decided I'd chance it being as your grandmother is off limits. It's so silly that I'm not allowed. After all we were always playing in the estate gardens when we were kids, weren't we?" Al grinned at his friend; his best friend, he'd always thought, though she didn't look that friendly today.

"True. They were good times, weren't they?" Lottie looked at him with an intensity that seemed odd somehow.

"The best, Lottie. It's about time we had some more." Al hoped his words would cheer her up.

"I think so too," Lottie lowered her voice and came closer to him.

Al backed away, feeling uneasy and unable to read her strange mood. He fiddled with the stem of a climbing rose, sunbathing itself on the warm stone wall next to him. It pricked his finger and he sucked at the blood spurting from it. "Ouch! So, what are your plans for the summer then, now you've finished school?"

Instead of showing concern for his finger, Lottie looked hurt, almost crushed. What on earth was up with her? Girls were so unpredictable.

"I don't know. A lot depends on Granny's health. I seem to be roped into nursing her a lot and Mummy wants me here all the time at the moment, so I'm not really free to do what I like. How about you?"

"Oh, I'm busy too. Driving the lorry, you know. Never a spare minute."

"That's not what I've heard."

"What do you mean?"

"Didn't you see Bella yesterday?"

"Maybe." Al didn't like the way the conversation was going or understand it.

"And you're off to Southampton today, I hear?" Lottie's chin stuck out aggressively.

"That's right."

"Thought you'd sneak off with Bella, did you?"

"I just thought it would give her a bit of a break, that's all. I know it's hard with your grandmother being ill."

"And don't you think it's also hard for me? I'm supposed to just carry on regardless, am I?"

Al stared at the ground and kicked another pebble, not risking a direct glance from Lottie's blazing dark eyes. "I thought you'd be too busy. "

"Oh, I'm busy alright. Did Bella tell you about Granny's operation? That she's had to have her toes cut off?"

"Um, yes." Al's finger throbbed uncomfortably.

"We're all very taken up in looking after her, so Isobel doesn't have time to go off on a jolly with you today. She's needed here."

"I see. I'm sorry about Lady Smythe. It must be awful for you all."

Lottie's eyes filled up, just as Isobel's had. In a voice almost too low for him to hear, she said, "It *is* awful, bloody awful. And it won't stop the inevitable, either."

"The inevitable?"

"Her death, of course. It can't be long, even with this dreadful operation, but I hope she'll last long enough to...oh never mind."

"I'm sorry, Lottie." He did look up then and was shocked to see the longing in Lottie's eyes. They were brown, so different to Isobel's cornflower blue ones, and matched her dark hair. Her build was unlike her sister's too. Where Isobel was slender as a willow wand, Lottie was well built, strongly made and shorter. Her face was her best feature, striking with its slightly beaky nose and strong jaw. Her mouth was full and would have been sensuous, if she would only let it relax a little.

Lottie broke the tense silence. Could she read his thoughts? In a choked-up voice she said, "Well, Albert Phipps, hadn't you better get going? That lorry won't drive itself."

Al nodded and fished the lorry's keys out of his pocket. "You're right. Give my best to your mother and I hope Lady Smythe recovers from the operation."

"No message for Bella?"

"No." He climbed into the cab and started the engine. The lorry thrummed into life. He swung it out in a big circle and drove off, sticking his hand out in a casual wave and steadfastly not looking at Lottie.

It had been so different when they were kids. They'd spent every school holiday together getting up to all sorts of larks. The three of them – no, four, once Lily had been born, had grown up together, had fights and adventures on the estate and rainy-day indoor games in the old nursery. He had other friends in the village of course, but both Isobel and Lottie had been part of the inner fabric of his life until that disastrous day on the river.

If Lady Smythe had been up and about, he still wouldn't have dared to go the manor at all. He'd only ever seen Isobel and Lottie in the village or down at the garage since that awful day and the old bag had come between his mum and theirs into the bargain for a while too.

No, however much Lady Smythe might be suffering now, Al could not find any sympathy in his heart for the old battle-axe, toes or no toes. And it was obvious looking after her was putting a strain on them all, especially poor old Lottie.

The heat wave continued, making any stay in the sickroom a trial. Lady Smythe insisted on having a fire blazing in the hearth, despite the warm weather. Lottie wasn't the only member of the family who stealthily opened the windows every time her grandmother dropped off to sleep.

Never a woman to withhold a complaint, Lady Smythe was a fretful patient. They took it in turns to sit with her and Cassandra engaged a night-nurse, so they could sleep.

"We can't do nights as well, my darlings. It's expensive but necessary, I think, don't you?" Increasingly, Cassandra looked to Lottie for verification of every decision. Lottie was already feeling under pressure. That piece of paper under her bed kept her awake at night, despite the extra member of staff.

But it was in the day that it happened. A bright day, refreshingly less humid with a welcome breeze lifting the leaves on the trees and everyone's spirits. Only that morning, Dr Benson had said Lady Smythe was making an excellent recovery and, on Lottie's specific questioning, was highly likely to live out the year, minus her toes but with everything else working satisfactorily. Lottie had relaxed for the first time in days. If Granny could only live until Christmas, she would insist that her grandmother openly declare her intentions in the will. Lottie had clung to this tenuous hope throughout the last difficult days and now it looked as if it would all work out after all.

She volunteered to sit with her grandmother for the rest of the morning while her mother and sister went out to do some shopping. Eager for a change, they had accepted her offer with alacrity and driven off to Woodbury, laughing and smiling together in the old

Sunbeam saloon. It being market day, Lottie didn't expect them back for lunch.

Lady Smythe dozed off after she'd eaten her midday meal on a tray. Lottie, too tired to find something else to do, sat by the window and allowed her mind to drift. She looked through the warped old glass upon the acres she'd been commanded to manage. The old doubts resurfaced. How would she ever explain to her mother and sister that their rights to share in the inheritance had been bypassed? Would it be legal for her to reverse her grandmother's will in December and share the burden with them instead? She still hadn't been to see Mr Leadbetter to check its validity. There never seemed to be a moment to call her own.

All too soon, Lady Smythe roused herself and commanded Lottie to read out loud to her.

"Don't you fancy a crossword instead, Granny?"

"No, not right now. We'll save it for later, my dear."

"My Graham Greene book?"

"No, let's have Agatha."

Lottie laughed. "Alright, then."

"And bring me those barley sugars. Your mother has put them quite out of my reach."

Lottie did as she was told. It was easier than arguing.

She cleared her throat and began to read out loud. Yet another Agatha Christie - 'Murder on the Orient Express'. It would be the second time she'd read it to her since the operation.

Lady Smythe adored this story but, as she knew the words off by heart, she was prone to interrupting.

"Of course, if people had kept to trains instead of noisy cars, everything would be different now." Lady Smythe was sucking so noisily on her boiled sweet, Lottie wondered how she could catch all the words when she did bother to listen. She marked the page and waited.

"Oh yes, everything changed with the motor car. I blame the Depression on all this so-called progress; putting men out of work with machines taking their rightful places. And That Woman down the road with her accursed factory. She's come through it all unscathed because of the dratted motor car. Oh, I can't stand the thought of it. To think she was nothing but a housemaid who threw her cap at my dear Charles."

Lady Smythe's colour had risen, as well as her voice, muffled by her boiled sweet, but still loud.

"My only consolation is that the grotesque monstrosity of her modern enterprise isn't on estate land, although no-one approaching the manor from the London direction can fail to miss the ugly collection of hangars and petrol pumps so close to our gates. Or smell that confounded rubber factory." Lady Smythe sniffed. "And all those gaudy advertisements plastered all over it. She always was common, and it shows."

Lottie had heard this old story many times and hid her smile by looking out of the window again. Lady Smythe had never forgiven Katy Beagle, the now prosperous Mrs Phipps of Katherine Wheel Garage and factory, for not succumbing to the workhouse, or preferably dying of heartbreak, after her grandmother had sacked her for flirting with Uncle Charles. She would have loved to have been a fly on the wall when Katy, only a housemaid at the manor then, answered her grandmother back all those years ago. She'd done it again, in front of all the staff when Lottie was a child. Lottie, Isobel, Al and Lily had ventured off on a doomed boat trip years ago. When they'd nearly drowned in Cheadle Lake, Granny had banished the entire Phipps family from the premises while Lottie had been getting cleaned up by the housekeeper, Mrs Andrews. Al had told her all about it when she'd finally managed to sneak off and see him, months afterwards. No one had dared challenge her grandmother since, especially not her mother, but at least Al's mother

41

and hers were friends again, even if it was behind Granny's back.

A choking sound broke her reverie. She looked across at the bed, horrified to see her grandmother flapping her plump hands and gasping for air, making ghastly sounds and writhing in pain. She rushed to the bedside where Lady Smythe was rapidly going blue and opening and shutting her mouth like a fish out of water.

"What's the matter, Granny?"

Lady Smythe shook her head and pointed to her throat.

"Are you choking on your sweet?"

Lady Smythe nodded once and then her face crumpled, and she clutched her chest.

"What is it? What's happening?" Lottie didn't know whether to stay or go for help. She started thumping her grandmother across the back of her shoulders and thought she'd succeeded in unblocking the hard sweet as Lady Smythe stopped gagging and slumped back on the pillows, trapping Lottie's hands.

Only then did it dawn on her that her grandmother had stopped breathing.

No amount of back-slapping, name-calling or cheek-rubbing could rouse the old woman. What should she do? Lottie prised her hands away, ran to the door and shouted for help, then came back in and tugged the bell-rope with such force it came away in her hands. She went back to the bed and felt for a pulse in her Grandmother's neck. Nothing throbbed under her searching, frantic fingers but then, she hadn't a clue what she was doing.

In answer to the ringing of the bell, the housemaid, Maisie, lurched into the room, took one look at her mistress and started screaming.

Lottie, still struggling to rouse her grandmother, had no patience with this hysterical response. "Shut up Maisie! Shut up!"

But Maisie, never very sharp-witted even though she was middle-aged now, continued to wail. Eventually old Andrews wheezed up the stairs and onto the landing.

He stood in the doorway, looking alarmed and very out of breath. "What's all this dreadful noise, Maisie?" The butler rarely ventured upstairs these days, and nobody had the heart to reprimand him, but Lottie was grateful he'd made the effort this time.

"Be quiet Maisie!" Andrews managed to gasp out and abruptly Maisie stopped her noise by stuffing her fingers into her open mouth.

The butler came into the room and turned to Lottie. "Miss Charlotte?"

"Oh, thank goodness you're here, Andrews. Quick. Telephone Dr Benson and get him to come here directly. Lady Smythe has stopped breathing. She choked on a sweet and then clutched her chest. I don't know what to do to bring her round."

At once, Andrews had command of the situation. "Maisie, go downstairs and get Mrs Andrews to telephone for the doctor and don't forget to say it's urgent. Go!"

He came over to the bedside and, with more confidence than Lottie, felt for a pulse on Lady Smythe's wrist. In the sudden hush while he listened for a heartbeat, Lottie understood that her grandmother had died and could not be resuscitated. She had died, not from the operation she had so bravely undergone, but from her voracious appetite for sweets.

After about thirty seconds Andrews turned to her. "I'm sorry, Miss Charlotte, but Lady Smythe has passed away."

Lottie let out a wail of her own. She stared at her grandmother, terrified she could have prevented the disaster. Not only had she lost her dearest relative but the estate would now be in jeopardy. Dear old Andrews, so faithful and loyal, would lose his job, his place to live. Her mother, worn out by care all these years, would be turfed out on the street too. And no one but her knew this. In that moment, Lottie felt overwhelmed by despair and sheer panic.

All she said was, "I think you are right, Andrews."

They both withdrew from the bedside towards the fresh air blowing in through the open window from the sunny orchard.

"She had been very brave, Miss, if you don't mind me saying so." Andrews extended his hand.

Lottie took it; was grateful for its reassuring squeeze. Andrews had been in the background for the whole of her life and she had never appreciated what security that had given her until the threat of its loss brought it home.

Maisie burst in the room, breathless and important. "Mrs Andrews 'ave telephoned the doctor and he's coming over right now. 'Tis the old doctor as t'other one's busy out and about but Mrs Andrews she says that's alright, sir."

"Yes, it's alright, Maisie. Thank you. Go downstairs and make a tray of tea for Miss Charlotte."

"Yes, Mr Andrews. Where shall I take it to?"

Andrews turned to Lottie, his eyebrows raised in enquiry.

"Put it in the drawing room, Maisie. I want to be ready to see the doctor when he comes."

"Yes, miss."

"Should we cover her face with the sheet, Andrews? Tell me what to do?" Lottie turned to look at her grandmother, whose still form frightened her.

"No, leave her now. The doctor will need to examine her ladyship."

Lottie nodded, relieved.

"I will accompany you to the drawing room, Miss Charlotte."

"Thank you, Andrews. Could I, would you mind if...if I took your arm? I feel a little unsteady."

Silently, Andrews extended his arm and Lottie leaned on it for the first time in her life. They went downstairs, arm in arm, united in grief.

CHAPTER SEVEN
CHEADLE MANOR
JULY 1939

Old Dr Benson stayed with Lottie until her mother and sister returned from their trip to Woodbury.

"We'll break the news together, Charlotte." Dr Benson had never bothered to address her as 'Miss'. He'd seen her with the measles and chicken pox.

They had a simple lunch. Lottie picked at hers and marvelled at old Dr Benson's robust appetite. They spoke little and for that she was grateful. Her mind was far too pre-occupied to manage conversation and Dr Benson seemed to understand. Lottie supposed he'd had enough experience of death and illness to know what people needed at times like these and left him to his cheese.

It was three o'clock before they heard the tyres on the gravel of the drive. Andrews opened the front door, leaving Lottie waiting in the drawing room with the doctor.

Cassandra and Isobel were still laughing and chattering as much as when they'd driven off. They'd obviously had a lovely, carefree morning.

Lottie sat in Lady Smythe's old armchair, so she could hear the conversation in the hall.

"Good afternoon, ma'am." Andrews cleared his throat. "There has been a, um, development in Lady Smythe's condition while you've been out. The elder Dr Benson awaits you, with Miss Charlotte, in the drawing room."

The laughter and chatter stopped. Cassandra and Isobel entered the room silently, still both wearing their hats and coats.

"Hello, Dr Benson. Why are you here?" She shook the doctor's outstretched hand and turned towards her mother's armchair. "Lottie? What has happened?" Cassandra drew off her gloves, looking from one to the other with an apprehensive face.

Isobel stood slightly behind her mother, one hand on her arm.

Lottie stood up and squared her shoulders. She swallowed hard and managed to blurt out, "It's Granny. I'm afraid she died this morning."

"What? This can't be true!" Cassandra's hands flew to her mouth. Her gloves dropped on to the floor. "But…but I thought she was making a full recovery?"

Dr Benson was already standing. "I can verify this, Cassandra. Your mother choked on a boiled sweet and had a cardiac arrest immediately afterwards. There was nothing anyone could do. It could have happened at any time. You must not reproach yourself."

"But…was no-one with her? Are you quite sure nothing could be done?" Cassandra turned to Lottie. "Were *you* not there?"

Stung, Lottie replied more angrily than she meant to. "Of course, I was there, Mummy. What do you take me for? I was reading one of her favourite Agatha Christie books to her. She started choking on this barley sugar - you know how she loved them - and I slapped her back and rubbed her cheek but then she clutched at her chest and stopped breathing." Lottie started to sob. "No-one could have done more. Could they, doctor?"

"No, dear child, don't upset yourself. You did all the right things." Dr Benson patted her shoulder.

Cassandra went white. She looked from Lottie to the doctor in disbelief. Her hands fluttered up to her face. "Oh dear, I don't feel very well. This has come as a…as a tremendous shock."

Dr Benson drew her to the sofa by the fireplace and Isobel quietly joined her, taking her mother's hand in hers. They sat there together, both staring at Lottie, their faces, so alike, serious and solemn, like judges.

Lottie felt excluded and as if she were in the dock, accused of some heinous crime.

"Can I fetch you some water, Cassandra, my dear?" Dr Benson leant over her mother with solicitous concern.

"Yes, no, I don't know. Perhaps we could ring for Andrews?"

Isobel got up and pulled the bell cord, then returned to her mother and put her arm around her.

Lottie remained seated on Lady Smythe's chair, set apart from the cluster of care around her mother, who was now weeping silently, her breath coming in short gasps.

No-one comforted Lottie, but *she'd* been the one to witness the distressing scene. *She'd* seen her grandmother die; *she* - who loved her more than anyone. Lottie had been the one who'd stayed with her grandmother through the operation, stayed with her all morning, tried to save her life, for God's sake! Lottie wiped her eyes with her sodden handkerchief; sat back in her grandmother's chair, pushing her spine against its upholstered, reassuring bulk. Alone she'd coped; *she* hadn't gone off to town to have fun; no, she'd stayed and done her duty.

Duty. There was plenty of that ahead.

And they didn't even know about the will yet.

Lottie had never felt more alone, more different, more bereft - or more guilty.

Next morning, Al came into the kitchen of the family bungalow after a long drive, ravenously hungry and ready for his lunch.

His dad came in behind him. "Have you heard the news, Katy?"

"What news, love?" Al's mother stood at the kitchen sink, peeling potatoes. That was normally Agnes's job, but his grandmother sat in the corner chair by the range, snoring gently, her head slumped to her chest.

"Is it about the kittens?" Lily had put up a sign on the garage forecourt, saying they were for sale and had high hopes of buying a bicycle with the profits. No-one had yet disillusioned her. They had all learned to wait for the penny to drop of its own accord with Lily.

Jem smiled and patted his daughter's shoulder. "No, it's not about the kittens, sweetheart."

"What then?" Katy ignited the gas cooker and set the pan of potatoes on to boil.

Al was silent, wondering if the news was from the manor. Rumours about Lady Smythe's health had been flying around the village lately.

"Never thought I'd see the day. I thought she'd live forever, just so she could carry on throwing her hefty weight about, but Lady Smythe has died." Jem took off his cap and neatly threw it on the hook by the door.

"She never has!" Katy stood still, with her mouth dropped open.

"Ah, so it is true, then," Al mumbled the worlds almost to himself. He wondered how Isobel and Lottie were coping with their loss, coming so soon after the strain of nursing the invalid - and all for nothing in the end.

"Yes, well, I suppose she must have been pushing seventy. Three score years and ten, just like the bible says. A lot older than my poor old Mum was when she died but

48

then, being lady of the manor, she never did a stroke of work, did she?" Jem sat down at the kitchen table and rubbed his good hand across his tired face.

"No, you're right there. She made my life hell when I was working for her as a girl. Always had it in for me, she did. Well, I'll be blowed. So, the old girl has gone at last. Was it that dia-whatsit thing?" Katy went to her prized possession, the new refrigerator, and took out a dozen sausages wrapped in brown paper.

At the sound of the fridge door shutting, Agnes's cracked old voice growled from the corner chair where she had been dozing. "You wants to let them sausages warm up a bit afore you cooks 'em."

Al marvelled at how his grandmother could wake up in an instant from one of her naps as if she'd never been asleep. She was always doing it and it was always unnerving.

"Oh, don't fuss, Mum," Katy held up the string of pink sausages and slit the twisted membrane between them with a sharp knife. As each sausage hit the frying pan with a sizzle, it began to spit.

"They wouldn't spit if they was at room temperature, like I said. Blooming refrigerators." Agnes heaved herself upright and Al heard his grandmother's knees crack as loud as his Dad's bird-scarer in the vegetable plot.

"Come on, shove over, and I'll do it." Agnes shuffled over to the stove, also new and distrusted.

"Thanks, Mum, God knows, I could do with a sit down. And this news takes a bit of getting used to. I wonder who else knows about it?" Katy didn't argue but sat down next to Al and Jem.

"Knows about what?" Agnes's hands never stopped chopping cabbage as she spoke.

Jem spoke a bit louder for her benefit. "Lady Smythe's died, Agnes."

The chopping knife stopped in mid-air. Agnes put down the knife and leant against the wooden draining board.

"You alright, Mum?" Katy went to her mother's side. "Come on, sit back down again."

"Maybe I will, at that." Agnes returned to her chair by the range. She shook her head. "Well, so the old tartar's gone before me, has she? Well, good riddance to her. When I remember that time she tried to throw me and your father out of our own home at West Lodge, what we had worked for and paid for with hard graft for so many years, it still makes my blood boil. I'll not weep for that one. No, I'm not sorry she's gone." Agnes gave a harsh, dry laugh. "It gives me some satisfaction to know I've outlived her, I must say."

"Oh, Mum, I know what you mean but you always told me it's not right to speak ill of the dead." Katy returned to the sausages in the frying pan. A cloud of blue smoke had begun to rise above the cooker.

"Here, give over and let me rescue those bangers. You've never had the least idea about cooking, my girl." Agnes heaved herself back up and took over at the stove. "*I'm* not dead yet, not by a long chalk. To think that Lady Muck has gone first." She chuckled again as she prodded the sausages.

Katy smiled at her and surrendered her position. "So, what else do you know about Lady Smythe's passing, Jem?"

Jem turned to his wife. "Not much. Heard it from Susan Threadwell when I went for stamps at the post office in Lower Cheadle. Seems young Simon Benson amputated her ladyship's toes a while ago. They had gone black with the gangrene apparently, nasty business, but all seemed well after the operation. Then the old biddy went and choked on a sweet, would you believe? It made her have a heart attack and she never come round after." Jem rubbed his own truncated limb.

Katy reached out and stroked her husband's arm above its wooden prosthetic substitute. "Bring it all back, did it, love?"

"A bit." Jem shuffled in his seat.

Al longed to ask what it really felt like, having bits chopped off, but he didn't want to hurt his father's feelings.

Lily, however, shared no such scruples. "What's amputate mean?"

There was a horrible silence and, surprisingly, it was Jem who broke it. "It means cutting off a part of your body. "

"Ugh! That's revolting!" Lily stopped stroking Tabitha, mother of the quartet of marketable kittens and stared at her father's wooden arm.

"It's better than the alternative," Katy said quietly.

"What do you mean, Mum?"

"Sometimes the body gets infected, see, Lily, and it can spread so you have to get rid of the affected part or you can die. That's what happened to your Dad in the war and it saved his life. Same thing's happened to Lady Smythe, up at the manor but she hasn't got away with it."

Jem reached out with his good arm and wrapped it around his daughter's waist, pulling her to him. "So, if it wasn't for losing my arm, young lady, you would never have been born at all."

"Why?"

Jem didn't seem to have an answer to that. "We'll explain about that bit another day." Al smiled as his Dad abruptly changed the subject. "Did your mother say you could bring that damn cat in here?"

"She needs feeding up, Dad. She hasn't got enough milk for the babies."

"And she wouldn't have had any babies if she hadn't been with that old Tom cat, would she?" Katy's mouth was hovering close to a laugh and Al could barely contain his, either.

Lily looked from her father to her mother and then it was her turn for her mouth to drop open in wonder.

Her mother gave Lily a hug. "Well, you're twelve now, Lily, so you may as well understand about these things. If you want to know more, ask me when we've a moment to ourselves, alright?"

Lily nodded silently.

Al laughed out loud and got up, ruffling Lily's curls. He turned to his grandmother who still stood by the stove, making gravy. "Want me to mash the spuds, Gran?"

Agnes nodded. "Yes, and it's about time someone noticed who's doing all the work around here."

CHAPTER NINE
CHEADLE MANOR
JULY 1939

"There's so much to do, girls, I hardly know where to begin." Cassandra sat at her desk in the drawing room early the next morning.

Lottie didn't answer. A sleepless night had drained all her energy. How could she sleep when that traitorous document lay beneath her bed and her grandmother lay stone-cold nearby? She paced the big room, chewing her already bitten nails. She didn't know how she could possibly explain about Granny's will. She couldn't imagine how to even broach the subject. She felt she was the holder of a stick of dynamite rather than a piece of parchment and was terrified of lighting the fuse, knowing the resulting inferno would be utterly unpredictable.

"What will happen to Granny now, Mummy?" Isobel stood by her mother's desk, her face soft with sympathy.

"Good question, Bella, and a good place to start. I should have asked Dr Benson yesterday, but I was so shocked, I forgot. I suppose she will go to the funeral parlour for now."

"When will the funeral be?" Isobel asked.

Lottie looked across at them, also interested in the answer.

"I don't know, dear, I'll have to telephone the undertaker. I suppose I'll have to call the vicar too and, oh, and the solicitor, Mr Leadbetter, of course. He'll have the will at his office. I don't think we have a copy here."

Lottie knew she should have told her then, she really should. "I'll make the calls if you like, Mummy. I don't mind."

"Would you? That would be a help, but I'll speak to the vicar. In fact, I think I'll walk down to the church, it will settle my mind; help me to think." Cassandra laid down her pen, the ink still wet and unused.

"Funeral director first?" Lottie got up from her chair.

"Yes, please, Lottie. The sooner the better, if you get my meaning."

Lottie understood only too well; but it was hard to think of Granny as just a dead body to be disposed of, no longer a person.

"Here's his card. I had it ready, just in case. Was that very wrong of me?" Cassandra held out a black-edged visiting card.

"Very sensible and...um...Mr Leadbetter?" Lottie looked at the sombre writing on the card and shivered.

"Ah, yes, here's his card too. Do you fancy a walk down to Lower Cheadle, Bella?"

Again, Lottie was excluded from the invitation. Again, she was left to do the real work. She left the room silently, biting her lip against the impulse to cry.

The only telephone in the manor was in the hall. Lottie watched Cassandra and Isobel drift off upstairs for their things, as she dialled the number of the funeral director. Mr Bailey promised to come within the hour for the 'dear deceased' as he called her grandmother. A blur of tears obscured the receiver as she replaced it. Granny *was* just another dead body to him, however much he couched it in respectful euphemisms. Her handkerchief was too wet to be of much use, but she blew her nose into it anyway.

Cassandra squeezed her arm as she passed her on her way out. "'Bye, darling. Thank you so much for doing the telephone calls. We won't be long. I'll try and get a date from the vicar and we can begin planning the funeral. No doubt the world and his wife will want to come." Her mother and sister, both dry-eyed and wearing new hats, left the front door open as they passed through it, and the warm summer wind whispered into the vacuum left behind.

Lottie nodded them on their way. "See you in a bit." She watched them disappear down the driveway, looking as if they didn't have a care in the world. Had neither of them loved Lady Smythe? Was she the *only* one grieving? How could they be so heartless? Was it her genuine grief and their lack of it separating them, or had they intuited the contents of the will and already were pulling away from her?

She was glad they had gone in one way; it meant they wouldn't overhear her call to Mr Leadbetter, although anyone passing through the hall would. There was no privacy at Cheadle Manor. Maybe she could do something about that when she was in charge. Have a telephone installed in her father's old study - a more modern one with a decent cradle - instead of this old candlestick variety. The random idea made her see how being in control might have its advantages after all, before her guilt rubbed it out.

Lottie picked up the earpiece and dialled the solicitor's number.

A woman's voice answered. "Leadbetter and Brown, may I help you?"

"It's Charlotte Flintock-Smythe here, from Cheadle Manor."

"Good morning, Miss."

"Hello, um, I wondered if Mr Leadbetter could come and visit us today?"

"Today? That's very short notice."

"I know, but, you see, my grandmother died yesterday, and we need to read the will."

"Ah yes, Lady Smythe's will." The haughty woman cleared her throat ostentatiously. "I can see why you would want Mr Leadbetter to be there for *that*."

"Can you?" Lottie knew a moment of distaste that this stranger would know her secret, had known it probably for much longer than she had herself. The frosty woman had probably typed it up.

"Would three o'clock this afternoon be convenient?"

55

"Thank you, yes." Lottie put the earpiece back on its stalk. A butterfly flew in from the garden. It must be searching for its fluttering mate in her stomach.

None of them ate much at lunch. Having witnessed the departure of Lady Smythe under a shroud of purple velvet into the black hearse, it wasn't only Lottie who picked at her food. Lumps of it stuck in her throat; nothing would go down. All her muscles had tightened up. Rigid and unyielding, they refused to bend to her will. She kept dropping things. She rummaged for her serviette for the third time on the floor. Andrews was too old to oblige.

"Don't worry, Lottie. The will is only a formality. There's nothing to fear." Her mother smiled at her from the head of the table.

Again, she could have told her the truth. She knew she should. It would be better coming from her before the crusty old lawyer read out the dry, yet volcanic words. She opened her mouth but, just as no food could squeeze down her gullet, neither could speech make an exit. She closed her lips, retrieved her napkin and laid her cutlery across her plate in silent defeat.

They gathered in the drawing room at five to three. Lottie wasn't cheered when Cassandra patted her shoulder on her way to the sofa by the empty grate. The day was hot again, but Lottie shivered at her mother's touch.

Mr Leadbetter arrived promptly five minutes later. Andrews announced him at the door and her mother got up to greet him. Immediately, Lottie recognised the gravity of her mistake. She should have told her mother and sister beforehand. This was too formal. She felt wrong-footed from the outset. And yet, none of this was her doing. She hadn't *asked* Granny to leave things this way. The thought strengthened her.

Mr Leadbetter, now in his sixties, cleaned his glasses with a white handkerchief before he began. He'd refused a chair and stood in front of the giant fireplace, flexing the large piece of parchment in his blue-veined hands.

He cleared his throat and began to read the stilted words out loud. There was a polite silence as the three listened to his clipped voice intoning the dry words. But then he came to the crunch.

"...Therefore, the entire estate of Cheadle Manor and its dependencies will become the sole property of Miss Charlotte Amelia Flintock-Smythe on the attainment of her 25th birthday..."

When he had finished, the quality of the continuing silence changed. Everyone looked stunned, even Mr Leadbetter. Now, the quiet space bristled with tension.

Lottie didn't feel she should be the one to break it.

But it was Mr Leadbetter who broke the deadlock. He coughed into the vacuum and polished his spotless glasses again. "Mrs Flintock-Smythe?"

Cassandra nodded, still mute.

Mr Leadbetter replaced his glasses on his bony nose. "I have to tell you that this arrangement is far from unique. It implies no slight upon your good management of the estate thus far. Indeed, it shows great foresight on the part of your, er, mother, the late Lady Smythe. You do understand why she has done this?"

Cassandra shook her head. "I confess I do not." Her voice sounded dry and cracked with controlled emotion.

Mr Leadbetter inclined his bald head in acknowledgement. "Ah, I see. And you had no forewarning of the contents of the will?"

"No." Lottie was dismayed to hear a tremor in her mother's voice. Was it anger? She knew it wasn't grief.

"Let me explain. You remember, after your dear father departed this world, when the excellent late Mr Hayes was still estate manager, that the death duties were so onerous you sold the house in London?"

"Of course, I remember. How could I possibly forget? It was my decision."

Again, Mr Leadbetter gave a deferential nod. "Indeed. Lady Smythe was making quite sure that wouldn't happen again. As current law stands, fortunately, the estate is exempted tax when a spouse dies following the death of a husband upon whose estate tax is already paid."

"Then why did she do this?"

"Your late mother wanted to guarantee exemption from death duties, should they fall due but also felt you had carried the burden of the estate for long enough. If you remember, Sir Robert made a similar arrangement whereby Lady Smythe had no authority over the running of the estate but still owned it outright. It is this precedent she wished to emulate. Further, she did not wish the estate to be broken up into separate parts."

"So, it's revenge." Cassandra had gone white.

"I think that is rather a, um, colourful way to describe it. I rather fancy your mother wished you to be free of the heavy responsibility after so many, may I say, valiant years of service?"

In a slow, uncharacteristic growl, Cassandra replied. "Then why, Mr Leadbetter, was *I* not the beneficiary? Why was I not even *told*?"

Mr Leadbetter whipped off his glasses again. He twisted the stems around so many times, Lottie feared he would break them. "That, I regret to say, was not in my jurisdiction. Lady Smythe was adamant the arrangement should remain a secret until either her death, which is unfortunately the circumstance we now find ourselves in, or Miss Charlotte's twenty-fifth birthday."

Cassandra glared at the solicitor, who had stopped his twirling and was now having a coughing fit.

Lottie squirmed in her grandmother's old armchair. If her mother was angry now, what would she say when she discovered Lottie knew all about it?

"Would you like a boiled sweet, Mr Leadbetter?" Isobel said.

Surely Isobel wasn't trying to be funny? Did she want the poor man to choke on it like his employer and the author of this dreadful will? Lottie stared at her sister in disbelief at her gauche remark.

Mr Leadbetter looked understandably alarmed and stopped his nervous coughing immediately.

"Ahem, there is of course a life annuity each for you and Miss Isobel, so you will not be, um, destitute. The estate will remain in *trust* to you, Mrs Flintock-Smythe, but will become solely owned by your daughter, Charlotte, on her twenty fifth birthday, which is the 26th April 1945 and…"

"I know when my daughter has her birthday!" Cassandra stood up. Lottie watched her pace the room; heard her heels digging into the parquet floor.

Lottie's stomach lurched against her pounding heart.

Predictably, Isobel got up and joined her. "Don't fret, Mummy darling. I'm sure there's a way around this."

Mr Leadbetter turned to Lottie, looking desperate for corroboration. Lottie felt unable to move. She might as well have been chained to Granny's chair.

Lottie took a deep breath. Her mouth was dry, but she forced herself to speak. "There is no way around it, Mummy; Isobel. Looks like the responsibility for the estate will fall on my shoulders in 1945."

Cassandra whirled around, knocking Isobel's arm from hers. Her face was no longer inscrutable but contorted with fury. "Your shoulders? Yours? Haven't mine been strong enough all these years? Did my own mother think I was useless? What's it all been for? Did she want to humiliate me even from the grave?"

Cassandra looked from Lottie to the solicitor and back again. "Did you have a hand in this, Charlotte? Did you put Mother up to it? You were always as thick as thieves and a thief you have become!"

Lottie had never seen her mother so angry. "No! For God's sake, Mummy! I don't want it!"

Cassandra threw out her hands, pleading for some explanation that Lottie felt entirely unable to give. "Then why? Am I to be thrown out on your twenty fifth birthday? Am I supposed to live in some little cottage in the grounds of my own home? This home, that I've scrimped and saved to secure. This white elephant of a house, with all its dependents and tenants, that I, and I alone, have kept going through the Wall Street Crash when we lost all our money and had all those death duties to pay. I had no husband at my side, and I did it for *both* you girls, not just *you*!"

Lottie, torn between anguish for her mother and for herself at the injustice of these words, felt her chin wobble and turned her face away.

"Charlotte! Did you know about this before today?" Cassandra stood stock still in front of Lottie.

Another pregnant pause hung between them. "Well? Answer me!" Cassandra was not going to back down.

Lottie could see no way out. "Yes, I'm afraid so. Granny told me when she gave me her ruby tiara set."

"You *knew*?"

"Oh, Mummy, I wanted to tell you so desperately, but Granny swore me to secrecy. It's been such a burden - I can't tell you how difficult it's been!"

"Obviously you didn't feel you could tell me! Me, your own mother! Haven't I been a friend to you all these years? Have I ever made it difficult for you to tell me anything? You've always had a secretive side to you, haven't you? Oh yes, don't deny it! You think you're cleverer than either Isobel or I, don't you? Well, apparently, so did Mother. You must have had a hand in this. You cooked it up between you!"

"No, no, that's not true! I had no idea until she told me." Lottie was appalled at this accusation. How could her mother even think that of her?

"And that was weeks ago! Why didn't you tell me after Mother died? You've had ample time to do so." Cassandra's face had turned from stony white to hot pink.

"I meant to…I tried…I really did, but I just couldn't find the words." Lottie was floundering now.

Cassandra dropped her hands back to her sides. "Hah! That's pathetic, Lottie. You have never, in all your life, been at a loss for words."

Lottie proved her wrong again by remaining silent.

Cassandra seemed unable to stop herself and more destructive words tumbled from her mouth. "How could you deceive me like this, Charlotte? How could you betray my trust like this? God knows, I've tried to be both mother and father to you both. Your father must be turning in his grave." Her voice caught. "Not only is my inheritance to be torn from me but all my efforts as a mother."

"You're a wonderful mother, Mummy. Oh, don't cry!" Isobel was once more at her mother's side.

"Excuse me, I must…" Cassandra clamped her hand to her mouth and almost ran out of the room, Isobel trailing after her.

Lottie let out a sob. "Oh, Mr Leadbetter, I never thought it would be as bad as this." Lottie collapsed on to the armchair, cursing the woman who had always sat in it, and covered her face in her trembling hands.

CHAPTER TEN
CHEADLE MANOR
AUGUST 1939

Over breakfast the next morning, Lottie tentatively enquired about the funeral arrangements for her grandmother.

Cassandra lowered the newspaper she was pretending to read. "As you are the sole heiress, I'm assuming you want to be in charge of them, and as far as I'm concerned, you are welcome to do so. I have no further interest in the matter."

So, it was Lottie who placed the black-edged advertisement in the local papers and posted off letters informing the great and the good throughout the county of Lady Smythe's demise. She consulted Andrews and his wife, the housekeeper, about the catering and domestic arrangements and liaised with the funeral director and the vicar, who insisted on inviting the local bishop. The atmosphere inside Cheadle Manor remained tense. Cassandra withdrew completely from her eldest daughter, and the harsh angry words she'd voiced when the will had been read out drove a wedge between them that Lottie could not bridge. Left to her own devices, it was a relief to take up the organisation of the funeral. There was so much to do, it left little time for idle talk, which Lottie found a blessing at a time when her personal grief was compounded by her mother's rejection. Isobel fluttered between them, trying to broker a peace but Lottie always sent her away, claiming she was pressed for time and patience and eventually, Isobel took the hint and spent more time than ever with their mother, or out on her pushbike.

Despite her unpopularity over the years, and the steady drizzle that had set in for the day, Lady Smythe's funeral was well attended. Lottie was glad to see that Jem and Katy Phipps were rallying around her mother, just like old times. Granny had a lot to answer for, but Lottie had loved her, irrationally perhaps, considering all the trouble she'd caused over the years. But still, it would be good to see Jem and Katy back inside Cheadle Manor instead of her mother always having to visit them at the garage.

There were a few smirks and nudges towards her throughout the service. Seeing the surreptitious sniggers made Lottie very angry. Why couldn't people be more respectful? Had word got out about her inheritance?

It didn't help that Al and Isobel isolated themselves in the soft rain outside after the service, unlike the rest of the sombre congregation, who mingled and chatted in subdued tones under dripping umbrellas, talking about how suddenly the heatwave had broken at last. Her mother, roused into being sociable, was busy making sure she spoke to everyone to thank them for attending the funeral. Some were invited back to the manor, only a short walk away across their parkland. Lottie couldn't stop glancing across at Isobel and Al, standing together, slightly apart from the crowd.

She detached herself from the worthies surrounding her (no doubt hoping for a free meal up at the manor) and went over to them. "Come on, Bella. I could do with your support."

"Hello, Lottie. How are you?" Al held out his hand.

Lottie shook it, thinking how stupidly formal the gesture was when they had always been such friends. Did Al, too, think her a gold digger, some grasping fortune hunter, trying to squeeze Isobel from her rightful dues? What had they been talking about? Was it her?

"I'm fine, but I'm breaking you two up, you know how people talk."

Isobel spoke in her soft voice. "Al was just being kind."

Lottie sniffed, trying to disguise the way her heart felt painfully squeezed. "That's as may be, but Mummy needs us both, Bella."

"Of course. How selfish of me. See you later, Al."
Isobel detached herself from Al's side. Really, they had
been standing much too close together for such an
occasion. Lottie mistrusted the way they looked at each
other too.

Al nodded and backed away to join his parents
who were talking to his uncle and aunt, Billy and Daisy
Threadwell. How Lottie longed for his support too. She
had her grandmother to blame for that estrangement as
well, after that dramatic day on the river a few years ago.
But they had got through that together. Why couldn't he be
here for her now? Had Isobel been twisting the truth? Was
she trying to keep him for herself in revenge for losing out
on the estate?

The interment took less time than the church
service, but the rain made it feel longer. As she bent her
head in prayer, Lottie felt the cool invasion of rainwater
slither down inside her black coat collar and shivered. The
men strained as they lowered her grandmother into her
final resting place. She watched the big coffin settle into
the soil of Cheadle Manor. Rest in peace, Granny, dearest.
A tear, warmer than the raindrops, joined the moisture on
her face. She blotted the water away with her handkerchief
and blew her nose fiercely before looking up at her
mother, who, like everyone else, remained dry-eyed.

Lottie did her best at the lavish tea after the
funeral, she really did. She chatted to everyone, from the
tenants on the estate in their Sunday best to the bishop
with his cultured tones and polite, insincere, sympathy.
No-one would have guessed that the leaden lump in her
heart threatened to engulf her, or that it wasn't only grief
for her grandmother that caused it.

***

Isobel walked home from the funeral, unaware of
the crowd of well-wishers surrounding her. The only
person she was aware of was Al. He had looked at her in

such a sympathetic way at the graveside, she felt sure he thought she was special too.

It had been such a strange time since Granny had died. Lottie had withdrawn into some hard shell she could not penetrate, and her mother wasn't much better. All the old harmony had died with her grandmother and she didn't know how it was going to turn out with Lottie as sole inheritor. She'd never seen her mother so upset. Isobel cringed when she remembered all the cruel things Cassandra had said to Lottie. It was no wonder she'd withdrawn from them. Isobel had tried to get close, tried to show she still cared for her sister, however unfair the will had been to her; indeed, however angry she might also be, but she'd had to give up when Lottie stonewalled her at every attempt. She supposed their mother must have been like this when her father died, but Isobel had been so young, she couldn't remember it. She could barely recall her father's face or his voice.

She glanced round to check Al was there. And he was, just a few people behind her, his eyes fixed on her – no-one else. She felt a wriggle of excitement flow through her, chasing her sadness away. She wasn't sorry that Granny had gone anyway but she hated the way her manipulative control of the entire family had ripped them apart. Poor Mummy looked ghastly. No make-up could disguise the bags under her eyes or the new way her mouth had compressed into a thin line, the corners always slightly turned down. Her eyes had a new, flinty look too. They were no longer smiling and crinkling in the corners in their usual gentle way, soft and benevolent, and full of love for her girls.

Had she, herself, contributed to this impasse? Isobel had had a few sleepless nights, raking her conscience for anything she might have done to deserve reproach. She loved both her mother and her sister with all her heart but, she had to admit, those affections were dwarfed by what she now felt for Al Phipps. With the restrictions imposed by her Grandmother now gone, she felt a rush of joy that Al could once again visit the manor in absolute freedom and had already asked her mother for his permission to do so, thrilled when the answer had been an unequivocal 'yes, of course'.

Unbeknownst to Lottie, they'd met up three times already since the reading of the will. Al had been full of sympathy for the situation but not just for her, he'd been concerned about Lottie too.

They'd been in the kitchen garden only two days ago, Isobel's favourite place, and Al was helping her pick the last of the season's raspberries.

"Poor old Lottie. That's a right old fix for her to find herself in and so unfair on you. But why didn't she tell anyone before Leadbetter turned up with the actual documents?"

"I don't know, Al, it's a complete mystery to me and I think that's what has really hurt Mummy's feelings." Isobel dropped a raspberry. It fell apart on reaching the ground, too ripe to withstand the impact.

"Yes, I think you're right. She drove down to the garage yesterday and was chatting to my Mum for hours in the lounge. They kept the door shut the whole time, but I did see her get into her car afterwards, and her eyes were all red from crying."

"Oh, poor Mummy!" Isobel felt a stab of sympathy for her mother all over again.

"At least they are friends and see each other any time they like again."

Isobel gave a wistful smile. "Yes, that's something, I suppose."

"Don't *you* feel angry about what your grandmother has done?" Al's warm brown eyes searched hers.

"Yes, actually I'm furious, except I do know she was trying to relieve Mummy of the huge burden of the estate." Isobel ate a raspberry at the peak of ripeness. It was quite perfect, perfumed and sweet. She crushed it between her teeth and swallowed its goodness.

Al frowned. "I can't understand why you were left out entirely. It seems completely unfair."

"It is unfair, Al. I'll have an annuity but that's all and the same for Mummy. It's much worse for her. A complete snub. I think it's Granny's revenge for Grandfather leaving Mummy in sole charge when he died. Granny's never forgiven her but I don't know what will happen to me."

They continued picking in thoughtful silence.

"My basket's full, Bella." Al lifted it up to show her.

"Oh, well done. I'll get Mrs Andrews to make some jam." Isobel took the basket from him. Their fingers touched, making hers tingle. She looked up at him, startled to find him gazing back at her with an intense, searching look.

"Bella…"Al began.

Isobel felt unequal to hearing what Al might say next. Her own feelings were jumbled up between grief for her family and these new, exciting feelings when Al was around. "Let's take them into the kitchen, shall we?"

Al had been so kind ever since Granny died, well, he always was. She did feel a bit guilty that Lottie wasn't receiving support from any of them, but whenever she saw her sister, she was so busy rushing around making arrangements for the funeral, looking and sounding important, she'd never stopped long enough to let Isobel ask her if she was alright. And now, the day of the funeral had finally arrived and, to look at Lottie, you'd think nothing was wrong. There she was, in total command of the situation, smiling and talking to people with just the right level of civil solemnity to fit the sombre occasion, as if Cheadle Manor was already hers. Lottie had the gift of being able to talk to anyone. Isobel always felt tongue-tied on these big social occasions and when the bishop, tall and forbidding, came towards her, she took fright and sought refuge in helping Andrews with the drinks.

Andrews raised his eyebrows at this breach of etiquette. "I can manage perfectly well, thank you, Miss Isobel. Miss Charlotte has provided me with extra staff from the village and there is no need for you to lower yourself to serving drinks. That's for us to do."

Chastened, Isobel turned back and found the bishop still expecting to give his condolences to her. She accepted them as graciously as she could and was hugely grateful to Al, who seemed to sense her discomfort and had come to stand at her side.

"And this is?" The bishop, inclined his head towards Al.

"Oh, pardon me for not introducing him, Bishop. This is Albert Phipps, my good friend. He is the son of Katherine and Jeremy Phipps – of Katherine Wheel Garage."

"Ah, yes, an impressive enterprise. You must be very proud of your parents, young man. They have created a great deal of employment in the area. Your mother, in particular, is a remarkable woman."

Al smiled. "Thank you, sir. I'm proud of them both."

"And do you work at the garage?"

"Yes, sir, I mean, your honour. I drive the lorry for the factory, doing deliveries and such-like."

"That must be most interesting. And, I gather, there is more work on, with the government building up armaments, and such like?" The bishop must be well informed because few people knew of the huge orders from the Home Office they'd had recently.

"I couldn't say, your honour." Al had been sworn to secrecy on the subject and wasn't going to break it, not even for such an eminent figure as the bishop.

The bishop inclined his head. "I quite understand young man, and I commend you for your discretion."

To the relief of both of them, the bishop moved on to Cassandra and stayed chatting to her for quite a while until his departure.

"Phew! That was a close shave." Al smiled at Isobel, making her heart flutter.

"What did he mean about big orders, Al?"

"Now, you wouldn't expect me to tell you when I wouldn't even tell the bishop, would you?" Al laughed. "Come on, let's see if Lottie's alright. She's being interrogated by our postmistress and no-one should have to undergo that on their own."

How typically sweet of him, thought Isobel, though she doubted Lottie needed any help in managing with the likes of Miss Threadwell.

CHAPTER ELEVEN
KATHERINE WHEEL GARAGE
AUGUST 1939

Al was kept busy in the immediate days after Lady Smythe's funeral by running errands on his bicycle and ferrying goods in the lorry to various army depots throughout the nearby countryside. He couldn't wait to see Isobel again and felt frustrated at the delay. Had his mother suspected something when she saw them together in the churchyard and kept him deliberately occupied for every minute of the day?

Did he? He'd been so flattered that Isobel had singled him out in front of everyone like that, but did it really mean anything? He was longing to see her again and find out.

Finally, on Sunday morning with the factory shut and silent for the day, he seized his chance. Katy and Jem had gone to church earlier and were staying in the village to have their Sunday lunch with the Threadwells. Agnes and Lily had gone with them. They'd asked him to go too, of course, but he'd come up with the inspired excuse of needing to mend his pushbike which had sprung a puncture and would be required for work the next day.

Jem and Katy seemed to recognise he was too old to be forced to come but Agnes hadn't held back her doubts about leaving him behind. "What're you goin' to do for your vittels? A young man needs a good Sunday lunch to set him up for the working week."

"Ah, but there's some of your excellent steak and kidney pie left, Gran. You wouldn't want that going to waste, now would you? And there's just enough for one. Your cooking is better than Aunt Daisy's any day of the week." Al gave his grandmother a cheeky wink.

"There be some truth in that. Make sure you has greens with it, mind." Gran folded her bulk into the family car, still muttering. They drove off, beeping the horn in farewell. What was that well-worn phrase? The bliss of solitude. Al reckoned he could use a bit of that.

The puncture was fixed in no time, leaving him with at least three or four hours to call his own before his parents were due to return. He pumped up the tyre and jumped on the bike to test the repair. It wouldn't do to take the lorry where he was going. Too noisy for his purposes and anyway, he could use the bike ride as an excuse for staying out longer, saying he'd had to check his handiwork would hold.

Satisfied the tyre was airtight, he went quickly back into the bungalow. In his room, he combed his hair and smoothed it with bay rum till the chestnut curls lay flat and shiny. He changed into his Sunday best but left off his tie. Wouldn't do to look too formal.

Al clipped metal bands on to his trouser legs to stop them catching in the wheel spokes, went back outside and hopped on to the leather bicycle seat. His legs pumped hard all the way to the manor, and he reached it in record time, blown along by a stiff breeze from the east. The wind had an unseasonal edge to it after the recent heatwave that had broken just before the funeral. Al didn't care or think about the return journey as he pedalled against its chilly resistance. As he cycled up the drive, forcing his muscles to contract even harder against the gradient, he wondered belatedly if he would be welcome on a Sunday, so soon after the funeral too.

Cheadle Manor stood grey and gaunt, smothered in ivy and honeysuckle. It didn't look welcoming. No-one was about, and the empty stillness was brooding, off-putting. Al felt like a thief stealing up to the big house without knowing if he'd be wanted or expected and he almost turned back. He supposed he should have telephoned first, but he didn't want Lottie giving him an earful again and desperately hoped he could find her sister first. Only the thought of seeing Isobel's lovely face gave him the resolution to carry on, right up to the back door. He leant his bicycle against the wall of the kitchen garden.

He knew it was her favourite place, amongst the fragrant herbs and vegetables. He took off his cap and stuffed it in his pocket, smoothed his oily hair and lifted the latch on the wooden gate.

And there she was.

His heart knocked in his chest, missing a beat and then racing too fast, faster than when he'd cycled up the steep hills on the way here.

Isobel wore an old jacket, a man's jacket, belted tight around her waist against the cool weather and her fair hair was contained in a bright headscarf that flapped like a sail. A basket at her feet was half full of carrots, their green tassels cascading over the wicker edge, already drooping from lack of water. As she turned to place her dark green crop on top of the orange carrots, she caught sight of Al and waved a muddy hand.

Al jerked his back in salute, startled out of his brown study of contemplation, his pleasure at watching her fluid movements, the hint of rose the cold wind had chivvied into her cheeks. He could have stood there all day, just enjoying the look of her.

"Come and give me a hand with these potatoes, Al."

He never gave a thought to his best suit as he plunged the garden fork into the moist, dark earth and extracted several soil-encrusted spuds.

"You need to swill them off outside, Bella. Wouldn't do to take half the garden into the kitchen with 'em." Al held out the clump by its leaves, and clods of mud fell onto his polished boots.

Isobel pointed to a cauliflower, so covered in thick leaves he couldn't see its white curd inside.

"Good idea. Use that bucket over there. Have you got a knife?"

Al never went anywhere without his penknife. His mother had given it to him on his thirteenth birthday and it was his most prized possession. He withdrew it from his pocket and flicked open the blade.

72

Isobel looked impressed as he cut the cauliflower from its stem and slashed away at the leaves, making it look pristine and neatly trimmed. It was intensely satisfying when he laid its pale white head on top of the other vegetables in an orderly row.

"Perfect! I can give these to Mrs Andrews now and she'll concoct something for lunch. You will stay, won't you, Al?"

Al's stomach rumbled. The bike ride had burned a lot of calories, but he'd never turned up unannounced on a Sunday before. He didn't count the funeral tea. Any old bod had received an invite to that.

"I don't know about that. I'm not expected, and your mother has enough to do, what with Lady Smythe being gone."

"Nonsense, I'll ask her. It will be lovely to have some company. We have been very low in spirits." Isobel darted a look at him. She looked so sad. He longed to comfort her.

"Come on, let's take these vegetables to the kitchen and find Mummy."

Al trooped after her. He wished his tongue would untie itself. They scraped their boots on the metal grid set by the back door for the purpose and entered the house.

There was no-one in the cavernous kitchen, so they left the basket and Isobel's scruffy coat in the scullery. Years ago, it would have been busy with boot boys and kitchen maids with a head cook to boss them all around, now the empty tiled space echoed as they clattered through it. It astonished Al to remember that his Mum and Dad had been part of it all.

Al followed Isobel's slender back. "Thought you had a cook to see to all your meals."

"Not for years. Old Mrs Biggs died five years ago, and we've never replaced her. Mrs Tibbet comes from the village every day, but she doesn't live-in and she doesn't work on Sundays. We usually have a roast cooked by Mrs Andrews, so don't expect anything fancy."

"Sounds lovely, but I really shouldn't presume, especially if you don't have help."

Isobel stopped abruptly so he banged into her. She looked straight into his eyes and Al's stomach flipped over. He wouldn't be able to eat anything if she kept that up, whoever cooked it.

"Please stay, Al. Stay for me?"

He mumbled something incoherent and nodded his head in quick assent.

She leant forward and kissed him on his flushed cheek.

"Thank you." Isobel grabbed his sweaty palm and pulled him towards the hall and into the drawing room. Her mother was sitting at the little writing desk in the corner, surrounded by papers, a worried frown on her tired face. Despite the cool day, no fire burned in the huge grate.

"It's alright if Al stays to lunch, isn't it, Mummy?"

"What? Oh hello, Al. How are you?"

"I'm well, thank you Mrs, I mean, Lady, um..."

"Oh, just call me Aunt Cassandra, like you always have. I wouldn't want to be called Lady Cassandra, so I'm glad the title didn't get passed on to me. Never been that ladylike anyway!" Cassandra pulled her big cardigan tighter around her middle.

"Are you sure? I don't think my mum would approve." Al twisted his cap in his hand, awkward in front of Isobel's mum for the first time in his life. Everything seemed different, not least the way he felt about her daughter.

"Rubbish. She'd be the first to agree and anyway, she's always called me Cass. Now don't stand on ceremony, Al, I've known you since you were a baby, even if we haven't seen so much of you lately. It's beef for lunch, I think. I warn you, Mrs Andrews always burns it to a crisp."

"There you are, Al. I told you you'd be very welcome, but lunch will be ages yet. Are you hungry? I'm sure there's a slab of cake in the nursery to keep you going." Isobel was tugging at his sleeve again.

Al looked across at Cassandra, but she had turned back to her paperwork and didn't seem to care what they did.

"Come on, slowcoach." Isobel grabbed his hand.

The old nursery, the shabbiest, friendliest room in the huge house, welcomed him like an old friend, as indeed he was. He had played in this room on many a rainy day as a child and knew every jigsaw and book on its teeming shelves. His awkwardness fell away and he relaxed in the familiar space. Isobel opened the big cupboard in the corner and took out a large cake tin. Lifting the lid, she crowed, "Bullseye - chocolate! Your favourite. I'll cut you a big slice."

Al sunk his teeth into the brown sponge. Its sweetness matched his mood and he knew a fleeting moment of sheer contentment. The nursery had always been a world within another world, away from adults and censure and formality. He sat back in the horsehair armchair and munched, relishing every crumb and allowing his stomach to unknot itself and receive the sweet stodge.

"Do you want a drink with that? I could fetch something from the kitchen." Isobel had curled up in the window seat. You couldn't feel the cold wind in the nursery and the sunlight outside looked deceptively bright and warm. The sunshine framed her perfectly, forming a bright backdrop to her delicate beauty, without casting a direct light on her features, leaving her oval face masked in secret shadows and difficult to see and her fair flyaway hair lit up like a halo around it.

"No thanks, the cake is enough. How are you? Your mum seems very busy."

"Yes, she's so worried about money. Things have turned out so strangely."

"Can't be easy, all on her own. But you haven't answered my first question. How are *you*, Bella? Are you

75

missing your grandmother? She must have left a big vacuum in all your lives."

Isobel looked away, out of the window. By turning sideways, the sun fell on her pale skin, illuminating it and revealing dark smudges beneath her eyes.

"I'm alright, a bit more tired than usual, perhaps. Lottie has taken it harder than I. In fact...oh Al, I can say anything to you, can't I? Please don't repeat this, especially to Lottie."

"Of course, you can. I wouldn't breathe a word to another soul."

"No, you wouldn't. I know I can trust you." Isobel gave him a brief, dazzling smile.

"Definitely. Tell me what's troubling you."

"You know about the will, about Lottie inheriting, but do you know about the debts?"

Al paused before answering. "I've heard rumours, nothing definite."

"I don't know how these things get out."

"Hard to keep a secret in a village." Al took another bite of the chocolate cake.

Isobel clasped her hands together. "Quite. Well, I want you to know the whole truth. A couple of years ago, before even she was really ill, Granny made a new will. She's left everything to Lottie."

"Yes, I know, you told me."

"It's in trust till she's twenty-five, so Mummy has to manage the estate until then, but the worst of it is the estate is heavily mortgaged and the payments are huge."

Al spluttered through the last crumb of cake. "Bloody hell – that sounds very difficult. How's anyone going to cope with that? And there's really nothing for you? What about your mum?"

"Nothing for either of us. Granny said to me, before she died, that I should marry into money. That was the fate she decreed for me."

Al swallowed the last irritating dry morsel of cake. "Oh, you need a rich man. I see."

Isobel turned to him, "No, I don't! Oh, God, Al, it's all such a mess. Mummy and Lottie aren't speaking to each other. The estate is in hock up to the hilt because of the massive debts we have accrued since the Wall Street Crash in 1929. It's all a complete shambles. Maybe I *should* marry a rich man to sort it all out."

Al felt suddenly cold. He couldn't think of anything to say, so he just sat there, watching her.

Isobel hesitated, still staring out at the apple trees, their branches now laden with fruit and swaying clumsily in the stiff wind. She sighed and on the deep out-breath turned back to him.

"It's all because of Granny. I'm so ashamed but all I feel is relief that she's dead. I never loved her, you see. She terrified me and was always so harsh and critical to Mummy." Isobel lowered her already quiet voice so that Al had to lean forward to hear her. "In fact, between ourselves, I think I always hated her and now, I know I do."

"Just because someone's your relation doesn't mean to have to like them, or even love them."

"But I *loathe* her for what she's done to us, Al! That's a sin, isn't it? I always found it hard being with her but that stench at the end, oh, I couldn't stomach it, and now she's left a legacy that has divided us right down the middle. I feel as guilty as hell but I'm still glad she's gone."

Al shuffled his feet. "She wasn't the most likable person in the world."

"But she was my grandmother - my own blood and bone."

"Even so."

Isobel turned to face him, her blue eyes shiny wet. "But the real reason I hated her was - you."

"*Me*? What have I got to do with it?" Al edged even further forward on his chair.

"Why do you think you've not been invited here for the last few years?"

"Well, after that day on the river when you and Lily nearly drowned, she banished me, didn't she? Then my mum and yours fell out over it. It's a good job they got close again, before your grandmother died. I'm glad my mum could comfort yours then. And anyway, you've been away at school most of the time."

"It wasn't that. Mummy loves you and all your family – look at how she's let you visit again since Granny died. Your mum is her best friend. It was Granny all along, even before that awful day. She didn't want you in the house, even when we were little. She tried to forbid it before, Al. That day on the river gave her just the excuse she needed. She always thought you weren't good enough. She hated your mum, really hated her. That's why Mummy always visited your parents at the garage and couldn't invite them here after Daddy died. You were only allowed to come when you were little because Lottie made her give in. Daddy could stand up to her, as well, but after he'd gone...I don't remember it that clearly, but Mummy's told me all about it. Granny hated both your parents and all because they were servants here when they were young. Granny was such a filthy snob. I don't think she ever forgave your Mum and Dad for doing so well for themselves."

Al knew he was hearing the truth, but he had not known how deep the vengeance had gone with Lady Smythe. He had not known that Lottie and Cassandra had had to fight Lady Smythe for the privilege of his visits when they were kids, but their shared childhood had created a bond that no avenging old woman could ever break, and he would always be grateful.

He got up and joined Isobel on the cushioned window seat. A sunbeam fell on his neck, warming his blood, already hot in his veins.

Al took Isobel's hands in his. They were cold, like the glass she leant against. He hoped his heat would transfer into hers. "It's history. What matters now is the future. Do you want to marry a rich man in order to save the estate?"

Isobel lifted her eyes, blue as cornflowers, and looked into his, openly, unabashed, trusting, soft.

"No, I don't. I don't care about money. All I know is how I feel about *you*." She squeezed his hand. Hers were warming up nicely.

"What do you feel?" His voice had gone all husky, his mouth dry and his throat suddenly tight.

"Don't you know that I love you? Can't you feel it too?"

"You do? Oh, Bella, I do feel it, I've always felt it, always loved you." Somehow, he'd got nearer, without even noticing. Her lovely lips had turned up at their rosy edges leaving him no choice but to kiss them.

Already smiling, her lips parted as they met his and their breath mingled. Al gathered her up in his arms, feeling a heavenly joy flood through him as Isobel clung to him and kissed him back with a passion that matched his own.

By the time they parted, breathless, the sun had retreated behind a storm cloud and a sudden August shower splattered against the glass window.

"I can't believe this is happening," Al raised his voice against the din.

"Shall we do it again, just to be sure?" Isobel giggled.

Desire, love, disbelief; all vied in his mind as he took her in his arms again and kissed her even more deeply, unaware that the rain had turned to hail which now hammered against the window in a deafening spray of icy stones that ricocheted off the sill like bullets.

The tirade of hailstones was no louder than the roar in Al's ears as he revelled in Isobel's sensuous embrace, unaware that another shadow, this time from inside the room, had fallen across them.

Isobel sensed it first. He felt a lessening of her hold on him, an infinitesimal withdrawal, before the shock

79

of realising Lottie was standing before them made him freeze and let go his arms.

She stood, white-faced and stony, her dark eyes blazing at them. In a shaking voice, she said, "What is going on here? What do you think you're playing at?"

Isobel broke off and stood up.

"I, that is, we..."

"I can see *what* you're doing. No need to explain that!"

Al found his voice. "We love each other, you see, Lottie."

"Love? You're just children. Infatuated more like."

"No, Lottie, darling. We really do and I'm not a child - I'll be seventeen in December and Al's less than a year younger than you." Isobel reached out for Al's hand and found it. Their fingers entwined, pulsing emotion from him to her.

Al stood up. He was a head taller than Lottie and looked down into her face, disturbed to see the anguish in her eyes. A sneaking suspicion dawned in the back of his mind, already reeling from Isobel's confession and his own bubble of happiness. He wasn't about to let Lottie puncture that.

Al let go of Isobel's hand reluctantly, confident it would be returned another time, and went and sat on the horsehair armchair he'd recently vacated. He tried to gather his thoughts, frame the right words. In front of him Lottie quivered with - well, what was it? Rage, shock, or, incredible though the thought was, could it be - surely not – rejection, jealousy?

How had he, such an ordinary bloke, inspired such devotion in these two women?

Lottie spoke before he could formulate a sensible sentence. "My sister is too young to be taken advantage of, Al, you of all people should know that. How dare you come in here and exploit our patronage?"

"Patronage? Who do you think you are? Your grandmother's dead and buried. No need to resurrect her

80

and take over her attitude just because the estate belongs to you now." Al's anger had supplanted surprise at her words.

"How dare you bring my grandmother and my inheritance into this? How could you, when she's only been dead two weeks? How could you use Isobel like this? Don't you know she's grieving too?" Lottie spoke in a low, barely controlled rumble.

Isobel gasped in shock. "He did not *use* me, as you so disgustingly put it. And I don't care about Granny. I'm glad she's dead! I never loved her; in fact, I hated her. Hated her snobbery and selfish abuse of Mummy's good nature. She wasn't kind to anyone. If anybody exploited a situation it was her, and that's what she's done now, even though she's dead!" Isobel had two bright pink circles on her high cheekbones but stood, resolute and strong.

"You spiteful cat! After all Granny did for you! You're so deceitful and two-faced and now you've stolen Al. I hate you both!" Lottie stormed out of the room, not bothering to shut the door behind her but running to her own bedroom nearby, slamming that door so hard the banisters on the big curved staircase shook.

The hailstones had ceased their yammering and a soft, silent rain now caressed the window. In the sudden hush, they could hear Lottie crying through the wall. The sound was muffled, as if she wept into her pillow. Al and Isobel stood, a couple of yards apart, staring at each other, mute with shock, their brief moment of bliss expunged.

CHAPTER TWELVE
CHEADLE MANOR
AUGUST 1939

Lottie flung herself on her bed and gave way to the avalanche of emotion that threatened to engulf her. More than anything, she wanted to run to Granny and tell her that Al loved Isobel. Al, the one man she thought might love her. Al, the boy she had loved since they were children together. They'd played together, laughed, argued and fought like brother and sister. But he hadn't been a brother to her. He was her life's love. She'd never love anyone else. Not that Granny would have approved; in fact, she'd have been horrified. It was Lottie's one big secret from her grandmother.

Lottie knew she was clever. She was top of almost every class at school; she'd been head girl for heaven's sake! How could she have been blind to this? Al had never betrayed his feelings by a whisker. She'd not had the slightest inkling that he loved Isobel or indeed that her sister loved him. How could these two quiet people have sneaked around behind her back? What was the use of inheriting the estate if she did not have the man she loved by her side? It would be her mother's sad situation all over again.

She felt utterly betrayed and there was no fond Grandmother to console her. Her mother would sympathise, but Cassandra's own grief was so persistent, so ever-present, so unfathomably deep for Lottie's dead father, there was never any room for other people's sadness. Lottie had never felt she could burden her mother with more. Granny was the only one who really understood her. She could tell her anything, knowing any confidence was never disclosed to another, especially to her mother. But then, this was and always had been her private torment; the one truth she could *not* share with her snobbish grandmother.

She had never felt more alone, more abandoned, more upset. A fresh bout of crying overtook her, shaking her robust body in convulsive sobs that hurt her ribcage. She couldn't control it, she, who prided herself on always being in control.

She lay there all afternoon, losing all sense of time, excusing herself from lunch when Sarah, the youngest maid, came to tell her it was ready. There was no way she was going to face those lovers over one of Mrs Andrews' burnt offerings.

"Tell Mother not to disturb me. It's just a headache, that's all."

She heard people coming and going downstairs. She supposed it must be Al leaving. More rain set in and the afternoon darkened, as if it was winter rather than summer. Vaguely, she thought there must a storm brewing. Lottie didn't care about the dimming light in her bedroom or hear the drumbeat of the heavy rain, brought on by the gale force wind. She didn't hear the tap at the door either. She didn't know her mother was in the room until she felt gentle hands rubbing the small of her back.

"Leave me alone," she managed to gasp.

"Lottie, please don't upset yourself so. I...I'm sorry I've been so distant, so angry. I can't bear you to be so upset. Granny was very old and was suffering so much. It is best she's gone, even though I know you will miss her."

How could her mother know what she was really crying about? What was actually breaking her heart in two? She could feel it cracking open, she had a great pain across her chest from it.

"Lottie, please. You'll make yourself ill like this."

Lottie couldn't formulate a sentence. She shook her head and tried to push her mother away.

"Listen, Dr Benson gave me some sleeping tablets. I think you should take one and rest. You've been so strong, helping me nurse Granny but that's all over now and you can sleep knowing she's out of pain at last. It's all been such a shock, um, about the will and everything," Cassandra added in a lower voice, "to all of us."

An insistent hand kept prodding her, trying to make her turn over but she couldn't, she wouldn't. Lottie buried her face in her pillow. Maybe she could make herself suffocate and sleep for ever, like Granny. Leave Isobel and Al to kiss each other for eternity without her having to witness it.

The hand left her back and came around to her bedside table. Water was poured into a glass and she heard the rattle of pills in a bottle, the twist of its cap.

"Come on, Lottie." Her mother's voice was firm now. "I insist you sit up and be sensible. You can't go on like this. Granny wouldn't approve, you know."

Lottie was beginning to feel dizzy. Involuntarily, she turned her head and took a proper breath. She inhaled a whiff of Cassandra's citrusy cologne and blinked. She took another breath and another, deeper this time. Her sobs ebbed away, unevenly and without dignity.

"That's it, good girl. Sit up now and have a sip of water."

She sat up and took the offered handkerchief for her dripping nose. She blew into it forcibly then looked up at her mother. Her chin wobbled at the compassion in Cassandra's brown eyes. They looked bottomless and ineffably sad, even more than normal and she hadn't thought that possible.

Meekly, Lottie took the sleeping tablet and swallowed it with some water.

"Well done. Now get some rest. Everything will seem better in the morning."

Cassandra smoothed Lottie's dishevelled hair, tucked up her bedclothes, and then departed.

Lottie submitted to it all. She knew she was exhausted, but she knew her mother was even more tired. They both had broken hearts but only hers contained an extra secret.

She did sleep, the drug made sure of that, but her mood was just as miserable in the morning. On waking, she stretched out in her big bed, groggy from the sleeping pill. It had taken some moments to remember the events of the previous day and when she did, tears welled up again.

Granny's death had been grisly and had looked horribly painful. No slipping away into the restful peace sung about in church. The pain she'd suffered immediately after the operation had been unbearable. Dr Benson had increased the morphine dose before she had finally quietened, her breath coming in grating rasps that had set Lottie's teeth on edge and made her so tense it wore her out. And she'd come through all that only to choke on a sweet. Granny had fought and gasped and strained; her huge body writhing in pain for those few agonising seconds until her heart stopped beating. Then there had been the dreadful scene when the will was read out and the funeral had been equally exhausting. And now, just when it was all finally over, just when Mummy was beginning to relent, she'd found Isobel and Al in that clinch. Oh, she couldn't bear the memory of witnessing that passionate kiss. They had not held back at all, they'd been all over each other. And they were both too young to know about real love, not like the love *she* felt for Al.

But then, Al had said he loved Isobel and she'd said the same. Who loved Lottie? No-one now Granny had gone. Every hope of happiness she'd ever cherished had slipped away. She felt empty as a desert. Numb. All the future promised was overwhelming responsibility and debt. Some coming of age she'd have.

Sarah, the timid housemaid, knocked briefly on the door and entered the room carrying a breakfast tray.

"Mrs Flintock-Smythe said for you to have your breakfast in bed, miss. See, there's toast and honey and an egg."

"Thank you, Sarah. Put it down there, would you? And draw the curtains, please."

"Yes, miss." The dumpy young woman did as she was told. "Is there anything else, miss?"

"No, I'll run my own bath. Unless, is there hot water?"

"I'll make sure the boiler's stoked for you downstairs."

"Thank you, Sarah. That'll do for now."

Sarah nodded and the floppy lace on her cap bobbed on top of her wide forehead, making her look like a daisy in the rain. When the door had shut behind her, Lottie looked over the contents of the tray she had brought in. The only thing she fancied was a hot cup of tea, so she poured one out of the silver pot and added some milk to it. She sat up in bed, sipping it slowly and staring out of the casement window through the spiral of white steam.

Slowly, her head cleared, and she knew what to do. She bathed and took her time whilst the plan took shape. Once dressed, she ate her toast, cold though it was, then rummaged in her desk for the letters from Françoise, her penfriend in Paris.

In the very last one, her friend had written an invitation for her to come and visit. Well, now was the time. Lottie looked in another drawer and found her passport. It was still in date; she'd renewed it only last year for a walking trip in Switzerland with another friend from school. It seemed ages ago, when she'd still been a child. She felt very different now. She slipped the little hard-backed blue folder into her travelling case, already open on her bed.

She slipped downstairs quietly and managed to reach the hall unnoticed. Andrews passed by with his usual soft shoe shuffle.

"Where is everyone, Andrews?"

"I believe Mrs Flintock-Smythe and Miss Isobel have gone out for the morning – Mrs Flintock-Smythe has gone into Woodbury and I believe Miss Isobel said something about going for a walk." Andrews stood, laden with a silver tray and a load of cutlery, shiny and polished.

86

"That looks heavy, Andrews. You'd better offload your burden." Lottie smiled at him, wishing him gone.

"Very good, Miss." He disappeared into the dining room and, thankfully, shut the door behind him. There was a decanter of sherry in there and no doubt he didn't want a witness while he raided it.

All the better. Lottie looked around to check no-one was within earshot and lifted the receiver of the telephone. Susan Threadwell's twangy voice spoke from the depths of the post office, "Number, please?"

Lottie gave her the number of Françoise's home in Paris.

"Oh, long distance, is it? It'll cost more, you know." Susan Threadwell spoke with smug authority.

"Never mind that, Miss Threadwell, just put me through, would you?" Lottie could summon up some authority herself when called upon.

The clicks on the line told her Miss Threadwell had accepted her command. Lottie fervently hoped she wouldn't listen in. Even if she didn't, the gossipmongers would soon spread her news around the village and beyond. Lottie just didn't want her mother to hear her plan from anyone's lips but her own.

A man, speaking in French, answered the call. Lottie made her request to speak to Françoise in the same language, grateful she had worked so hard on it at school. Speaking French had always come naturally to her, she seemed to have an affinity for its fluid beauty.

"Lottie! It's good to hear from you!" Françoise sounded so excited to hear from her.

Lottie's bruised heart softened. "Françoise, how are you? Do you need some company?"

"Why yes! That would be marvellous. Are you planning a visit soon?"

"As it happens, I am. Françoise, I've so much to tell you!"

CHAPTER THIRTEEN
KATHERINE WHEEL GARAGE
AUGUST 1939

Al lay on his bed, unable to sleep. He'd spent half the night dreaming up excuses to visit the manor during the working day. He'd offer to do all the errands and squeeze in a trip every opportunity he could, shave off time elsewhere to fit it in. And, until Isobel went back to school in a couple of weeks, they could go for strolls in the woods, where they'd have some privacy perhaps. Oh, the opportunities were endless when he thought about it, which he did for several more hours.

He only slept when the birds struck up the dawn chorus outside in the bungalow garden. His Dad had planted their patch not just with yards of vegetables in neat rows, enough to feed half the village by selling it in the shop, but also with roses and honeysuckle and all sorts of other flowers Al couldn't name. After yesterday's storm, the weather was making up for it today. The bees were as busy as their reputation in their garden and as soon as the sun rose the army of insects hummed into life. His Dad was never happier than when pottering about, pruning and digging and harvesting - and why he loved these chores remained a mystery to Al.

Al was more restless, more like his mother in that regard. He wished he had her knack with machines, but he couldn't take to that either. What Al really loved was the open road, the endless possibilities, exploring new territory, trying out short cuts and coaxing the lorry or the car around bends by easing the gears and accelerating away afterwards. He was a good driver, he must be, or his mother would have been sure to let him know. He knew he was a disappointment to both of them, but he had no idea how to fix that. School had been just as bad. He'd scraped through his School Certificate but staying on to do further education had been a complete waste of time. What had been the point? He was good with people. In time he was confident he could run the factory as a manager, even if he wasn't the top engineer.

And Isobel loved him. The truth of it washed over him afresh. Beautiful, gorgeous, wonderful Isobel. She looked up to him, trusted his judgement, listened to his opinions, believed in him. And that kiss yesterday; kisses. He'd relived them over and over since. The overwhelming bliss of it. When he was with her, he felt important and clever and capable of anything. In a couple of years, he'd ask her to marry him. He knew she'd say yes, that she felt the same way. Together they were safe forever, whatever the world thought about them being too young. The money side of it would sort itself somehow, wouldn't it? Who needed money when you had that much love anyway?

He got up late, something that didn't escape his grandmother's eagle eye. She was at her most alert in the mornings and there was no avoiding her if he was going to grab a bite to eat.

"What time do you call this?" Agnes doled out his porridge, stiff and slimy with age. Al hated the stuff.

He spooned some sugar from the tin over the grey sludge on his dish. "Couldn't sleep, Gran and then overdid it."

"Hmm. You're supposed to be working, aren't you? School holidays no longer apply, young man."

Al scooped up a spoonful of porridge and managed to swallow it down. "I know, I'll get this down me and go and see what needs delivering from the factory."

"Drink this tea and all, then."

Al took a sip. At least his drink was hot.

He found his mother in the office, frowning over some bills, a pencil stuck behind one ear. How pretty she still was, despite that wrinkled brow. He felt a rush of love for her, while she was unaware of his presence and before her tongue whipped the tenderness away. It was quite something, really, a woman creating a business like this, out of thin air and lately, she'd been working harder than ever on these new orders from the Home Office, however hush-hush they were.

"Hello, Mum." Al slid his arm about her thin shoulders and dropped a kiss on to her mass of greying curls.

"You're late."

Al smiled, his affection lingering still. "Overslept. Sorry."

"It won't do. Either you're working for the factory or you're not. I wouldn't allow anyone else to be so sloppy." Katy wrote a figure in the margin of the sheet of paper she was studying and replaced the pencil behind her ear. She pushed her chair back, so she could turn around and look at him. Al tried not to squirm under her quick appraisal.

"Don't you have a tie?"

"Didn't think I needed one."

"That's not the sort of impression I want my employees to give to the world at large. Go and put one on and then report to Len and see what needs doing."

Al bent down to kiss her again.

"That's enough of that. Get going and make up the time you've lost."

"Alright, Mum. Don't go on."

With tie knotted, Al sought Len and found him stacking shelves in the storeroom. The tang of rubber dominated the big space, but Len never seemed to mind. Now in his fifties, Len still did the work of two men every day. You'd never think he'd been wounded in the war, like Al's Dad. They had each lost a limb during that dark time, his Dad had lost his lower left arm and Len his right foot. Both men seemed almost proud of their prosthetic replacements, but Al had caught each of them rubbing the sore bits when they thought no-one was looking.

"Morning, Len."

"Afternoon, more like," came the reply from twelve feet up.

"Don't you start, I've had enough grief off Mum."

"I'll bet."

"So, what needs doing then?"

"Billy's got a list as long as your arm. He's in the machine room."

"Right-oh."

Uncle Billy had married his mum's younger sister, Daisy, when Al was still a baby. His sister, Susan Threadwell, now ran the Post Office in Lower Cheadle, just like her mother before her. Al could barely hear Uncle Billy above the roar of the processing machine but took the list he fished out of his pocket. Al read it, pleased to find there were errands in Woodbury, rather than farther afield. He could whizz round quickly and still manage a visit to the manor before lunch.

All went according to plan, and he roared up the drive of the manor house just before noon and parked up next to the old Sunbeam. Just as he was getting out of the lorry, he was startled to see Lottie coming through the front door loaded up with suitcases which she then proceeded to stack on the front step, as if preparing to leave for a long time.

"What's up, Lottie? Are you off somewhere?"

She gave him no friendly hello in return, but maybe that would be too much to expect after yesterday's scene in the nursery.

Lottie's face was mutinous, and she completely ignored his question. "I suppose you came to see Isobel."

"If she's around."

"No, as it happens. She's out."

"Out?"

"That's right. She's left you a note. I think it's in the hall." Lottie jerked her head back towards the house, but Al didn't rush straight off. He could smell a rat.

"Where's she gone?"

Lottie folded her lips and didn't reply.

"Come on, Lottie, tell me what's up."

He watched her struggle with her emotions and wondered if more anger would come bursting out, but instead she looked as if she would cry, something he'd rarely seen her do, although he'd heard her yesterday. In the end, her answer surprised and disarmed him.

"Do you need to ask, after what happened yesterday? When I saw you with Bella...I...I thought you and I might..." She fiddled with the strap of a big suitcase that looked perfectly well fastened to him.

Shocked, Al leant his hand for support against the bonnet of the lorry and found it still warm from dashing around Woodbury. "We're still friends, Lottie, aren't we? I always thought we would be."

Lottie seemed to have mastered the urge to cry and now had a strange look on her serious face. Determined, that was it. After a short, awkward pause, she broke it with words that astonished him.

"You want us to be friends? But can't you see Al, I love you from the deepest part of my soul, don't you realise that?"

"I...I'm fond of you too but just not in that way."

"You mean you don't fancy me."

Al drew on his resources, all of them. Into the silent vacuum, he said, "No."

Lottie let out a gasp. It sounded painful. "You really love Bella, don't you?"

"She's well named."

"Yes, my little sister is beautiful. But Al, I have other qualities - loyalty, intelligence, integrity. Don't they count for anything?"

Al went towards her, but Lottie stepped back.

He dropped his outstretched hand. "You have all of those things, and much, much more and I love that about you but it's not the same, oh, what's the word - chemistry - do you understand?"

Lottie nodded, "Yes, Al, I wish I didn't understand but I do. Isobel is pretty, she is kind, and I suppose she's clever - in her own way."

Al smiled at that last remark. "Lottie, it's hard to explain, but it isn't about the way Bella looks. We just sort of, you know, work well together. She understands me, and I understand her in a way that is effortless somehow. We share a sort of," again he searched for exactly the right word and came up with "harmony."

"God, Al, that's so corny!" Lottie had withdrawn into her shell, where she usually lived these days, he realised with a pang of guilt. Poor Lottie, he'd not given a thought to her. It must be tough being left out, but her words still stung.

Hurt, he also drew back, knowing from long experience that perseverance would not pay off. Better to leave it, Charlotte Flintock-Smythe would always work it out for herself. Sharp as a knife and quick to stab, Lottie was the best friend a man could have. He certainly wouldn't want her as his enemy.

Lottie bit her lip and nodded. She turned and walked swiftly away without a backward glance. He stood watching her retreating stiff back as she walked back to the house. He followed her up the terrace steps and easily caught up with her in the hall.

"There's your letter." Lottie pointed to the envelope balanced against the vase of gladioli on the central hall table.

He held it in his hands, reluctant to read it in front of her. She watched him, resentment in every line of her tense body. In an attempt to diffuse it, even though he knew it would probably be futile, he said, "I haven't asked where you're going with all those cases?"

"No, I don't suppose you're that interested. You'll be pleased to know I'm going to France, so, when Bella comes back, you can have her all to yourself."

"Is that wise with things the way they are?"

"Hitler isn't interested in France and anyway, I'd rather face him than stay here and watch you two together. Can't you see what you've done to me?" Lottie's voice caught on a sob and she turned her face away.

Al put out his hand to comfort her, but she shook her head and picked up a stripy hatbox that had been left behind and took it outside. Al ripped open the envelope and quickly scanned its contents.

"Al, darling,

Lottie was beside herself with grief for Granny and the will - and about us yesterday. She said she can't bear to look at me. She said some awful things that I won't repeat. I thought it best to get out of her hair this morning in hopes she will calm down when I get back.

I thought you might call, so this is to let you know you'll find me in our old secret place where we used to play in the bluebell woods.

I'll be waiting for you all day. I've brought a picnic we can share. I'm sure Lottie will come round once she's got used to things. Poor thing, I think she must love you almost as much as I do.

All my love,
Bella. xx"

Much as he longed to tear off and run up to the woods, Al realised Isobel had no idea Lottie was leaving for France. Was even their mother aware of what she was up to?

He ran back down the terrace steps.

"Lottie! Wait! Who knows about you dashing off like this? Does your mother know?"

She turned to face him, fuming. "Of course, she bloody knows, what do you take me for? At least, I haven't told her face-to-face, but I've left her a letter in her bedroom. I want to get away before she finds it. I was hoping to be gone before she got back from Woodbury."

"Well, judging by Bella's note, she obviously doesn't know."

94

"I don't care about that. I've just got to get away. So, if you'll excuse me." Lottie walked down the driveway with two of the cases.

At that point, Cassandra appeared in the double doorway above them, looking very distressed, and holding a piece of paper in her hand.

"Lottie, wait! I've just come home and found this note! What on earth do you think you're doing?" She turned and saw Al. "Oh, Al, it's you. What do you think of this mad scheme of Lottie's?" Not waiting for his reply, she clipped down the top stairs at a brisk trot and laid her hand on his arm. "Maybe you can persuade her to stay? France is no place for anyone with sense at the moment. Who knows what might happen? Oh dear, oh dear, I must stop her."

Just then, a black taxi-cab came up the drive and drew to a full stop next to Lottie. Although Cassandra walked quickly towards it, Lottie was already in the car before her mother reached it. Al ran ahead of her around to the passenger side and tapped on the glass. "Lottie, wait! Open this window. Don't go like this, let's talk!"

But the window remained locked shut. Lottie turned her head away. He could see more tears on her cheeks, but she did not look back. The driver silently loaded up the car.

Cassandra had reached them now and gripped his arm. "Oh, Al, make her stop. Say something to make her stay! She can't go with things like this! I never meant to make her run away."

Cassandra, too, knocked on the window of the car. "Open this window, Charlotte! Open it, I say. We must talk!"

Lottie brushed her hand across her face and turned around. She wound the window down and said through it. "It's no good, Mummy, I must go. I'll write to you."

"But, when will you be back?"

"I don't know, perhaps it would be better if I stayed away until my twenty-fifth birthday!"

"Oh, Lottie, darling, don't say that! I know you are angry but please, don't leave like this!"

The driver, who had not shown any emotion throughout this exchange, got in behind the wheel. "Where to, Miss?"

Lottie gave one lingering look at both her mother and at Al and then turned back to the driver. "Woodbury Station, please."

"You are sure, Miss?"

"Absolutely! Drive on."

Al could only see Lottie's profile, her mouth set and determined, her chin forward and her eyes trained on the back of the driver's head.

The driver shook his head, pressed the ignition button and the car moved away.

Al was left standing on the driveway, dumbfounded by the turn of events, unable to think or move until the vehicle had disappeared from view.

Cassandra stood like a statue behind him. She was white with shock. "Oh, Al, what have I done?"

Al put his arm around Cassandra and walked her back up to the house. He installed her on one of the sofas in the drawing room and she collapsed against it. He had no idea how to deal with the situation but then he realised the one person who could help would be his mum.

He went into the hall and picked up the telephone. "Put me through to the Katherine Wheel Garage please, Miss Threadwell."

"Is that you, Albert Phipps? Is everything alright?"

"Yes, just put me through, please."

His mother understood immediately. Always quick on the uptake, she promised to be at the manor within ten minutes.

Al went back into the drawing room and rang the bell for Andrews. "Some water for Mrs Flintock-Smythe, please, Andrews, and perhaps some brandy?"

"Right away, Master Phipps."

By the time Cassandra was nursing her strong drink, his mother had arrived.

"What on earth has happened, Al?"

In the hall, he quickly told his mother the whole story.

She patted his shoulder. "Alright, love. Leave Cass to me. I'll handle it from now on. Where's Bella?"

Relieved, he ran his hand through his hair and remembered the letter in his pocket. Bella! She knew nothing of this crazy adventure of Lottie's.

"She's gone out, Mum, but I think I know where to find her."

"Off you go, then, my lad. Leave the rest to me." His mum nodded briskly and disappeared into the drawing room.

Al stuffed the paper into his pocket and set off for the woods at a quick trot.

He saw her before she noticed him. She was picking wildflowers and bunching them up in her hands. She wore a white dress decorated with similar flowers. It gave the delightful illusion she was part of the landscape. The sun filtered through the trees, lighting her face as she bent down. Al's heart lurched. Isobel had never looked more beautiful than in that golden moment.

He forgot all about Lottie as he went to her and gathered her in his arms, showering her with kisses and holding her so tight she dropped her wild bouquet. The petals fell like confetti around them, scattering scent and colour at their feet.

It took a while before he could stop kissing Isobel and even longer to remember anything but the feel of this gorgeous girl in his arms, her lips on his, her passion matching his own. The bees hummed around them, their only witnesses, as they lay down amongst the roots of the trees to kiss and hug again.

It took all Al's resolve not to pursue things to their natural conclusion, but he loved this girl. He'd flirted with other girls from the village from time to time, but he'd never felt this overwhelming sensation with them. Although their breath was coming thick and fast and Isobel put up no restraint, he withdrew before his desire took them both too far.

"What's wrong, Al?" Isobel looked puzzled at his pulling away.

"Absolutely nothing, that's the problem." He grinned at her, determined not to hold her until he'd regained control of his senses.

Isobel laughed and blushing slightly, nodded her fair head. "That's so true, my love."

She reached towards him again, but he knew he wouldn't be able to hold back a second time. "Wait a minute, Bella, let's get our breath back, shall we?"

"If you want." Isobel hugged her knees and rested her chin on them.

She looked a little sulky. She was as frustrated as him! Al decided to change the subject and suddenly remembered Lottie's dramatic departure from Cheadle Manor. How could he have forgotten?

"Bella, did you know that Lottie has gone to France?"

Isobel's head jerked up. "What? What on earth are you talking about? She never even left her room all day yesterday. Mummy was so worried about her."

"She still is. I've just left her. She was in a right state and I had to call my mum to come and look after her."

"When?"

"About half an hour ago."

"Why didn't you say before?"

"Isn't it obvious?"

Isobel flushed. It made her look prettier than ever. "Yes, well, never mind that now, I must get back home and see Mummy."

"I'll come with you. Just one more kiss first?"

But this time it was Isobel who refused him. She rushed ahead through the woods and didn't stop running until she reached her home, with Al close behind her.

Smoke fumes from the man standing before her in the queue blew back in Lottie's face, making her cough. Even more annoyingly, her penfriend and host, Françoise Blanchard, couldn't stop giggling. She kept making eyes at the gaunt lad in the queue next to theirs. Lottie didn't join in. She no longer felt young but old, passed over, unwanted, rejected and very, very alone. She didn't care about being in Paris or that everyone here thought war inevitable.

The smoker went to the table to be fitted for his gas mask, leaving her and Françoise first in line.

She wondered if the Frenchman puffing on his Gauloises cigarette really needed that gas mask. Surely, he'd inhaled enough fumes to make himself immune to anything enemy planes might spew from the sky if war ever did break out.

Françoise's giggles had grated on Lottie's nerves but now the serious-looking, dark-haired young man in the adjacent queue smiled openly at her pretty, fair-haired friend. They introduced themselves, ignoring Lottie. That suited her mood. She had no desire to mingle with dubious strangers and anyway Françoise's smirks and smiles had become embarrassing. She wished she'd shut up. Lottie had to reluctantly admit that Françoise was less interesting to live with on a daily basis than she had been as a correspondent. Yet another disappointment.

Lottie was almost glad when it was her turn to be fitted with the rubber mask and goggles. She wondered if the rubber had come from Al's factory. Could be. They were working overtime these days. Even if she had been at home, she would barely have seen him, judging by her mother's letters.

100

Her thoughts were disrupted by the fat policeman's fingers measuring her from ear to chin. He smelt of stale sweat and tobacco. Every Frenchman she'd ever met smelt of tobacco. She probably did herself, having queued in this smoke-filled police station for an hour.

The policeman nodded his satisfaction with the fit of her mask and passed it to her in its cylindrical canister. At least she wouldn't have to look like a walking gargoyle wearing it all the way home. She sat and waited on a hard chair against the stained wall while Françoise got measured for her mask and the thin, delicate boy did the same on the next table. Lottie had to suppress a smile when both their heads were jerked back to look at the fitter at the same time instead of sideways at each other. Françoise's face was beetroot colour by the end.

Françoise babbled on about the boy all the way home along the tree-lined boulevard. Lottie listened to the stream of French, pleased she could understand it so easily. It had always been her favourite subject at school, and it was gratifying to find her hard work was paying off. She'd enjoy it a lot more if Françoise's conversation was interesting.

"His name is David and he lives near us."

"That's nice but it's odd you haven't met before, if he's local." Lottie noticed the leaves beginning to brown their edges above her. Horse chestnuts, always the first to turn. How worn out and fragile they looked. August was always a dusty, tattered sort of month, even in Paris.

"Yes, I suppose that's true, but he says," another giggle from Françoise, "he wants to see me again." She held up a ragged piece of paper. "Look, Lottie, he's written down where we're going to meet."

"He looked very young."

Françoise pouted. "He is the same age as me."

"Exactly." Lottie's penfriend was two years younger than her, which hadn't seemed to matter when they'd exchanged letters through their school days. Now, it was a gulf Lottie could no longer cross.

Françoise's lower lip grew so pronounced it distorted her attractive heart-shaped face into a scowl. Then her mouth broke into a gasp of surprise and she nudged Lottie in the ribs. Cross, Lottie turned to her, a retort at the ready but she never uttered it. A woman passed them from the opposite direction, chicly dressed à la Parisienne, pulling the leash of a dog. Nothing extraordinary about the pairing except the clipped white poodle was wearing a gas mask over its face.

"Whatever next!" Lottie said, loud enough for the smart woman to notice.

"He has to get used to it." The woman gave a delicate shrug and walked on past them, the dog hanging its head under the weight of the ugly gas mask.

"Well! I think I've seen it all now." Françoise, scowl erased, looked back at the woman and her dog trotting along beside her.

"Surely she doesn't think we'll be gassed before the war even starts?" Lottie faced forwards again, disgusted at the cruelty inflicted on the little pooch. Perhaps the woman thought she'd get more attention through the novelty. She looked the type, with her smart feathered hat and bright red lipstick.

They walked on in silence. Lottie glanced sideways at her companion. Françoise looked excited, too excited. In repose, Françoise's pale face became sulky. She might only be seventeen, but Françoise was mistress of the pout French girls seemed so good at when they couldn't get their own way. But, when she smiled, she dazzled. She was smiling now.

Lottie knew a moment of misgiving. "What are you so happy about, Françoise?"

"He's the one."

"Who?"

"David - the boy in the queue at the police station." Françoise turned her fair head towards Lottie, her big hazel eyes sparkling. "I'm going to meet him this afternoon. Say you'll come with me, Lottie? Oh, do come!"

"Why would you want me there? If you have met your match, all in a moment like a fairy tale, you won't want a gooseberry along." Lottie had never believed in love at first sight. Her love for Al had grown through her childhood into the all-consuming passion that now plagued her night and day. You couldn't just fall for someone instantly while waiting in a queue. There was more to love than *that*. She wondered for the umpteenth time what he was doing right now – and whether Isobel was with him.

"What do you mean - 'gooseberry'? Oh, I see, you mean to hold the candle. Pah! Of course, I'll need you - to make it respectable, for one thing." Françoise hitched her bag higher on her shoulder.

They crossed the quiet, tree-lined road. They were nearly home already. The tall blocks of apartment buildings had thinned out. Gardens now separated individual houses and each one was barred to the public by elegant metal gates between stone pillars.

Françoise clutched at Lottie's sleeve. "Do say yes, Lottie."

Lottie sighed, lifted the latch on the Blanchard's gate and walked inside their private world.

That afternoon, they sat together at a little table under shady trees in a café near the Odéon, as directed by David's note, sipping citron pressé.

"He's late." Lottie loved this drink, sharp yet sweet, the zesty lemon juice zinging on her tongue. She knew of nothing in Britain to match it, certainly not the weak, sugary lemonade Mrs Andrews made on the few really hot days Wiltshire wrung out of its summers. She added another shake of sugar to her glass and stirred the ice cubes with a long spoon.

"There he is!" Françoise squeaked, her voice sounding high pitched and to Lottie's mind, a little hysterical.

The tall young man, barely more than a boy, was strolling towards them, his gait graceful and his stride wide. He quickly spotted them and soon stood before a blushing Françoise who smiled back. Lottie looked him over. Slim, with hair and haunted eyes so dark they looked almost black. He wore a worn but well-cut suit, a battered Fedora hat and polished brogues. He didn't look exactly destitute, but he'd obviously fallen on hard times.

The felt hat came off and he gave a little formal bow.

"It's good to see you again, Françoise. I wasn't sure you would come after so short an acquaintance."

Lottie checked the sarcastic response she longed to give these star-struck lovers and instead said, "Do sit down. David, isn't it? I'm Charlotte Flintock-Smythe but you can call me Lottie like everyone else."

The young man nodded and obeyed, hooking his hat on the back of his chair and stretched out his long legs under the tiny table. A waiter appeared from the back of the café and raised his eyebrows in query.

"A coffee, please." David's French had a Germanic accent that set alarm bells ringing in Lottie's ears.

As Françoise's tongue seemed to be tied up at this juncture, Lottie decided to take up the role of inquisitor. "So, you are not Parisian, David? We haven't seen you in our arrondissement before."

"No, it's true, I have only just arrived."

"Oh?" Lottie left the little syllable hanging for him to fill the gap.

He took the hint. "I come from Austria. Vienna, actually."

Lottie took another sip of astringent lemon. How well its acidity suited her mood.

"How interesting. What brings you to France?" Françoise couldn't take her eyes off him but at least she had found her voice.

104

David raised his eyebrows. He looked astonished - downright shocked - but replied politely. "Can you not have heard of the Anschluss and Kristallnacht?"

"I, I think so. Isn't the Anschluss when Austria joined Germany last year?" Françoise murmured.

"You *think* so? In such times as these?" David still looked shocked, almost angry. "Do you not have a wireless?"

"My father will not let us listen to it, he keeps it in his study. I've been away at school. We never looked at the newspapers there." Françoise had gone pale now.

Lottie might find Françoise irritating, but she was fond of her friend. Sensing her disappointment, alarmed at his sudden ferocity, she defended her. "You must forgive her ignorance, David. Monsieur Blanchard, Françoise's father, is very protective. He wants to shield his daughter from the harshness of the world."

David downed his black coffee in one go. "I shouldn't have come. It was stupid. I must go."

"No!" Françoise shot out her arm and touched his.

David stood up. "I'm sorry, Françoise, but we are so different. You are so innocent and pure - a proper bourgeois French girl and I..."

Anger rose in Lottie at his rudeness. "Now listen, David, you can't just leave without explaining yourself. Françoise and I might be ignorant, but it doesn't mean we aren't curious. Please sit down and fill in the gaps in our knowledge. Waiter? Another coffee for the gentleman, please."

David stood, uncertain and wavering until Françoise touched his arm again. "Please stay, David. It is not my fault I do not understand."

Lottie kicked herself for not encouraging him to leave straight away but there was something about him that invited curiosity. Was he one of the refugees she'd heard about? Was that why he was so aggrieved, and if so, who could blame him?

David sighed, shook his head and capitulated. "It's just that I can't believe anyone in this world can remain unaware of events so near to them. Your father must be a tyrant."

Françoise pouted, her pale lipstick glinting in the sunshine. "My school was a convent and we were shielded from the outside world – and…and, um, my father is very concerned for my safety."

"Safe!" David gave a short laugh. "No-one is safe anymore, except perhaps someone of your beautiful colouring, Françoise, and, yes, perhaps locked away from the world in a convent. Please forgive my rudeness. It was your carefree high spirits that drew you to me this morning at the police station. You were a ray of sunlight in that dark place. And there has been so much darkness, I am hungry for sunshine, for simplicity."

His deep brown eyes rested on Françoise's delicate features and her mouth, always mobile, lifted at the corners.

Lottie felt uneasy. The anger simmering under David's thin veneer worried her. She pressed him further, wanting to believe he had a good reason behind his bad manners. "David, please share your story with us, if you don't mind?"

"Very well. Vienna used to be like Paris. Tranquil, prosperous, perhaps complacent would best describe it."

"Ouch," Lottie nodded her agreement. Françoise sat quite still, her big hazel eyes rapt with attention.

David didn't smile back. "It's how life should be in a normal world. But last November people turned on the Jewish community - of which I'm one - and smashed up shops and houses and synagogues all over my city. Resentment against my people had been building up for months, perhaps years, but they used the excuse of the assassination of a German diplomat here in Paris as justification. Did you not hear about that?"

"I did hear something of it, when I was in England." Lottie could not deny it just to save Françoise's face.

"How could you not? A young Jew, much the same age as me, shot him in the embassy here. The Nazis said Kristallnacht was their revenge for the killing but, in fact, the pogrom had already begun."

"Pogrom?" Françoise's brow had wrinkled to a frown.

Lottie answered. "It means to persecute and kill."

David took up his story again. The words came tumbling out of him now, in an unstoppable flow. He looked flushed, the anger rising to the surface. "Yes, that's exactly what it means. Since then, we've certainly suffered persecution and thousands of men have been rounded up and taken away to labour camps. There have been many beatings and murders."

Françoise let out an audible gasp.

David didn't stop for breath. Lottie felt she was witnessing a confession, that he needed to tell someone, anyone, his life story. He looked very young.

"My father, a musician like me, decided to come to Paris, leave his job behind and come to live with my mother's relatives here. My mother is French, you see, and her parents have an apartment here in Chaville. She met my father when he was working at the Paris Opera House. After they married, they went to live in Vienna, and he got a post in the Viennese Philharmonic Orchestra."

Lottie could hear the pride in his voice as he spoke of his father. He offered them a cigarette, which they refused, before lighting one for himself. He took a deep drag before continuing his story. "It wasn't easy to get permits to leave but my father knew some influential people who helped him. It still cost all his savings and we had to leave everything behind. The government had already cancelled our insurance policies, so we could not claim damages and our food was rationed. Living in

Vienna had become impossible and, from what I've heard since, we got out just in time."

The waiter arrived with his second coffee. David slumped back against his chair to allow him to place the little white cup down on the table and remove the used one. He looked tired now, older, empty. The cigarette trembled between his long fingers, casting its chimney of ash to the pavement.

"I'm sorry." Lottie had heard the reports, she wasn't as ignorant as she'd made out. She'd read the papers at home, but it had all seemed remote; unbelievable. She'd been so caught up in her own affairs. The death of her grandmother, her crazy inheritance and Al's rejection had wiped out the rest of the world's concerns for a while. She was ashamed.

"It is not your fault, but Hitler's." David sipped his coffee.

"So, you are Jewish?" Françoise's full mouth was a silent 'o'.

"I am proud to be so."

"Of course, you are." Lottie smiled at him, but Françoise went very quiet.

"This changes how you feel about me?" David looked directly at Françoise,

Françoise looked away.

Lottie saw her eyes fill with tears. "Françoise's father is very critical of your people, David. It makes it awkward."

"Awkward? Awkward? Such a polite term for the brutality and hatred my people face. I knew I shouldn't have come, but when you looked at me this morning, Françoise, my heart turned over. Didn't yours?" He stubbed out his cigarette in the ashtray.

Françoise turned back to him. A single tear trickled down her young face. Lottie definitely felt like an intruder now.

"Yes, David. I've never experienced anything like it. When you looked at me, I felt I knew you, soul to soul. You did too, didn't you?"

David reached out his hand and took Françoise's small one, enfolding it in his. "You have the face of an angel. You make me feel there is still beauty in this ugly world."

Lottie had heard enough and felt this young stranger should not have said so much. It was strange how he'd told them his entire life story on first acquaintance. It disturbed her that he'd opened up like that and it made her uneasy, especially about her gullible friend. She stood up, hoping Françoise would take the hint and join her. The speed of events rapidly unfolding between these two people was disturbing. They were barely adults.

Lottie tucked her chair in noisily, hoping to disrupt their trance. "Do either of you know where I could get an English newspaper? You've made me want to catch up with the news, David, and I have to admit, I find it easier to speak French than read it."

"I think most newsstands would have one, but you could also go to the English bookshop and ask them."

"Is there one?" Lottie straightened her hat.

"Yes, have you not heard of Shakespeare and Company? It is run by an American woman. It's not far away, just two blocks. I could show you, if you like."

"No, just give me directions, I'm sure I'll find it."

David told her how to find the shop.

Lottie nodded. "Thanks. Going to join me, Françoise?"

They both ignored her; gazing only at each other with an earnest feverishness that Lottie distrusted.

"Are you sure you won't come, Françoise?"

Françoise shook her head, barely glancing up.

"Please come with me, Françoise."

"No, I'm staying here, with David."

David smiled at Lottie while she hesitated, uncertain whether to go or stay. "I'll walk Françoise home.

Don't worry, I'll make sure she's safely returned. I do not live far away from her house and I promise I will behave. Forgive my indiscreet ramblings. I am still coming to terms with all that has happened. I should not have said so much, but I will take care of your friend, I promise."

At a loss to know what else she could do to break up the two lovers, Lottie put some money on the table, picked up her bag and straightened her hat. She had a lump in her throat that prevented speech, so she left in silence. She walked up the wide boulevard, grateful the traffic roared past her. If only it could drown out her thoughts. David's story had been deeply disturbing. Somehow, it was so much more unsettling hearing a real account of these atrocities. She made a vow to keep up to date in future. In her rush to get away, Granny's death and funeral but above all, Al's rejection of her love, Lottie had been totally preoccupied with her personal concerns. She really was mortified about her ignorance before David's account of his experiences. She was surprised Françoise's innocence hadn't put him off, but maybe that was exactly what he'd found so devastatingly attractive. Maybe, and it would be understandable, he harked back to a time when he, too, had been innocent of these ugly pogroms.

She bought a French newspaper but could find none in English. It was hard work not reading in her own language with so much happening in the world. She tucked it under her arm and marched on further in her quest.

The English bookshop was easy to find. She went inside and sniffed. Books. Her favourite aroma. The place was stuffed with them from floor to ceiling on every wall. Pictures of authors vied for space on whatever room was left. Tables and chairs groaned under piles of more books. There was a delightful untidiness to the place, encouraging creativity and ideas. She lost herself in the shelves of novels. Selecting half a dozen, she went to the counter to pay. Lottie was shocked at the total. The small amount of money she'd brought with her to Paris was fast running out.

"Um, I think I'll just have these two," she said, speaking in English in hopes of being understood.

"Of course, it does come to quite a bit, doesn't it?" The middle-aged woman at the till replied in English and smiled, her button-bright eyes warm and brown and intelligent.

Lottie, grateful for the kindness, smiled back finding it delightful to speak in her native tongue for once. She counted out her francs and passed them over. "Is there anywhere I could sit and read for a while?"

"Yes, there's a little corner there." The bookseller put the two volumes in a bag and gave them to her. "Are you on holiday in Paris?" She had an American accent. It struck a chord with Lottie, a dim and distant memory of her father's beloved voice.

"Sort of. I'm staying with a penfriend, but she's not so interested in reading books as I am, and certainly not English ones!" Lottie thanked her and settled into the chair in the corner. She opened her book, 'The Rainbow' by DH Lawrence. She'd forgotten all about buying a newspaper with all these books to tempt her.

None of the teachers at school had encouraged their pupils to read the famous author. 'Far too racy for young girls', her English teacher had said. All the more reason to discover his work now. Lottie was soon engrossed and didn't notice an older woman, of about forty years of age, sit down on the chair next to her until she spoke.

"Sorry, what did you say?" Lottie had to drag herself back to the present.

"I said, how do you do?" The woman wore unusually informal clothes and also spoke in English with an American accent in a deep, rich voice. The fabric of her coat was expensive and brightly coloured. It reminded Lottie of some curtains her mother had bought from Liberty's for her bedroom, inspired by the designs of William Morris. The lady wore a bright orange scarf around her neck and an equally vivid purple hat that

111

clashed magnificently. Lady Smythe would have described her outfit as 'rather fast'. Lottie loved its brazen anarchy and felt immediately drawn to the large woman.

The woman lifted pince-nez to her eyes; she wore them on a golden chain. "What are you reading?"

"It's a DH Lawrence book, 'The Rainbow'." Lottie lifted it up to show her the spine.

"Ah! What a perfect age you are to be reading Lawrence. Read them all, my dear, and learn all you can about love before it smites you down." She gave a low laugh, which rumbled from somewhere deep under the Liberty print.

Lottie felt strangely uninhibited in this intoxicating company and told the truth. "Already smitten, I'm afraid."

"Is it the real thing? Or just an infatuation? At your age, honey, I'd already lost count of the number of times I'd thought myself in love."

"I've always loved him. Ever since I can remember. I've never found anyone else remotely interesting."

"Him? Pity." The woman mumbled the words, as if to herself.

Lottie wasn't sure she'd heard them right. "I'm sorry? What do you mean?"

"Oh, nothing." The lady removed her little spectacles and let them fall across the large expanse of her colourful coat. "Tell me about him. I want to know if he's worth loving."

Lottie raised her eyebrows. "Don't you think we should be properly introduced to each other before we talk about such things?"

"Heavens, no, why should I? I feel an instant rapport, don't you?"

"Well, yes, I suppose I do!"

That rumble rippled between them again and, this time, Lottie laughed too.

CHAPTER FIFTEEN
PARIS
AUGUST 1939

Mabel Miller – "Oh honey, just call me Mabs," - transformed Lottie's life in Paris overnight.

Instead of going out with Françoise every day, she abandoned her to David's seductive charms. The disquieting qualms she'd had when she'd met him never really went away, but she could not persuade Françoise to stop seeing him, and after a while, she gave up trying and ignored the nagging guilt that pricked her conscience every time she saw how deliriously happy Françoise seemed.

Lured by Mabs's formidable charisma, Lottie let her sense of responsibility for her young penfriend dissipate and allowed herself to have fun instead, expressing her misgivings whenever Françoise spent time with her as a sop to her conscience and listening to her tedious monologues on David's many virtues with increasing impatience. Françoise was obviously deeply in love for the first time in her life and it would take more than Lottie to dissuade her from her passionate obsession.

In Mabs, Lottie had found a soul mate, a woman of the world so different from her inexperienced penfriend as anyone could be. She learned so much from her new American friend, despite, or maybe because of, their age difference of almost twenty years. They met every morning at the bookshop and had lunch either at the Café de Flore or at Les Deux Magots alongside the intellectual élite of Paris. She overheard animated conversations from their tables that sent her mind reeling into unknown realms of radical thoughts and ideas. It refreshed and renewed Lottie's crushed spirit. She felt she had finally found where she wanted to be and soaked up every new experience like a dry sponge submerged in an infinite lake.

113

Lottie spent more money on books in Shakespeare and Company and its sister shop opposite, run by the lover of Sylvia Beach, the proprietor who'd been so kind on her first visit. A world had opened up to Lottie she'd never known existed, where women loved other women, men flirted with other men, where you didn't have to be pretty to be interesting, because an alert and curious mind was more of an asset in this highbrow, liberal milieu.

Though apparently unmarried, Mabs hinted at a failed relationship, but never expanded on the details and Lottie didn't dare to enquire further. She was lonely, she said, and glad of a friend. Obviously affluent, Mabs was always eager to pay the bill but Lottie's pride prevented it. She insisted on going halves – going Dutch, Mabs called it – and, towards the end of August, ran out of funds. One lunchtime, sitting outside a café in the late summer sun, full of omelette and wine, she confessed.

"I'm skint." Lottie sat back, pushing her cane chair away from the table. Her purse was quite empty except for a few small coins. "Look, I only have enough for the Métro back to the Blanchard's house."

"Honey, let me pay. You know I don't mind. It's so delightful to have your young company."

"No, well…I say no, but you'll have to this time. I've been meaning to ask you about something. I have a mission to fulfil. I have some jewellery I want to sell."

"No! Surely it hasn't come to that?" Mabs lit up one of her cheroots.

"It's not a problem. I want to sell them anyway. I shall never, ever wear a tiara."

"A tiara? My word, that does sound glamorous."

"And very old hat. My grandmother gave it to me before she died, just this summer, actually. It seems an age ago now." Lottie ran her finger round her empty wine glass, making it sing.

"I'm sorry to hear that. Were you very fond of her?" Mabs blew blue smoke towards the busy street.

"Yes, very. Not everyone loved Granny. To be honest, I think I was the only one and even I had secrets from her. She was such an incorrigible meddler, but I do miss her." Lottie, startled by the tears that suddenly pricked her eyes, blinked them away. "But I shan't miss the tiara. I was wondering, Mabs, do you know a trustworthy jeweller who might buy it? I think it's worth a bit – it's got rubies and diamonds – not huge ones, but it is pretty."

"Heavens! It must be worth a fortune."

"Probably not but that's why I must find an honest goldsmith."

"Leave it to me, I'll make enquiries." Mabs winked.

"Discreet ones, please."

"Naturally." Mabs chuckled. "Now, you will come to dinner tonight, won't you? At my hotel? There are some charming people I want you to meet."

"That will be the third time this week. The Blanchards will think I've left home."

"Well, you could stay with me all the time. I'd adore that." Mabs stubbed out her cheroot.

"Tempting, but no. At least, not until I've sold the family heirloom." Lottie got up from the table. "I'll see you tomorrow then?"

"Alright, I'll let you off this once and I'll find out about you-know-what in the meantime."

Mabs, true to her word, promised to take Lottie to Cartier's, whose jewellery store dominated the fashionable rue de la Paix in the second arrondissement. Lottie had slung the plush red jewellery case into her bag at the last minute when she left Cheadle Manor in such a hurry, and in such a temper. She hadn't expected to have to sell them at all, let alone so soon, and felt a pang of remorse as she slipped the velvet box into a small suitcase.

"Where are you going with that valise, Charlotte?" Madame Blanchard asked her in the hall, as she drew on her gloves. Like her daughter and Lottie, she was rarely at

115

home in the day and Ricci, the Italian chauffeur, was already waiting for her in the car on the drive. "Not leaving us, are you?"

"No, no, of course, unless…do you wish me to go, Madame? You have been very generous with your hospitality." Lottie gripped her case tighter.

"Nonsense, I am glad you are here to chaperone Françoise. She needs someone to look out for her. Françoise has always been, shall we say, a little gullible. It reassures me to know she is with someone older and more mature all the time." Madame Blanchard checked her appearance in the elaborate gilt mirror in the large hallway.

Lottie experienced a familiar stab of guilt. She hardly ever spent time with Françoise, but they usually left the house together. It must appear that they were still united throughout the day. How was Madame Blanchard to know they got out at very different stops off the Métro? She hadn't set out to deceive her hostess, but that was exactly what she was doing. "Um, thanks."

The moment of truth was saved by Françoise skipping down the staircase. She was wearing a new turquoise blue dress, and under her jaunty yellow hat, her happy face wore a fresh, becoming glow.

"You're looking well, Françoise, I must say." Madame Blanchard presented her cheek to her daughter for a kiss.

"Thank you, Maman. D…I mean, Lottie chose it for me, didn't you?" Françoise directed a fierce beam at Lottie, warning her not to betray her secret.

Lottie squirmed at this further deceit. "It's a very flattering cut."

"Yes, lovely." Madame stood back and admired her daughter. She turned to Lottie. "You seem to be developing a very individual style?"

Lottie knew another frisson of discomfort. It was true. Under the Bohemian influence of Mabs, she now dressed in wildly exuberant colours. Today, she wore a new red silk jacket over a deep saffron coloured frock, neatly tailored so it accentuated her waist, and she'd not be able to resist buying a stick of bright red lipstick to match. Her hair, now cut fashionably short, was tucked under a silk scarf shot through with orange and yellow stripes and her feet were encased in kid leather red shoes. Another reason she had to sell the contents of her case.

Aware of her appointment at the jewellers, Lottie directed an equally meaningful look back at her friend. "We'll be late, Françoise. Remember - we're going to the cinema?"

"Are we? Oh, yes, of course we are. See you later, Maman!" Françoise tugged Lottie's spare arm and they tripped lightly down the front steps of the villa before crunching across the pebbles to the grand entrance gates. Ricci had parked the big Citroën saloon in the drive and lounged against its bonnet, waiting, as ever, for Madame. He gave them a knowing smile. Lottie had seen Madame and her chauffeur together in the garage when looking for the tennis rackets some weeks ago, when she'd still spent most of her time at the chateau, bored enough to want to play. Monsieur Blanchard worked as a manager in the local Citroën factory and as a result kept the latest shiny model there, but the big Citroën car hadn't been big enough to hide them. Their compromising situation had left her in no doubt of the true relationship between her glamorous hostess and her young, handsome Italian driver.

"Oh, la-la! That was a close-run thing!" Françoise giggled. "If only Maman knew what we got up to!"

Lottie thought it just as well Françoise didn't know what was happening between her mother and the handsome Ricci. But Françoise's mother was not her responsibility. In fact, neither was Françoise, even though Lottie had assumed that role at first. Now she had reneged on that assumption and, remembering Madame Blanchard's trusting words, Lottie asked, "And what *are* you getting up to, Françoise? Are you seeing David every day?"

117

Françoise pouted. She was so very good at it. "Oh, Lottie, what if I am? He was so sad when I met him. He says I make him forget all the horrors he's seen. He says, when he's with me, the world goes away, and he can pretend everything's alright. And it will be, won't it?"

"Everyone seems to think that the British troops and the French will sort it out between them, if it ever comes to a fight. No-one I talk to thinks the Germans can get past the French troops guarding the border. I'm sure your David is safe now."

"I do hope so. I love him, you know, Lottie."

"You know your mother thinks I'm your chaperone, don't you? So, promise me not to do anything silly."

"What do you mean?" That pout again.

They reached their Métro stop and clattered down the steps into the underground station. A whoosh of cold air lifted their skirts. Lottie clutched at her dress with one hand and her case with the other. She hoped none of the other passengers would guess her precious cargo.

They sat inside the train carriage. "Don't play the innocent with me, Françoise."

Françoise adjusted her gloves, avoiding Lottie's gaze. "Well, who knows what you are getting up to in town every day with your new American friend? All those risqué books you read. Some of them wouldn't get past Papa's scrutiny if he saw them."

"That's beside the point, and anyway, he can't read English. Please don't change the subject. Don't do anything stupid with David. He's very intense and troubled. His feelings for you might make him go too far. It's up to you to make sure he doesn't." Lottie settled her case on her lap, holding it with both hands.

"David wants to marry me."

"Does he? And does he know how young you are?"

"I told a tiny, weeny fib about that."

"Oh, Françoise. You idiot!"

118

Lottie wanted to say a lot more on the subject, but the train eased into the next station and Françoise gave her a quick kiss and left before she could utter another word of caution.

Preoccupied with her errand, Lottie forgot all about their brief conversation when she was both impressed and surprised at the amount of money Granny's jewels fetched at Cartier's.

Even world weary Mabs looked shocked. "My word, darling. I think lunch is on you today! Have you got a bank here?"

"No, I just brought some cash and the jewels with me."

"Oh, you innocent child! You were lucky not to be robbed. Come with me, we'll open an account for you at The Westminster Foreign Bank. They'll know what to do with you." Mabs hailed a cab and they piled in.

Inside the hush of the marble building, Lottie banked the cheque. To be fair to the clerk, he didn't bat an eyelid at the large amount. Lottie suppressed an embarrassed giggle as she signed the forms. What would Granny have said if she was still here to witness the jettison of her heirloom? But then, that's why she'd given them to Lottie.

Granny had seen this coming.

After an elderly, more senior clerk, had rubber-stamped her application, on the strength of the cheque coming from Cartier's, Lottie was given his blessing to make a withdrawal.

Whilst he had his back to them, she turned to Mabs. "He probably thinks I'm a jewel thief!"

Mabs gave one of her familiar rumbles of laughter. "Better withdraw a fat wad to splurge out on then, honey, now you have your stash."

The clerk gave a decidedly contrived cough and shuffled his papers.

Lottie stuffed the crisp notes into her purse. There were so many, she struggled with the clasp. "Come on, Mabs, I need a drink!"

"I think this calls for champagne, Lottie darling. An entire bottle!"

They took the Métro a couple of stops to the Pont Neuf and walked across the bridge along the wide pavements. Lottie clutched her bag tight to her side and gazed down at the Seine flowing below her, marvelling at the sensation of power a full purse gave her.

Her mood was lowered when they bought a newspaper on the way to Les Deux Magots.

Lottie read it out loud over lunch. "They talk of peace and talk of war on these front pages in a political see-saw. I can't make head nor tail of who wants what, Mabs."

"I know, honey. I've been following it for months. First one country and then another exchange rhetoric and agreements. I have the general impression that no-one but Hitler wants another war. After all, he's already annexed Austria and taken over Czechoslovakia and you'd think that would be enough, but he's seems determined to create one. More champagne?"

"Thank you." Lottie broke off. "By the way - have I told you my mother drove ambulances in France in the last one? You know, the so-called Great War - the one to end all others?"

Mabs filled her glass from the bottle and returned it to the metal ice bucket. "Did she? No, I didn't know that, good for her. It seems naïve now that we all believed it would be the end of world conflict at the time. I was too young to serve but helped my mother with the Red Cross in New York. Your mother must be a bit older than me."

"Yes, she was in the FANY's. She met my father in France."

"Oh? Was he French, you didn't say?"

Lottie took a bite of her artichoke. "No, American, like you. He's dead now. Motor-racing accident. I was only seven."

Mabs reached out her hand and stroked Lottie's. "How difficult for you, my dear."

"Yes, it was, but even harder for Mummy. She's never really got over it. She adored him. Granny didn't help; she loathed him while he was alive, then never forgave him for dying young."

"That sounds complicated. Where in the States was your father from?"

"Boston. His father was a lawyer, I believe. I met him once when I was very young. All I can remember was that he was terrifying."

"Boston isn't so far from New York. Maybe we've even met."

"I doubt it, Mabs. My American grandfather was more interested in the church and upholding the law than art, but my paternal grandmother was lovely. She came to our house in Wiltshire once, with my Aunt Rose. She was very beautiful, tall and blonde, like my sister, Isobel. I'm afraid I didn't inherit her genes. I'm more like my short, stout other grandmother."

"Well, I find you perfectly charming, whichever grandmother you resemble."

They finished their meal and ordered coffee. Mabs opened out Le Figaro and perused the middle pages. "Oh, my word, they are now telling us how to fix black-out curtains."

"That sounds to me as if they mean it."

"Newspapers are always full of hot air, but it's not just the coffee that's sobering me up." Mabs folded the broadsheet and slung it back down on to the café table with a resounding slap. "I tell you what, my dear, I need to forget about all this for a while. I think we should go to an art gallery this afternoon and look at some paintings."

Lottie laughed. "You're probably right. After all, the Germans are still a very long way away and in

L'Humanité, the Communist Party's rag, they reckon the German and Russian ministers have signed the Hitler-Stalin pact of non-aggression."

"Well, the Communists would be all for the socialist Russians, wouldn't they? I can't honestly say I find it that reassuring myself. There's too much movement on the maps of Europe for my liking. Hitler is such a greedy little man."

"Yes, let's go and see some art, Mabs."

Lottie came home one sultry afternoon, a few days later, to find a telegram on the hall table from her mother.

Lottie read the stark message out loud:

"Telephones soon to be requisitioned by BEF STOP
Hope this reaches you as Letters may stop soon STOP
Come home Love Mummy STOP"

She showed it to Françoise.

Françoise scanned it over her shoulder. "Oh, Lottie. Do you want to go?"

"No, not really. I think Mummy's just feeling guilty about the way she treated me after Granny died. It was awful after the will was read and I got all the blame. It was so unfair."

"But what if war does break out? Won't you be stuck here in France?"

"Your French troops are guarding the Maginot Line, aren't they?"

Françoise shook her head. "Maybe - I don't even know where that is."

"Oh, Françoise. You really should read the papers. Hitler would have to cross it to enter France from Germany and he'd never make it past the French army. They're ready for him and so are the British troops – that's what the BEF is – the British Expeditionary Force. With the two armies between us and the Germans, I'm sure France will be safe. And anyway, I like it here. I'm having so much fun. There's no point in my going home five whole years before my inheritance comes due."

"But your mother has asked you to go back."

Lottie scrumpled up the telegram in her hand. "Can't say I'm convinced about my mother, after the way she spoke to me last time I was there, or my sister, come to that. No, Françoise, I'll wait and stay a little longer, if you'll have me. And then, if old Adolf invades, I'll pack my bags and run like hell." Lottie pushed thoughts of Al kissing Isobel from her mind and ran upstairs to her bedroom, where she threw the telegram in the wastepaper basket.

Lottie stayed home with Françoise the next day, as Mabs had a dental appointment. Apparently, David wasn't available either. To distract her friend, she suggested a game of tennis. They hadn't played in ages. Lottie hoped the exercise would do them both good. The edginess pervading both the house and the city made her feel restless and unable to relax. Bashing a tennis ball would provide some much-needed relief.

Françoise's pout became pronounced at Lottie's suggestion. "I don't feel like it."

"But we can talk freely down by the tennis court and Bertrand mowed the lawn only yesterday."

"Oh, very well."

They walked down to the Blanchard's court, situated in a shady dip below the house.

"We'd better actually play a game; your mother is watching us from the balcony." Lottie bounced a ball up and down on her flat racket.

Françoise scuffed the short grass with the toe of her tennis shoe. She glanced up at the house and sighed. "I suppose you are right."

Despite Françoise's reluctance, they both quickly became engrossed in the game. Lottie, whose frustration had borne fruit in a fierce overhead smash, won the first point. She looked up at the villa, but Madame Blanchard had already disappeared back inside. The big Citroën was parked in the driveway, but Ricci was nowhere to be seen.

They played on. Françoise gave back as good as she'd got, and soon the two girls became locked in a competitive battle.

"Deuce!"

"Oh, not again, Françoise."

"The ball was out, Lottie."

"Damn!"

Lottie picked up the tennis ball and returned to the base line. As she threw the ball in the air and swung her racket down on to it, their game was interrupted, making her serve also go outside the line, this time by a country mile.

"Mademoiselle Smythe?"

"Oui?"

Sophie, the plump young housekeeper, was out of breath, pink with exertion. "C'est le téléphone. Votre maman!"

What on earth did Mummy want? She never telephoned.

She sprinted up to the house, leaving Sophie panting far behind with Françoise.

The Blanchard's Parisian villa stood on a little hill, overseeing its small park in a satisfied, complacent manner, which typified the bourgeois suburb it inhabited, just like David had surmised. Tall, with long French windows on all sides and an exaggerated pitch to its roof, its architect had seen fit to embellish its facade with countless fol-de-rols that had been fashionably chic in the heyday of 'la belle epoque'. When she had first seen it, she had fondly remembered her grandmother, as it had been her who had introduced her to the Blanchards. Granny had met them through a mutual friend during her Parisian honeymoon in that halcyon era. Somehow, it was easier to picture Granny looking young and happy here, than at Cheadle Manor.

The telephone was an old-fashioned candlestick one, just like at home. She lifted the listening trumpet from its cradle, placed it against her ear and spoke breathlessly into the mouthpiece on the fixed stand.

"Mummy? Is that you? What's wrong?"

"Didn't you get my telegram? I have had no answer from you, and I was frantic. I've had a tip-off from Katy Phipps about the telephone lines being requisitioned for the BEF, so I thought I'd try ringing you before they're cut off. Katy's had a massive order for rubber seals from the army and the government official gave her a convincing hint about it. Charlotte," her mother never called her by her full name, "you *must* come home immediately."

"No one is worried here." Lottie had never felt less like going home.

"I can't answer for Paris, but I can tell you that Kate's information is rock solid. There's no doubt that things are going to get ugly. We've got the wireless down in the drawing room now and we have it on constantly. You must get back to England before the borders close and war is announced. Lottie, please, I'm worried about you."

"Oh, are you? You do surprise me. I thought you wouldn't want to see me before my twenty fifth birthday." Her mother's pleas just brought back her earlier rejection and suddenly, irrationally, Lottie saw red. "With any luck, I'll get shot or bombed and you can keep the whole damned estate to yourself."

"Lottie! This is no time for childish tantrums! Don't joke about being killed! You've never lived through a war; you don't know what you are saying. Lottie, please come home. We need you."

Lottie hesitated at that. Something melted in her heart, something that had been frozen from the day she left Wiltshire. Tears stung her eyes.

"Lottie? are you still there?"

Lottie heard her mother click the telephone, but the line remained open.

Lottie swallowed hard. "I'm sorry, I didn't mean that. Listen, Mummy. I'll...I'll think about it. Alright? I'll let you know. It'll probably be weeks yet before the borders shut and I'll have to make arrangements to catch the night boat, if I can find one running. It'll take time and...and I'm still not sure. Françoise, well, let's just say she needs me."

"*Françoise* needs you? What about *us* needing you? I'm having to borrow more money, you know - to pay the mortgage on the estate. The repayments are a terrific strain. Lottie..."

The line went dead.

Slowly, Lottie replaced the receiver and blinked back her tears, refusing to let them fall. She supposed she should go back. She didn't want to. The thought of Isobel and Al together made her feel physically sick. And she was just beginning to find herself in Paris. Find out who she really was, and she wasn't at all the person she'd thought. She'd never felt so liberated, so exhilarated by all Mabs was helping her to discover. She didn't want to end it and return to the narrow rural life she knew awaited her at Cheadle Manor. She thought about the money she'd got for Granny's jewellery. Perhaps she could send some to her mother to ease the strain? But how?

"Lottie?" Françoise came into the hall. "Who was it on the telephone? Was it David?"

Irritated, already struggling to contain her conflicting emotions, Lottie snapped back, "No, it wasn't bloody David. Other people do exist, you know."

She went up to her room and sat on the bed. Her suitcase stared back at her from the top of the wardrobe.

CHAPTER SIXTEEN
CHEADLE MANOR
AUGUST 1939

Isobel gazed out of the nursery window at the rain. An apple fell from a branch with a thud and joined the rotten ones scattered around the base of the tree.

She turned away from the depressing scene and sat again at the table in the nursery. She looked at the paper on the blotting pad.

"Dearest Lottie," was all that she'd written on its white, empty surface.

She hadn't got any further with her letter to her sister. It was her third attempt this week. The crumpled evidence lay scattered across the table. She picked up her fountain pen and chewed its end, already indented with her teeth marks. What could she say to Lottie? Should it be the truth – that her mother was distraught, distracted, worried sick and not well? That she wasn't sure she could leave her and go back to school once the autumn term started?

She couldn't possibly tell Lottie about how much closer she and Al had become since she'd left. That would simply pour salt into what was obviously a very deep wound. They were still getting over the shock of discovering that Lottie was in love with him whilst falling deeper in love with each other. She didn't know how she would have coped these last few weeks without him.

He was busier than ever at the factory and rarely had time off. He still wouldn't talk about why they had such a massive increase in work or even why they'd recruited two more people to work on the production lines, but it was clear to everyone that things had changed. There was a lot of gossip in the village about preparing for war. Isobel couldn't bear to think about what it might mean for Al. She'd tried to talk to him about it when they'd snatched a few hours together at the cinema at Woodbury last week.

"Let's sit at the back and canoodle." Al had whispered the invitation in her ear while they waited in the queue for tickets outside the cinema.

"It's such a lovely evening, we should be going for a walk by the river or something, not going inside in the dark."

Al kept his voice low. "I can kiss you more in the dark."

"Oh, Al!" But she hadn't refused him.

They sat together, hand in hand, fingers entwined and heads touching, turning now and again so their lips could meet, press together, feel the warmth, exchange breath. Isobel found it enchanting and exhilarating and forgot all about the balmy weather outside. Other couples were doing the same either side of them the minute the lights went out. She felt liberated, uninhibited by the mutual clandestine fumblings around them. Al slipped his arm around her neck and drew her in for a proper kiss.

Below them, the screen flickered into life and the soundtrack for the Pathé News blasted out. Isobel barely registered the trumpets blaring out the beginning of the newsreel until some latecomer barged through their aisle and made everyone get up off their seats so they could sit in the middle. The disruption startled Isobel from her sensuous relaxation. When she sat back down, she smoothed her hair and readjusted her hat, pushing Al back in his own seat so she could focus on the screen and the enthusiastic voice of its narrator.

"But Bella, no-one can see us."

"Ssh, I want to see this bit. It's about the launch of a ship, look." Isobel ignored his brushing lips and concentrated instead on the footage. To her horror, the film graphically showed how, by breaking free of its moorings too early, the huge new ship, aptly named Formidable, had killed one of the men who had built it. The Pathé News announcer went on to speak of how the aircraft carrier was only part of the build up to war happening through Britain. The man spoke throughout the bulletin in a thrilling voice, as if war was something to be welcomed and celebrated!

His perfect diction had the exact opposite effect on Isobel, who found it hard to concentrate on the film that followed. 'Goodbye Mr Chips', despite the affecting story and the excellent acting, couldn't blot out the real drama threatening their world outside the cinema. She kept feeling for Al's hand and gripping it tightly in her own.

All this talk of war frightened her. One of the boys on the estate had volunteered for peacetime conscription. Thank goodness Al was too young for that yet, for all his dreams of flying. Al had kissed away her fears in the lorry after the film had finished. That memory wiped out all the others.

She touched her lips where Al's had been and smiled. She looked back at the table and fished out the few letters Lottie had sent to her mother. Isobel had received none of her own and relied on their mother for news. When she'd said she'd try and write to her sister, her mother had been so pleased, she'd loaned her Lottie's correspondence.

Lottie's letters spoke formally and briefly of her adventures in Paris, her anger still obvious between the lines. This Mabel Miller person she'd met dominated the last ones. Isobel thought she sounded an oddity. What was an American woman of her age doing alone in Paris anyway? Why hadn't she got any family with her? Wasn't she afraid of Hitler's strutting across Europe? Why wasn't Lottie?

Isobel knew what she wanted to write. She wanted to tell Lottie exactly how miserable their mother was and how much they both missed her. She wanted to beg her to come home, make her peace, make amends, realise they didn't care about the inheritance, well, not much anyway.

Both Isobel and her mother wanted Lottie home and safe above everything else.

But Lottie, apparently, was too busy partying and playing tennis and going to art galleries and cafés. Isobel wasn't even jealous. She'd never been hungry for adventure. She loved being at home and, although she could only admit it to Al, she was relieved that Granny was no longer here to criticise and hector her. Her unfair legacy lived on without her, though, but Isobel had to admit it wasn't the only reason Lottie was abroad. Of course, she understood why any girl would fall in love with Al. He was so handsome and kind, and such good fun, but she'd never guessed Lottie's secret. It still astonished her that Lottie had kept her love for Al to herself all these years but then, she'd done the same, hadn't she? Had they both always known, deep down, that one day they'd make him choose between them?

Isobel shook her head. Life as a grown-up was mystifying. She thought about her sister again, about how clever she was, how well she'd done academically, as well as on the sports field – in fact, at everything. Lottie's school reports had always been chock-full of glowing praise. Perhaps Lottie would always have gone to Paris after finishing school. A lot of girls in their social circles did, but this year, most had stayed home. Isobel picked up her pen and filled it from the ink bottle.

"I hope this finds you well." Her words were so bland, so meaningless. She gazed out at the rain again, hoping for inspiration. Nothing came except doodles on the blotting sheet. She'd been working on a painting of the orchard and all that appeared were sketches of apple trees. After half an hour, she gave up and went downstairs.

She found her mother sitting at her desk in the drawing room as usual. Cassandra had never adopted the study for her paperwork. It remained exactly as Sir Robert had left it when he'd died, all those years ago.

Isobel sighed. So many gone and only her mother left to pick up the pieces.

"Hello, Mummy, how's it going?"

Her mother turned around. Her eyes had deep shadows beneath them, and her mouth still bore the lines that had emerged after Granny's will had chased Lottie away and brought the heavy burden of the estate debts solely on to Cassandra's shoulders, without hope of reward.

"Oh, I'm not getting very far. I have managed to get an appointment at the bank, though, and persuaded Mr Leadbetter to come with me." Cassandra, too, laid down her pen.

"That's good, then."

"It's something, I suppose."

"You know I'm happy to sell Granny's sapphire set, if it would help."

"Oh, I don't think it'll come to that, darling." Cassandra turned the subject, often discussed and always discarded. "What have you been up to this morning?"

"I was trying to write to Lottie, but I didn't get very far, either." Isobel sat down on the sofa and crossed her long legs.

"I do wish she'd come home. It says in the paper that Chamberlain is talking to the Russians, but nothing's been resolved. It's so worrying when he's already guaranteed to protect Poland. Some people think Hitler's going to invade that country as well as Czechoslovakia." Cassandra picked up the newspaper to show the headlines to Isobel.

"I'm not sure I understand any of it, Mummy. It won't really come to war, will it?" Isobel willed her mother to give a negative answer.

Her mother gave a weary smile and dropped the newspaper back down on to her bureau. "No, probably not, my darling."

Rumours continued to rumble around the streets of Paris, but it was still a taboo subject for discussion in the Blanchard household whenever Monsieur was home. Whenever his wife mentioned the latest gossip about the possibility of the Germans invading, his standard reply was to remind them all of the parade on Bastille Day, on the fourteenth of July, when the French army and its colonial colleagues had marched through the streets of Paris with thousands of onlookers watching.

"Of course, Charlotte, you were not with us then, but it was quite a sight. The best army in the world. Even your Monsieur Churchill said so. Hitler won't dare to invade us." Monsieur Blanchard, a firm but not always fair, force of nature, was not someone to be trifled with. Lottie had never attempted it.

So, it was a shock when, a few days later, on the third of September, Madame Blanchard, normally such a slim and elegant Parisienne, always immaculately turned out, came running up the garden, hairpins flying and almost too breathless to gasp out: "Mon dieu! Girls, they say war is declared! Françoise, Lottie – I don't know what to do! Please, come inside, where you will be safe."

She clutched at them with quivering hands, pulling them towards the house. In the salon, Madame reached for the cigarette box and, unthinking, offered them one each. Neither of the girls had ever smoked; Monsieur Blanchard frowned on young girls wreathed in blue fumes. When they shook their heads, she tried to put the box back down on the armoire but missed its marble top. The box fell to the floor, its lid still open, littering the Aubusson carpet with cigarettes, as if they were playing a game of spillikins.

Madame Blanchard, uncharacteristically, swore. "Merde! Oh, where's my lighter? I can't find the damn thing. I need a smoke!"

The silver engraved lighter was right next to Madame, but her eyes were darting everywhere but on the armoire. Lottie picked it up and lit her cigarette for her, the way she had seen Monsieur Blanchard do, but it was hard to marry the flame to the wobbling white stick of tobacco while Madame's painted lips tried to grip it through chattering teeth. Eventually, Madame Blanchard sucked on the cigarette, inhaling it deeply and blowing a great cloud of acrid smoke in Lottie's face. Françoise was scrabbling round on the floor, picking up the scattered ones.

Lottie looked at the two other women, neither had anything to say to the other, even in this moment of crisis. Suddenly, she longed for her own family. Lottie turned away and ran upstairs to her room, her heart pounding and guilt about ignoring her mother's pleas flooding her whole being. What if she got stranded and never got home? Why had she shouted at her like that on the telephone?

She already had her suitcase open on the bed when Françoise found her.

Lottie opened a drawer at random, her shaking hands making the handle rattle against the varnished rosewood. "Can you book a taxi to the station?"

"No need, I will ask Maman to get Ricci to drive you in our car and get our manservant, Bertrand, to book you on the night ferry to London. He's a genius at organising things like that but, Lottie, I don't really want you to go. Must you?"

"I suppose I must at least try."

Françoise gave her a brief hug and left her alone, her eyes full of tears, and her hand over her mouth.

Lottie scribbled a note for Mabs explaining how she had to go and advising her to do the same, maybe catch the same boat together that night. She hoped Bertrand would deliver it for her. She was halfway through stuffing things in her case, when there was a knock at the door and Françoise's mother entered without waiting for permission, a habit Lottie had found unnerving ever since she'd arrived in the Blanchard household.

Madame seemed to have collected herself. Perhaps tobacco was more therapeutic than Lottie had realised. "Ma chérie, Françoise has just told me you want to go home. Why not wait a while, ma petite? Let us see how far Herr Hitler gets – I, I've thought about it now. My husband has telephoned me to reassure me. He doesn't think the Germans will reach Paris."

To Lottie's surprise, as she had never done it informally before, Madame kissed her on both cheeks, leaving a hint of Chanel No 5 and a dusting of face powder.

"Merci, Madame, but I must take the very next boat train, so please excuse me for this evening's meal."

"Surely not? Can't I persuade you to stay? Françoise will be bereft."

"No, Madame, I have to try to get back to my own mother."

"You are sure? It will be dangerous, perhaps. Why not leave it a few days?"

"The Germans could be here in a few days, Madame! If I don't go now, I might never be able to get home." Lottie's voice caught.

Madame dropped her hands from around Lottie's arms. Defeated, she nodded. "I understand your desire to return. But you must eat, mon petit chou. I will have something sent up to your room and a pique-nique for your journey. Ah, it is a long way. I will arrange for Bertrand to book your passage on the boat and onward train in England. I would give you the car and the chauffeur to take you all the way, but I fear I am too selfish to do without him, I mean the car, for so long, but Ricci shall drive you to the station."

Lottie smothered a smile, despite her anxiety, and turned her face away to the ornate dressing table on the pretext of gathering up her brush and comb set.

"I will leave you to pack, mignon. Ah, Françoise will be lost without you." Madame sighed, sounding more annoyed than upset now. Lottie wondered who she would find to distract Françoise now, so her affair with Ricci could continue unobserved by her innocent daughter. Lottie had not had the heart to reveal the truth to her naïve friend. Some things were best left unsaid. Madame seemed entirely unaware that her daughter was conducting an affair of her own.

Lottie used the telephone in the hall to contact Mabs's hotel, but the concierge couldn't find her. Lottie had to be content with leaving a message and the note she'd entrusted to Bertrand.

Before she had time to stop and think about it, Lottie was cruising along in Madame's Citroën towards the Gare du Nord, gazing at the back of Ricci's head where his glossy black hair curled rebelliously from under his chauffeur's cap.

Lottie got out of the car and Ricci unloaded her bags. She tipped him extravagantly, not needing her French francs anymore. He flashed a grin, revealing teeth so white, she could easily understand why the aging Madame Blanchard had found him irresistible.

It was bedlam at the station. She barely recognised the place from its normal orderly routine. Crowds of frantic people crushed together. No-one seemed to have any sense of direction but swarmed this way and that in utter chaos. Babies cried in distress, as their parents held them too tight and older children clutched at their hands, their eyes wide with shock and fear. She instantly regretted not asking the handsome Italian chauffeur to accompany her.

Lottie carried a suitcase in each hand, no porter being available, and plunged into the throng. Hundreds of people pressed in on her, all desperate to clamber onto a train. She lost count of the number of men and women who knocked her shoulders and she gripped her heavy luggage tightly in hands that quickly became weary. The ticket office had a queue that stretched the length of the building. She stared at it for a few minutes before registering it hadn't moved along by even one person.

Fear began to curl its insidious chill through her body. A harassed porter turned around in front of her. Abandoning one suitcase to the floor, she grabbed his uniformed arm.

"S'il vous plait, monsieur?"

The man scowled. "Oui?"

"Is there a train going to the night boat, please?"

"The night boat is cancelled, Mademoiselle. Did you not know that war has been declared? There will be no sailings to England until it is over."

"Cancelled? For the duration of the whole war? I don't believe you! It can't be true." Lottie knew a moment of sheer panic. She stared at the middle-aged man, but he wasn't interested, had already turned away, using his elbows to barrel his way through the crush. Someone else was clutching his sleeve now. A child tripped over her case on the floor.

"What do you think you're doing, leaving that on the floor in this crowd!" The child's mother looked as panicky as Lottie felt.

"I...I'm sorry. Excuse me." Lottie grabbed her case and battled her way out of the station against the flow of the hundreds of people pouring in.

Out in the fresh air, she took deep, shuddering breaths. How stupid to ignore her mother. Her mother! How she longed to see her now. In that moment, home was exactly where she wanted to be.

Like most Parisians, Lottie held her breath in the next few weeks, waiting for life to change. Strangely, there was little drama. Sandbags piled up next to monuments; paintings disappeared from The Louvre, wrapped up and exported incognito to who knew where.

Mabs told of her outrage that the stained-glass windows of the Sainte-Chapelle, the Royal Chapel on the Île de la Cité in the middle of the river Seine, were being taken down as a precaution against air raids. "Such folly, my dear, they'll never be able to put them back as perfectly as those early craftsmen. Ah, so much beauty would be lost if Paris was bombed."

But ordinary, everyday life carried on after the initial panic began to fade. Letters from home became more insistent, but it seemed that affairs in Wiltshire remained likewise remarkably calm. 'La drôle de Guerre' Parisians began to call it and Cassandra wrote that it was the same at home - a phoney war. Paris slipped back into its normal routine, but the streets became unnaturally dark for such a big city at night. The resulting quiet had a sinister tone, as the black-out curtains killed the house-lights and the streetlamps remained extinguished. Shadows prowled silently in the eerie silence, making most citizens stay inside behind closed shutters until the sun exposed them again.

The fear and home-sickness Lottie had experienced at the chaotic train station dissipated, as life resumed its fascinating new dance with Mabs and her interesting acquaintances. After a while, she forgot all about going home and Cheadle Manor receded into a distant memory, almost a different life.

The biggest drama turned out to be a domestic one and involved, not Françoise and David, as Lottie fully anticipated - indeed dreaded - but her friend's mother. A few weeks after war broke out, Ricci decided to go back to his native Italy, leaving Madame Blanchard distraught and tearful as she watched his departure from the front steps, Françoise and Lottie by her side. He marched out through the pillared gates, a suitcase in each hand; his handsome face, without its habitual ingratiating smile, set into stony, determined lines.

The family supper was more subdued than ever that evening. Always turgid, with conversation hard to maintain, the first family gathering in Ricci's absence presented a daunting challenge.

Lottie had only ever seen Monsieur Blanchard at the evening meal and lately, seldom then, as she was often still out with Mabs in the evenings, at least until it was fully dark, taking taxis if it was later. The blackout made the city streets threatening and unfriendly to a young girl alone and Mabs insisted she didn't travel on the Métro at night.

Françoise's father was his wife's senior by twenty years. He had married Mireille Perrot late in life, after his first wife had died, leaving him childless. Françoise had arrived unexpectedly a year later but the trauma of giving birth had rendered Madame unwilling to repeat the experience – she told her husband – and, since her birth, they had slept in separate bedrooms.

Madame Blanchard's fork trembled as she raised it to her mouth. Her eyes were swollen and red and no amount of powder could disguise the fact. Her face underneath her make-up was white and two patches of ill-applied rouge on her cheekbones simply emphasised her pallor. She was silent through the entrée. Lottie and Françoise kept up a dialogue on a tennis party they had attended but it was hard going.

Monsieur Blanchard, his bald head shiny with perspiration, broke into their chatter. The interruption was startling, as he was generally a man of few words.

"So, we have no chauffeur now?"

Madame's fork stopped its shovelling, and she held it in a hesitant hand for a fractional pause. Eventually, she shook her head. "No."

"He has gone back to Italy?"

"Yes." Madame laid her fork down, giving up the attempt to feed herself.

Lottie and Françoise both spoke at once, in a bid to rescue the floundering older woman.

"Papa...?"

"Monsieur Blanchard..."

"Silence!" He glared at the two girls. "Mireille?" Monsieur Blanchard addressed his wife directly. "How do you propose to get about now? Or will your entertainment stop, now *he's* gone?"

"I..."

Lottie had never heard Mireille Blanchard stutter before. She felt an unexpected stab of sympathy for her hostess.

"You will just have to walk, won't you, my dear? Or take the Métro, just like everyone else. I will not be employing another chauffeur. In fact, I may sell the car. After all, petrol is rationed now. Soon it will be food." Monsieur Blanchard carried on eating. His noisy chewing dominated the dark, candlelit dining room and there were no streetlights outside to lift the gloom.

"Excuse me, I feel a little unwell." Madame lurched to her feet and fumbled out of the room, her serviette clamped to her painted lips.

Françoise turned to her father. "Do not sell the car, Papa. Who knows when we might need it? I could learn to drive."

Lottie was surprised at Françoise's boldness and decided to concentrate on her rapidly cooling chicken.

Monsieur Blanchard threw down his fork. It clattered on to his plate, temporarily drowning out the disgusting sound of his mastication. "No! You will not drive the car, Françoise. I can borrow one from the factory when I need it. We do not need to have one of our own. I give you too much licence already. I have heard rumours you are seeing a young man. Is this true?"

It was Françoise's turn to squirm.

"We see lots of people, Monsieur Blanchard. Françoise has many friends." Lottie felt duty bound to intervene and gave up the pretence of eating.

"When I want your opinion, Charlotte, I shall ask for it. I have heard you have made some eccentric new friends of your own, but that is your affair. In the meantime, I would ask you to refrain from comment while I speak to my daughter."

"I beg your pardon, Monsieur." Lottie had never felt unwelcome until that moment. She dropped her hands to her lap.

Under the table, Françoise grabbed Lottie's hand and squeezed it. Lottie felt like copying Madame and leaving the room but could not deny support to her friend now.

Monsieur Blanchard pressed on. "Is it true, Françoise? I insist on an honest answer."

The manservant, Bertrand, came in to clear the table but Monsieur Blanchard waved him away.

"Françoise? Tell me!"

The hand holding Lottie's gripped harder. She tried not to wince.

"Papa, it's true what Lottie said, we see all sorts of people, maybe not as many as before, but we still play tennis with other neighbours, go to cafés and things."

"But is there someone in particular?"

There was a small movement in Françoise's hand. Later, Lottie found out she'd crossed her fingers while she told the lie.

"No, no-one in particular, Papa." Françoise shook her fair head.

Monsieur Blanchard grunted. "That's not what I heard. Madame Brodeur told me you had been seen frequently with a tall, dark haired young man, new to the neighbourhood. She said he looked Jewish. It is not wise to associate yourself with Jewish families at this time, Françoise. In fact, if it is true, I forbid it, do you understand? I forbid it!"

Françoise gave a little gasp only Lottie could hear. In a small voice she said, "Yes, Papa, I understand."

"Good. Now go to your rooms, both of you, and leave me to eat my supper in peace."

They both got up and obeyed silently. By the time they reached her bedroom, Françoise was in tears.

"Doesn't seem right, me not joining up, now the war's official." Al was making the most of having his Dad to himself, a rare opportunity these days. "After all, if they're sending kids out of London in case of air raids, why shouldn't I go off and leave my bedroom free for one or two of them?"

"We need you here at the factory, Al," Jem's face was a mask of control. Al couldn't read his father's normally open countenance. "We've never been so busy. Your mother is rushed off her feet with this big order for gas mask parts. She's told the Local Invasion Committee we can't take on young evacuees as well."

"Has she? Makes sense, I suppose. Aunt Cassandra's taken on six up at the manor. Proper little tikes they are, Isobel says. Crawling with lice till Mrs Andrews scrubbed them senseless."

Jem laughed. "I'll bet, but it's different when you've got servants to help, isn't it? Listen, conscription will be here soon enough. I only hope your job is a reserved occupation. Should be."

"I know, Dad, but you did your bit in the last bash, I think I should be allowed to do mine."

"I understand how you feel, son, really I do, but it's not all it's cracked up to be, you know. Soldiering's not as glamorous as it sounds, believe me." Jem tapped his wooden arm.

"Yes, but at least you've got your honour. You know your conscience is clear and all that. I don't want to be thought a coward."

"Working in the factory *is* war work. Just as valuable a contribution as having your head blown off." Jem picked up a cauliflower and settled it among others in the wooden tray.

Al, commissioned to cut the big leaves off the creamy white curds, handed him another. "Other blokes are signing up. Geoff Holt is talking about going next week. He's trying for the RAF. I think I'd rather be a pilot than a foot soldier too."

"Geoff hasn't got a job, has he? Probably joining up is the only way that lazy oik can get regular pay." Jem took the trimmed vegetable from Al and tucked it in with the others. "Good crop this year, isn't it? Nice white heads on them."

Al didn't share his father's love of horticulture. Weeding and hoeing didn't have the same satisfaction for him, never would.

"Carrots next." Jem picked up a bunch of muddy roots and held them under the outside tap, next to the potting shed. "Turn on the tap for me, then."

Al twisted the tap till the water flowed good and strong over the carrots and into a bucket underneath. He watched his father swish off the clay and lift them up, bright orange and shiny.

"Smashing. Not a sign of carrot fly. I'll use them low nets between the rows again. It's worked a treat." Jem smiled and passed the wet carrots to Al for tying up.

Al couldn't help thinking how he'd much rather spend the afternoon with Isobel in her vegetable garden. Somehow even lifting carrots with her was exhilarating. Isobel had surprised them all by refusing to return to school to sit her Higher Certificate after war was declared on the third of September - the same date as the start of the new term. She'd been packed up and ready to go, but after listening to Mr Chamberlain's announcement on the radio, she'd unpacked it all again and refused to leave. She'd told Al how, at first, Cassandra had pretended to be cross at her decision. Then her mother had confessed how relieved she was that Isobel would be staying home with her at Cheadle Manor now that war had broken out and Lottie had point-blank refused to return.

He had a moment's guilt about that. It wasn't right, Lottie staying abroad in a foreign country with a war going on. Not right at all. Isobel kept asking him to write to her sister in Paris and beg her to come home but try as he might, he couldn't find the words. His wastepaper basket was full of abandoned attempts. He hadn't even sent a postcard, though he'd received several from her. He just didn't know what to say. He was hopeless at putting feelings onto paper.

"Al! Are you bunching them carrots or counting sheep?"

"Sorry, Dad."

"Listen, lad, see how it goes before you go signing your life away, alright? Promise me you'll wait a while. You're not old enough yet anyway and after all, nothing much is happening, is it? Oh, I know Hitler's marched into Poland, but Poland is a long way from Wiltshire. Maybe it'll all fizzle out and come to nothing."

"Didn't they say that to you in the last shout? I remember Gran saying everyone thought it would be over by Christmas last time." Al tied up the last bunch of carrots and swilled his hands under the tap.

Jem grunted. "That's as maybe. All I know is a lot of young men never made it home. Your Uncle Albert, who you're named after, he died in Passchendaele. Your Gran never got over it. You'd never know, she made the best of it - she always does - but a light went out of her eyes. They all thought I was dead as well because I was in the prisoner of war camp in Germany and couldn't write home. Had the Spanish influenza there too, so it's a wonder I did come through but if I hadn't, you wouldn't be here now so, please Al, understand that you are very precious to us."

Al turned his face away at the emotion written large on his father's, where the mask had long since been stripped away. "I bet Mum wouldn't miss me."

"Don't you ever let me hear you say that again! How dare you speak of your mother like that? She might have a sharp tongue, but she loves you and Lily with her whole heart. Why do you think she works so hard, if not for you? I've a good mind to clip you round the ear, even if you are an inch taller than me these days."

"I'm sorry, Dad, honest. It's just that I never seem to get anything right in her eyes. I know she wanted me to stay on at school and try for my Higher Certificate again, but I knew it was no good. Sometimes she makes me feel I'm no good at anything."

"Then make her proud, you idiot! Work hard and show willing. That's what's needed now. We've got more orders than we can deal with. Roll up your sleeves and give a hand. She'll be proud of you then. She *is* proud of you already. You're the best driver we've ever had. As good as Douglas Flintock ever was but a damn sight safer. Now get along with you and see what needs delivering and let's have no more talk of not being good enough or throwing your life away in the army. Do you hear?" Jem's brown eyes bored into Al's, unblinking and bright with anger.

"Yes, Dad. Sorry." Al shoved his hands into his pockets and walked away to the factory, not in the least bit mollified.

Over the next few days, Al tried to hide his frustration by digging out an air raid shelter in the only spare bit of ground next to the vegetable plot. Slowly, the leaves fell from the trees and the days shortened, making it impossible to complete deliveries before dark and he had less and less time to visit Isobel.

"I don't like you driving through the blackout, Al." Katy scribbled a note in the margin of her ledger and looked up. She had big shadows under her eyes these days that never seemed to shift.

"I've got used to it, Mum. It's not too bad when you know the road and there aren't that many I'm not familiar with now, which is just as well now they've taken the signposts down."

"But a fox could run in front of you at any time, or worse, somebody on a bike not looking where they are going. And what if a German paratrooper did land next to you?" She tucked her pencil behind her ear where it nestled amongst her dark curls, now streaked with white.

"There's a war on. We all have to take risks. I've painted the bumper and the running boards white so at least other people can see me better." Al had seen other lorries done this way and had taken it upon himself to do the same. With just a slit mask on the headlamps and dimmed side lights, it made sense to be as visible as possible.

"Have you? That's a really good idea. Well, we have no choice with the daylight hours so short but to send you out at night, but I can't say I'm happy about it." Al knew a moment of pride as his mother gave him one of her rare, lovely smiles.

"It's all them carrots Dad grows. I can see for miles." Al laughed and gave his mother a quick peek on the cheek.

To his surprise she hugged him back, a fierce, quick compression with her strong arms. "You take extra care anyway. Promise me?"

"I promise, Mum."

"Off you go then. This lot is bound for Salisbury to the army depot there. Make sure they sign for them." Katy blinked rapidly as she released him.

To save her embarrassment, Al picked up the papers and marched off to the factory sheds.

The road to Salisbury had also been painted with white lines down the middle and Al found it much easier to see than he had before. The delivery was completed in record time and he took advantage of it by nipping into Cheadle Manor on the way home. He hadn't seen Isobel for days and days.

Andrews let him in without the old interrogation. That formality had been dispensed with after Lady Smythe died. The regime under Aunt Cassandra was a lot more

145

casual these days, especially since they'd taken in some evacuees. He could hear a child's voice coming from the servants' quarters across the hall and Andrews, who must be seventy if he was a day, winced at the sound. The old man looked too worn out these days to protest about Al's visits and he made the most of it every time he could snatch a rare moment. He ran up the stairs and to the nursery, where he knew he'd find Isobel.

Rain had set in after the long night had fallen and the temperature had dropped with its arrival, but there was no fire in the nursery grate. Isobel sat huddled up in the big old armchair, wearing an old jumper and a blanket over her knees. A single electric lamp lit the pages of her book. She looked up when Al entered the room. Her smile made the fatigue of his day melt away.

"Don't get up, you look so cosy there." Al went and sat on the wide arm of the armchair and dropped a kiss on her upturned lips.

"Lovely to see you, Al. It's been ages."

"I know. We're run off our feet at the factory. Got a massive contract for the rubber component of gas masks. We're making millions of the horrible things." Al slid his arm around Isobel's shoulders, just to reassure himself she was real.

Isobel laid her head against his arm. "That must be worth a bit."

"I think so. I wish Mum would let someone else help her with the management of it all though. Although we've taken on six extra staff, she's worn out. What are you reading?"

"It's about land management."

"Sounds like dry stuff."

"No, it's fascinating." Isobel flicked over the next page.

"Shall I leave you to it? You look engrossed."

Isobel shut the book with a laugh. "Oh, don't be cross, Al, although I think you will be when I tell you what I've decided."

Al tensed up, ready for the blow.

"I'm going to volunteer for the Land Army."

"Will that mean you'll be going away?"

"It could do. There's a training base in Winchester where I'd stay for about six weeks, I think, then I could be posted anywhere." Isobel's blue eyes were fixed on his face.

He hoped his disappointment wasn't too obvious. "Anywhere in the country?"

"That's right." Isobel eyelids fluttered but she didn't look away.

"You're fixed on this idea, are you? Definitely not going back to school then?"

"No, but if I did, I would be away just the same. This way I shall feel I'm doing my bit. The only thing I'm good at in school is art. I love gardening, you know I do, don't you? So, this seems the right choice for me, if I get in, of course. Do say you understand, Al?"

Al swallowed, took a breath. "I'll miss you, but I understand."

"I knew you would."

"When will you apply?"

"Tomorrow. I'll go into Woodbury and find the recruiting office. I think it's on the High Street, next to the newsagent." Isobel got up and drew the curtains tighter. She looked back at Al with a smile. "That little gap has been worrying me for ages, but I was too warm and snug to get up and close it."

"You haven't got much light on in here anyway, I doubt the Germans would spot it." Al went over and stood behind her and wrapped his arms around her slim body. "Maybe they won't take you. You're too delicate for work like that. You'd be out in all weathers, you know, slugging it out in the mud, planting potatoes. It's rough work on a farm."

Isobel slipped out of his grasp and turned to face him. For once, she looked irritated with him. "I'm tougher than I look. Our kitchen garden doesn't dig itself, you know."

"No, but you still have a gardener to do the heavy work and who's going to keep Aunt Cassandra and those little evacuees fed if you go?"

"She can buy vegetables from your Dad, can't she? And all but one of the evacuees have gone back to London. As soon as the government made their mothers pay a bit towards their keep, they were off. Without the air raids everyone warned them about, they wanted their kids home - and who could blame them? The one that's left is such a poor dab even his own mother doesn't want him back. He's a penny short of a bob but Mrs Andrews makes him useful. Says she needs his young legs to run errands for her."

Al couldn't smile. He let go his arms. "Is that a fact? Poor kid."

Isobel pulled him back. "Don't be like this, Al." Isobel echoed the words he'd given his mother that morning. "There is a war on."

"I'm sorry. I know you're right, but you could end up in Scotland or Cornwall - anywhere!"

"I will miss you, but I need to do this. I'll write - you will write back, won't you?"

He took her in his arms again, smelled her hair. "Oh, God, Bella. This war! It's changing everything."

"Isn't that what wars do? But I can't just hang about and not take part." She leaned into him and kissed his lips.

"No, of course you can't."

Al left shortly afterwards. He climbed back in the lorry, suddenly weary. It was pitch black now with only a toenail moon to guide him home. He didn't believe the Women's Land Army would turn Isobel down. They were more likely to snap her up. She *was* strong really, he knew that, and she knew how to grow stuff; loved gardening just like his Dad. Isobel loved everything in nature. She was good with animals too. The land army would be a perfect fit. She would go, and he would have to stay put at the factory, same as always.

CHAPTER NINETEEN
PARIS
WINTER 1939-1940

All through the long, cold winter that birthed a new decade, Lottie, like the rest of Paris, tried to turn a blind eye to world events.

Madame Blanchard recovered her aplomb and her husband relented about the car. It sat like a beached whale in the garage, unused and unloved. Madame took to walking to the local cafés and shops; but walking to meet her friends took time, meaning Françoise and Lottie were left to themselves for increasingly long spells. Lottie ignored her conscience about Monsieur and Madame Blanchard not knowing that the two girls rarely spent time together. Instead she frequented the cafés, art galleries and concert halls with Mabs with undiminished curiosity.

After the initial panic, most Americans and their British counterparts stayed on in Paris, as unwilling as Lottie to give up their creative lifestyles. Artists continued to paint, musicians played their instruments, and writers carried on writing. Lottie drank it all in and tentatively started to write poetry of her own, which she read aloud to an enraptured Mabs, who encouraged her to read her favourite one in Shakespeare and Company one Sunday afternoon at one of their regular tea parties. Lottie, terrified, somehow got through the reading and was listened to politely, but not being asked for more work told her how much she needed to improve.

Mabs, devoted but undaunted, kept up her unqualified support and Lottie scribbled away the dark afternoons in her room at the Blanchard's chateau trying to encapsulate her renaissance into fewer words than she could manage. She and Mabs attended many other readings, but these only served to convince Lottie that she was no poet. Instead she read voraciously, spurred on by glimpses of the famous writers who frequented the bookshop and cafés she and Mabs loved. Ernest Hemingway, the forbidden fruits of Ulysses by James Joyce and, her favourite, the sensuous, astonishingly frank works of DH Lawrence. Deep within her absorption into art and literature, the winter passed quickly, the time passing almost unnoticed.

What Françoise got up to, she kept increasingly to herself. The two girls drifted further apart as the cold weather bit into winter, only seeing each other a few evenings a week over family suppers as Lottie now avoided the interminably long Sundays she had previously endured within the Blanchard's domestic domain.

Françoise's father worked longer hours at the factory and they barely saw him either, for which they were both grateful. When they did see him, he talked obsessively of a new car Citroën was developing, a little workhorse, he called it – needing only the equivalent power of two horses to function.

"You'll see, this will knock spots off that wretched man Hitler's Volkswagen. Hah! The 'people's car' indeed. He's only ever produced a few and we're going to beat him to it with our little 2CV beauty."

Lottie had never seen Monsieur Blanchard so excited about anything. "Ever since Boulanger took over the company, he has been innovative. This new model will revolutionise car ownership in France. Every family will be able to afford one. The world will open up!" The project certainly took his mind off his family and he left them in peace.

Lottie welcomed the arrival of spring, just like the rest of the Blanchard family. The days lengthened, buds formed on trees and bulbs pushed up towards the sun. She, like everyone else she knew, forgot about the war, as 1940 burst into life in the traditional way and the French troops safeguarded the impregnable Maginot Line.

Having never lived in Paris before, Lottie could not compare other years, but Madame Blanchard constantly grumbled that no-one was giving parties

151

anymore to celebrate the arrival of the warmer days and neither could she host one with all the rationing. Lottie's friendship with Mabs was the centre of her new life and when Mabs invited her to stay with her in her new apartment after Easter, she was sorely tempted.

"Oh, do stay with me, honey. Then you won't have to go back to that dreary villa in the suburbs every night. I worry about you going home alone in the blackout. You can hardly see the landmarks for the sandbags, either. Ugly things."

"I think I know my way around by now, Mabs. Don't fret. I often take a taxi anyway."

"I know – such a waste of money! But imagine, my dear, if you just stayed with me. My apartment is so sweet. It's not large and it's four floors up but the view across the rooftops is divine. I'm all alone there and I miss the comings and goings at the hotel. I long for some company." Mabs fiddled with the tulips that sat between them in a colourful jug on their dining table.

"I'll stay for a few days, once I've cleared it with Madame Blanchard, and we'll see how we get on. That do you?" Lottie smiled at her friend.

Mabs's face relaxed, uncreasing the lines around her dark eyes. "Marvellous. Come tomorrow and I'll cook you something on my tiny stove and we'll baptise the little kitchen with champagne!"

Françoise pouted, and Madame sulked, but Lottie managed to convince them her stay in the city centre was essential. She told them the truth; it seemed the best option. "I'm staying with an American friend for a few days while she settles into her new apartment. I'll be back on Saturday."

Mabs's enthusiastic welcome quickly dispelled the lingering cloud under which she left the Blanchard's gloomy villa. The kitchenette was indeed tiny but Mabs had lit candles in the large salon and thrown open the elegant French windows. They stepped out onto the narrow balcony to sip champagne.

"Welcome to your new home, Mabs." Lottie chinked her glass against her friend's.

"Thank you, dear girl. It's lovely to have you here." Mabs leant over and kissed Lottie's cheek, leaving a hint of expensive, musky perfume.

"What's for supper?" Lottie sipped her drink and looked out over the dramatic view of the city. She could see the spires of St Germain's church easily and pick out the trees in the square nearby.

"Well, I'm no chef, so don't expect too much! I've kept it simple. We've soup to start with and some of that lovely bread from the local bakery, then I'm going to whip up an omelette. I tried to get some chops, but meat is hard to get these days. However, I have begged Étienne from the little café on the corner for dessert – a slice each of his heavenly chocolate roulade - and I have a ripe Camembert to follow the main course. And at least they aren't rationing wine!"

"It sounds fabulous, Mabs. Tomorrow, I will take you out for dinner as my treat. Then we can be fair and square."

"Oh, let me indulge you for once, Lottie."

"No, I insist. Now, let me help you."

"No, sit down, dear girl, sit down and let me wait on you." Mabs bustled off towards the bubbling pan on the stove. Lottie concentrated on identifying rooftops and wondered where she would sleep.

The meal was delicious, if simple, and washed down with copious glasses of wine.

"Goodness, I feel quite tiddly. I think I'd better go back out on the balcony and get some fresh air." Lottie stood up and tottered towards the French windows. She went to draw back the curtains.

"I'll have to dim the electric lights before we open the curtains, honey." Mabs clicked off the lamps dotted about the salon.

"Oh, yes," Lottie hiccupped, "Silly me."

"I suppose you have servants at the Blanchard's place to do that sort of thing for you."

"Yes, I'm leading a very irresponsible life." Lottie stepped outside and inhaled. Wafts of cigarette and chimney smoke mingled with more delicate aromas of daffodils from the little window-box. Mabs added to the mix with her floral perfume when she joined her.

They stood together in silence for a few minutes, drinking in the night air, listening to the city murmuring goodnights. An accordion played a few streets away; its chords plangent in the still air.

"There's nowhere like Paris, is there?" Mabs said. She was standing just behind Lottie. Lottie could feel her warm breath against her cheek.

"Nowhere I know, but then, I haven't been anywhere much."

"Yet."

Lottie laughed softly. "Not yet, no."

"Who knows where you might go in your life? It's all ahead of you, my dear. Ah, I wish I was younger, more your age." Mabs sighed.

"Do you?" Lottie turned to the other woman.

Very gently, Mabs put her arm around Lottie's shoulders and drew her close. "Can I kiss you, dear girl?"

Through the fuzziness of the wine, a warning gong sounded in Lottie's mind. Mabs's kind, lined and familiar face swam before her eyes, but it was too close, suffocatingly close. Lottie froze, unsure what to do.

She took a step back. "I…I'm, sorry Mabs, I think you've got the wrong idea."

A spasm of anger flashed across the older woman's face. She dropped her hand and turned away abruptly. "I see. I'm sorry. I thought you an intelligent, open-minded sort of girl. I thought you knew why I asked you here; why I asked you to stay. Why, in fact, I took this damned apartment in the first place!"

"Mabs! No, I didn't realise. I'm so sorry. I've been a fool. I must go."

"You can't go now. It's too late and you're too drunk."

The boozy sense of relaxation was fast evaporating from Lottie. She reached out for the solid stone edge of the balcony and gripped its railings. Reassuringly cold, inanimate and immovable, their rigid iron bars steadied her. "Maybe you're right, but I will go home tomorrow. I could go to a hotel tonight. There's one on the corner, next to Étienne's café."

"And make me look even more of a fool than I feel? No, take the chaise-longue over there. There is only one bedroom. I had hoped we would share it." Mabs faltered.

Lottie braced herself for more.

Mabs schooled her face back into its more usual, soft lines. "You won't reconsider? I could teach you so much, my dear. I wouldn't hold you to a long-standing relationship, but we could share one night of bliss, couldn't we? Any future husband would be charmed to find you skilled in the things I can show you. I could pleasure you in ways you've never dreamed of."

"No!" Every part of Lottie recoiled at this invitation. "You are a good friend, Mabs, but I don't want that sort of intimacy. I'm sorry if I ever gave that impression but it was the meeting of our minds I enjoyed. I…I don't want to be intimate with you in that way. You've already shown me so much – art and music and books – but that's all I want. Please believe me."

Resignation supplanted desire on Mabs' face. "I understand. Take the couch. There's a bathroom off the hall, by the front door. It's basic but will suffice for," her voice caught, "for one night."

Lottie bolted for the bathroom and rammed the lock home once inside the small cubicle. Her breath was coming thick and fast and she plonked down on the toilet, feeling close to tears, but grateful Mabs' wealth had provided this unusual level of hygiene and privacy. Other apartments she'd visited in Paris only had a Turkish toilet,

155

or more often, none at all. All sorts of emotions sought for dominance in her whirling, befuddled brain. Words from the poets she loved haunted her. Lines she hadn't questioned before suddenly made sense. Romance wasn't always between opposite genders. What a simpleton she'd been. She should have guessed Mabs wanted more than friendship by the way she'd introduced her to other same-sex couples.

If only Al had loved her back was the thought that surfaced above all the others. If she had his protection, his love, she wouldn't have got into this awful fix.

Lottie took a deep breath and splashed water on to her flushed face. She tidied herself up, used the facilities and headed for the sofa in the salon. To her immense relief, Mabs had already gone to bed and was nowhere to be seen. One candle had been left alight, the curtains closed, and the table cleared. Some rugs had been thrown on to the makeshift bed. Lottie didn't undress but kicked off her shoes and lay down, pulled the covers over her. She lay on the horsehair mattress all night, listening out for footsteps that never came.

When the dawn broke, Lottie finally dropped off into a light doze, but she woke immediately when Mabs appeared with croissants and a jar of cherry jam, a couple of hours later.

Mabs looked just the same as ever and Lottie took her cue from her cheery demeanour.

"Good morning, my dear. I'll lay the table, shall I?"

"Good morning, Mabs. Those look nice."

"Yes, don't they? I'll make some coffee."

Across the breakfast table, an awkward silence stretched between them. Lottie dunked her pastry in the bowl of milky coffee, hoping, if it was wet enough, she could get it down. She couldn't think of a single thing to say. Sunshine streamed in through the French windows, leaving nowhere to hide.

"About last night," Mabs pulled her croissant apart but none went in her mouth.

"Perhaps we said enough then." Lottie sniffed the delicious aroma of coffee, craving normality.

"I think not. I've decided to go back to New York. Paris gets terribly hot in the summer and I'm not convinced that Hitler won't come knocking on the door. If things had turned out differently between us, it would have been worth staying. Whatever ghastliness that horrid little man inflicted on France, we could have faced together, but as it is..."

"You're going back to America?"

"I might have to charter a private plane to get there. No doubt I'll have to pay a fortune. But, I'm not an enemy of the Germans yet, unlike you, so my passport is still valid anywhere. I'll see what flights are still available. I have a friend who's bound to know. Money usually gets results, if you spend enough dough."

"Are you going right away?"

"As soon as I can arrange it. Oh, I know we had the chance to visit the hallowed apartment of Gertrude Stein and see her gorgeous collection, but I can't face it now. I'm embarrassed, to tell you the truth, Lottie. I misread our friendship badly. I've never had a rejection before but have always managed to reach an understanding by this stage. I suppose it's because you are so much younger than me. You have no experience, and, because of your intelligence, I assumed you understood, as have others before you. I'm sorry if I offended you."

"No, no, please! You haven't offended me! I should be flattered you felt that way. I'm not as innocent as you think." Lottie attempted a smile. "I just don't feel the same way."

"Quite. So, it's been fun, but it's over. I'll see about transport out of the city today. Don't come again, Lottie. I'd rather we ended it now."

Lottie felt completely out of her depth at this announcement, but she said, "I understand, Mabs," even though she didn't. She got up and fetched her coat and hat. She stretched out her hand. "Goodbye, dear friend. I hope we can stay in touch."

Mabs leaned in and kissed both her cheeks, one by one, in the French manner – impersonal and brief. "I think not. Experience has taught me that it's best to quit while we're ahead. Goodbye, dearest girl."

Mabs turned away on a sob. Lottie wanted to comfort her but didn't know how.

She picked up her small case and made for the door. Before going through it, she looked back. Mabs stood at the window, her shoulders heaving, her back turned away. Lottie closed the door softly behind her.

CHAPTER TWENTY
PARIS
MAY 1940

"You're back early." Françoise looked up from the magazine she was idly flicking through. Lottie had found her sitting in the warm sunshine on the terrace in front of the chateau.

"Yes, my, um, friend had to dash back to New York. It was a, a sort of, emergency." Lottie stumbled over her explanation, wishing she'd fabricated a story on the Métro on the way home.

"Oh? What sort of emergency?" Françoise looked up.

"Some aunt or other taken very sick, I think." Lottie tried to keep it as vague as possible.

"Let's hope the aunt is obscenely rich and dies peacefully, then." Françoise shut her magazine.

"It's not like you to be so cynical, Françoise? Is everything alright between you and David?"

"Shush! Don't say his name out loud!" Françoise scanned the garden, then looked back at the house.

"Sorry, didn't know it was a state secret."

"Well, it is, silly. What do you care, anyway? I've hardly seen you for weeks."

"I know, but that's all about to change, now my friend has gone. She was the one who introduced me to everyone and got the invites to parties. I shall spend more time with you from now on, I promise." Lottie smiled at Françoise, but only received a scowl in return.

Lottie went into the house, her mood lower than ever after the brief exchange. What *was* she to do with herself without Mabs? Should she stuff her pride in her pocket and go back to her friend, beg her to take her with her to America too, where she would be safe? Would Mabs have already left? Mabs's crumpled face, constrained by unshed tears, flashed across her mind. No, she really couldn't; both Britain and France were at war, unlike America. She'd have to find another way.

The following few days dragged by; the slow, quiet hours such a contrast to the heady days she'd become accustomed to in Mabs's gregarious company. In desperation, she went to Les Deux Magots for lunch on her own one day, half hoping to see Mabs there but, when questioned, the waiter informed her that her friend had not been seen for a couple of weeks. He raised his eyebrows in disdained surprise that she didn't know where her friend was. He made her feel a fool. Did he think they had been lovers? Were the other diners wondering the same? She caught one or two darting sly looks at her, sitting so conspicuously alone, and whispering to each other. It made her feel intensely embarrassed; too aware of the other diners conversing so easily together and too intimidated to join in without Mabs to chivvy her.

It was the same at Shakespeare and Company. Acquaintances nodded hello but no more than that. One woman did stop and enquire after Mabs but turned away with an expressive shrug of her elegant shoulders when Lottie couldn't give a forwarding address for her erstwhile friend. If anything, it emphasised her isolation, her sense of being a stranger in a foreign land.

Letters from Britain had dried up and, without news of her family either, Lottie felt stranded. She imagined her sister with Al, blissfully happy and spending every day together. She couldn't get home now, even if she wanted to.

She missed her mother more than she cared to admit, even to herself, and began to resent the increasing sense of imprisonment in the big, fussy villa. She had to distract herself somehow, so she sought refuge in the local library and sunk herself into reading all the French classics she could lay her hands on, stretching her mind and her vocabulary to ease the boredom and loneliness. She read the newspapers there too, dismayed when Hitler offered the protection of the Reich to Scandinavia, knowing that protection was not what he was offering at all, judging by his forceful invasions of Poland and Czechoslovakia. Lottie read the developments avidly, as Denmark immediately capitulated but its neighbour, Norway, resisted. From then on, she followed events daily, as the Norwegian and German navies battled it out on distant northern seas, aided by British naval ships, but it all still seemed comfortably remote from Paris.

David, apparently, had found work helping out at his father's orchestra and his free time was limited to mornings on days when there were no rehearsals. Françoise moped about the house when she couldn't see him, driving Lottie to distraction.

It was bad enough being away from home, cursing each lost day Lottie could have been there, helping the war effort, feeling part of things again, but Françoise made the lengthening days of May, usually the most beautiful of months, unbearable. Without being able to see David very often, she seemed lost and grew wan enough for even Madame Blanchard to notice.

"What is the matter with you these days, Françoise? You don't look well. Go out and get some sun on those pale cheeks."

"Yes, Maman." Listless and apathetic, Françoise drifted about the villa until Lottie felt she could strangle her.

Instead, she tried to cheer her up. "Come to the library with me, Françoise. There's bound to be a story to divert you there."

"Alright."

The day was warm at last and even in the city it was impossible to ignore the burgeoning spring. The buds on the horse chestnut trees looked ready to burst open after their winter incubation and primroses peeped around their base in the park. Although nature was asserting herself, everything was too ordered, too prim, too regulated to Lottie's critical eyes.

Lottie longed to be back in Wiltshire amongst its effusive, untidy hedgerows. There would be daffodils and tulips blooming there and forsythia colouring the cottage gardens with streaks of vibrant yellow. The orchard in Cheadle Manor would soon be awash with pink apple blossom too. She even wondered what Isobel would be planting in the kitchen garden of the manor, something that had never interested her when she was there. Had they had a hard winter too?

Françoise muttered something and broke her nostalgic reverie.

"Hmm? What's that?"

"Oh, nothing. It's ages since I've been to the library, that's all." Françoise ran her fingers along the metal railings of the park.

"Yes, why did you never come with me before?" Lottie swung open the door of her favourite place.

"I had something else to do when you were gone." Françoise gave a little smirk.

"Really? What was that?" Lottie held the door open for her friend.

"I saw David." The door swished shut behind Françoise.

"Oh, of course. Where - not at your house?"

Françoise's pretty face flushed with rare colour. She nodded.

Inside the library, they sat at a wooden table in a corner amongst the shelves of books and spoke in whispers.

Lottie inhaled the smell of books, instantly comforted by the regimented rows of words in alphabetical order. What wouldn't she give for some new ones written in English? She returned to their previous subject. "You never told me he'd been to your house."

"No. It was our secret. Maman was always out and so were you. Bertrand knew, but as long as I ignored his raids on father's cellar, he kept quiet."

"I suppose it was a bit cold to keep meeting in the park during the winter months." Lottie was losing interest, itching to thumb through a new book.

Françoise sighed. "I never felt the cold then."

Irritated, Lottie got up and started browsing the spines of books.

The next morning, she caught Françoise heaving into a basin in the bathroom and remembered the casual conversation in the library.

"How long have you been like this?"

Françoise wiped her mouth and looked at her face in the mirror. She talked back to her own image, rather than Lottie. "Six weeks."

"Françoise, did you and David...?"

A smile broke through the sadness on Françoise's face. "Yes, David and I made love every time you and Maman went out. It was glorious. I'll never regret it, never. I love him with all my heart and I'm proud to carry his child."

"His *what*? And you're proud? You reckless little fool! What will your parents say? Does your mother know?"

"No, no one knows, only you. Even David doesn't know." The smile faded.

"Oh, Françoise. What have you done?" Lottie slid down the wall to her haunches and stared at her friend. She watched as Françoise wiped her face clean with a wet facecloth and then patted it dry on a towel. Pregnant at nineteen. Unmarried and with a lover whose background was unknown to the family. The Blanchards didn't even know he existed! How could Françoise have been so stupid? Was love truly as blind as legend had it? Was what she felt for Al actually the real thing? Because there was no way she'd have given herself to him without a gold band on her finger but then, Al would never have tried it on in the first place.

What a pickle Françoise was in. Lottie could imagine the uproar when her father found out, let alone her

163

mother. At least Madame Blanchard, with her own louche lifestyle, might have some sympathy for her young daughter.

Françoise refused to tell her mother. Refused to talk about her pregnancy even to Lottie but withdrew, and the secret smile she parked on her complacent face infuriated Lottie.

Lottie let it go that day, while she got over her shock at Françoise's confession, but then her conscience won the internal battle it was waging with her temper. She resolved she had to get Françoise to listen to some advice. She knocked on her friend's bedroom door the next morning. It was raining hard outside, too hard to go anywhere. The house was steeped in gloom as the rain battered against its long windows.

Françoise opened the door. She looked pale, thinner rather than fatter. Lottie hadn't noticed it before. "What do you want?"

Lottie was unprepared for such a confrontational greeting, but doggedly carried on. "Françoise, we must talk."

"Why?"

"Because of your situation, silly." Lottie regretted her words almost before they left her mouth.

"Don't call me silly!" Françoise tried to shut the door, but Lottie pushed against it.

"I'm sorry, I didn't mean to call you that, but I'm worried about you."

"Why? I'm not." Françoise pouted.

"Look, can I come in?"

"Frankly, I'd rather you didn't."

Lottie was shocked. Françoise had never barred her from her room before. She tried a different tack. "I bought a new hat last week. I wondered if you'd like to see it. You can tell me if you think I've wasted my money."

Françoise paused. Then she shook her head. "No thanks." Before Lottie could say more, her friend shut the door. Right in her face.

Lottie felt lonelier than ever in the big empty house.

An alien.

Towards the end of a what was, to Lottie if not her friend, a strained and tense month, not least due to Hitler's tramping across Belgium, Luxembourg and getting closer and closer to northern France, Françoise seemed better, and relented when Lottie suggested a walk. They went together to the park and the warm May sunshine defied the knowledge that German troops now hovered near the French north eastern border. Lottie bought le Figaro and settled down to read it. Françoise seemed content to watch a little boy playing with a toy car along the kerb of the flower beds. Lottie let her relax and bided her time before embarking on the tricky subject of the baby.

The newspaper headline was so startling it blew all other thoughts away. The British Expeditionary Force were in retreat at Dunkirk with the German army snapping at their heels. Surely, it couldn't be true? The BEF were supposed to be the bulwark against invasion by the Germans. Lottie felt betrayed, deserted, bereft.

She looked up from the paper. The tranquil scene blurred before her eyes. A knot clamped together in the pit of her stomach. She looked back at the photograph. All those men. British men – her fellow countrymen stranded like beached whales waiting for ships to scuttle them home to England. How had it come to this? There were thousands of them. France had comforted itself on their defence of their country, and so had she. Who now would stop the Germans from entering the rest of France? These British soldiers, like her, were trapped in France, unable to escape. Were they as frightened as she was? Did they feel naked and exposed too? For a moment, she wondered if she could simply run away and join the massed soldiers on the vast beach pictured in the paper. Surely the navy would come and rescue them? Could she get on one of those boats and get home? Home! She'd never known homesickness at school. Now she felt as nauseous as

Françoise at the thought of her family back at Cheadle Manor.

Françoise. She couldn't face tackling her about her pregnancy now. Lottie got up. "I think it's time to leave."

"So soon?" Françoise had started to play with the little boy and his toy car. Her face had softened from its usual sulkiness and she looked pretty again. Lottie felt a stab of compassion for her friend, stupid or not. What a time to bring a child into the world. She had never felt less safe.

Lottie was silent on the way home, trying to digest the enormity of what was happening on that northern beach at Dunkirk, calculating the miles between there and Paris. Françoise, obviously relieved to be left alone rather than hectored, did not break the peace.

Lottie took the newspaper up to her room and read it over, and over, again. This evacuation of troops, the abject failure of these soldiers, changed everything. Her mind was still in a whirl when the gong sounded for dinner.

"I hear a lot of the richer Jewish families are leaving Paris." Monsieur Blanchard said, in his blunt way, as he carved a scrawny looking chicken.

"Are they? Why?" Madame Blanchard took a sip of claret.

"It's this British retreat. Some people don't think our army can cope without them and our Jewish neighbours are running for the hills in Switzerland, those who can afford it." Monsieur Blanchard snorted his disdain.

"So, it's true, then, sir? They're caught on that beach in Dunkirk?" Lottie hoped her host could tell her more than the papers.

"I'm afraid so, my dear. You should have gone home while you had the chance. You'll have to stay in France till the fuss dies down now."

"And do you think it will?" Lottie laid down her fork.

"Oh, I think so. Our troops won't let Hitler invade, you know. He might have conquered Poland, but he won't get France! The fortifications of the Maginot line are impregnable, and the Germans could never get through the Ardennes forest. Remember the parade last July? Ah, no, I forgot again, Charlotte, you were not with us then. Well, my dear, it clearly demonstrated we have the best army in the world! Not only French troops, but our colonial cousins from Africa, and never forget the Foreign Legion!" Monsieur wiped his mouth on his linen serviette and finished off his wine in one go. "No, you won't get *our* lads running for home or French families running for cover. Forgive me, but I think we can manage without your BEF."

Françoise had blanched white.

Madame Blanchard looked irritated at her husband's confidence. She turned instead to her daughter. "Are you unwell, Françoise? You are looking so peaky these days. I've a mind to take you to see the doctor."

"No, Maman, I'm fine, really I am."

Upstairs in Lottie's bedroom, her previous cold rejection forgotten, Françoise confessed her fears to her English friend. "I haven't seen David for a week and then, when Papa said some Jewish families had left Paris, I wondered if he had gone too."

"But wouldn't he have told you first? Left you a note or something?"

"Maybe he didn't have time? From what Father said, it seems lots of Jews are running away."

"But haven't you met his family? Gone to his place? You've been seeing each other for months now."

Françoise flushed, the red colour of her cheeks hectic against her white skin. She shook her head.

Lottie went cold. "What? Never? Why?"

"He...he didn't want me to, and I didn't push it, knowing how Father feels about...those sorts of people. We came here instead or went into the city. And lately, he's been busy with the orchestra. Oh, Lottie, what if he's gone to Switzerland? I'll never see him again!"

"Françoise, does David still not know about the baby?"

Françoise shook her head a second time. "I didn't want to worry him. I was frightened he would leave me, and now he has!" She burst into tears.

Lottie held her in her arms, feeling Françoise's body go limp against her as she wept. "Then I think it's time he was told."

The next morning, Lottie went into Françoise's well-appointed bedroom before breakfast, determined not to show how worried she was. "Hello, sleepyhead. I've been thinking about your young man, and I've decided we'll have to investigate his mysterious disappearance."

"Investigate?" Françoise held a flannel to her mouth. She looked a bit green.

"Yes, we'll be amateur sleuths and track him down. If he's found another girl, you ought to know." Lottie tried to laugh.

Françoise didn't respond. "I don't think he would do that. David loves me as much as I love him. You wouldn't understand, Lottie."

That hurt.

"Oh, wouldn't I?"

The image, so often repressed, of Isobel wrapped in Al's arms flashed across her brain. The pain centred around her heart. She took a breath, swept it from her mind and concentrated instead on her friend.

Françoise shook her head. Her eyes filled. She dabbed at her mouth with the flannel.

Lottie lost patience. "Well, if he hasn't gone off with a floozie, let's find out what has happened to him. Come on, we'll take the Métro to the concert hall. Someone there is bound to know where he's got to. We'll probably find him deep in the orchestra pit, cleaning up the sweet papers."

After a perfunctory breakfast, they walked to the Métro steps and down to the station. They got out at the nearest stop and walked for half a mile to the Salle Pleyel on the rue du Faubourg Saint Honoré, where David worked.

The box office cubicle was empty, and the front doors locked.

"We'll go around the side to the stage door." Lottie lead the way, holding Françoise's hand.

They had to knock several times before the battered door opened to reveal a middle-aged man with a cigarette dangling from the corner of his mouth.

Lottie gave him her brightest smile. "Bonjour, are you the concierge for this theatre?"

"Oui?" he growled, his cigarette firmly wedged against his tobacco-stained teeth.

Lottie knew Françoise wouldn't have the courage to ask for her lover's whereabouts. "We are looking for Monsieur David Blumenthal. He works here in the orchestra, like his father."

The man shook his head mournfully. "You'd better come in."

The two girls entered the lobby, carefully avoiding the clutter of dusty props leaning against the grubby walls. They followed the man's bowed back into the pit of the orchestra where the musicians huddled together, not playing but speaking in low voices, as if at a funeral.

The concierge pulled at his braces as he waited to be noticed. At last, a tall, grey-haired gentleman got up from the piano stool and spoke to him. Lottie and Françoise waited in the shadows, watching. The concierge took his damp cigarette from his mouth and used it between thumb and forefinger to point to the two girls loitering against the wall. The tall gentleman looked across and frowned. Instead of coming towards them, he returned to the group of muttering musicians and a bent old man leant his cello against his chair, withdrew from his colleagues, and joined him. The tall man leant down and spoke softly into his ear. The bowed old cellist ran his hand over his eyes and took a deep breath, before coming over to Lottie and Françoise.

Before he reached them, Lottie's increasing sensation of foreboding solidified into fear. She felt for Françoise's small hand and enclosed it with her own.

"You must be Françoise, Mademoiselle, and this is your English friend, no?" The old man's wrinkled face was kind, but his polite manners could not hide his distress.

"How...how do you know that?" Françoise's voice was muffled, faint.

"You are looking for David, are you not?"

Lottie came forward, away from the shadows. She wanted to observe his expression more clearly. "Yes, we are. Do you know where he is?"

The little man shook his head. "No, no-one does. His father was very anxious last week, talking about some friends in Switzerland and they never showed up for work the next day."

"But why not?" Françoise's voice was now barely a whisper.

"More to the point, where are they?" Goosebumps broke out on Lottie's flesh. She could guess the answer to her own question.

"We do not know. A pity, Monsieur Blumenthal was a fine violinist and we have no-one to replace him. It will be difficult to perform tonight for the string section."

"Have you an address for them?" Lottie slipped her arm around Françoise's waist. Her friend started shivering.

The old man shrugged and scribbled down an address. Françoise almost snatched it out of his hand.

Lottie smiled at the old man as he turned to go back to his cello. "Thank you for your help."

"I wish it were different and I could do more." He waved his long fingers in salute.

Lottie pulled Françoise towards the door and they walked through the untidy corridor back into the daylight, blinking at the sun's rays after the dark interior of the theatre.

"No wonder David was so pale," Lottie looked at her friend whose own colour was no better. "It's black as night in there."

"So, we go back home, do we?" Françoise looked non-plussed.

Lottie nodded, hoping she looked more in control. "Looks like it. How far is his apartment from your house, do you know?"

"No, I never went to his family home, remember?"

"Well, we can ask for directions, now we have his address, can't we?"

Lottie showed the scrap of paper to Françoise. "Ah yes, it's in the same arrondissement as my house."

They were silent on the train back and got out at their usual stop, glad their line was still running. Many had closed because of the war. Lottie strode up to the news kiosk with the scrap of paper. The newspaper seller gave her a strange look when he read it but pointed them towards a street to their left, saying it wasn't too far to walk.

"Come on, Françoise." Lottie took her friend's cold hand in hers.

Françoise met her stride and, after asking for directions once more from a street sweeper, they arrived in front of a blue door in an apartment building on a quiet tree-lined avenue.

Lottie lifted the elaborate knocker and rapped on the door.

A shifty-looking, middle-aged man pointed them up the stairs to the fifth floor. They began to climb the first half flight, turned half a circle and mounted the next. Lottie counted ten half flights and went along the landing till they found the right door. They knocked several times but got no answer.

"Let's try the apartment opposite." Lottie faced the opposite door and knocked twice. They waited. When they were almost on the point of giving up, a young girl eventually opened it a crack. Dark eyes, their whites showing, peered at them through it.

"Is that the apartment of David Blumenthal opposite?" Lottie held the address up for the girl to see.

She nodded a fraction.

"Do you know where he is? We are his friends." It was Françoise who spoke, her voice gentle.

But the girl looked even more frightened.

Lottie stuck her foot in the door and made it widen enough to see more of her face. "Don't be afraid. We really are friends."

"He, he's not here. He's gone." The girl had the same guttural accent as David, the consonants harsh. French was obviously not her first language.

"Are you related? You look just like him." Lottie let Françoise speak.

The girl shook her head. She couldn't have been more than fifteen. "No, but we were friends."

"I am Françoise Blanchard. Did David not tell you about me?"

The young girl nodded again and this time her mouth quivered at the corner.

"The whole family has gone. They said they had to go first to make sure we could join them. It was the same in Berlin. I don't understand any of it." Tears welled up in the girl's face and began to trickle down her sallow cheeks. From inside the house they heard an older voice, cracked with age. "Who is it, Gisela? Who is there? Shut the door. We don't want to speak to anyone."

"I must go. My mother is not well; she needs me. I'm sorry. I cannot tell you anymore. Please, move your foot so I can shut the door. You never know who might be listening."

"But maybe we can help you?" Lottie left her foot in the door-jam even though the girl was pressing the wood against it, causing her pain.

"No one can do that anymore. Please, I must shut the door. Don't come again."

The pressure on Lottie's foot increased and she pulled it away slightly. Instantly, the door slammed shut. Lottie stared at the glossy blue paint for a few seconds before turning to her friend.

"Looks hopeless. Sorry, Françoise."

Françoise burst into tears for the second time that morning.

CHAPTER TWENTY ONE
A HILL FARM IN FLINTSHIRE
MAY 1940

Isobel never thought she would look back on her training days for the Women's Land Army with such fondness. Now she was on a real farm, the beds in the dormitory at the training centre seemed like feathered nests in comparison with the makeshift wooden constructions she slept on here and she began to doubt her decision to enrol. The whole process had taken ages. She'd had to wait until she turned seventeen before she could apply and then had to have a medical examination and an interview before a rather formidable panel of women who asked searching questions about whether she was tough enough for a farming life. She'd been so pleased to have finally been accepted in the spring of 1940. She'd felt guilty about leaving her mother to cope with the manor on her own, especially with Lottie gone, but even more about Al, slogging away at the factory without the joy of their snatched times together. She longed for him every day and soon regretted her impulsive decision when the novelty of farm work wore off and the ache of missing him hit home.

She thought she'd learned a lot at the Land Army centre. She'd heard lectures about growing potatoes and milking cows, even rat-catching had been briefly touched on. Isobel had donned her brown breeches and her Land Army badge with pride when she qualified at the end of four short weeks. The training had stirred excitement and inspired confidence, sadly misplaced here in North Wales, when the reality of farm life clearly demonstrated how sketchy those lessons had been.

Although the big industrial port of Liverpool, and its satellite town of Chester, were only thirty miles away, you would never guess it at the remote farm where Isobel was posted. She and the two other girls got up at dawn, whatever the weather, and worked eight solid hours – it would be ten in the summer, Mr Williams told them with glee - with nothing but four slabs of bread stuck together by beetroot slices to keep them going through the working day. The beetroot leaked its juice into the bread, making it both wet and a deeply unattractive pink. They only got cheese on a Saturday.

They slept on hard wooden makeshift beds in the dark and draughty old stables at Pen y Bryn. Elsie snored, and Lilian's chronic catarrh meant she was always blowing her nose. It was all very different to the healthy outdoor life the glamorous posters had promised.

Mrs Williams, the farmer's wife, who never took off her greasy wrap-around pinny, had resented rather than welcomed them. "All these extra mouths to feed, as if I didn't have enough to do."

Mr Williams had been more welcoming, managing to smile while keeping his stained teeth clamped on his pipe, but after Isobel had spotted him peering through a knothole in the wooden wall of their so-called dormitory, she had kept her distance from the small, taciturn Welshman.

Glamorous it was not.

She pulled on her corduroy breeches; they were stiff with the cold. She put on two vests and decided to forego a wash at the improvised washstand. Breakfast in the farmhouse kitchen was bread and butter and weak tea, over too quickly and only on offer once thirty cows had been milked.

Steam rose from her breath as she hit the cold air in the farmyard. Mr Williams sat on the tractor waiting to take the land girls to their work in his trailer. He gave her his usual welcome to the working day, a wordless grunt.

"Come on, Miss Posho. Climb aboard." Elsie held out her hand to help Isobel clamber on to the back of the wooden cart.

Mr Williams smirked as she missed her step and half fell into the wagon.

"Don't listen to 'im, love." Elsie, a cockney, had a heart of gold.

Isobel didn't know what she'd do without her or Lilian to keep her going. Lilian was late, as usual. She came running across the farmyard, still tying her scarf over her bright red hair.

"That hair is as genuine as my silk stockings," Mrs Williams had said when she'd met Lilian. The farmer's wife always spoke as if she thought no one could hear her.

"Too much time alone up on these Welsh hills," Lilian said afterwards, not the least bit put out. "We hear worse in Yorkshire, believe me." Robust in body and mind, it took a lot to shake Lilian.

"What are we doing today, Mr Williams?" Elsie shouted above the roar of the old Fergie as they trundled out of the yard and over the stony, bumpy path.

"I'll do the milking today because you'll be lifting beetroots," came the terse and dreaded reply.

Isobel groaned. "Not again." She looked at her hands, still raw from yesterday.

"Can't we wait till the frost is off 'em?" Elsie yelled.

Mr Williams steered around a bend in the track. "No, it's dry and the sun'll be out soon enough."

"Sun? Can't remember what that looks like." Elsie muttered below the level of the tractor engine.

Mr Williams left them to it once they got to the beetroot field. Frost still rimed the hedgerow, each leaf edged with white crystals, despite the lateness of the season.

"If I saw that hedge on a Christmas card before I joined the WLA I'd think it was beautiful. Now my hands sting just looking at it." Lilian shoved her hands in her pockets.

"I'm going to ask Mrs Williams about gloves again. It's not right. My hands are red from the beetroot and raw from the frost. And look at the size of this field!" Isobel blew on her fingers.

"Two days' work, I reckon."

"And no hot drink all day."

"I'm going to complain to our supervisor on Sunday, after church." Isobel had made up her mind.

"Good for you. We'll all go."

Mrs Hopkins, the local organiser of the Women's Land Army, didn't openly criticise Mrs Williams when they showed her their hands, but she looked very sympathetic. "I see what you mean, girls. I'll call on the Williams's tomorrow morning - first thing. You can't work in these conditions without a hot drink all day. And I'll supply the gloves - I'll bring them with me."

Things improved after that, including the weather, except for Mrs Williams's temper.

"I'm sure Mrs Hopkins was polite, but you'd think we'd shopped Mother Williams for murder the way she's treating us." Lilian grumbled one May morning before milking, just after dawn.

"At least we've a Thermos of tea to call our own." Elsie combed her hair in the cracked mirror.

"If you don't mind drinking out of a jam jar." Isobel had spilt some of her precious tea the first day of tea-drinking because the jam jar had been too hot to hold in hands still frozen despite the gloves.

"Come on, girls. At least the beets are in." Lilian pulled on her Wellington boots.

"More bloody beetroot sandwiches." Elsie was really down in the dumps.

After milking the cows, they trooped into the farmhouse kitchen.

Isobel's stomach rumbled. "Anyone know what we're doing today?"

The farmer's wife poured hot water into the big brown teapot and plonked it in the middle of the table. A loaf of bread was cut already, and Isobel took two slices, ignoring Mrs Williams's tutting.

"No idea. Looks like rain, just to add to the joy. You'd think the month of May would be sunny at least." Elsie sniffed.

"It's the same in Yorkshire, lass. Warmer weather means more rain, not less." Lilian scraped her plate with her roughened forefinger and licked it.

"Time for work, girls." Mrs Williams started clearing the table, her pursed lips brooking no argument.

They walked into the yard, where Mr Williams already had the tractor and trailer waiting. "You're going to a neighbour's farm today. Their potatoes need planting, in fact they're well overdue. Hop on the trailer and I'll take you there."

"How far is it, Mr Williams?"

"Only a couple of miles. Come on. Get up on the trailer." Mr Williams was wearing his gabardine mackintosh, not a good sign.

"Do you think it's going to rain all day?" Isobel asked the farmer.

"Looks like it. I'll have to check my ditches once I've dropped you lot off."

Mr Williams took them to an isolated barn amongst untended fields, which housed a small tractor. He filled the tank with petrol from a can put ready. "Follow me to the fields you're to plough and plant. One of you can drive the tractor and the others can sow the potatoes. Look, here they are in trays, already chitted and sprouting. Come on, you can load them up on to my trailer while I finish getting Mrs Jones's tractor ready."

He turned over the engine with the starting handle while the three girls hefted the heavy trays of potatoes on to the trailer.

"So, who's going first with the cushy tractor driving, hey?" Lilian asked.

"Bags I go first," Elsie said quickly. "I've had the official training. I could show you my proficiency certificate if I had it on me."

"Oh, go on, then." Isobel hadn't done that part of the training and had always regretted it. "Can you teach me how to drive, Elsie?"

"Yes, of course I can, nothing to it."

Lilian and Isobel bumped along in the trailer over the rutted lane to the potato field, huddled between the trays of potatoes and kept busy by stopping them from spilling. Elsie grinned at them from her tractor seat.

"Don't bloody gloat!" Lilian shouted at her.

"Now then, I won't have language like that on my trailer, Miss." Mr Williams turned around, face like thunder.

"Talk about double standards," muttered Elsie under her breath. "Old lech."

Mr Williams lost no time in driving off and leaving them to it. The neglected field stretched ahead of them and the rain did keep up the whole day, coming in swirls of soft droplets off a sea shrouded in mist. They set to work but were soon soaked.

"It's like working inside a bleeding cloud." Lilian pulled her hat down over her red curls, now limp with the wet.

"At least it's not so cold."

"Which is worse, would you say? You know, marks out of ten. Freezing to death or dissolving in rainwater?" Elsie wrung out her scarf ends, as she got down from the tractor to take a turn at the back-breaking potato planting.

"Ten for rain!" Lilian and Isobel agreed.

"Hello, who's this?" Elsie stopped her wringing and looked over to the gate.

A short, stout woman in a gabardine raincoat and Wellingtons got out of an old Austin Seven and came towards them, a large wicker basket on her arm.

"Hello girls! What a day for you to be outside. I've brought you some tea and apple-cake. Made it myself from apples from that orchard over there. Always keep a store for the winter. I thought you might like to know what the fruits of your labours could taste like. I'm Mrs Jones, from the farm, and I'm that glad to have your help. Mrs Hopkins arranged it and I hope Mr Williams doesn't mind lending you to me for the day."

Mrs Jones was as different to Mrs Williams as two women could be. Plump and red-cheeked, Mrs Jones doled out large chunks of fruit cake to each of them.

"This is lovely, Mrs Jones." Isobel said through the sweet nectar.

"Well, you can't work on empty stomachs, my dears, now can you?"

Elsie looked at Lilian, then at Isobel, a mute question in her brown eyes. Isobel nodded back at her. "That's exactly what we are doing over at the Williams's."

"Hmm, can't say I'm surprised, cariad. Now you do another hour on the potatoes - those rows you've done are looking good, I must say. And I'll come and fetch you in the car for lunch up at the house - how's that?"

"That is the best news I've heard in ages."

"Thank you!"

"Sounds lovely."

Isobel planted more potatoes in the next hour than she had managed the whole morning. When the little black car reappeared, she straightened her aching back, downed her tools and, with Lilian and Elsie, trudged through the mud to meet it.

"Hop in, my dears, hop in! Scrape your boots on the grass verge first!"

Isobel couldn't believe the difference between Mrs Jones's warm and welcoming farmhouse and the cold austerity of their hostess's one. The smell of the food reminded her of Al's grandmother's cooking. Agnes always made sure everyone got fed, just like this lovely lady. How she longed to be back in that kitchen, with Al by her side. Doing your bit was all very well but Al's letters were no substitute for his kisses.

On the range, which warmed the entire room, bubbled a cauldron of savoury smelling cawl.

"This cawl is so tasty, Mrs Jones." Elsie echoed Isobel's thoughts. The chunky meat stew actually tasted of mutton and the rich gravy glistened amongst leeks and potatoes and herbs. Mrs Williams's version was as grey as her hair, consisting mostly of water and lots of swede.

"Can I have another piece of bread to dip in it?" Lilian's hand hovered over the thick slices.

"Of course, you can, cariad. They don't ration that yet!" Mrs Jones stood at the range, a ladle in her hand. "More cawl anyone?"

Isobel held her bowl out for more and laughed as she saw her friends do the same.

"Do you need some land girls here all the time, Mrs Jones?" Elsie winked at Isobel.

"We could use some help, it's true. Our Gruff's just joined the army, even though farming's a reserved occupation. Said it was an opportunity to get on in life. He's not my son, you see, but I think of him as my own. Jobs are piling up around the place. Like those potatoes you're planting a month late. It's a good job I have Dai Morgan to look after the sheep, or I don't know what I'd do. He's getting on in years and his arthritis plagues him but at least he's too old to desert me and join up, like Gruff. I hope to God the dear boy will come home." She shook her head, looking sad.

Mrs Jones filled her own bowl and sat down. "My husband died five years ago, see. Without Gruff, I'm not sure how I'll manage but Mrs Williams would never forgive me if I poached you lot. She'll still be my neighbour after this dreadful war is over. I wouldn't want to fall out with her," she added in a low voice, "not that we are close friends, her being chapel, and that."

"I'll come!" Lilian and Elsie said together.

"Well, that would be lovely, my dears, but like I say, I don't want to upset anyone."

"You won't - you'll be saving our lives. We'll ask Mrs Hopkins."

Isobel wiped her bowl with Mrs Jones's excellent soda bread. How many land girls would she need on this small farm? She doubted it would be three.

CHAPTER TWENTY TWO
PARIS
JUNE 1940

Lottie put down the newspaper in the library, and stared at the wall opposite, trying to digest the shocking news about the massive retreat of British troops from northern France. The BEF was now encircled by the Germans, whom they had failed to defeat, and were, unbelievably, a whole week later, still stranded on the beach at Dunkirk, in Normandy. A massive flotilla of boats from the south coast of England were, even now, on their way to rescue them, bit by determined, gruesome bit.

On the twenty-eighth of May Prince Leopold of Belgium had surrendered and Belgian refugees now flooded into France, said another report. Other contingents of the German army had gone on to bypass the French troops bravely trying to defend the Maginot line. Hitler's Wehrmacht had then slyly slipped past them through the thick forest of the Ardennes, left unguarded by the French, who had believed it impassable. Was there no stopping them?

Now, in early June, there was nothing between them and France. So much for Monsieur Blanchard's confidence in his compatriots, the fortifications and the forest and the famous Maginot defences.

Lottie finished the article, hardly believing its stark summary of recent dramatic events. So much had happened this last week in the theatre of war a few hundred kilometres from where she sat in the quiet library. This war was no longer 'drôle' or phoney and danger was knocking on the door. *Her door.* As a British person in France, she would probably be considered an enemy alien. The Germans might shoot her on sight if they discovered her identity! Lottie darted a furtive look at the other members of the library. There were far fewer than normal, and all kept their heads down. She looked at the librarian.

He had always been her friend, helping her choose books, stamping their return. He looked away, wouldn't catch her eye.

She had to get home. No more wasting time. She would do whatever it took. Bribe officials, sneak onto trains, find a boat, any boat. She couldn't stay here a moment longer. Granny's will had shrunk into insignificance now. Who cared who had what? What did it matter who was in charge of Cheadle Manor? All that really mattered was that Cassandra and Isobel were her family, and she missed them like hell.

And she missed Al the most.

Françoise wasn't her responsibility. If the silly fool had got herself pregnant with David, it was nothing to do with Lottie. No. Not her problem. Françoise had two parents and no siblings. It was up to them to sort it out. They were wealthy, protected, and they could look after her.

Cursing the days, weeks, she had already wasted, Lottie hurried back to the Blanchard's villa. Once again, she packed her suitcase, counted out her money, luckily she'd had the foresight to withdraw another chunk of it from the bank, and prepared to go home.

Home - the best word in the English dictionary. Chez-moi didn't have the same resonance at all.

Lottie thought of all those British troops being rescued by boats of all kinds off the coast at Dunkirk. If they could make it home, why couldn't she? Now she had made up her mind, she was itching to depart. If she made it to Dunkirk, she could get on one. She'd read about thousands of refugees, just like her - for wasn't she one - doing just that. There must be a way through the Germans surrounding the area, there just must be. The flood of displaced people wasn't only in one direction. People were leaving France too. The evacuation had begun on the twenty-sixth of May, it was now the third of June and still not over. If she left today, she had a chance.

Françoise came in as she was packing. "What are you doing?"

"Leaving. I can't stay any longer, Françoise. You know the troops stranded at Dunkirk?"

Françoise looked blank.

Lottie tutted impatiently. "The British Expeditionary Force that's in retreat?"

Françoise nodded but her hands fluttered in denial.

"I'm going to try and join them. Get on a boat, any boat."

"But I need you, Lottie!" Françoise held on to the door frame for support.

"I'm sorry, Françoise. Look," Lottie sat down on the bed, "you must tell your parents about the baby. You are their responsibility - not mine. You are a dear friend, but I miss my family. That silly row about the legacy. It was stupid of me to get so angry. I want to go *home*, Françoise."

Lottie looked at her friend, standing stock still in the open doorway, her spare hand on her belly. For the first time, Lottie noticed it's gentle swell through her thin summer dress. "Françoise. Tell your mother about the baby. She might be cross, but she will stand by you."

Françoise started to cry. "Don't leave me, Lottie. Please!"

A shadow passed by in the hall. Madame Blanchard crossed the threshold. "Why are you crying, Françoise?" She looked across at Lottie sitting amongst her scattered clothes on the bed, her suitcase open against the pillow.

"What is going on? Why are you packing, Charlotte?"

"Hello, Madame. I was going to come and find you to explain. I feel I must try again to get home. The BEF is still at Dunkirk and boats are coming from England every day to rescue them. I'm going to try and get on one, get to England before it's too late." Lottie stood up and squared her shoulders ready for a protest.

But there was none. Instead, Madame Blanchard simply nodded. "I quite understand. You wish to be with your mother. Frankly, I'm surprised you have stayed so long but Françoise was glad of your company. Since she left school last summer, she has been...shall we say, without direction. And this war..."

Lottie looked at Françoise who stood motionless, a hand still on her convex belly. "Françoise, this would be a good time to..."

Françoise shook her head violently.

Madame looked from one girl to another, her eyes narrowed, her lips thin.

"To what?"

But the sentence was never finished. A distant rumble from the direction of Paris distracted each of them. Madame Blanchard was the first to reach the window. She pulled back the lace curtain and looked out.

"Ah, mon Dieu! Aeroplanes!"

"Are they British?" Lottie strained to see them.

Françoise stood apart, her fingers over her mouth but Lottie craned her neck, pressing her nose against the glass, feeling its faint vibration.

Madame Blanchard shook her head. "No, I think they are German." She suddenly gripped Lottie's arm. Her fingers were surprisingly strong.

Despite the pain, Lottie didn't shrink from her grasp. "Oh, no! They are bombing the city!"

"But why are they attacking Paris?" Françoise came closer.

"What are they targeting?" Lottie strained her eyes. "Look, they are flying over the Seine, close to the Citroën factory. Oh no! They are heading straight for it!"

"Édouard! He is at the factory! Oh, please God, may they miss it." Madame Blanchard's other hand flew to her throat.

Lottie drew back the nets completely and Françoise sidled up to her, drawn to the sight.

Seconds later flames shot up in the distance. A moment after each flare, they felt the impact as the sound followed. The panes of glass rattled in their wooden casements.

Horrified, the three women watched as more bombs fell from the sky. They could hear sirens wailing like seagulls in mournful flight. Then Bertrand ran into the garden below them, and stood, staring up at the sky, his mouth hanging open in disbelief.

Madame Blanchard threw open the French window and stepped on to the balcony.

"Bertrand! Are they German bombers?"

"Oui, Madame."

"Isn't that the direction of my husband's factory?" Madame now gripped the balcony railings, looking down at Bertrand and then back at the orange sky.

Bertrand nodded, without looking up. "Oui, Madame. It looks like a direct hit."

Lottie felt a hand sneaking into hers. Françoise had joined her on the balcony. She was trembling.

Lottie put an arm around her friend. "The bastards."

Madame Blanchard did not reprimand her words. Lottie looked at her hostess. Tears tracked down through the powder on her cheeks, leaving pale tramlines among the wrinkles.

It was two days before Édouard Blanchard's death was confirmed; one day after the last boat left Dunkirk for Britain.

In the confused aftermath, Lottie's hopes of escape faded away. Françoise had become hysterical, her mother stony-faced and unresponsive. Lottie was the only one who could function normally. Madame had been telephoning everyone she could think of to find out about her husband. Bertrand had been sent to the factory but came back without an answer. Then, forty-eight hours after the bombing, the telephone shrilled through the hall.

Bertrand handed the receiver to Madame and Lottie took Françoise into the dining room to wait. Somehow, they all knew what the caller would say.

Madame replaced the telephone mouthpiece on to its stand in the hall and came in to join her daughter and Lottie.

"It's definite. Your father's office took a direct hit. He wasn't the only one. They think about two hundred and fifty people were killed and another couple of hundred are injured. The factory had been singled out. Perhaps the Germans knew of Papa's new 2CV." Madame Blanchard's voice caught on a sob. "He had such hopes of that little car."

She sat down and clasped her white hands together, resting them on the polished surface of the table. They shook slightly. Madame silently stared at them.

"Oh, Papa!" Françoise looked bewildered.

Lottie had thought no love existed in this family but perhaps you don't know you love someone until they are gone. "What are you going to do, Madame?"

Madame Blanchard looked up. Her eyes swam with tears. Lottie wasn't sure if she could see through them.

"I do not know."

"But Maman, why was father's factory singled out? In all of Paris? Why?" Françoise mumbled the words.

Lottie answered for her mother. "It was right on the Seine, Françoise. An easy target and an important one. It must have been a doddle to pick out against the river, so big and white, right on the water, and the sheer size of the factory behind would have given it away. Who knows where they will strike next? Paris is bound to be their number one target."

Madame Blanchard took a deep shuddering breath. "You speak sense, Charlotte. Perhaps it is not wise for us to remain in the capital. I must think what to do. Oh, if only Édouard was here. He always knew what to do."

Lottie spoke again. "Madame. Where is Monsieur's wireless? We need to listen to it, keep abreast of events. Can it be moved into the salon?"

"I...I don't know." Madame Blanchard, usually so cold and sarcastic, so in control of herself, appeared to be unable to make any decision, however small.

Lottie turned to Françoise. "What do you think?"

"I don't know what to do! Why ask me? I've enough to think about without moving wirelesses. I don't care what happens anyway." Françoise began to sob quietly, despairingly.

Lottie looked at the mother and her daughter. Hopeless.

"Right, I'll go and find Bertrand. He can move the wireless. No one can stop us listening to it now and we must find out what's going on." She waited for a response, but Madame had got up and slid an arm around Françoise. Grief had finally united them, but would they stay that way once Madame knew Françoise's secret?

She had to leave them to it. Lottie went in search of Bertrand. Pulling the bell cord hadn't yielded a result. She went below stairs. The kitchen smelt of cabbage and boiled ham. There was no one there.

She found him in the garage, poking about the big Citroën saloon.

"Bertrand?"

The man spun round, a guilty look on his face.

"What are you doing?"

"What is it to you?"

"Don't speak to me like that." Lottie was shocked, she'd never seen that shifty look on his face before. Bertrand had always seemed the perfect manservant; his countenance always impassive, impersonal.

Bertrand gave a Gallic shrug. "Do you think things will be the same now? Monsieur is dead. The government doesn't know what to do. We must all think for ourselves."

Lottie heard the chink of car keys. "Give me the keys to the car."

Bertrand looked uncomfortable.

"Bertrand! Give me the keys. You have not become the master in this house just because Monsieur Blanchard has died. If you want your wages paid, hand the car keys to me." Lottie held out her hand.

He hesitated, making her doubt he would obey her command. Then he passed the keys over in silence. His eyes betrayed him. He didn't look the least bit like an obedient servant anymore, in fact he looked downright dodgy as he dropped the keys into her open palm.

"Thank you. Now, I need you to do something for me. Madame has asked that the wireless be brought from Monsieur's study into the salon. We can all listen to the news there, including you and the other servants."

"What other servants? Only Sophie is left. The others left this morning. You won't see them again. I told you, it's each man for himself now."

"Did they? I see. You are right, Bertrand, we must all look out for ourselves but there is no reason why we can't do that together." Lottie turned and lead the way upstairs. There was another moment's pause before she heard his heavy footsteps following her. She let out her breath as she mounted the stairs.

She helped Bertrand, white faced and cursing, to shift the heavy wireless into the salon. He plugged it in and Lottie tuned it up to the right station. Through the crackles they heard the announcer talking about the bombing of the Citroën factory.

"So many dead," Madame said.

"And the suburbs got hit too; no wonder it sounded so close. We could have been hit ourselves." Françoise murmured.

"The cowards." Lottie clenched her fists. "Two hundred and fifty-four dead. My God."

Once installed, the wireless quickly became the focus of their world as events unfolded. Over the next few days they listened to every bulletin. The Prime Minister of France, Paul Reynaud, appalled at the defeat of the French army, dismissed his supreme military commander, Maurice Gamelin.

Madame Blanchard shook her head in disbelief when he was replaced by an old man, the seventy-three-year-old Maxime Weygand. "But he is too old to lead our troops! Oh, mon Dieu."

When Monsieur Reynaud made a further appointment of the even older eighty-four-year-old Phillipe Pétain as his deputy Prime minister, none of them could understand what their leader was thinking.

"He might be a hero of the First World War but he's too old to be in government!" Bertrand ran his hand over his eyes. "At eighty-four, he's a geriatric! He should be at home by the fire, warming his slippers. He'll have no stomach for a fight. Are we just going to let the Germans walk all over us?"

"But maybe these elder statesmen will broker a peace?" Madame Blanchard looked to the only man left in the household.

Bertrand snorted. "Peace! That always comes at a heavy price."

CHAPTER TWENTY THREE
PARIS
JUNE 1940

As the political manoeuvrings unfolded, Lottie became increasingly dismayed as it dawned on her that the French government were not going to put up any fight against the invading German army. A veteran of the Great War, Pétain did indeed seek peace and had no stomach for another conflict. The French army had already been trounced despite valiant efforts by pockets of French troops, enduring flak from the Luftwaffe and losing much equipment in their retreat to the north of Paris.

Over the next couple of days, Paris was besieged. No bread could be bought anywhere, and a rising sense of panic spread throughout the streets. Oblivious to it all, Madame Blanchard kept obsessively worrying about a funeral for her husband, becoming angry when no-one could or would assist her.

"Everyone tells me without a body, it is difficult." Madame Blanchard told her daughter over dinner, a simple cheese omelette with vegetables from the villa garden and the last of the ham. "I will ask Father Pierre at church and order a Requiem Mass be said in honour of Édouard."

She spent the next couple of days fussing about flowers and printed invitations and telephoning all her friends to come and fill the church. She kept Françoise busy too, calling on their friends to let them know about the service when other means of communication hadn't worked. Françoise, shocked into submission by her father's death, quietly acquiesced.

Lottie reluctantly went with her friend whose brooding silence pervaded every meal. Françoise had cried only once after Monsieur Blanchard's death had been confirmed.

Lottie had been drawn by the sobbing noises coming from her bedroom. Françoise had been weeping profusely, abandoning herself to the throes of grief.

"Françoise, please stop, you'll hurt the baby." Lottie put her arm around her friend's shaking shoulders.

"There's no-one to help me now, no-one. Who will look after me now? Who will protect my child? Oh, Lottie, if only I knew where David was. Now Papa will never know the father of his grandchild and my child will never meet Papa! Oh, is nowhere safe anymore?"

Lottie had no answers to any of these questions, but she held Françoise for a long time until her friend had no tears left.

As they walked along the street, Françoise voiced her doubts. "We shouldn't be doing this. Everyone is worried for themselves since the bombing. Papa wasn't very popular. He was always at work. It's embarrassing because these are Maman's friends, not his."

Every door they knocked on opened furtively. They were ushered into familiar drawing rooms in hushed tones.

"It may not be possible to attend your father's service, Françoise."

"We are worried about the Germans."

"We've heard they are marching towards Paris."

"We do not know what to do for the best."

Everywhere people said the same thing. Madame Blanchard became single-minded about the memorial service, unwilling to be distracted by external events or anything else.

"It's guilt, isn't it?" Françoise said to Lottie, on the way back from another fruitless round of rejected invitations.

"What is?"

"Maman. All this fuss about poor Papa. She was carrying on with Ricci behind his back for months."

"You knew?" Lottie stood still, unaware her mouth had dropped open.

"Of course, I knew. That oily Italian made up his mind to ensnare Maman the minute he set eyes on her. And she, faded old thing, couldn't resist. Don't blame her either." Françoise pulled a leaf from a bush as they carried on walking.

"Françoise! I didn't think you knew about it." Lottie was genuinely shocked at this revelation.

"So, you knew all along, and you never told me?" Françoise pouted.

"You always seemed so innocent, I didn't want to upset you and then, when war was declared, Ricci went back to Italy and there didn't seem to be much point."

"No, well. I'm not the fool you take me for. Except I am, aren't I? David used me just the same way Ricci used Maman. And now they are both gone." Françoise tore the leaf into shreds, leaving a green trail on the pavement behind her.

"But you love David, don't you?"

"I thought I did." Françoise looked away, her face no longer soft and trusting. Her jaw was set in a new, harsher line. She was too young for wrinkles, but Lottie could suddenly see where they would appear when she was older.

"Come on, Françoise. Let's stop for a citron pressé." Carefully avoiding the café in the park, Lottie turned the corner and walked briskly to a little bar they had previously scorned as too scruffy.

The proprietor didn't remove the cigarette from the corner of his mouth as he served them.

"These glasses are smudged." Françoise wrinkled her dainty nose.

"Taste it. I think it's better than the one they serve in the park café. Go on. It's really good." Lottie didn't care about the smudges. She was still wondering where Françoise's innocence had gone.

"Oh dear, sounds like thunder. Funny, there's not a cloud in the sky." Françoise looked up at the blue expanse above them.

Lottie's hand froze. She was about to take another sip of the refreshing lemonade. Slowly she put her glass down. The café owner stopped wiping the next table too. They all stayed motionless, listening.

After a few moments they all looked at each other at the same time. The rumbling noise was getting louder by the minute.

"Sacré bleu!" The café owner threw down his cloth. "Les Allemands!"

Françoise clapped her hand over her mouth; her eyes stared at Lottie. She looked horrified.

The distant roar increased.

"It must be the German tanks." Lottie nodded across to the café owner. He nodded back, only once, and disappeared into the back of the café, calling for his wife.

"Come on, Françoise. We must get back home to your mother."

Abandoning their drinks, not even bothering to pay for them, they got up and ran the short distance back to Françoise's villa.

Other people jogged beside them. Everyone's face looked white and panicky. Swarms of people crowded in the streets with suitcases and bundles of clothes piled up on anything that would carry them. Horses, carts, cars, bicycles and even wheelbarrows were stuffed with bits of furniture, bags of clothes and small children.

"What is happening?" Lottie asked one old man.

"It is time to leave, Mademoiselle. This pathetic government is letting the Germans stroll into our beautiful city. I advise you to go, too. Get out before the bastards get here."

The panic was contagious.

"The Germans are coming! Get home as fast as you can! Leave Paris at once!" The cries reverberated around Lottie's ears and she increased her pace.

Françoise was clutching her sides by the time they reached the big house.

"Oh, slow down, Lottie! I've got a stitch," Françoise panted.

"No time, come on!" Lottie pounded up the steps to the front door. Madame Blanchard was in the salon, hunched over the wireless.

The announcer blared out confirmation of the German approach, pleading for calm.

"Oh, mon Dieu. What should we do? Lottie?" Madame's hands were quivering signals of distress.

"We must leave." The panic on the streets had left Lottie in no doubt of what they should do.

"Leave? But where should we go? What about Édouard's memorial service?"

"Too late for that now, Madame. Your husband would understand, I'm sure. What's important is our safety. Where is Bertrand?"

No answer came.

"I will look for him." Lottie turned to Françoise. "Take your mother upstairs and pack bags for you both. Just the essentials and don't forget your identity papers."

Françoise seemed rooted to the spot, still panting from running.

"Go! Françoise. Now!"

Françoise grabbed her mother's wrist and dragged her towards the stairs.

"But the service, Françoise...." Madame's voice trailed after her daughter.

Lottie went into the kitchen. There was no one there. Suddenly she heard the sound of a car revving outside. She ran to the front steps and saw Bertrand backing the big Citroën out of the garage. Sophie, the young housekeeper, was with him in the car.

Lottie ran across the drive and hammered on the car window. Bertrand looked up, scowling, but it was Sophie who wound down her window.

Lottie shoved her face through the aperture. "How did you get the keys? You cannot take the car! You have not got Madame's permission!"

"Permission? who needs that now? And there was a second set of keys in the garage." Bertrand grimaced. "Haven't you heard? The Germans have reached the outskirts of the city. They could be here by tomorrow. Our brave government has already left. They've destroyed all their papers and fled. "

"Of course, I've heard! But you cannot just steal Madame's car! We need to get out too." Lottie clamped her hand down on the glass.

"It's every man for himself in times like these!" Bertrand revved the engine again.

"No! We must stick together. Wait for Françoise and her mother. There is plenty of room. It is not your car but theirs. The Germans won't be here in the next five minutes."

Sophie turned to Bertrand, laid a hand on his thick thigh. "Please wait, Bertrand. Mademoiselle Smythe is right. We have time to wait. We must not behave like the Germans. We are French. We look after each other, don't we?"

Lottie saw Bertrand's face soften. So that was the way the land lay, did it? "That's right, Sophie. Thank you. Please, wait here. I will get the others and some things of my own. I'll be no more than ten minutes, maximum. Bertrand? Promise me you will wait?"

She saw Sophie's plump hand squeeze his leg again.

Bertrand let out an irritated sigh. "Oh, very well. But you must be quick, Mademoiselle. We do not have long. The tanks are getting closer every second!"

Lottie nodded at him and sped back into the house. She found Françoise dithering in the bathroom. "Do I need to bring bath salts as well as soap, do you think?"

"For goodness' sake, Françoise! Just soap, just soap!" Once inside her own bedroom she shut the door behind her and leant against it. How could this be happening? Noise from the street filtered through the window. Her room faced the front and only the garden separated it from the tree-lined street. She went to the French window and opened it, stepped out on the balcony. From there she could see a stream of people wending their way northwards in a haphazard melée.

She must think quickly. The car would give them a real advantage but how much petrol did they have? Lottie seized her suitcase and flung it open. Grabbing things at random, including a few beloved books, she threw them into it and shut it with a snap. She made sure she had her passport and all the cash she could lay her hands on and stuffed them into her handbag. Lottie grabbed her thickest coat, despite the summer warmth and shoved it on, checking she had gloves in the pockets.

She went back down to the kitchen and into the scullery and scooped up whatever she could. Frantically, she opened the larder door and grabbed cans and jars, threw them into the housekeeper's shopping basket. There was no bread because of the siege but at the last minute she saw a big slab of cheese on the marble counter wrapped in greaseproof paper and a large dried sausage. She lobbed both into the basket and tucked a tea towel over them but left the basket of eggs. Too fragile. She found a few wizened apples from last year's crop and added those with a couple of bars of chocolate she found stashed on the shelf above. It would have to do.

She dashed back to the landing, calling out to the others. "We have to go now. Bertrand has taken the car and he's waiting for us, but he won't wait long! We must go, this instant!"

Madame appeared lugging an enormous suitcase. "Madame! Do you need so much? Oh, there's no time to argue but you must carry it yourself. Françoise? Are you ready?"

Françoise nodded. She had sensibly divided her burden into two smaller cases and held them one on each side. She looked quite grey.

"Right, come on, into the car with you before your manservant leaves us high and dry." Lottie trotted down the staircase.

At the hall door, Madame Blanchard hesitated. She looked back at the house, her charming big house, as if saying goodbye. Madame's hair had escaped its chignon on the nape of her neck and strands cascaded down her bony back. It made her look at once younger and more vulnerable; undone.

Françoise put one of her cases down and slipped an arm around her mother's waist. "Come on, Maman. Time to go."

Madame Blanchard nodded and started to drag her large case down the front steps.

Bertrand revved the engine, put it into gear. He and Sophie were yelling at each other inside the car, but she couldn't hear their words.

Lottie looked at the car, horrified to see it moving off. "Wait!"

Bertrand shouted through his open window. "How are you going to stop me, Mademoiselle? Eh?"

Lottie couldn't answer him. He was quite right. She had no idea how to stop him. Just then Madame Blanchard reached the driveway, her suitcase in one hand and dragging Françoise's arm by the other. She dropped both and broke into a run until she stood in front of the big Citroën saloon, one imperious hand held up, forcing Bertrand to stop or run her over.

"Bertrand Paget! I command you to stop right there!"

There was a screech of brakes. The nose of the Citroën halted inches away from Madame's black silk dress. Lottie went to stand next to her hostess in solidarity. Bertrand wound the window down to its fullest extent and stuck his head out. "Get out of the way, Madame. You are no longer my employer. I am not responsible for you or them. I am saving myself and my girlfriend. You can't tell me what to do any more."

"How dare you speak to me like that! That is *my* car you are driving. This is theft!"

"Oh yeah, and where are the police? eh? Who's going to stop me?" Bertrand withdrew his head and started to reverse the car. Lottie ran around the side, trying to reason with him but then Sophie, the quiet, plump housekeeper, yanked on the handbrake.

Bertrand slewed round in the driver's seat towards his only passenger. "What are you doing? We have to get out of here before the Germans come!"

Sophie had one hand on the steering wheel, another on Bertrand's sleeve. "We have room for the Blanchards. Don't be ridiculous, Bertrand. Have you no heart? Let them come with us. We cannot just abandon them. Monsieur was always good to me." She got out of the car and opened both the rear doors.

"Please, get in, Madame." Sophie gave them a brief, tight smile.

Lottie didn't hesitate. She grabbed Françoise's cases and shoved them deep into the boot. Lottie went to the driver's window and glared at Bertrand. She nodded towards the roof rack. With a begrudging grunt, Bertrand got out and helped her lift the bigger case on to it, strapping it down with some rope he found in the boot.

Then she ran back for hers and the basket of food and crammed them on top of the others in the boot and shut it with a bang.

Sophie waited until the rear doors were shut before she got back in the car. Bertrand glared at her and cursed the whole time, stretching Lottie's vocabulary into areas she'd never encountered before. He mimicked Sophie, "'Monsieur was good to me', huh! I'll bet he was, the old lecher."

Barely had Sophie shut her door when Bertrand depressed the accelerator and, still cursing, drove through the elegant gates of the Blanchard's villa and out on to the crowded street. "I am taking Sophie to her mother's house. We will have to find room for one more."

"There is no more room!" Madame's old authority had crept back into her voice.

"Then you will have to make room, Madame!"

When they joined the main road, they found pandemonium on the streets. Other cars, vans and lorries, laden down with luggage and furniture, just like theirs, were jammed together in the road. The long line of vehicles was further hampered by people on foot or horses. Everyone was surging towards the south away from the city centre.

"Where have all these people come from? Why won't they get out of the way?" wailed Françoise.

"They all want to escape the Boche, just like us." Bertrand growled.

The car crawled along the congested road.

Bertrand started arguing with Sophie. "Madame is right, Sophie. There is no more room in the car. I'm not sure I can even stop in this crowd."

"I cannot leave without my mother." Sophie's mouth was set in a thin, firm line. She stared at Bertrand.

"Merde! Do you think this is a bus? How many women can we squeeze in? We are full to capacity."

"Down here, Bertrand, please." Sophie pointed down a smaller road.

Bertrand groaned. "If I go down there, Sophie, I'll never be able to re-join the traffic on the main road. You must get out and fetch your Mother. I'll park up on the pavement." Bertrand leaned across and opened the passenger door, narrowly missing a young mother carrying a baby. He gave Sophie a shove. "Go on but be *quick*."

Sophie hesitated, bit her lip, then climbed out of the car. She ran to a small house in a row of others just like it down a side street at right angles to the main road. She disappeared inside for a few minutes.

"Where is the woman?" Bertrand fumed.

Sophie returned, breathless and alone. "She won't come, Bertrand."

"Who?"

"My mother. She insists on staying. She has a heart condition and wouldn't make it."

"Then you must come alone."

"No. I cannot leave her. She says she is not frightened of a few Germans. She lived through the last war and she's staying put. I can't shift her." Sophie's round cheeks were flushed from running.

"But, Sophie, what about me? I'm not staying in Paris and I want you with me." Bertrand pleaded through the car window.

Lottie felt he might have more chance of persuading Sophie if he showed some affection and got out of the car.

Sophie shook her head. "I'm sorry, Bertrand. I cannot leave."

"But..." Bertrand stopped talking as a little boy, no more than two years old, ran out from the house and caught up with Sophie. He tugged at her skirts. "Maman! Maman!"

Sophie bent and picked him up; settled him on her wide hip. Her eyes implored Bertrand to understand.

"This is your child? Who is the father?" Bertrand looked flabbergasted.

"Yes, Pierre is my child. You do not need to know about his father. Go now, Bertrand. Keep safe. If you make it through the war, come back and find me. I will be here." Sophie kissed the little boy's grubby face and he hugged his mother tighter.

"You never told me."

"No, I never did and now it's too late. I will stay with my child and my mother. We will be alright. It is better you go."

"Did you know about Sophie's child?" Françoise spoke softly in her mother's ear.

"Oh yes, I knew." Madame Blanchard's face was inscrutable.

Sophie looked into the back of the car and exchanged a meaningful look with Madame Blanchard.

To Lottie's amazement, Madame Blanchard reached into her handbag and took out a wad of notes. "Wind down the window, Charlotte."

Lottie did as she was told.

Madame Blanchard handed Sophie the notes. "He has no father now, Sophie. Take this from Édouard. It is all you will ever get."

"You knew?" Sophie mouthed the words almost silently.

Madame Blanchard nodded. "Of course. Goodbye. Keep Édouard's child safe."

Sophie hitched the boy up on her hip with a brief nod. She took the money and stuffed it down the front of her dress.

"You may drive on, Bertrand." Madame Blanchard said to the back of Bertrand's head. He sat behind the wheel staring ahead at the procession of cars and people still streaming southwards out of Paris. Then he leant across and called out through the open passenger window, "Sophie! Don't go! I'm sorry. I didn't mean it!"

But she had gone.

"Bertrand!" Madame Blanchard had now fully regained her authoritative tone. "Keep going! Shut the window."

"Agh!" Bertrand recoiled as a hand thrust through the window and tried to grab the steering wheel. "Get off! Imbecile!" He put the car back into gear and went forward again, winding the window up as fast as he could by stretching across, making the car career wildly.

"Idiot!"

Lottie didn't know if he was referring to his lost girlfriend or the woman clamouring to get in and take her place. The woman withdrew her arm smartly as the window glass connected with it. Lottie winced as she saw the cut on her forearm, before she was lost behind them.

Bertrand dashed his hand across his eyes, his mouth still hanging open in shock. They lurched forward and bumped down off the pavement. The car behind tooted its horn in protest but Bertrand ignored it and slewed the car into line with the great crocodile of humanity and vehicles stretching ahead as far as Lottie could see.

Hands clawed at their windows. "Take us too!" Mothers, exhausted with the weight of babies and toddlers, peered in. One spat. "Bourgeoisie. Always the same! Look after themselves.

Madame Blanchard astonished Lottie and Françoise for the second time. With an agility that surprised everyone in the car, she clambered over the gear stick and sat in the front seat, alongside Bertrand.

Bertrand looked across at her. "You cannot trust anyone, can you, Madame?"

"No, Bertrand, no-one." Madame Blanchard looked out of the window, lost in thought.

"Have we got extra petrol?" Lottie peered over Bertrand's shoulder and looked at the gauge, relieved to see there was plenty left in the tank. No one had used the car since rationing began and Monsieur Blanchard had boasted of his private supplies from the factory.

"In the back."

"How much?"

"A few gallons, no more."

"How far will that get us?"

"How should I know? I'm not a fucking chauffeur."

Lottie knew that swear word in French. "I'm sorry about Sophie."

Another grunt. "Not as much as I am. I thought we had a future together. She said she would come with me. Start a new life in the country. Pah! Her old mother wouldn't have lasted long anyway. I would even have taken the child."

"She felt she had to stay, I suppose."

"Pah!" Bertrand steered around a cyclist who had wobbled towards the middle of the road suddenly.

"Could we stop and help him, do you think?" Lottie winced as she looked at the old man, who looked like he might faint.

"No. He must fend for himself. He has a bicycle. He should have brought food."

"Did you pack some? I brought a basket of some things from the kitchen, but it's not much."

Bertrand gave his first smile. It was so humourless it could have been a grimace, Lottie couldn't tell. "There is a crate of wine, some cheeses and a cold chicken but I'm not stopping for a picnic until we're well clear of these other bastards."

Al drove along the dark road, following the painted white lines by the dim light of his shielded headlights. There was half a moon gleaming white in the dark sky, so it was easier than some nights. He still found it hard to concentrate. All his thoughts were of Lottie not Isobel, for once; stubborn, obstinate, angry Lottie, stranded in Paris. Why, oh, why hadn't she come home when she'd had the chance? Stupid, stupid girl.

Everyone had gathered round the wireless yesterday, listening to the newsreader reading out Churchill's speech about the rescue of the BEF at Dunkirk. What was it the old gaffer had said about fighting on the beaches and in the hills and never giving up, never surrendering? It had stirred everyone up. Maybe Lottie had grabbed her chance with the British soldiers getting rescued and was already on her way home? But then, surely, they'd have heard by now?

Aunt Cassandra had called round to the garage shortly afterwards. His mother, busy as she was, had left off work a second time that day and taken her friend into the bungalow. When Al had come in for lunch, he'd found Aunt Cassandra in floods of tears in his mother's arms. And little wonder.

He'd grabbed a hunk of bread and cheese and slipped quietly back to the factory. He'd had a letter from Isobel the day before.

He took it out of his jacket pocket and held it up to the moonlight. He could hardly make out the words, but it didn't matter, he knew them off by heart. He laid it down on the seat beside him, as gently as if it was Isobel herself.

"Dearest Al,

How are you? I'm thinking about you all the time while I go about my farm work. I don't know how I'd get through the days, if it wasn't for Lilian and Elsie. The Williams's aren't a very happy couple, I think. Mrs Williams had a black eye this morning. She said she'd caught it on a cupboard door but I'm sure she got it from her husband. He's a miserable little man. Mrs Williams doesn't give us much to eat but I don't like to complain in case he takes it out on her.

We went up to another farm the other day, a Mrs Jones. What a difference! She was so warm and friendly. Lilian and Elsie say they're going to try to get a transfer and go to work for her as her farm hand has signed up. That will leave just me here on the Williams's farm until another WLA girl can be found. I wouldn't put it past them to refuse more help, so they don't have to pay.

Oh, don't listen to my moans! Write and tell me your news, dearest Al.

I hope you are well and not working too hard. I expect Aunt Kate's factory is busier than ever?"

He didn't want to go home, even though it was late. He pulled into a wide lay-by by a farm gate and stilled the engine. A fox barked, breaking the sudden silence. On the prowl, just like those fucking Nazis. A fox on the hunt was legitimate. Everyone had to eat but those bloody Germans wanted more. Greedy bastards.

He glanced down at the piece of paper and picked it up. The next few lines had obviously been written in haste, almost scribbled and barely legible.

"Oh Al, I've just heard about the BEF on the radio! It's so worrying about Dunkirk, isn't it? I never thought the Germans would defeat all those thousands of soldiers. I can't stop thinking about Lottie. I do wish she'd come home and I pray she's safe. I know it's mad, but I keep wondering if she could somehow make it to Dunkirk and cadge a lift with the soldiers being rescued – is there any chance, do you think?

Anyway, better go, those cows won't milk themselves.

All my love, write soon, and please, if you hear any news, let me know. I'm frantic about Lottie now.

Your Bella. Xxx"

So, she'd also heard about the Germans beating the British troops hollow on that beach in Normandy. A selfish part of him hoped it might draw her back to Wiltshire. Wales might not be as far as France, but it felt like it.

Al picked up his packet of Woodbines, took one out and lit up the fag. The glow of the match illuminated the dashboard, now so familiar to him. He'd never felt so lonely. All his life Lottie and Isobel had been around, always there in the background when he was little and then more distantly as they grew up. But they remained part of his inner fabric even when they were away at school. His other friends never occupied that special corner of his heart. And their home, Cheadle Manor, with all the privileges and resentments that came with it, was part of the reliable scenery, a symbol of the continuity of time, the head of the structure that governed their little world. Now, nothing seemed fixed or safe. People were talking about the risk of invasion everywhere he went. There weren't so many jokes about the blackouts now and his job was a lot harder without road signs. Good job he'd learned his way about before they'd been confiscated. Never mind confusing invading Germans, you couldn't tell where you were these days.

He longed to see Isobel above all. He couldn't picture her lifting beetroots in a sodden field, even though she'd described it so well. He worried his returning letters were boring. Despite the drama elsewhere, all he seemed to do was trundle up and down these Wiltshire roads and lanes delivering or collecting bits of rubber and parts of cars in an endless round that was anything but merry.

He chucked his cigarette stub out of the window, pleased to hear a faint sizzle as a puddle extinguished it. He didn't want the ARP warden after him for starting a fire for the Luftwaffe to target. He fired up the engine. If only it was a plane, not a lorry. He'd shoot the bastards out of the sky alright.

He hadn't had his conscription papers yet. He knew his parents were hoping to keep him at the factory, train him up and call him an engineer. They had been preparing a letter asking for him to be exempted by saying his job was a reserved occupation. Bugger that. If he didn't get his call up papers before his twentieth birthday in December, he would have to register as fit and able soon after. They said you had a choice of which service to join.

He'd already made his choice. He was heading for the skies.

He drove home slowly and crept indoors, hoping everyone else would be asleep and relieved to find they were. He lay on his bed, staring at the ceiling, willing his mind to shut up and let him rest but all he could see were the faces of the Flintock-Smythe girls, each so different, each so far away.

CHAPTER TWENTY FIVE
A HILL FARM IN FLINTSHIRE
JUNE 1940

Isobel turned the letter over to look at the back, hoping for more. There was nothing but a greasy thumbprint on the reverse. She turned it back over and read it again.

"I miss you so much, Bella. Your Mum does too, though I'll bet she won't say in a letter. She's worried sick about Lottie in France. Hasn't heard from her in months. I know the work you are doing in the Women's Land Army is important and I don't want you to stop but isn't there any way you could do it at home? I think your Mum needs you here, more than ever. I'll bet Farmer Stubbs could do with someone with your skills at Home Farm. I don't want to pressure you, my love, but please think about it, won't you?

They've painted white lines on the roads now, which helps driving in the dark. I'm doing deliveries all times of the day and night these days, with the factory so busy. I've got slit covers on the lorry headlamps so it's hell if there's no moon. I like the quiet of driving at night though. Helps me to think. And it's always <u>you</u> *I'm thinking about! There's not much traffic on the roads, with the rationing but we get extra petrol because of the factory work for the army.*

Have you got any leave? I can't really take time off at the moment, or I'd come and see you in Wales. Has it stopped raining yet? Did you get those beets up alright? Has Mrs Williams been feeding you enough? Blimey, I sound like I'm your mother!

Truth is, I miss you - did I say that before? Well, it's true. What's the point of fighting a war if not for each other?

I've not had my call-up papers yet. Mum keeps trying to train me up in the factory. She's hoping I'll get reserved occupation status, but I'm not keen. I've a mind to apply for the RAF when it's my turn. What do you think? I wish you were here, so we could talk it through together.

All my love, Al
Xxxxxxxxxxxxxxxxx

The RAF? Oh, Al! Isobel couldn't bear the thought of Al up in an aeroplane, a target for German planes and shot down. Or, for that matter, dropping bombs on the enemy. It was all dirty, dangerous work. He'd obviously not had her letter asking for news of Lottie. She was even more anxious about her sister now the news had come about the Germans invading Paris. Where was she? Why hadn't she come home?

She got another letter from Wiltshire the next day. The post boy, Dai Thomas, gave it to her when she was sweeping out the yard. She ripped it open with a grubby finger. It was from her mother.

"Darling Bella,

How are you, my dear? I hope all that fresh air is doing you good. There is much talk of invasion here and Andrews has put blackouts in all the windows now, even the small ones in the servants' quarters. It makes it very gloomy of an evening. There is talk of houses like Cheadle Manor being requisitioned by the Government to train troops against the invasion. I'm not sure I like the sound of that!

We have had no news of Lottie. I'm so worried about her now we know that the Germans are on French soil. The Citroën factory was bombed in Paris – had you heard? That's where Monsieur Blanchard worked. I do hope he wasn't involved. I feel like driving over to France myself to try and find her and bring her home. Not knowing where or how she is makes me very anxious. But what can we do? Unless she gets in touch, I've no way of knowing. The telephone lines are off limits and who knows if our letters get through? I've not heard from her in months. It's enough to drive one mad.

Something nearer to home may interest you. Both Farmer Stubbs's sons have joined up. On the same day too! They've both gone into the army and have already left to do their training at Aldershot. Poor old Farmer Stubbs is finding it hard without them. I was thinking, he's going to need some land girls, just like you, to give him a hand. Is there any chance you could ask for a transfer? It would be so lovely to have at least one of my girls home again.

Sorry to sound so feeble! If you are happy where you are, of course I will understand completely and I'm sure Home Farm will get help elsewhere, but please, darling, do think about it, won't you?

Everyone else is fine, including your Al. He's always dashing about in that lorry, delivering things for the factory so I hardly ever see him. The garage is doing well, although with the petrol rationing, there are far fewer cars on the roads these days, so I think Aunt Katy is concentrating on the factory production. She's got some enormous order from the army, I think, and has had to employ a lot more staff, all young women like you.

I'm having the groceries delivered now and walk down to the village if I need to rather than waste my miserable ration of petrol.

Looking forward to hearing from you soon,
Love always, Mummy.
Xx

Isobel looked up from the page to see Mr Williams leaning against the door post, staring at her through narrowed eyes. At least she was fully clothed this time, the dirty old man, not like the other morning when she was getting dressed. She'd had to stuff a precious sock in his peephole in the wall of her wooden dormitory. She folded up her mother's letter and tucked it in the pocket of her jodhpurs.

"That's two letters in two days, Isobel. Something up at home, is it?" Mr Williams always talked with his pipe in his mouth. It made his teeth clack horribly.

"Sort of. Listen, Mr Williams, I'm going to ask for a transfer back to Wiltshire. I'll cycle into the village and see Mrs Hopkins about it after I've finished here. I'm sure they can find you a replacement."

"Maybe I don't want someone else." He strolled towards her.

She picked up her broom again and began to sweep the yard. Slurry washed over her boots in brown, smelly waves.

"We're just getting to know each other, aren't we?" Mr Williams attempted a smile, but it looked like a leer to Isobel.

"Nevertheless, Mr Williams, I think you need more than one land girl anyway. There's too much for me to do on my own with Lilian and Elsie up at Mrs Jones's place."

"And why is that? Those girls had no right to shove off like that in such a hurry. Old Mother Jones's farm is a lot smaller than mine and she's less livestock. It's all sheep up by there – no cows to milk."

Isobel squared her shoulders. "Quite frankly, Mr Williams, the food is better, and Mrs Jones says thank you."

Mr Williams took a step back. Emboldened, Isobel added, "And she doesn't spy on you when you get undressed!"

"Now look here, you've been well looked after. There's no call to tell lies. I go to chapel like everyone else and I'm a God-fearing man."

"Well, you don't frighten me. I'll let you know what Mrs Hopkins says."

Mrs Hopkins sighed when she spoke to her later. "I have a feeling no girl is going to want to stay long at the Williams's farm. I shall never forgive Mrs Jones for poaching your colleagues. Doesn't she know there's a war on? We all have to do our bit, wherever we are."

"I know, Mrs Hopkins, but the thing is, my mother has written to ask me to return. Looks like our house is going to get requisitioned for war work and she's going to need support. And our Home Farm needs a land girl. Both the farmer's sons have joined up for the army. I think I'm needed there as much as here."

"Alright, alright, but you're not to go until I've replaced you, do you hear?" Mrs Hopkins smiled. "Go on

214

with you, you've done a good job, Isobel, and I know it hasn't been easy. I'll have to have words with Mr and Mrs Williams though and I'm not looking forward to giving either of them a lecture. Very well, off with you and be careful on those roads, it looks like it's going to rain."

"Thanks Mrs H. You're a marvel."

Isobel cycled home in a euphoric mood, barely believing her luck. She wouldn't write home with empty promises. She wanted to see their faces when she turned up unannounced.

The next day was, for once, dry and sunny. Isobel had been commissioned to check the ewes on the highest point of the farm. Mr Williams drove her up as far as the tractor could go but then stopped as the track narrowed into a pathway between two flint dry-stone walls.

"That's as far as I go. I want you to do a rough count of the ewes and report back to me. It's time they were checked since the lambs were separated."

Isobel dismounted from the tractor. "How many do you have, Mr Williams?"

"There's only fifty or so. You can count, can't you?"

Isobel didn't bother to reply. She hitched up her rucksack and nodded her goodbye, glad to be out of the lecherous gaze of her employer and free to roam the hillside. She'd brought her paints and some paper. It had been so long since she'd had the chance to use them.

An easy day. She couldn't remember the last time she had one of those. Had Mr Williams got wind of her desire to leave and given her a soft task, hoping she'd stay?

She didn't care. It was enough to be out in the June sunshine with the wind in her hair.

Isobel climbed further. She could see the sheep in the distance, grazing contentedly, no lambs to worry them.

Mr Williams had said to take her time and not to hurry back. It was almost a day off. She climbed the hill, aiming all the time towards the placid sheep but then stopped to take a swig from her water bottle. The sun, seen so rarely in these parts, was making up for lost time and her face felt hot under its fierce rays. She flung herself down under the shade of a hawthorn tree. With its deeply lobed leaves bedecked with white flowers and its branches bent by the prevailing westerly winds, it formed a perfect parasol. Isobel lay back on the springy turf, using her knapsack for a pillow and closed her weary eyelids.

She dozed until the sound of heavy boots ringing on stone infiltrated her dreams. Momentarily disorientated, she sat up, groggy with sleep.

Looking a short distance down the hill, she could see a man plodding up towards her. His head was bent to the task so she couldn't see his face, only the top of his battered canvas hat. She tried to gather her scattered wits, still barely awake. Isobel rubbed her eyes and when she looked up, the man was in front of her, looking as surprised as she was.

"Good day, to you."

"Good day, sir." Isobel scrambled to her feet. The man wasn't a tramp, as she'd first thought, but dressed in good quality tweeds and plus fours. He must have been at least six feet tall, maybe more, and his shoulders stooped slightly as if to compensate for his height. He carried an easel slung in a canvas holdall and a small wooden case.

"Please, don't get up on my account. You looked so peaceful lying there. I'm so sorry I disturbed your rest." His voice was cultured and mellifluous; his face regular and kind, its moustache neatly trimmed above a firm, full mouth. His eyes were shaded by the brim of his hat. As if sensing her gaze, he took it off and gave a little bow.

"I shouldn't have been sleeping but the day is so warm, I couldn't help it." Isobel put out her hand.

The stranger replaced his hat and took her hand, giving it a gentle shake. "Makes up for all the rain we've had. He smiled. "Geraint Lloyd at your service."

Isobel dropped her hand. "How do you do? I'm Isobel Flintock-Smythe."

"And not from these parts, I take it?"

She laughed, "No, I'm a land girl."

"Ah. Now I understand the jodhpurs."

"Yes, the uniform has to be practical." She smoothed her trousers down with the flat of her sweaty hand.

"I'm sure, and it's quite admirable." He put his burden down against the stone wall. "May I join you? It's quite a climb."

Strangely, Isobel didn't feel at all uncomfortable with this idea. Geraint Lloyd wasn't the least bit threatening. She judged he must be well into his thirties – almost old enough to be her father.

Geraint took off his hat and laid it on top of his canvas bag. "I've brought a picnic. Fancy sharing it? Painting is a lonely occupation."

Isobel laughed again. "Only if you'll have some of mine."

"I can't think of anything more delightful." He rummaged in his bag and brought out a bottle of ginger ale and various paper bags.

Isobel had a small dry piece of cheese, an apple and two slices of bread spread so thinly with margarine it was barely visible.

"Is that it?" Geraint looked at her meagre repast.

Isobel nodded and her stomach rumbled so loudly, they both burst into laughter.

"Then you must definitely share mine." He spread out fat slices of ham, a jar of chutney, a small cottage loaf and a large wedge of cheese on to the tea towel he'd brought. "Do they expect you to do a full day's work on that tiny lunch?"

"Well, I've an easy day off today but yes, I'm afraid it's just the same on normal working days. Does wonders for the figure."

"I can see that. Let me make you a ham and chutney sandwich." He worked quickly and deftly before passing it to her.

Isobel bit into the fresh bread. Chutney oozed out of the sides on to her cheek. "Excuse me," she giggled.

"I can see how hungry you are. Don't mind me. Here, use my handkerchief."

A starched white square was handed to her, neatly folded and pressed. The letters GL were embroidered on one corner.

"Are you sure you don't mind me messing up your fine linen?"

"Not a bit. And munch away, you look like you need it." He turned away, sensitive to her embarrassment, and fiddled about making another sandwich for himself.

Isobel wolfed down the food. She'd been feeling so dizzy when she woke up and the sight of the fresh picnic had made her realise how truly ravenous she was.

They ate in companionable silence. Isobel finished first and wiped her face with his handkerchief. "Thank you, you're a life saver."

Geraint shook his head. "It's very pleasant to entertain such a nice young woman so unexpectedly. What are you doing out on the hillside in such glorious isolation?"

"Counting sheep," Isobel began and then roared with laughter.

Geraint laughed too. "No wonder you fell asleep!"

Isobel nodded towards his easel. "What do you paint?"

"Landscapes, sometimes portraits. Watercolours mostly. I only dabble."

"I love painting in watercolours myself."

"Do you? I see we share a common bond. It's an exacting discipline, isn't it?" Geraint leant his head to one side in query.

Isobel nodded, overjoyed to meet a kindred artistic spirit. "Can I see what you've done?"

"Not worth it. Haven't done anything today. Of course, you have to have a good subject."

"Like sheep?"

Geraint laughed again. It made him look much younger. More her age. "I prefer humans. I would love to paint you. That's what I was thinking when you were sleeping under the tree."

"You were staring at me?"

"Only briefly and from a distance. At first I thought you might be wounded but I can't see anything wrong with you."

"Sound in wind and limb and a lot stronger than I look."

"I suppose you'd have to be, working on the land."

"Yes, it's hard work alright. And I'd better get on and check up on those ewes or I'll be in trouble."

"Stay a moment longer, won't you?"

Something in his blue eyes made Isobel stay. After a moment, she said. "Where do you live? You don't look like a hill farmer from around here."

"No, I'd make a terrible farmer. I live in the big bad city of Liverpool, but we have a country estate just south west of Chester, on the border between England and Wales. My father owns a few factories near the docks, and I'm expected to follow in his illustrious footsteps."

"You don't like it?"

"No, I don't like it, but I will inherit it one day and must learn the ropes. Father is getting on now and I've been allowed to travel and do my own thing, but he had a heart attack a few months ago and I've been reeled in to take it over. Not my cup of tea but, with the war on, I, too, must do my duty."

So that explained the expensive tweeds.

"Where do you hail from, Isobel?" Geraint started to pack up the remains of their lunch.

"Wiltshire. A little place called Cheadle in the depths of the countryside."

"Sounds idyllic."

"It is, really."

"Then why the qualification?"

"Oh, my father died years ago, and it's left my mother in a bit of a fix financially. Death duties, you know. She'd sold our London house, you see, and put the capital into stocks and shares. Lost the lot after the crash in 1929. She's had to borrow against the estate to get us out of hock since my grandmother died last year."

"That's happening to so many people with land, isn't it? Maybe it's not so bad to have my fingers in dirty trade."

"Maybe not." Isobel got up and brushed crumbs from her trousers. "It's certainly been hard on Mummy and with Lottie …" She trailed off.

"Tell me?"

Somehow, it all came tumbling out. Granny's death, Lottie's angry departure to Paris but for some reason, Isobel didn't mention Al once.

Geraint was a good listener.

CHAPTER TWENTY SIX
SOMEWHERE IN FRANCE
JUNE 1940

"I have to stop, Maman, I simply have to."

"Oh, Françoise, can't you hold on like the rest of us?"

"No, I'm sorry, but...no." Françoise looked at Lottie next to her on the back seat of the Citroën with pleading eyes.

She looked desperate.

Lottie sighed and looked out of the window. The caravan of refugees had thickened even more as they turned further south towards the sun. Lottie didn't fancy getting out and facing the resentful stares of those without a car, face to face. "Bertrand? Don't we need to refuel?"

Bertrand's eyes flicked down to the dashboard. Lottie craned forward to see the petrol gauge. It was almost on empty.

"Merde." That seemed to be Bertrand's favourite word. It meant shit and she couldn't help but agree it was appropriate to their situation. "Yes, I'll pull off the main road, see if I can find a quieter one and pour some more petrol in the tank. We'll get lynched if people see we have spare petrol. So many cars have already run out of fuel. Hold tight, ladies."

At the next turning, Bertrand tooted his horn at some weary pedestrians and edged the car past them down a little lane. He drove round the first bend before stopping. There was a little brook running clear and true in the field next to the road.

"How about a little lunch, Madame?" Bertrand gave a grim smile.

"Oh, Maman, let's stop, please! I'm so hungry." Françoise was already out of the car, one foot on the farm gate but turned back to entreat her mother.

"Very well. There is no train to catch after all and it is good to be away from all those other people crushing in on us." Madame got out of the car.

She and Françoise disappeared behind the hedge.

Bertrand tucked the car into the verge on the side of the little lane and he and Lottie got out. Bertrand went to the boot and retrieved the drum of petrol and a metal funnel.

"I'll help you, Bertrand." Lottie watched as Bertrand unscrewed the petrol cap and placed the funnel into the aperture.

"Hold it steady, Mademoiselle."

Lottie watched as the thin, noxious fuel glugged into the tank. "How did you manage to get so much petrol?"

"Don't ask awkward questions." Bertrand lifted up the drum as high as he could till it was almost vertical and shook out every last drop. As he screwed the lid back on the tank he nodded with satisfaction. "That should get us far enough away from trouble."

"Do you know the right road to take?"

"I have no fixed destination now. I don't suppose Sophie's family in the Auvergne would be pleased to see me without her. There is a map in the glove compartment. We'll look at it over lunch and stick a pin in it."

"Good idea. Oh, what's that noise?" Lottie looked up at the sky, following the noise.

"Planes. Merde."

"German or British?"

"I can't see through these trees. I'll go back to the road and have a look."

Before she could stop him, Bertrand marched back down the lane towards the main road they had just left. She couldn't follow him, or Madame Blanchard and Françoise would think they had been abandoned. Deciding to ignore the overhead noise and pay attention to the more immediate rumbling coming from her stomach, Lottie focussed instead on getting the food out of the car.

How typical of the man to disappear when you most needed him. The food baskets were right at the back and she had to really stretch to reach them. Above her, the drone of the engines grew louder, closer. They must be heading towards Paris. More bombs, probably. Just as well they'd joined the exodus, away from danger. She'd never forget the plumes of smoke after the Citroën factory was bombed. Lottie wondered what their target was this time. It was hard to feel real grief over Monsieur Blanchard, he'd been such an enigma, but it was shocking about Sophie and her little boy. What a strange attitude these rich Parisians had to fidelity. She was sorry he'd been killed though. Françoise needed his secure protection now, more than ever. They all did.

Lottie found the cold chicken in the basket. Sophie must have packed it. It was done beautifully with a little jar of mayonnaise tucked inside the snowy white napkin. Lottie's tummy growled loudly but not loud enough to drown out the sounds of the planes, now directly overhead.

Clutching the basket, she went to the farm gate, calling for Madame and her daughter. She found them shouting at each other, both looking distressed. She couldn't hear what they were saying over the drone of the aircraft, but she could hazard a guess at the topic. Madame must have seen Françoise's growing belly when they'd relieved themselves in the field. This was not going to be a relaxing picnic.

Suddenly she forgot all about Françoise's baby. There was a strange whine, coming from the aeroplanes above her. She looked up at the sky, shielding her eyes, but, as Bertrand had said, the trees blocked her view. Seconds later, she heard the staccato sounds of machine guns...and screams.

She looked back at the two other women. They had stopped shouting and now stared at her, open-mouthed.

"Come back!" Lottie cried. "They are shooting the other refugees!"

Françoise and her mother ran over to her and climbed over the gate together, making it rattle on its hinges.

"Quick! Get under the car." Madame pointed to the vehicle.

"No, we've just filled it with petrol." Lottie shook her head. "If it gets hit, it'll go up like a torch. Come on, we'll go under the trees – the biggest we can find."

"Where is Bertrand?" yelled Madame, as they crossed the road into the forest.

"I don't know – he went to see whose planes were flying overhead." Lottie panted as she ran.

"Not hard to guess their identity, I'd say," Madame Blanchard muttered.

They crouched down under a massive oak tree. Lottie pressed her back into its ribbed bark. How normal it felt. How natural and strong and stable. Oh, why did people *do* this to each other? All those defenceless mothers and babies in the long file from Paris! How could this be happening?

The strafing lasted for ten, maybe fifteen minutes at the most. The planes would fire their wicked bullets then they could hear them swoop off, their engines sounding fainter, only to return with more, their engines screaming as they dived.

Françoise began to sob quietly. Clutching her stomach, she slid to the ground and curled up into a ball. Her mother stroked her back and leant protectively over her. Lottie sat apart, more aware of their guardian tree than the other women. She shut her eyes and prayed, focussing on the ridges of the wood sticking into her spine, gripping the hand of the wicker basket, its tasty contents forgotten.

They sat there for at least another quarter of an hour after the aeroplanes faded into the distant blue sky. Such a hot summer's day. After the whine of the aircraft ceased, the birds took up their song again, as if nothing had happened. They trilled above them in the branches of the oak tree, same as ever, but moans and cries could be heard faintly in the distance above their delicate cadence.

"I want to move, my leg's gone to sleep." Françoise lifted her head.

Lottie spoke more quietly. "Do it slowly and carefully. No sudden movements."

Madame Blanchard moved out of Françoise's way and helped her sit up. She looked at Lottie, her plucked eyebrows raised in query.

Lottie nodded back at her. "Wait here with Françoise. I'll go and look. If anyone approaches, hide in the ditch behind the trees. Understood? I'll leave the basket here."

Madame signalled assent.

Lottie got up, her hunger forgotten. She walked down the lane, back towards the main road. She had to find Bertrand. As she approached the end of the lane, the crying grew louder. She dreaded what she might see.

She braced herself, took a deep breath and broke into a run. As the lane opened out on to the main road she came to a dead halt, aghast at the scene before her. Bodies lay scattered on the ground, their loved ones huddled over them, crying or pulling at their clothes, hugging them. Some of the people on the ground were obviously wounded. Some were bleeding, others moaned in pain. But where was Bertrand?

She called out his name, softly at first, her throat dry and tight from fear. "Bertrand? Where are you? Bertrand?" She cast about, calling more loudly now. "Bertrand?"

Suddenly, she found him, slightly apart from the others at the entrance to the lane. He lay completely immobile on the ground, his mouth open in shock, just as it had been when he'd seen Sophie's little boy. His eyes were open too, wide open, disbelief still discernible in their expression. Lottie knelt down and slipped her hand inside his waistcoat over his heart to see if it was beating. Nothing. Her hand came away stained with blood. She wiped it on the grass, then felt his neck. No pulse. She sat back on her heels, revolted by the feel of death. Bertrand had no disease like Granny. It had not been his natural time to die. What *was* the world coming to?

Lottie dropped her head on to her chest, closed her eyes, willed herself not to cry and tried to ignore the way her body had started to tremble.

She clenched her fists, took another deep breath and looked up. Reaching out, she closed Bertrand's eyes with shaky fingers, leaving a trail of his own blood on his face. What should she do about the body? Should she bury him?

An older woman came up to her. "Is this your father, ma petite?"

Lottie looked up at her and had to shield her eyes from the glaring sun. "What?" She shook her head. "No, no, he is not my father. We're not related at all. He worked for my friend. He was driving their car."

"You have a car which still has petrol? Then what are you waiting for? Get in it and get away from here. You can do nothing for him now."

"But...all these wounded people. Maybe I should take them to a hospital."

"Most are dead. No doctor could save them. Save yourself, little one. Go."

"But what about you? Don't you need a lift?"

"You couldn't give a lift to my whole family. I will stay with them, we must stay together now. Are you with your family?"

"With my friends, yes, they are up the lane over there."

"Then waste no more time but escape from here and may God protect you."

The woman hauled Lottie upright and pushed her in the direction of the car. Dazed, Lottie stumbled back in the direction she'd come from. She willed her unsteady legs to walk forwards, blinking away the tears that blurred her vision. She found a handkerchief in her dress pocket

226

and blew her nose. Walking helped return her heart to some sort of rhythm from the uneven bounding pace it had assumed since seeing the devastation wrought by the enemy planes. So many dead bodies, so much crying and grief. Little children and babies struck down as they walked. A wave of nausea made her stop and retch into the grass verge. She wiped her mouth with her handkerchief and plodded on.

She found Françoise and her mother exactly where she'd left them. At her approach, Madame Blanchard peeped over the ditch. If the circumstances had been different, Lottie would have laughed at her dishevelled appearance, her comical dismay.

"Is it you, Charlotte?"

"Yes, it's me. You can come out now." Lottie went back to the car and reloaded the food. She had no taste for flesh now.

The others joined her. "We must go. Come on, get back in the car."

"But…" Françoise pointed in the direction of the main road.

"What about Bertrand?" Madame pushed her straggling hair away from her face.

"Bertrand is dead. And so are many others – women – children – babies. You don't want to know."

"Oh, mon Dieu! The planes?"

Lottie nodded.

"German, I suppose?" Madame bundled Françoise on to the back seat and shut the door.

"Yes, German. A woman spoke to me. She told me to get out of here before they came back."

"Of course, we must go! What if they came back? Hurry, hurry!"

"No regret for Bertrand?" Lottie remembered the manservant's staring, sightless eyes before she'd closed them and shivered involuntarily.

"Pah! He was a fool."

Lottie blinked the ghastly image away from her whirling brain but felt no surprise at Madame Blanchard's cynical reaction. "Can you drive, Madame?"

"Me? No, not at all."

"Then it seems I must." Lottie got in behind the wheel. She stared at the controls, the gear lever, wondering where to start. What was it her mother did? Her brain refused to think.

Madame Blanchard leaned across and pressed the starter button. The luxurious car purred into life.

Somehow, the sound of the engine clicked a memory in Lottie's tired, shocked mind. She reached out with her foot and depressed the accelerator. Nothing happened.

"I think it has to go into gear first." Madame Blanchard frowned.

"Oh yes, of course. I remember now. I used to drive our old Sunbeam around the grounds at home." Her voice caught on the last word. "At Cheadle Manor, with Mummy."

She blinked away a tear.

What had her mother said? Clutch – yes, that was it. Lottie put her left toe on the clutch pedal and pressed. Keeping it flat on the floor she fished around with the gear stick, eventually finding first gear, after a lot of horrible crunching sounds. Lifting her left foot slowly, she pushed her right one down in a corresponding opposite direction. Magically, the car inched forward.

She turned to the woman next to her. "So, Madame Blanchard, what direction do you want me to drive? Maybe we should carry on heading south, like everyone else," Lottie swallowed, "those who are left, that is."

Madame had been quiet for a few minutes while Lottie crunched the gears. "No, I think not. We will go to my mother's house in Normandy. She has a little smallholding. It stands alone, surrounded by trees. We will be safe there. It seems we have a new life to consider now." Madame sounded decisive, back in control.

Françoise had been silent, huddled into the back seat, arms folded protectively across her distended stomach, shock and fear making her face white. "Thank you, Maman, for not scolding me about the baby. I have been so afraid to tell you about David."

Madame Blanchard's face was strangely impassive. Lottie, like Françoise, had expected anger, rejection, even outrage, when Françoise's mother knew her secret. This calm acceptance was strange, but then, this whole situation was bizarre; bizarre and terrifying. It dwarfed everything else.

They drove along the road in silence, Lottie concentrating hard on her driving. The others apparently either lost in their own thoughts or trying not to distract her.

After a while Françoise's voice, tinged with hope, emanated from the back of the car. "I have never met my grandmother. Where is the nearest town to her house, Maman?"

"It is between Caen and Bayeux, not far from the sea."

"The sea? You mean the English Channel?" Lottie felt her heart leap.

"La Manche, we call it," Madame turned her head to answer her. "I suppose it could be called the English Channel. Certainly, the south coast of England lies on the other side."

Lottie couldn't keep the excitement from her voice. "If we could find a fishing boat, I could take you back with me to England - to safety."

"England? Why would I want to go there? There soon will be guards all along the coast who would shoot us dead at first sight, thinking we were Germans invading."

"Maman, I'm frightened."

Madame Blanchard turned to her daughter in the back of the car. "Shut up, Françoise." Madame looked

229

back at Lottie. "Why not find a telephone and order a private aeroplane? You've as much chance of that as a boat to England."

CHAPTER TWENTY SEVEN
NORMANDY
JUNE 1940

Lottie let out a sigh of relief. The petrol gauge had crept perilously close to the red empty line for the last few miles. She'd been dreading having to get out and walk along the bewildering criss-cross of lanes down which Madame Blanchard had unerringly guided her. Having never driven more than a few miles before, the challenge of coordinating her feet and hands while looking at the road had given her scrambled mind something to focus on in the aftermath of the massacre she'd witnessed. She'd stalled the car at least half a dozen times and once nearly put them in the ditch. Traffic had lessened dramatically once they'd turned northwards and refugees were few and far between. They saw more cows than people. The lack of food all day long and the trauma of the slaughter of refugees by the German machine guns caught up with her and her hands, so steady while she'd been driving, trembled on the steering wheel.

Madame Blanchard looked across at her. "That way." She pointed a painted fingernail towards a rutted farm track between two limestone walls. Wearily, Lottie steered the car along it and parked up next to a field of trees planted in symmetrical rows.

Lottie switched off the engine and let out another long sigh. She rubbed her hand across her gritty eyes and looked around her.

"There is my mother." Madame Blanchard nodded towards the wall on the other side of which an old woman stood in her apple orchard, chickens clucking around her sturdy black lace-up shoes. Strongly built and of less than average height, Bernadette Perrot bore no resemblance to her elegant daughter. She wore a wrap-around flowered apron over her faded dress and her grey hair was drawn back into a tight knot at the nape of her neck. She didn't

231

look like she'd ever been to a hairdressing salon for one of Madame's long, indulgent sessions.

"Is that old peasant woman really Grandmère?" Françoise had woken up when Lottie switched off the engine.

"She is. Wait here, both of you. I will go and talk to her alone." Madame Blanchard got out of the car, straightened her blouse and tucked the wayward strands of hair behind her bejewelled ears.

Lottie watched her approach the older woman, her back ramrod straight, her hands drawn up into tight fists, her high heels sinking into the turf. If Françoise had never met her grandmother, this was a long overdue and momentous meeting.

She couldn't hear the conversation from the car, even with the window down, but she could read the body language clearly. No embrace. None of the traditional kisses exchanged. The two women stood apart, like stags about to fight; eyes locked on each other, faces wary.

Madame Blanchard did all the talking. Her mother's face remained impassive. Eventually, the older woman nodded and came towards the car.

Lottie got out to greet her.

Françoise stayed in the back of the car a fraction longer before joining her and going to stand beside her mother. "This is Françoise, Maman. She looks like you."

"Pah. That was a long time ago. And who is this?" Bernadette Perrot jerked her chin in Lottie's direction. "She doesn't look like family."

Lottie held out her hand, then let it drop when it was not taken up by the old woman. "My name is Charlotte Flintock-Smythe. I'm from England. Françoise and I have been penfriends for many years and I was staying with the Blanchards over the winter, before the Germans invaded."

"That was stupid of you. Why didn't you go home before war was declared?"

"I tried, twice, but it was impossible. I left it too late, didn't take it seriously, I suppose."

"Then you were a fool."

Lottie couldn't help but agree. "Yes, I think I was."

Bernadette gave her a brisk nod. "Hmm, but I must admit, your French is very good. Parisian accent of course. You'll stick out like a sore thumb around here."

Bernadette looked back at her daughter. "So, left your fancy villa in Paris, have you? Running away. You were always good at that."

"Édouard is dead, Maman."

"Dead? How?" Bernadette's piercing grey eyes narrowed.

"The Citroën factory was bombed. His office took a direct hit. The Germans invaded Paris soon after. Everyone has left the city, not just us." Madame Blanchard looked worn out.

Lottie tried to back her up. "It's true, Madame. Even the Government has gone."

"Did I ask you?" Bernadette looked directly at Lottie then at each of them in turn.

Lottie felt she was being assessed; that they were all being weighed up, evaluated. She'd never experienced anything like it, not even when standing before the stern headmistress of her school when she'd absconded to the village to buy sweets for a midnight feast. How long ago that seemed now. A different life, and such an easy one.

"You'll be hungry." Bernadette turned away back to the farmhouse Lottie could see on the other side of the orchard. Most of the other houses they'd passed along the way had been of pale, yellow stone too but this one looked older, medieval perhaps. Wooden beams, twisted and silvered with age, ribbed its rendered walls and it fitted into the landscape seamlessly, as if a part of it. Dormer windows poked through a tall pitched roof of black slate.

"Um, we have some food, actually." Lottie volunteered the information.

Bernadette looked at her with interest for the first time.

"What have you got?"

"Lots. A chicken, some cheese, a saucisson."

"No bread?"

Madame Blanchard answered that one. "No, there was none in Paris."

Bernadette grunted. "That must have been difficult when you don't know how to cook. Come, I'll help you carry it."

They all went to the rear of the car and Lottie opened the boot. She handed the other women the baskets of food and the crate of wine.

"We usually drink calvados or cider." Bernadette nodded at the orchard. "From our own apples."

"I'm sure that must be very healthy." Lottie tried to smile.

Bernadette grunted. "Didn't save my husband from the pneumonia."

"That was ten years ago." Madame Blanchard almost dropped her burden. "Anyone would catch pneumonia if they stayed out all night in the snow trying to shoot foxes."

"How would you know?" Bernadette walked up to the house without looking back.

Madame Blanchard hurried after her. "Father always had a weak chest, since he was gassed in the war. He should have taken more care."

"I did take good care of him, but you never even visited."

"If I'd known he was ill, I would have come but you didn't tell me anything until it was too late. I came to the funeral."

"Pah, too little, too late." Bernadette turned to Lottie and Françoise. "This way."

They had reached a cobbled yard inside another wall. Low stone buildings lay along one side and the farmhouse stood at right angles to it.

Madame Blanchard lagged behind. Lottie looked back at her. She looked very upset and her box of groceries wobbled precariously.

Lottie put down her basket and went back to Madame Blanchard. "Here, let me carry these for you."

"Thank you." Madame Blanchard took out a delicate handkerchief from her pocket and wiped her eyes. She offered no explanation, so Lottie didn't ask for one.

They went into the farmhouse together, straight into a large kitchen, dominated by a big table covered in a gaudy oil cloth, with eight chairs around it. A range pumped out unnecessary heat into the room. A kettle sang on its hob. Bernadette went and shifted it across, away from the fire.

"Bring those things in here. There is a cool larder in the corner of the scullery."

They trooped after her in silence and placed their various offerings down on the flagstone floor.

Bernadette inspected the horde. "You did well. So, Mireille, you're expecting to stay here, are you?"

Her mother's use of Madame Blanchard's Christian name made Lottie look differently at her old hostess. Suddenly she could see Mireille as a little girl, here on the farm, bossed around by her stern mother, perhaps bullied by her dead Papa. It cast an altogether different light on the woman she had largely ignored in Paris and whom she had criticised for her shallow lifestyle. Her new awareness that Sophie, the housemaid, had borne Édouard's son further complicated her view of her former hostess.

She remained silent. The air between Bernadette and her daughter crackled with tension in the dark, cool space. What on earth had happened between these two women to make them hate each other so?

Mireille didn't flinch. "It is not safe in Paris and we have nowhere else. I must think about Françoise's safety."

"Especially as she is pregnant." Bernadette turned to look at Françoise's pale face.

Françoise gasped out loud. "How could you know?"

"It's obvious." Bernadette turned back to Mireille. "How long do you intend to live off me?"

"I don't know. It's not up to me, ask Herr Hitler."

"You'll have to share a room with your daughter. I take it she's not married?" Bernadette turned back towards the kitchen and headed towards a door. Opening it to reveal an enclosed, turned staircase, she placed one foot on the first step. "Well?"

"No."

"So, like mother, like daughter. Typical."

Bernadette stomped up the stairs, her heavy shoes loud against the bare wood. Lottie had the curious thought that it would be difficult to creep down them without being heard.

Bernadette showed Françoise and Mireille into a large bedroom over the kitchen. It had two beds covered in chintz bedspreads and was a pretty room with floral curtains and good furniture. Lottie was surprised. She'd expected something more rustic.

"You, come with me. I have another room for you." Bernadette took Lottie across a large landing and up another flight of stairs, not much more than a large ladder. When they reached the top, she could barely see, it was so dark, and she fumbled her feet on the floor, feeling her way, reluctant to release the handrail. She leaned her back against a wall until her eyes adjusted. Bernadette walked ahead confidently, the stomp of her stout shoes against the floorboards the only guide Lottie had to her whereabouts. She obviously knew every inch of her home by heart. Bernadette clattered open several shutters and let in the strong sunlight, revealing a big raftered room in the eaves, with a pitched roof and long, narrow windows under dormers overlooking the apple orchard on one side and some fields on the other. There were rag rugs on the floorboards and four single beds in a square formation. Though bare, it looked comfortable and there was a large wardrobe and a couple of chests of drawers. It was dusty and hot so high up in the roof, but Lottie loved the amount of space she'd been allotted – and the privacy.

"I use it for the pickers in the harvest season. There's a chamber pot if you need it and a jug and basin for washing. You'll have to carry the water up yourself and empty both in the soak-away. I'll show you where that is later. You'll have to brush out the spiders and there's no electricity up here, only oil lamps or candles. Any questions?"

Lottie shook her head. "Thank you, Bernadette. It's a lovely room. You are very kind to put me up as well as your family when we've turned up out of the blue like this."

"Humph. Come down when you are ready. I'll make some soup." Bernadette clomped back down the steep wooden stairs.

Lottie lay on one of the beds. The coils of the springs connected with her back through the thin mattress. Soup? In this heat?

She closed her eyes, longing for sleep. Images of dead bodies immediately spilled into her mind, so she opened them again, blinking in the fierce sunbeam shafting across her body. She had a headache and a terrific thirst.

It would be so easy, so welcome, to just lie here, blissfully alone, and simply rest.

CHAPTER TWENTY EIGHT
THE KATHERINE WHEEL GARAGE
LATE SUMMER 1940

Gathering round the wireless for both the six o'clock and nine o'clock news had become a routine activity for the whole Phipps family, but they had never heard Churchill deliver his own speech before. It brought solemnity to the occasion. For Al, it made the war even more real and closer to home. And that was before the Prime Minister had spoken.

The long speech continued for half an hour. Even Lily listened intently, huddled close to the crackling set.

When Churchill said, *"What General Weygand has called the Battle of France is over ... the Battle of Britain is about to begin,"* Al felt a frisson of thrilling fear. He leant nearer to the wireless to catch the next momentous words.

"Upon this battle depends the survival of Christian civilisation. Upon it depends our own British life, and the long continuity of our institutions and our Empire. The whole fury and might of the enemy must very soon be turned on us. Hitler knows that he will have to break us in this island or lose the war. If we can stand up to him, all Europe may be freed, and the life of the world may move forward into broad, sunlit uplands.

"Please God," Agnes murmured.

"Ssh, Mum," Katy frowned at her mother.

Churchill's unique voice intoned further through the Bakelite box.

"But if we fail, then the whole world, including the United States, including all that we have known and cared for, will sink into the abyss of a new Dark Age made more sinister, and perhaps more protracted, by the lights of perverted science. Let us therefore brace ourselves to our duties, and so bear ourselves that, if the British Empire

and its Commonwealth last for a thousand years, men will still say, "This was their finest hour."

When he had finished, Al found he had gripped his mother's hand tightly, without even realising it. He looked across at her, shocked to see her eyes brimming with uncharacteristic tears.

Jem cleared his throat. "That was comprehensive. Good for Churchill telling us what's what and not leaving us guessing. We never heard the like in the last shout."

Agnes nodded. "True enough but I don't like the sound of us sinking into some 'abyss' and what's he mean about 'perverted science?'"

"Yes, Mum, I wondered about that too. As for the rest, at least we know what we're in for and he's left us in no doubt that the weight of the world lies on our shoulders. That's quite a responsibility." Katy looked up at her husband, who had stayed standing throughout the broadcast. "We'll have to camouflage the factory, Jem. Don't want that being spotted by the Luftwaffe."

"That's true, love. I'll get on to it. We'll need to find yards of netting from somewhere."

Katy nodded. "I'll ask Cass if she knows someone in the army who could spare some."

Jem smiled at his wife. "Good idea, or I'll ask old Sam Fleming next time I go to the Local Defence Volunteer meeting. He claims to know everything. Time he was put to the test."

Al was thinking about what Churchill had said about looking forward confidently to the exploits of the fighter pilots. Al rather fancied being one of *"these splendid men, this brilliant youth - who will have the glory of saving their native land, their island home, and all they love, from the most deadly of all attacks."* His skin prickled with a mixture of fear and pride. He pictured himself inside the cockpit of a Spitfire, gunning down some German bastards; being one of that gang of brave youths defending the skies.

Over the next few weeks, the summer sun shone as bravely as any pilot, mocking Churchill's dark, sombre words with day after day of glorious weather. The news on the wireless, however, did match the Prime Minister's dour prophecies with regular bulletins describing the destruction of the convoys of ships importing precious supplies to Britain, as the German Luftwaffe's aeroplanes cut them to shreds. Italy declared war on France and Britain. It made Lottie feel closer somehow, united in the fight.

Al wondered whether to mention it in his letter to Isobel and decided against it. He tried to keep his letters light but found it increasingly difficult. Early in July, Cardiff was bombed, and Al felt really alarmed about Isobel. His knowledge of the geography of Wales was vague at the best of times.

When they heard the announcement on the news, Jem got out his old Atlas and they pored over it together.

"I don't even know how you pronounce Rhydymwyn, let alone find the bloody place." Al peered closely at the map.

"Isn't Chester the nearest city?" Jem traced his finger along the main road, marked in red.

"That's right and the next town is Mold. At least I can get my tongue around that one."

"Here it is. Look - Chester is miles away from Cardiff and it's not even in Wales, but England." Jem pointed to a dot on the map.

Al found the bigger city of Cardiff and they measured the distance between. "Must be well over a hundred miles, don't you reckon, Dad?"

"A good bit more, I'd say. Cardiff's on the south coast and Chester way above. Now, if they targeted Liverpool docks, there might be cause for concern. Don't worry. A bomb would have to be completely off target to reach north Wales when they're aiming at Cardiff, or even Chester. Look Rhydymwyn is right over there in the middle of nowhere and she's not even in the town but in the depths of those green hills. She's as safe there as anywhere, Al."

Al knew his father was right. Isobel couldn't be in a more secure spot, but nothing could rid him of the notion that the safest place of all would be right under his nose, where he could keep an eye on her.

News came thick and fast after that, and the ritual of listening to the daily news became a fixed, tense highlight of the day. Al went with his dad when Jem scrounged some camouflage netting off the local army depot, who agreed their factory could easily be a target, small though it was, compared to the big Avon rubber tyre factory some thirty miles north.

When Jem signed for the bundle of netting he said to the Sergeant, "I never thought we'd be glad of our big competitor being so close by."

The Sergeant nodded. "Still, can't be too careful these days. I'll get some of our lads to load it on to your lorry. You'd be surprised how heavy this stuff is."

Al drove the lorry back to the garage and tooted his horn as they drove into the forecourt.

Jem opened the passenger door. "Come on, then, lad. It's all-hands-on-deck to get this up on the roof."

Al collected up every ladder they possessed while Jem got all the men at the factory into the yard.

Once they'd unloaded the netting, Jem addressed the men. "Right, let's gather it up on one side and, working together, with two of us in a line, take it up the ladder and on to the roof. The other two, grab those hooks we use for the rubber bales and, when we've thrown it across, you pull it down and across towards the other side."

"How are we going to secure it, Jem?" Len, always practical, asked the question.

"I've got these staples, so you'll each need a hammer to bang them in, with the net caught up inside. Got it?"

241

There were murmurings of assent as each man grabbed a hammer and went to a ladder. Some of the factory girls came out to watch.

"What are you gawping at? Haven't you got work to do?" Billy Threadwell looked cross as well as hot.

Al supposed his uncle's temper went with his red hair, even though it was thinning on top these days.

Jem shook his head. "Leave 'em be, Billy. This shouldn't take long. All part of the war effort."

Katy emerged from the office too and squinted up at the roof, shielding her eyes with her hand. "Take care everybody! I don't want any accidents on my patch!"

The operation, under the careful guidance of Jem, went like clockwork. Soon the factory roof was covered in camouflage netting.

"Good job everybody! Now everyone get back to work, the show's over." He turned to his son. "Except you, Al."

A ragged cheer went up as the other workers, including Katy, trooped back inside.

"What do you want me to do, Dad?"

"You and me are going around the woods at the back to cut off bits of leaves and twigs. Then we're going back up on the roof to tuck it into the nets. Oh, I know they've got imitation leaves and that on it but it's not a good enough disguise. I don't want any German planes thinking they've got an easy target. I'll need you to be my left arm and pass 'em over."

"But Dad, in this sun, they'll soon be dried up twigs and won't cover anything."

"That's right, good thinking, Al. We'll take only evergreens. Come on."

It was weary work taking the cuttings up to the hot roof, but Jem wasn't satisfied until the sun was setting in the west and the rest of the workforce had long since gone home after their day's shift. Hot and tired, they gathered up the ladders and hammers and put them away in the old Nissen hut. Then they stood back to look at their efforts.

"You'd have to be in a plane to judge whether it's worked for sure." Jem mopped his forehead with his handkerchief.

"Give me half a chance and I'd check it out from up there." Al took one last look, and headed indoors, feeling disgruntled that he couldn't do just that.

Towards the end of the month, Jem came home from a Local Defence Volunteer meeting grinning from ear to ear. They sat round the table for tea. As Agnes doled out the mashed potato, Jem said, "Extra portions for me, Agnes, as I'm now a member of the 'Home Guard'."

"What's that when it's at home? I can only give you two sausages whoever you are, what with the rationing. Have an extra carrot."

Jem laughed. "It's exactly the same as the Local Defence Volunteers but Churchill's given us a new name. Let's hope he'll give us some firearms so we can live up to it."

"How come you old duffers can do your bit when people my age have to sit tight?" Al poured gravy over his pile of potatoes.

"You'll have your turn all too soon." Agnes tweaked his ear as she passed.

"Will you have to fight the Germans when they invade then, Dad?" Lily looked impressed.

"Yes, I'll be ready if they come." Jem dipped his fork in his mash.

"What? Armed with a broomstick? I'm sure a German paratrooper would be terrified." Katy reached for the gravy jug.

"It won't always be broomsticks, love, and anyway, I've got my rifle. Quite a few of the blokes in our group have some sort of firearm. We're all countrymen at heart. Most people have a pop at a rabbit for the pot." Jem sliced some bread.

"And there's knives, I suppose." Al looked at the lethal blade his father was using to cut the loaf of bread.

Jem's slicing paused, and he wagged the knife at his son. "Don't you go getting ideas, young Al."

"I'm not so young, Dad. I'll be signing up in a few months."

"Don't remind me," Katy laid her fork down, her plate still half full.

As the month wore on, reports of airfields being bombed and British pilots fending off the German planes in dogfights over the channel made Al fume he wasn't six months older. By mid-August he felt more impatient than ever, as the RAF announced more and more losses of Spitfire pilots. They seemed to be alone in defending their shores, as the Battle of Britain raged above them in the sunny skies.

"Where's this lot going then?" Al looked at the delivery note Len had passed to him one Friday afternoon.

"Southampton, I think. It's a bit late to be setting off, isn't it?" Len checked the webbing on the lorry and nodded, satisfied.

"Right-oh, needs must." Al swung up into the cab. "I'd better get going before the light fades. And you'd better get off home. Doesn't your wife mind you being late on a Friday?"

"This lot won't wait but I'll be ready for my tea when I get home, I can tell you."

"Want a lift? I'll be going right by your place."

Len hesitated, looking tempted. "If I leave my bike here, I'll have to walk into work tomorrow morning."

"Sling it on the back then. You can rope it on to the webbing."

"You're on!" Len went to the back of the lorry and Al joined him. They lifted the bicycle up against its back wall and roped it fast.

"Can't have you missing your grub, now can we?" Al pressed the starter button and the engine roared into life.

"My stomach's already rumbling." Len laughed.

"I'm not surprised, you've been here since seven o'clock this morning." Al steered the lorry out on to the main road.

"True, but I'm glad we've got this lot shipped out. The RAF are losing planes so fast, they need more rubber components for the new ones. And the army have upped their demand for brake seals too. One thing you can say for this damned war, it's been good for business for the Katherine Wheel factory. Your Mum's taken on two more girls for the production line."

"Yes, and we get more petrol allowance than anybody. There's hardly any traffic about these days. Makes my job easier."

"I'll bet. And more factory work must make up for the loss of car and petrol sales for your Mum."

Al overtook a couple of blokes on bicycles. "They look a bit wobbly. Been down the pub, I should think."

"Who can blame them? We all have to relax when we get the chance." Len gave them a cheeky wave, making one man weave alarmingly into the middle of the road.

"Does your wife mind you working these long hours?" Al changed gear.

"I'm sure she does but she doesn't say much. The extra money comes in handy. Working for your Mum and Dad has been the best thing that's ever happened to us. Even Ethel's asthma is better. She was that thin before." Len smiled across at Al.

"I'm glad it's worked out for you, Len. I know they both think very highly of you. Mum says she couldn't run our place without you."

Len coughed. "I don't know about that. Your mother is a remarkable woman, you know, Al. I've never met another like her. She's so clever with machines and she works as hard as any man I've ever met, harder than most."

"I know." Al lowered his voice. "Sometimes I feel...oh, nothing."

"What is it, lad?"

"It sounds daft."

"No, go on."

"Well, I sometimes feel that I'm not good enough, you know. Mum is so amazing and Dad so, sort of, solid, and all I've ever managed to achieve is driving this old lorry. It's hardly the stuff of Biggles, is it?"

Len laughed. "Some would say you're very brave, driving alone, especially at night in the blackout. After all, you're only nineteen, lad."

"I quite like it actually. Gives me time to think."

"I know what you mean. We all need a bit of time to ourselves sometimes. But don't you go running yourself down, Al. You just don't know what you're capable of yet. With this war on, you're bound to be called up and I'm sure you'll do your parents credit."

"Thanks. I'll do my best. I'll have to register in the new year, when I'm twenty."

"Have you thought which service you'd like to join?"

"I fancy the RAF, if I could get in."

"Don't you have to be posh for that, begging your pardon?" Len pointed Al at the next turning.

Al turned the lorry up a little lane into a small village. "Maybe. I think there are exams and that. I've been studying the different types of planes, both ours and the ones the Gerries fly. It might help in the tests but to be honest, exams aren't my strong point!" He grinned and pulled up outside a tiny terraced cottage, thick with thatch. The front garden frothed with flowers within a neat white fence. "Nice place you've got here, Len."

"My Ethel keeps it lovely. Now her health is stronger, she's able to do the garden as well. It's been such a hot summer, she's got masses of blooms. Her asthma isn't from pollen but dust and smoke, so living in the country has done her the world of good." Len opened the door and jumped out, limping slightly from the impact. "I'll get the bike myself, no need for you to get out."

"Don't be soft." Al hopped down from the cab and went around the back of the lorry. Between them they soon had the bike released and back on the ground. "Hmm, something smells good, Len."

"Got time to come in? I'm sure we could stretch to another plate."

"No, better get on. Gran's cooking fish and chips for us tonight. I shan't miss out and I've got a sandwich to keep me going."

"Alright then. At least they haven't rationed fish yet. Thanks, kiddo. See you tomorrow."

"Enjoy your evening and say hello to the family for me."

"I will. Safe driving, now, lad."

"Don't you worry about me!" Al re-ignited the engine and did a three-point-turn in the village lane. A black cat scuttled across his path as he headed back for the main road. He tried to remember if that foretold good or bad luck. Agnes would know. He was lucky to have such a tightknit family, but he missed Isobel like hell. No talk of a transfer back to Wiltshire in her letters. It was now the middle of August and he'd had hopes she'd be back before now.

Being a Friday afternoon, the roads were emptier than ever, and he made good time to the army depot. He offloaded the goods into the hangar and got the foreman to check off the delivery note. The drone of aeroplanes interrupted their work.

The foreman swore. "Oh, not again. Look!"

Al looked up at the sky. "Blimey! Are they bombers?"

"Yes, looks like it. Heinkels."

"Heading for London again, do you think?" Al shielded his eyes with the palm of his hand.

"Wrong direction. Looks like they're heading straight for the city."

"What? Southampton?"

The older man nodded. "Probably aiming for the docks. Bastards. My house is just this side of the city centre." He shoved the piece of paper back at Al. "Put this in the office, will you? I'm getting off home. My shift's ended anyway. My missus is all alone and she's that nervous with all these bombs flying about."

Al nodded and took the clipboard from him. The man ran off to a large shed and got on a bicycle. He pedalled off furiously in the same direction as the German planes.

Al lifted the clipboard up to his forehead, using it as sun visor. He leant against the side of the lorry and watched in amazement as, seemingly out of nowhere, three Spitfires attacked the heavier German bombers. Agile as wasps, they swooped and dived around the attacking fleet of aeroplanes and took them out, one by one. Al couldn't believe their manoeuvrability in the sky and the speed of the turns as they foiled the lumbering Heinkels time and again. Then some Messerschmitts joined the fight and engaged the Spitfires with bullets of their own, followed by a Hurricane, bringing more firepower to aid the Spitfires. He was transfixed by the battle raging above him.

The sun had not yet started to set, and the sky remained blue with just a hint of pink in the west. Against the azure background white trails of smoke streamed out of the planes. His eyes fixed on a Hurricane under fire from a Messerschmitt. Al screwed his eyes tighter. He'd swear it was a Bf 110 and wished he had binoculars to make sure. It was giving that Hurricane hell, bombarding it with fire from its guns.

Al gasped. The Hurricane had caught fire in the cockpit. He strained his eyes to see if the pilot would bail out but instead the British aeroplane turned on the Messerschmitt and opened fire right back at its attacker. The air was so still, Al could pick out the shots fired in the dogfight. He held his breath as the Hurricane swooped down on the German, firing all the time. Surely, he was going to explode? What if the fire caught the petrol tank? He hardly dared to blink in case he missed the outcome. Suddenly it was the Messerschmitt catching fire and, unlike the Hurricane, the flames spread along the spine of the plane and along one wing. The German plane started to nosedive down towards the sea below. Al switched his gaze back to the Hurricane, still on fire, then quickly back to its attacker. The Messerschmitt spiralled below and burst into flames just before it hit the water. No bodies had jumped clear, as far as he could see.

The Hurricane was now veering downwards too. Faster and faster the plane fell out of the sky. Unwittingly Al clutched his mop of chestnut hair, tearing it at the roots as he watched, paralysed by the tumbling fighter plane. Then, through the fiery blaze blooming out of its nose, a black figure, orange flames licking around his outline, appeared against the cerulean sky. Then a white parachute mushroomed above him; cool and serene, it floated down more slowly, gliding gently towards the channel guided by the gravitational pull of the earth. The Hurricane hit the sea, exploding into shards of fire, red against the white plumes of water.

The pilot floated down at a more leisurely pace above the inferno. Al could imagine the agony he must be suffering and when the airman ditched into the sea, he hoped it would soothe his burns rather than drown the poor bugger. There was no way he could see if the man survived his dunking. He doubted he'd be in a fit state to swim ashore after being burned, how could he have any strength left? But many men had done just that and made it back to shore but then, they probably hadn't been on fire when they hit the briny waves. It all depended on the extent of his burns and if he was rescued by the lifeboat, if they could find him in those cold waters.

But what a fight! That Messerschmitt wouldn't destroy any more British planes.

How he longed to be a part of it.

CHAPTER TWENTY NINE
A HILL FARM IN FLINTSHIRE
SEPTEMBER 1940

Mr Williams lowered his newspaper and shook his head.

"Anything the matter?" His wife topped up his mug of tea with her big brown pot.

"I should say there is."

"Can I see, Mr Williams?" Isobel held out her hand imperiously. She'd found the only way to keep him at arm's length was to play up her poshness, knowing both the Williams's were a little in awe of her aristocratic background.

The front-page article read: "Yesterday, the 7th September 1940, London suffered its worst bombing yet. Mothers are being urged to evacuate their children amid fears of the bombing intensifying."

"I'm sorry to hear about the bombs, but we don't want Londoners here." Mrs Williams pulled the knitted, stained tea cosy over the spout of the teapot.

Isobel couldn't let that go. "You do surprise me, Mrs Williams, I thought you were a chapel goer? Don't they preach Christian values of hospitality to refugees at your chapel?"

She'd gone too far. Mr Williams stood up. "That's enough cheek off you, Isobel. I'll not have you talking to my wife like that. She's a good Christian woman, I'll have you know." He clamped his pipe between his yellow teeth and glared at Isobel.

Mrs Williams sniffed and stalked out of the kitchen.

Isobel sighed. She'd done it again. It was getting harder and harder to keep her mouth shut at the hypocritical attitude of her hosts.

"You can muck out the pig sty, Miss High-and-Mighty. Let it be your penance." Mr Williams nodded at the door. "Now, get going."

Evacuee children began arriving in the area looking for billets soon afterwards and Mr and Mrs Williams were the only farmers not to offer accommodation, until the minister's wife called one day, while Isobel was in the kitchen cleaning harness.

"Mrs Williams, you have no choice in the matter. We will all have to do our bit and take in these unfortunate young souls. I'm taking in three children myself. Hitler is bombing London now, you know. Tons of bombs are falling at night and destroying whole streets. We cannot turn these poor children away and not protect them, now can we?"

Mrs Williams looked to her husband, who chewed his pipe in silence. Eventually he said, "Do we get paid for feeding these evacuees?"

Mrs Owens let out a sigh. "You will be paid ten shillings and sixpence for the first unaccompanied child, and eight shillings and sixpence for any subsequent children."

"What, every week?" Mrs William's tight little mouth was open in a perfect 'o' shape.

"Is that so?" Mr Williams took his pipe out of his mouth. "Well, it wouldn't be Godly to refuse, now would it?"

But Mr Williams wouldn't agree to Isobel leaving, even after Geraint Lloyd paid a visit and put him in his place.

Isobel had been cleaning down the milk shed with only a bucket and broom for tools, when a shadow had cut the light from the shed doorway. Frowning, she looked up, expecting the scrawny outline of Mr Williams to be blocking the sunlight. She was astonished to see Geraint Lloyd's tall form lounging against the door jamb.

251

"Goodness, I never expected to see you here!" Isobel put down her broom. "Hello, Mr Lloyd. I'm surprised you found this farm."

"Oh, I'm no stranger to these parts and please, call me Geraint, as one artist to another." He walked towards her with his easy stride.

Isobel put her broom to one side and held out a mucky hand. "That's kind. I warn you my hand is filthy."

Geraint shook it warmly, undaunted, despite his immaculate suit. "That looks like very hard work, Isobel."

"Actually, this is the easy bit."

"Do you ever get time off for good behaviour?"

Isobel laughed. "Very rarely."

"You look worn out, if you don't mind me saying so."

"I don't mind because, quite frankly, I am."

Geraint frowned. "It shouldn't be like this, Isobel."

"Shouldn't be like what? And who might you be?" Mr Williams came into the shed, looking like a dog guarding its territory with its hackles raised.

Isobel was surprised he didn't growl at the taller man when he came up to him so close, she could smell the farm odours that reeked off his none-too-clean overalls and was embarrassed that Geraint couldn't avoid them.

"Geraint Lloyd. I'm a friend of Miss Isobel's. And you are?"

Mr Williams spread his legs wide and put his hands on his hips. "I own this farm, see."

"Do you? And is this land girl your only staff? Seems a bit unfair."

"Don't you tell me my business. Your kind don't know nothing of farming."

"Now, that's where you're wrong. I have a farm on my estate, near Chester, not so far away."

"An estate? Well, I expect you have plenty of staff there. Can't see you mucking out a cow shed." Mr

Williams pulled his pipe out of his pocket and started to chew on it, unlit.

Isobel knew this to be a bad sign. "Um, shall we go for a stroll, Geraint? I'm finished in here, Mr Williams. All the cows are milked for the evening. I'll only be half an hour." Not waiting for an answer, Isobel guided Geraint out of the milkshed and past the malodorous Welshman.

"Are you really the only member of staff for that obnoxious little man?" Geraint followed Isobel out into the meadow at the rear of the yard.

"Afraid so. I've asked for a transfer but our WLA local officer, Mrs Hopkins, said Farmer Williams had refused point blank to release me."

Isobel leaned on the farm gate and looked at the meadow. "I tried to paint it when it was in flower. It was so lovely, you know."

Geraint joined her at the gate. "I'll bet. Even the seed heads are quite architectural, in their own way, but they must have been magnificent when they were in full bloom. Where does this Mrs Hopkins have her office, Isobel?"

"Hmm? Just in the village, why?"

"Oh, no reason, just wondered how the whole land army thing worked, you know."

They chatted about this and that and Geraint gave her a painting he'd done of the hills where they'd met. She felt sad when he left without a promise of seeing her again.

Isobel decided not to tell Elsie and Lilian about Geraint's visit when they met up the next Saturday at the harvest supper dance. The little village hall, built just after the last war, smelled of damp, even at the end of summer.

There was no band, but Mr Hopkins had some old '78's he was cranking out on the wind-up gramophone. He kept getting distracted by nattering to all and sundry, so the records revolved too slowly making them sound out of tune and in lower keys. Lilian thought it hysterically funny.

"Come on, Isobel, don't you think it's hilarious?"

"I might, if I wasn't so bloody hungry." Isobel's stomach growled. It did a lot of that, living at the Williams's.

Elsie grabbed Isobel's hand. "Come on, let's have a dance anyway, it'll take your mind off your empty tum."

Isobel let herself be drawn into the centre of the little hall.

Elsie said, "Listen, it's Glenn Miller. Mr Hopkins has finally found some new stuff to play. Don't you just love 'Moonlight Serenade' – it's so…sort of… creamy."

"Don't talk to me of cream. I've forgotten what it looks or tastes like."

"Poor Isobel. Come on, I'll be the bloke." Elsie, tall and lanky, took her in her arms and swung her round.

By the end of the number, Isobel had forgotten her hunger and was smiling too but she still couldn't forget about wanting to leave. "I applied for a transfer way back in June, but the miserable old duffer won't let me go. You were so lucky to get transferred when you did to your soft lodgings with Mrs Jones. It's just not fair."

"I know, I'm sorry. I think the Williams's were promised replacements and that's why we got away with it. He'd never have agreed otherwise. He always had a soft spot for you, though, so I'm not surprised he won't let you go. You could leave the Land Army and just go anyway, I suppose." Lilian licked her finger and corrected the pencil line she'd drawn on the back of her calf. They'd all worn out their old stockings and there were none to be had up on the hills of north Wales.

"I know, but I really don't want to quit the WLA. I like belonging to something official while the war is on." Isobel lowered her voice and leaned in towards her friends. "Mrs Hopkins had a word with them back in July about the rations, but it's made no difference. I don't give much for the chances of any evacuees who end up on their doorstep."

"Bad luck." Elsie and Lilian exchanged sympathetic looks.

"It's good to know you are pulling your weight and all that, but I fainted in the milking parlour yesterday." Isobel went to the little serving hatch and got a cup of tea in a chipped cup.

"Do you want a biscuit with that, dear?" The minister's wife spoke with a cheery smile.

"Yes please, um, I couldn't have two, could I?" Isobel ventured.

"There is a war on, you know."

"Yes, yes, of course, sorry. Oh, Rich Tea, lovely." Isobel bit into the dry biscuit. The whole thing disappeared in a second.

"Blimey, you'd better have ours too." Lilian took Elsie's biscuit off her saucer as well as her own and passed them to Isobel, who scoffed them down as quickly as she'd eaten her own.

"You can't go on like this, you know." Elsie looked at Isobel. "I don't mean to be rude but having held you in my arms while we danced, I could feel how thin you are."

"You won't survive the winter at this rate! Come up to ours next Saturday and Mrs Jones will fatten you up." Lilian winked at her.

"Thanks, I'll take you up on that."

Over lunch the following Saturday, Mrs Jones clucked at Isobel's thinness. "There's slim you are, Isobel. That's not right. I've a mind to go down to the Williams's and give 'em what for. Making you do the work of three girls and on no food. Duw, duw, how can they have the nerve to go to Chapel and behave like that on the quiet?"

Isobel couldn't answer because her mouth was full of bread and golden Welsh butter, made by Mrs Jones and never talked about off the farm because of the rationing. Where she got the cow's milk from was a secret, even to Lilian and Elsie. Its salty fat oozed goodness on her tongue. She wasn't going to waste the moment on words.

Elsie and Lilian roared with laughter. They had plumped up since moving to Mrs Jones. Their landlady looked happier too.

Suddenly, Isobel felt angry. Why had she got the short straw? "You know, you're right." She swallowed her food down. Her hollow insides clawed at it uncomfortably. "I'm going to write to the WLA's head office."

"Hear, hear!"

"It's human slavery, that's what!"

"Have another faggot, cariad."

Isobel kept her vow and took pen to paper the minute she got back to the farm.

She wrote, 'Dear Madam', and then paused. If she went home, gave in to her mother's and Al's pleas to return, wouldn't that be giving in? Giving up her independence? She wouldn't see Geraint Lloyd again, if she did. Isobel shook her head. So what? It was Al she loved and, if she went home, she'd see him every day. Geraint Lloyd didn't mean anything to her. She looked up at the painting he'd given her of the Welsh mountains. She'd hung it on a nail above the table in her dormitory. It was so evocative of that lovely sunny day she'd spent with him. The hairs on her neck prickled. Isobel looked around at the door, which she'd left ajar. A shadow moved furtively away. Mr Williams had been snooping again.

Isobel renewed the ink in her fountain pen and pressed its nib to the page.

She posted the letter off with the others she'd already written to her mother and Al. She never told them about her short rations and made no mention of a possible return home. They each had enough to worry about without fretting about her and it wouldn't do to raise expectations that might easily be dashed.

To her surprise, an inspector of The Women's Land Army turned up a few weeks later and roundly denounced Mr and Mrs Williams for underfeeding and overworking her.

"You cannot expect our gals to work like slaves on these rations! I am relieving Miss Flintock-Smythe of her duties forthwith and unless you can assure me that you will adhere to the guidance rules of the WLA, you will not receive a replacement. In fact, you need at least two of our staff for the level of work involved."

"You can't do that!" Mr Williams had even taken his pipe out of his mouth, it had dropped so far open.

"I think you'll find that I can." Mrs Steeple's voice was firm.

"Oh, don't go, please," whispered Mrs Williams from her chair in the corner.

"How'm I s'posed to milk my cows?" Mr Williams ignored his wife, as usual.

"That is your concern. Mine is Miss Flintock-Smythe. You should have thought of your cows before, Farmer Williams. Perhaps you could have shared some of their produce with Miss Flintock-Smythe here. Why, the poor girl is wasting away and if I don't remove her before the winter's in, she'll become ill. That won't help the war effort!"

"I'll get my things." Isobel wasn't going to let Mrs Steeple go without her.

"But…" Mr Williams's voice faded as Isobel leapt up from her chair and ran to her dormitory.

She grabbed her clothes. There weren't many, just the regulation Land Army uniform. The bulkiest item was her overcoat and the most precious, her letters from home. She took Geraint's picture from the wall and shoved it into her rucksack, strapping the flap carefully over it to keep it dry. She put on the overcoat rather than carry it. It was raining, as ever, anyway.

Back indoors, a tense silence stretched between visitor and hosts.

Isobel held out her hand, first to Mrs Williams, who pursed her lips and looked away. She took the hint and didn't offer it to her husband. "Goodbye, Mr Williams. I'm sorry it's turned out like this."

Mr Williams had clamped his yellow teeth back over his clay pipe. He grunted his farewell, no more.

"Right, let's be off, then!" Mrs Steeple nodded to the older couple.

They let themselves out through the door and latched it shut behind them.

"Phew!" Isobel felt her shoulders descend to their normal position for the first time in months. Isobel felt a pang for the cows in the barn. A few were crying out to be milked. She hoped Mr Williams wouldn't ignore the poor creatures.

Mrs Steeple glanced across at her. "Don't worry, child, I'll get the farm inspected properly. I know the local magistrate quite well and we had a bit of a tip off from a friend of yours - Geraint Lloyd? He has quite an influence in these parts. He'll get the Ministry to come and look at the place. And I will get the representative to strongly suggest his wife pays the doctor a visit. She doesn't look at all well. Did you see that bruise on her arm? What a miserable little man."

"Yes, it's not the first bruise I've noticed. I do hope Mr Williams doesn't take it out on his wife now and I hope he milks those poor cows today." Resolutely, Isobel turned away from the melancholy lowing of the cows and climbed in the waiting car. "Thank you, Mrs Steeple. I had no idea Mr Lloyd had put in a word for me."

"Word gets around, my dear, even in wartime."

They bumped down the rutted farm track and soon gained the road. Isobel felt cheerful looking out of the window at the Welsh hills. Even the perpetual rain couldn't dampen her mood, her euphoric sense of release.

"I'll give you a lift to the village. You can catch a bus there to Chester and the train station. Aim for a connection to Crewe, I would, that'll get you further south, but you'll need to change trains several times, my dear. Have you enough cash for the journey?"

"Yes, I've saved my wages. Thank you, Mrs Steeple. You are very kind."

"All part of my job. I hope you will stay in the Land Army? Most postings are not like this. You will always work hard but not be unfairly treated, by and large. You were unlucky this time."

"I was wondering if I could work on the home farm next to my house at Cheadle Manor in Wiltshire? I know that the farmer's sons have signed up and he's in need of help. Or would that be considered cheating?"

Mrs Steeple gave a rich deep laugh. "Not at all! Kill two birds with one stone, more likely. Would you live at your family house?"

"I think that would be best. I could support my mother at the same time."

"Splendid idea! We wouldn't have to pay for your upkeep!"

To Isobel's surprise, Mrs Steeple broke into song.

> *"We're girls, girls of the land are we,*
> *When working we're happy and free*
> *We work for its pleasure*
> *We've no time for Leisure*
> *So join in the Land Army!"*

Dutifully Isobel joined in the chorus, having learned it at the training base in Winchester:

> *"England will need us and how!*
> *For someone to sow, to reap and to hoe,*
> *And someone to master the plough!"*

Mercifully Mrs Steeple didn't venture into the second verse, but their singing had broken the tension.

"Have you heard the WLA version of 'Coming Round the Mountain'? Isobel asked her driver.

"Oh, do tell, Isobel!"

Isobel launched into the ditty she'd sung with Elsie and Lilian through wind and rain:

"If you wanna go to heaven when you die
You must wear a green pullover and a tie
You must wear a khaki bonnet
With WLA on it
If you wanna go to heaven when you die!"

Mrs Steeple hooted with laughter. "My dear girl, I had no idea!"

Isobel didn't go on to sing the really rude version. Mrs Steeple might be a good sport, but everyone had their limits.

Mrs Steeple stopped the car outside the WLA office in Mold. They walked together into the building, passing a young girl in a Land Army uniform in the hallway. She nodded in deference to Mrs Steeple who wished her a good morning and said, "Two teas, Ethel, please, quick as you like. It's been a busy morning."

They walked upstairs to her office on the first floor. "Sit yourself down, Isobel. Now, have you the number of that farm you're interested in?"

"I have, actually. I know it off by heart." Isobel told her the number.

Mrs Steeple dialled it straight away. Luckily, Mr Stubbs was in the farmhouse at Home Farm and answered immediately.

"That's settled then," Mrs Steeple put down the telephone receiver. "Mr Stubbs was very keen to have you and hasn't got anyone else yet. I rather got the impression the situation is urgent. I'll write out the forms and you can take them with you straightaway. No point wasting any more time. Mr Stubbs sounded a bit desperate." She laughed loudly. "Poor man. He'll be glad to see you."

The young girl they'd passed in the lobby downstairs came in, with a tray of two mugs and a packet of biscuits.

"Thank you, Ethel, put them down there. I'll have some post for you shortly. Are we alright for stamps?"

"Yes, ma'am."

"Good girl."

Ethel smiled and went back downstairs.

Isobel sipped from her hot tea and ate three biscuits in quick succession. By the time her mug was drained, Mrs Steeple had finished her paperwork.

"There you are, my dear. All sorted, and I'll send a copy to HQ in today's post."

"Thank you, Mrs Steeple. I'm really grateful."

"Nonsense, it's the ideal solution. Now, you'd best be off. The bus comes on the hour for the station and you don't want to waste any more time. Good luck, keep yourself safe, won't you? Are you quite sure you have enough cash on you for the journey?"

Isobel nodded. "Yes, plenty, thanks. You are so thoughtful, Mrs Steeple."

They shook hands.

"Do keep in touch when you get home, won't you, dear girl? Let me know how you are getting on."

"I will, and thanks again." Isobel picked up her things.

"Good show! Safe journey home!" Mrs Steeple nodded her dismissal.

Isobel walked to the bus stop at the end of the road, as directed by the girl in the office. There was no sign of the bus or even anyone waiting.

Isobel sat on her suitcase, content to wait for the bus to turn up.

She was going home.

CHAPTER THIRTY
NORMANDY
OCTOBER 1940

Lottie lay on her bed, watching a fly flitting about her attic bedroom. She was feeling too lazy to get up and swat it, however much it annoyed her. The small black insect had the same effect upon her as her friend Françoise, now swollen by her unborn child and as restless as the fly.

At least Bernadette seemed happier with the apples gathered in. No extra helpers turned up for the harvest. Bernadette had announced the four women could easily cope as casual workers were thin on the ground these days. Lottie, being younger than Bernadette and not pregnant like Françoise or idle like her mother, had taken the brunt of it. Her back still ached but she'd been glad not to share her attic with strangers. Vats of cider now bubbled in one of the barns. Françoise complained of the smell of it, saying it turned her stomach acid. Most foods seemed to do that although she couldn't get enough of greens, oddly. Bernadette said, with tedious repetition, Françoise needed iron. Once the apples were safely gathered in, Bernadette rewarded them with a tiny glass of two-year-old calvados each, the more palatable end-product of the fermentation process, to celebrate the harvest.

Mireille Blanchard, even though she was Françoise's mother, took less interest in her child than Bernadette. Lottie longed for her own mother, her own home. She even longed for Isobel. The ache for Al was a constant pain; it had become a part of her. She often wondered if she'd be lost without it.

She should sleep, she knew she should. Bernadette would expect her to get up and milk the goats at six tomorrow morning. Neither of the others would do it. Mireille had a knack of absenting herself when there was any work to be done and Françoise could no longer do anything other than complain. Bernadette worked so hard to keep them fed and the farm running, Lottie felt obliged to chip in.

She turned over to her left, away from the fly. Immediately, it flew to the other side of the big attic room, so she still could not avoid its buzzing. She shut her eyes and ignored it; tried to relax, but the image of those German soldiers in their local village only a couple of kilometres away kept sleep at bay. They had swept into Normandy in their cars and trucks, guns at the ready, and their presence had terrified her even at a distance; but now they were really close. Their proximity terrified everyone, even tough old Bernadette.

At least she had resurrected the ancient bicycle she'd found in one of the barns. Dusty and covered in cobwebs, Lottie had prised it from amongst some rusty old tools, relieved to find its tyres stayed full once she had pumped them up. With the aid of some oil to lubricate them, she got the wheels turning and freed the brakes with brute force. It had given her hope when she'd taken it out on the lane, and it hadn't fallen apart. Today, on her way to buying their one meagre loaf in the village square, she'd witnessed the Boche entering the village for the first time, and their strange way of marching. What was it called? The goosestep. Geese were the fiercest creatures you could find. They'd run at you, hissing, unafraid and persistent. Did the Germans model their army on those aggressive birds?

Lottie shivered, although the attic was always warm in the summer; indeed, unbearably hot, when the heat generated underneath rose up and gathered amongst the oak beams and dusty floorboards until it felt like a furnace. If she forgot to close the shutters during the day, adding the sun's rays to the mixture, it was impossible to sleep. But tonight, it was just right. A soft breeze, no longer hinting of ripe apples, rippled through her lofty bedroom. There was no rain drumming on the roof; autumn mists had yet to form, it was quite comfortable really and yet she could not rest, and it wasn't entirely the fly's fault. She could read one of her few books, but she knew them all off by heart now and had only the stub of a candle left - and there was no electricity installed in the attic.

The scene in the village square returned to her mind's eye. She'd witnessed the takeover when coming out of the baker's shop. Dominating it all were the long blood-red flags, their swastikas strutting black on the white circle in their centres, hanging down from the roof of the Mairie, where the local council had their administration and usually hung the French flag with such pride. Their village had been transformed by the presence of these soldiers, walking around as if they owned the place. She, and the two Blanchard women, had come to Bernadette's farm for refuge. It no longer felt like one with their enemy around the corner. Perhaps they should have gone south to the unoccupied zone, like those other refugees.

It had been impossible to ignore the huge German flags. Perhaps that was the point. The Germans had looked like impassive tin soldiers with no expressions on their serious faces. Didn't they have feelings, like the French villagers staring at them, clearly fearful and dismayed? Were they robotic machines like something out of HG Wells' fantastical stories? If only all this *was* fictional. Oh, if only she could close the book and return to normal reality! She willed her mind to picture Cheadle Manor instead. What would her family have been doing today? Out riding? Would Mummy have been visiting the tenants? Would Isobel have spent the day with Al? Ah, that made the heartache worse.

She must think of something else if she was ever going to get to sleep. An owl hooted in the woods beyond Bernadette's fields. Hunting a mouse probably. The natural order of things; the balance of nature. Kill to eat, that's all. As it should be.

Someone stirred in the room below. Françoise and Mireille's bedroom. She heard low voices. That was unusual. Mireille usually ignored anyone making demands upon her. A chair scraped on the wooden floor and she heard a deep moan.

The baby!

Françoise must be having the baby! No wonder she couldn't sleep.

Lottie swung her legs out on to the floor and into her makeshift slippers. Bernadette had made them from some old carpet. They were rough, but they were warm. Lottie slipped on her biggest cardigan, cast off from Mireille's dead Papa. Not the most glamorous garment she'd ever worn but again, it was comfortably warm. She lit her night candle and held it by its brass handle, the saucer catching the dripping wax, turned and climbed one-handed down the ladder-like stairs with the ease born of practice.

She met Bernadette on the landing. Her hair was plaited down her back and she wore a flowery dressing gown. She looked softer dressed like that; Lottie caught a glimpse of Bernadette's younger, prettier self before life had stripped it of joy. Now, she looked excited and a little alarmed.

"How long has she been like this, Bernadette?"

"A long time, it seems. Mireille has been up with her some hours."

"Is there a doctor we could call out?" Lottie held her candle higher, the better to see Bernadette's wrinkled face.

Bernadette shook her head. "There's no-one. And if there was, we couldn't fetch them during the curfew."

"Of course. Do you know what to do?"

"I have had two children of my own and seen many animals enter this mad world, heaven help them. Yes, I know what to do. You," Bernadette never addressed Lottie as anything else, "boil water on the range. Build up the fire. Get clean linen from the cupboard in the hall. Towels and sheets."

Lottie nodded as a howl of pain issued from the other bedroom. Galvanised, she tore down the lower stairs and switched on the one electric light in the centre of the ceiling. She soon had the range fired up and a full kettle on its hob. She fetched in more firewood and put the clean linen over the wooden airer above the range, using the string pulley to take it above scorching height.

Loud wails could now be heard from upstairs and she wondered whether to go up and offer help or stay out of the way.

She thought about what Bernadette had just said. She'd given birth to *two* children? Did Mireille have a brother or a sister somewhere? Lottie winced as a much louder scream pierced the silence of the night. Poor Françoise. Was it always like this? She'd never heard anyone give birth before. The animals at Cheadle Manor had never made a fuss like this.

The kettle came to the boil. Maybe Bernadette and Mireille would like a tisane? Lottie lit a small oil lamp and carried it upstairs.

She knocked softly on the door, but no-one answered. Softly, she opened it and peered round. Françoise, legs bent up and spread wide on her bed, was red and sweating, gritting her teeth in pain, her hair clamped to her head with perspiration.

Françoise's mother stood at the bedside grim-faced, her mouth, for once bare of lipstick, a thin line of compression. She was holding Françoise's hand. Bernadette bent over the foot of the bed and lifted the sheets.

"Um, sorry to intrude. Just wondered if I could bring anything?" Lottie averted her eyes as Bernadette put her hand under the sheet.

Bernadette's head whipped round. "What's that? Yes, bring up some hot water in the kettle and rip up an old sheet into large squares. Bring fresh towels – have you aired them?"

"Yes, Bernadette, I…"

"Good. Now, go."

Lottie nodded and quickly shut the door behind her. Poor Françoise! She looked like she was in agony. Another scream echoed her thoughts and she raced back downstairs to fetch the cloths and water.

As she tore a frayed sheet into strips, more screams ripped through the house. The donkey whinnied in sympathy from the attached barn. Lottie felt beads of sweat under her own hairline and her skin prickled in fear. What if Bernadette didn't know what she was doing? What if the birth wasn't straightforward? Those screams didn't make it sound as if it was. Damn the blasted curfew, she'd offer to fetch a doctor on the pushbike. No-one would see her. They were buried in the country and it was only just over a mile to the village. There was no moon to speak of. Who would know?

She gathered up the linen and placed it carefully in a wicker basket, bracing it against her hip with one hand and took the heavy kettle up in the other. She pushed the door open with her foot and entered the bedroom.

Françoise was panting. She looked exhausted. Sweat was running down her face which was contorted with pain. Lottie had no idea childbirth was this bad.

Bernadette turned to her. She looked worried and tense. "Put them over there, child. Now, pour some hot water into that bowl and soak a couple of cloths in it, then bring them to me."

Lottie did as she was told. Bernadette took them with a steady hand and gave one to her daughter. "Wipe her face, Mireille, can't you see she needs it?" Bernadette held Françoise's legs and braced herself against the foot of the bed. "Now push, little one. Next time it hurts, push."

Lottie didn't know whether to go or stay. No-one seemed interested. She stayed put.

Another grimace and Françoise screwed her face up and groaned.

"That's it, little one. Push as hard as you can."

267

Françoise lay back after her effort. Bernadette looked at her. "The baby's head is out, mon petit chou. The worst is over. When the next pain comes, push again and your baby will be born."

Françoise gave her grandmother a look of sheer loathing before the next contraction. Lottie looked on, fascinated, as a red, slithery baby slipped out of Françoise and on to the bed.

Bernadette glanced over her shoulder. "A towel, stupid!"

Lottie grabbed one and brought it over.

"Well, wrap the child in it, then!"

"What, me?"

"Yes, you! I must cut the cord."

"Oh." Lottie looked down. A grey twisted cord pulsated from the baby's belly back into Françoise. She slipped the warm towel under him while Bernadette tied two linen ribbons about three inches apart around the cord and snipped it cut between them. A tiny spray of fluid sprang from the scissors.

Bernadette looked at her; smiled. "Go on then, wrap him up and give Françoise her son."

As carefully as if he was made of the finest china, Lottie scooped the baby up and took him round the side of the bed to Françoise, who gathered him to her breast.

The baby's hair was black and his skin red.

"He doesn't look like you at all," Mireille said, peering down at him.

"He looks like his father. I shall call him David." Françoise looked up at them all over her new-born baby and treated them to a radiant smile.

CHAPTER THIRTY ONE
CHEADLE MANOR
OCTOBER 1940

Cheadle Manor waited patiently for Isobel in the brooding silence of the October night. There had been no taxi to hire at Woodbury station, it being a Sunday evening as well as wartime, and she hadn't wanted to surprise her mother on the telephone with the request of a lift. Her leaden feet trudged the last few yards towards her old home, but her heart lifted as she finally turned off the main road and slipped quietly past the empty lodge house at the entrance gates. She wanted, for some reason she didn't understand, to see her mother's face when she sprung her arrival on her.

At first, she had relished the solitude of her long walk after the push-and-shove of the journey. Her suitcases didn't weigh much. There had been little to buy on a Welsh hill. The air was cold and crisp, hinting of frost. Not one light welcomed her through the windows but then she hadn't expected any because of the blackout. The stone gables triangulated three deep shadows against the night sky. A quarter moon was her only guide as she took the last weary steps to the servants' back door, praying it wouldn't yet be locked.

She put down her suitcases with relief. Their weight had, after all, dragged her down for the last mile, despite all her newly toned muscles. She'd had so little to eat for such a long time, the pie she'd had at the station where she had changed trains also felt like a lead-weight in her shrunken tummy.

She reached out for the doorknob and gripped its familiar moulded shape. The sensation of it against her hand overwhelmed her and her throat constricted with emotion she could barely control. She knew its ornate markings so well; had touched them every day of her life when she wasn't at school. This reliable old friend undid her as it turned in her roughened hand and let her into her home once more. Blinking back tears, Isobel picked up her luggage. It felt lighter now as renewed energy strengthened her body.

The lingering stale aroma of a roast dinner assailed her nostrils in the servants' quarters. Burnt beef and boiled cabbage. Mrs Andrews had obviously done her worst that day.

No lights greeted her inside the massive building. Everyone must have gone to bed. Isobel supposed there was little to keep her mother or Mr and Mrs Andrews up in the evenings, now they were the only ones living under the vast slate roof that had once housed nearly fifty people, if you counted the ground staff, and double that when they'd hosted country weekends. Her footsteps echoed through the hall, underlining her thoughts. She put down her cases and popped her head round the doors of the drawing room. It struck cold. No fire had been lit there for days, weeks even, and no-one lounged on the sofas around the empty grate. She closed the double doors and turned for the staircase. Picking up her cases again, she mounted the grand stairway. Ghosts from the past whispered of happier times. Once, she thought she heard her father's American drawl, his easy laughter, drawing her upwards to the cosy comfort of her feather bed. How she longed to lay down under clean white sheets again.

She reached the top of the stairs where it branched to left and right along the galleried landing. How strange that Granny wasn't here anymore; her long skirts would never swish against the curved banisters again. No walking stick would be used to point out the faults in her clothes, nor its owner command her to stand up straight and be proud of being so tall. Why did things never stay the same? She had lived in fear of her grandmother's censure and yet, coming home to its absence felt hollow, almost as if this big old house wasn't really home anymore. And there would be no Lottie to chide and tease her in the morning either. She had no way of even knowing if her sister was still alive.

But her mother was here and Al just a mile or two away. Isobel smiled at the thought and the whispering voices from the past quietened enough for her to hear padding footsteps and her mother's bedroom door open. A flickering candle cast shadows against the wall.

"Who's there?" Cassandra sounded scared but determined.

"Mummy!"

"Isobel! My darling, darling girl! You're home!"

Cassandra put her candle down on a little table against the wall and opened her arms wide. Isobel dropped both her cases and ran into her embrace.

"My dear girl! What has happened to you? You're as thin as a rake! I can count every rib you possess. Come down to the kitchen this instant and I'll make you some cocoa. I want to hear all your news. Are you on leave? How long have you got? Here, let me put your cases in your bedroom."

Isobel's face was as wet as her mother's as their tears met. She wiped her eyes with the heel of her work-hardened hand and smiled.

"Oh, Mummy! You are so kind. I had forgotten how good you are!"

"You have had a rough time, haven't you?" Cassandra lifted her candle up to examine her daughter's face. Isobel read the shock reflected back in her mother's.

"What have they done to you? Come, I'll call Mrs Andrews and she can make up your bed while we have our hot drink."

"Oh, don't disturb her, Mummy. Isn't she asleep?"

"Nonsense! She would never forgive me if I did it myself and didn't tell her you were home. You're *home*! Oh, Isobel, you don't know how much I've longed to have you here!"

They went into Isobel's old bedroom and, once she had drawn the curtains across, Cassandra flicked on the bedside lamp. Looking around the softly lit room of her childhood, Isobel marvelled at the space she had taken for granted all those years. The luxury of the quilted bed with its silk hangings, her own water-colour paintings on the wall, the pretty dressing table with its three-sided mirror and enamel-backed brush and comb set. All was dust-free and immaculate. Someone had taken care to keep it in order; everything had been waiting for her return. She was undone. A great sob welled up inside her and wrenched her thin body.

"Oh, my dear child! Come here, let me hold you."

Isobel leant against her mother and let the tears come.

There was a knock on the door a few minutes later.

"My lady? Is something wrong? I heard voices. Oh, it's Miss Isobel home!" Mrs Andrews, looking older than Isobel remembered but still thankfully as robust as ever, peered around the door, an oil lamp in her hand.

Cassandra released Isobel. "Ah, Mrs Andrews. I'm glad you are here. See, we have our prodigal daughter back, well, one of them at least. Isn't it wonderful? Now, I'm going to take her down to the kitchen and make her some hot cocoa. Could you make up the bed for her and, I think, a hot bedpan to warm the sheets would be a good idea?"

"Ay, my lady, of course, and may I say Miss Isobel, it is very good to see you home."

"Thank you, Mrs Andrews. I can't tell you how good it is to be back but I'm sorry if I've got you out of bed. I didn't mean to arrive so late, but the trains were awful, it being a Sunday."

"Och, never you mind about that, Miss. I can't think of a better reason to be up and about at this time of night. If Miss Charlotte were back too, it would feel like Christmas!" Mrs Andrews blinked rapidly, then bustled away muttering about airing linen.

"I'll put the kettle on the hob downstairs for the bedpan, Mrs Andrews." Cassandra called out to the housekeeper's retreating back. "Come on, darling. Let's get that drink. You need something nourishing by the looks of you."

Isobel submitted with gratitude.

Over cocoa, Isobel poured out her experiences to her mother, who sat gazing at her with focussed attention, not speaking much but nodding and murmuring encouraging noises, as Isobel told her of the meanness of Mrs Williams's housekeeping, the lecherous stares of her husband and the sheer hard graft of a hill farm.

"Mind you, I don't blame Mrs Williams. I think he hits her, you know. Once or twice I saw bruises on her arms and red marks on her sallow cheeks. Wretched man. I feel sorry for any evacuees that end up there."

"How dreadful, darling, but he didn't hit *you*, did he?"

"Oh, no. I soon learned to keep him at a distance. A pitchfork makes a good weapon." Isobel sipped her cocoa, relishing the milky richness of it.

"Good for you! But what next?"

"I've written to Farmer Stubbs, asking him if I can be a land girl there and Mrs Steeple has also requested my transfer to Home Farm and spoke to him on the telephone."

"Why didn't you tell me? I could have put in a word for you. I can't think of a better arrangement."

"There simply wasn't time, it all happened in a rush at the end and anyway, I didn't want to bother you or raise your hopes if it didn't work out. It's a bit of a cheek requesting a specific posting like this. I'm supposed to go wherever I'm put really, but Mrs Steeple, the WLA officer, was very understanding and swung it for me." Isobel pulled a crumpled letter from her coat pocket. "I didn't even wait for the confirmation from HQ but hopped on the train straightaway. It was all set up with Farmer Stubbs in one telephone call. I start next week."

"That's marvellous. I think we'd better build you up a bit before you go back to work." Cassandra smiled, then sighed. "I have news of my own."

Isobel drained her mug and wiped the chocolate liquid from her top lip with the back of her hand.

Cassandra frowned. "I can see your manners have slipped a bit, living on a farm."

Isobel laughed. "It's done me good, really. I met some lovely land girls, Elsie and Lilian. I must write and tell them where I am. They worked at the Williams's too but bunked off to the farm up the hill. Soft billet there, alright! But what's your news, Mummy? Have you heard from Lottie?"

"I wish I could say yes to that with all my heart but, no, it's about our home. Cheadle Manor has been requisitioned by the army. It's going to be a hospital, can you believe?"

"Oh, my goodness! Somehow, I never thought it would really happen."

"Sadly, it will. There's no way I can refuse."

"Maybe you'll be able to help them?"

"Perhaps, although I think they'll see me as more of a spare part. We may even have to move out."

"And how's everyone else?"

Cassandra chuckled. "I expect you mean the Phipps? They are so busy at the rubber factory, you wouldn't believe!"

"Are they making stuff for the war?" Isobel put her empty mug down on the table.

"Goodness me, yes! The army have put in some massive orders – parts of gas masks, windscreen seals, parachute fixings – you name it. They've taken on six, no eight, more staff – all girls of course." Cassandra picked up Isobel's mug and took it to the sink.

Over the sound of the tap running, Isobel asked the question uppermost in her mind all along. "So, Al's busy too, then? And has lots of girls eyeing him up, I'll bet."

Cassandra smiled. She picked up a tea towel and dried the mug. "You've been dying to ask about him, haven't you? Yes, he is busy but I'm sure he'll find time to see you tomorrow, darling. He's never shown any interest in anyone but you, as far as I can see. Now, let's get you up to bed so you can get some beauty sleep before you see the dear boy, shall we?"

Isobel needed no encouragement. Soon she was tucked up in her own bed, as if she was six years old again. How simple life seemed looking back. Excited though she was at the prospect of surprising Al tomorrow, she was asleep within minutes.

The next morning, she was woken by the sun streaming into her bedroom. She blinked sleep away from her eyes and gazed around at the familiar space. She got up quickly, glad to wash properly in a real bath at last, even if the water was tepid and shallow, and raced downstairs for a hearty breakfast. In broad daylight, her mother looked washed out and Isobel could see that she had aged years rather than the months she had been away. Outside, as she went to get her bicycle from the old stables, her home also looked worn out, shabby and neglected and the gardens unkempt. Woodbine and ivy clambered up its walls in a disorganised scramble. Isobel was glad she was home. It was time she did something about it.

Al's face, when she turned up at the Katherine Wheel Garage after pedalling as hard as her weary legs could go, was as flabbergasted and pleased as she'd hoped.

She found him pumping up the tyres on the Bedford lorry with a foot pump. He had his back turned to her as his leg forced the air into the tyres in rhythmic compressions.

"That looks like hard work."

Al wheeled around at the sound of her voice. The pump fell over sideways against the tyre. Isobel heard the whoosh of air escaping. "Isobel? Is it really you?"

"It's me alright!"

They both started running towards each other and collided halfway. Explanations had to wait while their lips met and spilled out their feelings in a long, passionate kiss. She stopped for breath, withdrawing her face but throwing her arms around Al instead.

"My God, Bella, you're like a beanpole! Oh, but it's so good to see you!" Al mumbled into her ear and squeezed the remaining breath out of her.

"And you, and you, my love," Isobel kissed his neck, damp from exertion. She was no stranger to sweat these days after working on the farm and found it sexy rather than distasteful. She wanted to kiss him all over, if she was honest.

Breathless, she stood back, before she disgraced herself and then was very glad she had, as Katy Phipps appeared from the garage workshop.

"Isobel! How lovely to see you, my dear. How was Wales? Are you home on leave? Al never said you were coming." Katy treated Isobel to one of her rare but ravishing smiles.

Isobel ran her hand through her wavy blonde hair, trying and failing to tame it, as ever. "Hello Aunt Katy. Nice to see you. Al couldn't tell you I was coming, because he didn't know! I'm not on leave, I'm home for good. I'm going to work at Home Farm as a land girl there."

Al let out a whoop of joy. "That's wonderful! Are you going to live at the manor?"

"For the time being, I think so, but it's being requisitioned by the Government, hadn't you heard?"

"No, this is big news. What's it going to be used for?" Katy squinted into the sunshine.

Isobel shrugged. "A hospital, Mummy said. I think we might have to move out – wouldn't it be a great joke if we went to your old house?"

"West Lodge? Surely not?"

Isobel nodded. "It's a possibility - it's the only place vacant at the moment and it'll be convenient for

Mummy to keep an eye on things - but I'm sure it won't come to that. I expect we'll squeeze into a corner of the manor house."

"But what about the Andrews? Surely your mother isn't planning on having no help at all?" Katy looked shocked.

"You'll have to ask Mummy all the details. I think it's all in the planning stages at the moment."

Al chipped in. "And anyway, Mum, the main thing is, Bella's home." He slipped his arm around her waist and squeezed.

Katy laughed. "Oh, young love! I'll leave you in peace. Tell your mother I'll pop up to the manor later today and get the full story, won't you? Oh, and feel free to stop and have a cuppa. I think I can spare my son for an hour or two." Katy kissed her on her cheek. "Good to have you back. It'll mean the world to your mum. Pity Lottie hasn't returned from France. Cass is worried sick about her now it's occupied. She doesn't even know where Lottie is. I'm glad she's got one of her girls with her at least. See you later."

Katy turned to Al. "Two hours, no more, mind. That lot of components must get to Portsmouth this afternoon." She nodded to the lorry. "I'll get your Uncle Billy to load it for you."

"Thanks, Mum."

"Get on with you." Katy disappeared across the yard and disappeared into the factory from where a constant thump, thump noise proved it was in full production.

"Come inside and I'll put the kettle on." Al took her hand, kissed it and drew her indoors. "Gran's out visiting. We've got the place to ourselves. Come here, you."

CHAPTER THIRTY TWO
CHEADLE MANOR
CHRISTMAS 1940 - NEW YEAR 1941

While the autumn of 1940 was blissful as far as Al's personal life was concerned, his bubble of happiness at having Isobel back at home was punctured by the extent of the Luftwaffe's blitzes, not just on London but Coventry and Birmingham in November and, just before Christmas, Liverpool got badly hit.

And for some reason he couldn't fathom, it was the Liverpool bombings that bothered Isobel.

"Don't tell me you're fretting about Farmer Williams and his miserable wife, Bella?" It was a Sunday morning, crisp with frost, and they were enjoying a rare moment of leisure, walking through the woods above Cheadle Manor with no-one to interrupt them.

Isobel gave a shaky laugh. She looked away from Al, towards the trees, as she answered, "No, of course not, but obviously I'm concerned about Lilian and Elsie."

"Oh yes, I'd forgotten about them. I'm sure they'll be alright, though, tucked away at Mrs Jones's farm. It was only the docks that were targeted."

"Hmm." Isobel didn't look very reassured.

Al soon forgot the unsettling conversation, once he returned to work on the Monday morning, but driving the lorry no longer satisfied him. More and more, Al chafed at not being part of the bigger fight. Although the skies had quietened and the threat of immediate invasion had receded, at least for now, he still itched to play his part against the increasingly aggressive Hun, but then felt torn because he didn't want to spend a minute longer than he had to away from Isobel. They were both kept so busy, there was little enough time to see each other as it was. When they did, he could barely keep his hands off her.

One freezing cold night just before Christmas, Cassandra put on a modest dinner party to celebrate the solstice. Soon, Cheadle Manor would be given over to medical staff as a hospital. Everyone was aware it could be the last time they sat around the polished dining room table together.

He arrived early so he could snatch a moment with Isobel. "So, who's coming to this do, then, Bella?"

"Oh, the usual crowd, you know, and, um, someone I met in Wales. A painter, actually, who was very kind to me and who's going to stay over the Christmas holiday."

"Oh?" Al pictured an elderly spinster daubing a canvas and giving Isobel tea in a little cottage but, before she could say more, his parents turned up and their intimate moment was lost.

So, Al wasn't best pleased to find a handsome male stranger amongst the more familiar faces. He was even less so when Isobel introduced him to Geraint Lloyd while the sherry glasses were being filled by Andrews before dinner. Having made the introduction, Isobel was called away to meet some new guests arriving. Left alone, Al felt at a disadvantage standing opposite this tall Welshman, whose cultured manners showed he was very much at ease in the drawing room of Cheadle Manor.

Cassandra seemed especially keen on the newcomer and came over to join them. "Isn't it marvellous, Al? Isobel met Geraint in the wilds of the Welsh hills when she was posing as a shepherdess. Rather a romantic image, don't you think?"

Al didn't think that at all, not for one moment. And then, alarmingly, he realised it could well have been. "Pleased to meet you, Mr Lloyd." He mumbled the greeting rather incoherently.

Geraint inclined his head graciously. "You too. Albert, um, Phipps, isn't it? I assume that lovely lady over there is your mother?" He had a rich baritone voice, damn his eyes.

"That's right. Owns the garage and rubber factory on the London Road."

"Does she now? How enterprising. My father has some factories in Liverpool but we're in paper manufacture. Luckily we escaped the worst of the bombing."

Aha! – Liverpool was it? – now he understood Isobel's concern about the blitz there. "Only some? So, more than one, then?" Al knew he was being rude, but he no longer cared.

"Just a few. And what do you do, Albert? Not joined up yet? I'm a bit past it for this one."

"I can see that."

Geraint smiled wryly. "Is it so obvious?"

Cassandra, who had remained silent through this exchange, watching with narrowed eyes, now laughed and stepped between them. "Nonsense, Geraint, you're in the prime of life and I'm sure you're doing valuable war work up in Liverpool. It's just as important to keep the cogs of industry turning as it is to fight."

"Excuse me." Al couldn't bear to watch his hostess cosying up to this rich industrialist and detached himself from them.

He went over to Isobel, who was talking to old Dr Benson, now bent with age but with his great shock of white hair as thick and luxurious as ever.

"Excuse me," Al said again, nodding at the elderly doctor. "Isobel, might I have a word?"

Dr Benson smiled. "Oh, don't mind me, you two. I need a chair anyway."

Isobel immediately steered the doctor into a sofa by the fire and bent her blond head over his white one with solicitous care. Dr Benson waved her away. "Never mind the old men, go and see to that young one!"

Isobel smiled and straightened up. She walked towards Al and his heart felt like it flipped over, but his words came out all wrong. "So, who's this middle-aged friend of yours, then? You've never mentioned him before."

Isobel looked across him over to where Geraint Lloyd still stood chatting amiably to her mother. Cassandra was nodding and smiling. She looked very relaxed, almost happy. "Haven't I? How silly of me. He's called Geraint Lloyd and we met when I was a land girl in Wales. He's such a nice man and very artistic. He wants to paint a portrait of me, so that's why he's come to stay over the Christmas holidays."

"Does he now?"

"Yes, he did a few sketches in Wales, but there wasn't time for more, I was always so busy. There's not much farming to be done at this time of the year, so it seemed an ideal opportunity."

"It's certainly given him an ideal opportunity."

"What do you mean, Al?" Isobel's eyes widened in surprise. Surely, she couldn't be as innocent as she was making out?

"Oh, come on, he might be over the hill, but the way he looks at you leaves nothing to the imagination about the way he feels."

"Oh, it's not like that! I see him more as an uncle, and a very kind one at that. He really put old Farmer Williams in his place and made my placement there easier to bear."

"Hmm. Very kind of him, I'm sure. Funny you never mentioned it."

Andrews called them into supper, and they all took partners. Isobel went in on Al's arm, but it was stiff with anger and they were the only pair walking through the hallway to the dining room in awkward silence.

The evening passed pleasantly enough, but Al had no further moments alone with Isobel. She seemed determined to keep him at arm's length and suggested cards after dinner, which prevented all but the most general of conversations. Eventually, the party broke up amongst sincere wishes for a happy Christmas, despite all the hardships and bereavements of war.

Al stayed on after his parents and the few other guests had left.

"Well, I say goodnight, my dears." Cassandra kissed them both lightly on the cheek.

"I think I'll turn in too," Geraint held out his arm to his hostess.

"Thank you, Geraint." Cassandra took his proffered arm, and to Al's deep relief, they departed together.

As soon as the big house hushed, he grabbed Isobel's hand and drew her towards the fire, still blazing away in the hearth.

Bella cuddled up to him on the sofa and Al finally relaxed. "Phew, we're alone together at last."

He decided he'd jump straight in. These private moments had become rare.

He kissed her on the mouth, then drew back slightly, holding her lightly in his arms. "Let's get married now, Bella. What's the point of waiting? We might be out in the sticks, but a stray bomb might get the lorry one day and catch me out near Southampton or Portsmouth. They're both target ports. Or I might drive the lorry into the ditch one of these long, dark nights."

"How cheerful you are tonight." Isobel, usually so free with her kisses, withdrew from his embrace.

Al pulled her back and wouldn't let go. "Just facing facts. Working on the farm isn't without danger either. Agricultural accidents happen all the time."

"Charming." Isobel insisted on wriggling free of him. She turned to face him. He marvelled at her beauty all over again. For once, she wasn't in her manly Land Army uniform, but wearing an old blue velvet dress that emphasised the colour of her eyes. He could drown in those eyes.

"I don't mean to be pessimistic, Bella, but it's true that anything could happen in wartime. I love you and I want to love you properly before I…"

"Before you what?" Isobel folded her arms.

"I wasn't going to say anything till after Christmas," Al began.

"Then you haven't got long. It's Christmas Eve in a couple of days – your twentieth birthday and my seventeenth. Oh, I wish we knew if Lottie was alright. It's awful not being able to celebrate with her; she would have loved this evening." Isobel reached past him and expertly nudged a smouldering log with the toe of her shoe.

Immediately, it burst into flames, lighting up the drawing room of the manor house, which only had one lamp on in deference to the long hours of black out. How short the days were at this time of year. How little time they had left before he had to go.

Al drew her back to his side. He turned his face towards her, memorising every little detail of hers.

"Oh dear, Al. You do look solemn, and it's not about Lottie, is it?" Isobel faced him squarely and held both his hands. "You're going to sign up, aren't you?"

Al nodded, glad she had saved him from spelling it out. "Yes. I've decided to go for it in January. As you said, I'll be twenty years old and I've had enough of waiting to fight. It's time I did my duty. I can't stand not being part of it."

Isobel nodded. He watched her Adam's apple move up and down, barely discernible in her long, smooth neck as she swallowed. She blinked but she didn't cry. He'd been half hoping she might. Was that because her heart was no longer his, but belonged to the tall, suave Geraint?

"I see." Isobel looked away towards the fire. The bright light from the flames flickered over her face.

"Do you, my love? Do you really understand?" Al squeezed her hands.

"I think so, but of course I don't like it. It will be unbearable with you not here." She gave an answering pressure within his grasp. He pulled her closer and spoke softly into her ear.

"I know. I hate the thought of not being with you all the time, but I couldn't live with myself if I stayed home for the duration. I'm not a conchie." Al released her again, so he could look at her. "But that's why I want to get married now, don't you see? Then we could be together properly, you know, as man and wife, not all these fumbles on the side, snatching a few minutes here and there when we can be together."

"You must do what you think is best, Al, I won't stop you, but I don't want to get married yet. I'm too young to make that commitment – oh, don't look at me like that! I will never, ever love anyone else but, if we were together, properly as you said, I might have a baby and I'm just not ready for that responsibility. Let's face it, the world is in too much of a mess to bring another poor soul into it."

"There are ways around that, Bella."

"Yes, I know, Lilian and Elsie explained all that to me, but they also said none are fool-proof."

"Not completely, but would it matter? If I did die," Al placed his finger across her lips to silence her. She kissed it. "If I didn't come back, wouldn't it be a good thing if you *were* expecting my baby?"

"Not for me, Al, much as I love you. In normal times I would love to have a dozen of your babies. We have to face the fact that we are at war and it's not a time to be building families. We will just have to hope that we both come through it and then, who knows? We'll have all the children you want. How many is that exactly?"

Al tried to laugh. It didn't work. "It's because I'm not good enough, isn't it? You don't want to start a family with a no-hoper like me. I suppose Geraint Lloyd is dripping in money."

"Now that's just silly. I love you just as you are, you know I do. I wouldn't care if you didn't have a button to share."

"Well, I'll show you, and everyone else. I'm going to sign up for the RAF. I saw those Spitfires giving the

Germans hell and I knew then that's what I wanted to do. The one thing I am good at is driving and flying a plane can't be that different, can it?" Al dropped her hands and got up. He plunged his hands in his trouser pockets and stood with his back to the fire, comforted by its warmth, until he remembered that the pilot of that Spitfire had dropped into the sea with his uniform in flames.

"You'd be a brilliant pilot, Al, but their casualty rates are the highest of all the services. Won't you consider the army?"

"Nope. I've made up my mind. We'll have a bloody good Christmas and New Year, well, as best we can with rationing, and then I'll sign up. I was hoping we'd have a winter wedding too but that takes two and you don't want to marry me so, as quickly as I can, I shall apply to the RAF. I'll be called up soon anyway."

Isobel didn't join him by the fire. She sat, looking cool and composed. Different, like an adult twenty years older than her years. "If that's your decision, Al, I will respect it. I do want to marry you and I hope I will, but not yet."

"Fine. That's settled then."

They stayed apart.

After five minutes of hoping she'd relent, Al left. The sound of the lorry tyres scrunching the stones on Cheadle Manor drive drowned out the angry doubts clamouring for attention in his head as he accelerated away, far too fast, wishing it was already an aeroplane in flight. Part of him longed to escape and another dreaded what might happen in his absence.

CHAPTER THIRTY THREE
NORMANDY
DECEMBER 1940

The baby was crying again. Lottie lay in her bed up in the attic, counting the minutes before Françoise got up to feed him.

Too many.

When silence descended once more, Lottie couldn't get back to sleep. She got up to fetch her overcoat and laid it on the bedcovers to insulate herself against the bitter cold.

Socks. They might help thaw her feet. She drew on a pair donated by Bernadette's dead husband. They were far too big for her, but they were made of pure wool. It was worth the itchiness to feel their warmth. Before returning to the icy sheets, she went to the window, opened a shutter a crack and looked out. The frost had already bitten into the frozen ground when she'd gone to bed. Now, little shards of snow cascaded down from the blackest sky she'd ever seen and immediately settled on the cold, metal-hard earth. She shivered, retrieved her coat from the bed and put it around her shoulders. Falling snowflakes always fascinated her. They amplified the deep hush only found in the nadir of a winter's night.

Good job she'd put extra straw in the goats' barn. She sniffed the glacial air. The smell of snow, recognisable anywhere, assaulted her nostrils with astringent purity. It smelled like fresh linen off the washing line, full of oxygen, clean and unsullied.

How inappropriate in this Godforsaken place. Everyone was remarking on how well the German soldiers were behaving. Correct. That was the universal term being bandied about. Correct, my foot. Lottie hadn't trusted the uneasy peace between the occupiers and those they thought subdued. Today's events had borne out her suspicions.

That morning, Lottie had cycled the two kilometres to the local village to buy fresh bread. As she approached the boulangerie, she'd noticed a schoolteacher leading a troop of children across the village square towards the linden trees in its centre. One of the children mimicked the occupying soldiers parading up and down the square, copying their jackboots marching in perfect time like a single metronome. The officer in charge of the men broke away from his troop and went to clip the young boy around his ears, but the youth neatly dodged the blow. The teacher, a blonde young man wearing horn-rimmed glasses, immediately stepped between them. Lottie couldn't hear what was said, but the German officer, a thick-set middle-aged man, much shorter than the young teacher, looked threatening and wouldn't stop shouting. Everyone in the street stopped in their tracks and watched as the soldiers immediately reached for their rifles and raised them at the crocodile of children.

At children!

The teacher spread his arms wide and low to protect them. None of them could have been more than eleven years old and each looked terrified, except the one who had play-acted the German march. He still looked mutinous. The portly officer glanced over towards Lottie and the other bystanders. He looked furious at all the attention; the disruption to the routine calm his troops had so carefully crafted.

An old man, with a scar down one side of his face, standing next to Lottie, muttered, "Keep moving. Don't look at them. It might save Monsieur Thibault."

He shoved Lottie in the back, and she pulled her eyes away from the drama. Other villagers did the same, instantly united, tacitly understanding an audience would only escalate events.

The German officer returned his angry gaze to the teacher, who stood his ground. Suddenly, the older man with the facial scar fell to the ground and thrashed about, as if he was having an epileptic fit.

"Oh la, la! It's Monsieur Dubois again. That's the second time this month he's had one of his sessions." Madame Leroy came hurrying out from her boulangerie, flapping her floury apron, creating puffs of white clouds around her substantial frame.

The German officer whirled around at all the disturbance. He strode over. Lottie let out her breath.

The German spoke in French with a strong guttural inflection. "What is happening with this man?"

"He's having one of his fits, officer." Madame Leroy knelt on the cobblestones and leaned over Monsieur Dubois who was still performing his rendition of an epileptic seizure.

"A fit? What sort of a fit?"

"Monsieur-le-docteur calls them, 'une crise grand mal', monsieur.'

While the German officer was interrogating Madame Leroy, Lottie left the scene and walked discreetly across the square to where the young teacher still stood with his children in the line of fire.

"I think you should walk the children quietly away." Lottie stood near the schoolchildren, pretending to search for something in her basket. "Monsieur Dubois can't keep up the show for much longer. Make yourself scarce."

"I will not back down." Monsieur Thibault looked fierce behind his spectacles.

"Think of the children." Lottie still rummaged in her basket.

There was a fraction of a moment's pause. "You are right. Thank you. Come on, you lot. Back to school."

The young man's jaw clenched tight, but he forced a smile and encouraged the children to move away.

Lottie decided to risk more advice. "Go quickly. Actually, I'll come with you. I'll walk behind the last of the children."

Monsieur Thibault nodded at her. "If you must. I can manage perfectly well on my own."

"I'm sure, but the children look terrified. Go on, I'll bring up the rear."

Monsieur Thibault gripped the hands of the two children at the front of the queue and walked briskly to the corner of the square, towards the church.

A German subordinate broke away from the soldiers still standing to attention, their guns raised and pointing at the teacher, waiting for orders. None of them appeared to know what to do as the children moved away. The younger officer strode towards his senior officer, who still stood, apparently fascinated by the writhing Monsieur Dubois on the pavement. Quite a crowd had gathered around the star of the show and formed a tight-knit group around his prostrate form. They surrounded the German officer and obscured his view of his soldiers.

As the last child reached the corner of the square, Lottie looked back. The younger officer had only just reached his elder colleague through the cluster of villagers outside the boulangerie. He was muttering into the ear of the senior German, who turned around but, being short, he couldn't see over the heads of the French people encircling him. Before he could catch sight of her, Lottie slipped into the lane between the church and the school, whisking the last all-too-curious little girl along with her who was walking too slowly, craning her neck trying to see what was happening in the square.

As soon as they gained the narrow lane that ran between the church and the presbytery, Monsieur Thibault broke into a trot. "Come on, kids. We must run to the school."

The children, excited and frightened, eagerly followed suit and ran towards the school at the end of the little lane. Within three minutes, no more, they were all inside the school and Monsieur Thibault locked the door behind them.

The smell of ink and chalk, reminiscent of her own carefree school days, instantly calmed Lottie. She bundled the children into the classroom and told them to sit at their desks.

"Are you a teacher too?" Monsieur Thibault turned around from locking the door.

"No, I'm not."

"You seem to have the knack of getting the children to obey you."

"It's a fluke because they are so scared."

"I doubt it."

One of the little girls began to cry. Monsieur Thibault went to the dais and stood behind his desk.

"Do not fear, children. We are safe now. We must learn from this lesson. Although we may not like the German soldiers telling us what to do, we would be wise not to make fun of them. Jacques! Come here."

Lottie went to comfort the little girl who was so upset, while the boy who had caused the trouble by his accurate miming of the Germans, shuffled his way to the teacher's desk, his head hanging down and feet dragging.

Lottie put her arm around the girl and rubbed her back. The girl leaned into her and put her shaking little arms around Lottie's waist. A few other girls joined them, and more tears began to flow.

Monsieur Thibault made them all jump. He clapped his hands. "That is enough crying, girls. Return to your desks. We must not lose our courage. Thank you, Miss...I'm sorry I don't know your name?"

"Charlotte, um, Perrot."

"Perrot? Are you related to Madame Bernadette Perrot who keeps goats?"

Lottie nodded.

"I have never heard of you."

"Distant relative from Paris."

"Ah yes, so many relatives have rediscovered their rural roots since the Germans invaded, haven't they? Quite the miracle."

Monsieur Thibault seemed to lose interest in her. He turned to Jacques. "You must wear the dunce's hat and stand in the corner for a whole hour under the picture of Maréchel Pétain. I want you to reflect during that time about the stupidity of mocking the German soldiers. You have put all your classmates in jeopardy. Do you understand, Jacques?"

The boy nodded but didn't look up.

"Here, put the cap on and stand over there. We will talk again once the hour is up." The boy walked over to the corner after pulling the cap on to his head and stood with his back to the class.

"Good. Now let us resume our work. We will turn to literature today and I will read to you, while you all sit down and recover your courage and your calm. Miss Perrot? You are free to leave us. We thank you for your assistance. Say thank you and goodbye to the lady, children."

The children obediently chorused, "Merci et au revoir, Mademoiselle Perrot."

Lottie was left with no choice but to depart.

As she passed by the teacher's desk, he nodded at her. "Thank you for helping us, Mademoiselle. We are obliged to you."

"I am glad you are all safe and nothing awful happened." Lottie spoke softly, so the children couldn't hear.

"Not this time, perhaps. Goodbye, Mademoiselle Perrot."

"Goodbye, Monsieur Thibault."

Lottie let herself out of the school room. As she passed through the school gate, she almost bumped into the German officer in charge of the troops stationed in the village. He walked purposefully towards her with some of his men. They were on the march again and this time they had a quarry. There was not room for them all in the narrow passage between the church and the school.

"Out of my way mademoiselle, if you please."

Lottie, outnumbered, gave way and pressed her body flat against the stone wall. The soldiers filed past her, looking neither to right nor left. Were they automatons? Had they no feelings? Did not one of them care about the children inside the building? Some of them didn't look much older than schoolkids themselves.

The short officer banged on the door. When it opened, all the soldiers, bar two, disappeared inside with their weapons held high and ready for action. Lottie couldn't leave. She waited and listened.

She heard loud voices but couldn't make out their meaning. Five minutes later, Monsieur Thibault appeared, a soldier on either side, frogmarching the teacher up the lane back towards the church.

"What are you doing?" They ignored Lottie.

The officer was the last to appear. He stopped when he saw Lottie and addressed her, echoing the words of his captive a few minutes ago.

"Are you also a teacher in this school? You went with the children just now."

"Not really, I…"

"No matter. You should go back to them. There is no adult left in there. The other teacher has been sacked. She was Jewish and not suitable to teach impressionable young children."

"But where are you taking Monsieur Thibault?"

"He is coming with us to our headquarters for interrogation."

"But he did nothing wrong! He only protected his schoolchildren."

The officer frowned under his peaked cap. "That is for us to decide. We cannot have our soldiers ridiculed."

"But..."

"Goodbye, mademoiselle. See to the children if you want to be helpful, or would you rather come with us? Where are your papers?" The officer's cold eyes looked very uncompromising.

"I don't have them on me."

"Next time, you will be inspected."

Lottie waited a moment, dreading more questions, but the soldiers didn't stop. They pulled Monsieur Thibault along roughly. He tried to resist but it was hopeless. He was a slight young man and one against many.

Lottie shook her head in disbelief at the swiftness of events. Then she went inside the school again.

The children were gathered around the windows, their noses pressed against the glass. Some of the younger girls were crying again, huddled together in the corner underneath the portrait of Maréchel Pétain, hero of Verdun and Chief of the whole of France, now safely ensconced in Vichy out of harm's way.

As soon as she appeared, they all clamoured around her, seeking reassurance. She didn't even know their names, only Jacques, the boy who had caused it all.

"What will happen to Monsieur Thibault, mademoiselle?" It was Jacques, his young face white with shock, who spoke.

"I don't know, Jacques. We must wait and see. Now come on, little ones. What story was Monsieur Thibault reading to you? Let's find it, shall we?"

Lottie stayed with the children all morning until their parents came to collect them at lunchtime. A few had left earlier, hurried home by anxious mothers. When the last child left, she didn't know whether to lock up, and if she did, where on earth to deposit the key. She tidied up the schoolroom and closed the windows. Whom should she notify? What was happening to that young teacher? She shuddered to think. She couldn't stay in the village indefinitely; she would already be missed at the smallholding. They would have missed their bread even more.

She decided to write a note and take it to the church. Someone there would surely know who to give it to. She sat at the teacher's desk and took up the fountain pen that rested in the wooden groove, next to the inkwell.

She tore a piece of paper from an exercise book in a pile on the desk.

But to whom should she address it? She filled the pen with ink and began to write.

The sound of the door opening startled her. She turned around, shocked to see Monsieur Thibault, both eyes puffy with bruises and his lip oozing blood from a cut, standing in the doorway.

He swayed, looking like he might faint. Lottie threw down the pen and went to him.

"Ah, Monsieur Thibault! Come and sit down before you fall."

"Are you inviting me to sit at my own desk?"

"I suppose I am. Come." Lottie put her arm around his slim waist and lead him to the teacher's chair.

Monsieur Thibault limped as he walked, obviously in considerable pain.

"The Germans did this to you?"

Monsieur Thibault nodded, wincing as he did so. "The bastards." He took off his spectacles, laying them on the desk with trembling fingers.

"Let me get you some water." Lottie had found the little kitchenette earlier when searching for water for the children. She took the jug she'd used then and refilled it afresh. Coming back to the school room, she poured out a glass for the young man. He drank a great draught straight down, emptying it in one go. Lottie poured out another.

"Thank you." Monsieur Thibault took another gulp.

Lottie waited. After a few moments the young teacher revived. He ran his fingers through his blonde hair, now matted and dark against his scalp and ran his hand across his brow, avoiding the bruises around his blue eyes.

Through swollen lids he looked at Lottie a long time, studying her face thoughtfully. "You have been very kind, especially to the children. Did you stay all morning with them?

"Yes, it was nothing. I couldn't just leave them. A lot of parents came early and took them home."

"Ah, yes. I doubt anyone is in ignorance of my foolishness by now."

"I don't think you were foolish. You were simply protecting the children in your care. And it looks like you paid for it." Lottie fetched another glass and poured herself some water.

"I was stupid to take them across the square. I should have remembered the Boche always march at that time of day, they are creatures of habit it seems, but we were studying the barks of trees. I was showing the children how to identify them, even in winter. Stupid, stupid! I should have stayed indoors and kept them safe."

"None of them came to any harm."

"Not this time but Jacques won't escape their notice twice. And they'll keep an eye on me now. Good job I had my identification papers handy. If they'd thought I was Jewish, I wouldn't be sitting here now, I'd be out of a job like poor Mademoiselle Mayer, or worse."

"At least you have been released and your cuts will heal. Excuse me, but I must go, Bernadette will wonder where I am." Lottie got up to leave.

"What relation did you say you were to Madame Perrot? You don't look the least bit alike."

"I didn't."

"Ah."

"Goodbye Monsieur Thibault."

"Thanks again, Mademoiselle…Perrot."

"I'll let myself out."

"I think you'll have to; I'm not sure I'll ever move again!" Monsieur Thibault gave a grunt. It might have been an attempt at a laugh, Lottie couldn't be sure. She smiled a goodbye anyway and shut the door quietly behind her.

The village square was deserted. An air of suspenseful tension lay across the cobbled expanse. The three linden trees, bare of leaves, stood sentinel in its centre, bearing silent witness. She could swear blinds twitched in the windows, but no-one appeared. She found her bicycle and pedalled back to Bernadette's, her basket empty and her mind struggling to believe that the drama she had witnessed had been real.

It was a relief to return to the smallholding, and her knees shook as she propped the bicycle against the ribbed old walls of the farmhouse and went into the kitchen.

"Where's the bread?"

Not, 'how are you; are you okay?' Trust Bernadette to keep focussed on her stomach.

"I haven't got any."

"But that was why you went to the village."

"Something happened."

Françoise looked up from breastfeeding little David and even Mireille stopped reading her magazine and glanced at Lottie with interested eyes under the pencilled brows.

Lottie's stomach rumbled. The debris of their lunch - soup dishes, cheese rinds, walnut shells and apple cores - littered the table. No-one offered Lottie any. She was famished after her morning's adventures. She sat down at the table, suddenly weary, the bones of her legs still feeling more like jelly than solid supports. Three pairs of eyes fixed upon her.

"Well? What happened?" Bernadette fetched another soup bowl from the dresser and placed it down in front of Lottie.

"Thank you, Bernadette. I am very hungry."

"We all are, without bread."

"I'm sorry about that. It was outside the boulangerie that it happened."

"For heaven's sake, Lottie, what?" Françoise put the baby over her shoulder and tapped his back. She was a natural mother, surprisingly.

"The school children were out in the square, when one of them mimicked the soldiers marching in that stiff way they have. Their senior officer took exception to it and went to hit him. The teacher, Monsieur Thibault, came between them and, before you knew it, the Germans had their guns pointed at him."

"And the children were next to him?" Françoise clutched David even tighter to her chest.

Lottie nodded. "Another man, Monsieur Dubois, older with a scarred face, had a seizure on the pavement outside the boulangerie."

"Dubois?" Bernadette snorted. "He's as fit as a flea, never had a seizure in his life. That scar is from the first war and was only a surface scratch. Michel Dubois could get thrown in a midden and come out smelling of soap."

"I don't think it was a genuine fit."

"He was pretending? How extraordinary!" Mireille's over-plucked eyebrows were even higher than normal.

"Yes, it was to distract attention from the teacher and children – and it worked. The German major, or whatever he's called, had a morbid fascination for Monsieur Dubois's condition, but his soldiers never lowered their guns until another officer called him back. I...I went over to the children and helped Monsieur Thibault get them back to school." Lottie looked longingly at her bowl of soup.

"That was stupid of you." Bernadette stood, hand on hips, looking more interested than her terse words would suggest.

"Maybe, but the little girls were terrified. We took them back to the school, but the Germans came for Monsieur Thibault shortly afterwards and took him away for questioning."

Talking of the young teacher seemed to have touched a nerve in Bernadette. "Did they now? Well, I've no time for teachers anyway. They give kids ideas above their station. If they didn't have so much education, we'd have more young people staying on the land, keeping the

297

farms going, keeping the traditions up. In my day, we had nuns and they drummed some discipline into you and some respect for God and the church. I've never held with schools being run by civil servants. I didn't stay in school a moment longer than I had to, and I make a good enough living. Are you going to eat that soup?"

"Yes, of course, Bernadette." Lottie could have eaten the bowl itself.

"There you are then." Bernadette belatedly plonked a spoon down in front of Lottie. "So, that teacher is in the hands of the Boche now, is he?"

Lottie shook her head, holding the spoon of soup still for a moment, hungry though she was. "No, I stayed in the school as the other teacher wasn't there – apparently she's been sacked. The children left at lunchtime and I told them not to return."

Françoise's eyes widened. "Their parents must have been terrified for them." David, having been winded, now slept in his mother's arms, blissfully unaware of her concern.

"What do you mean, no?" Bernadette took another wrinkled apple from the larder and put it on a plate in front of Lottie, with a couple of walnuts and a fresh circle of white goat's cheese.

Lottie swallowed some soup. It was so good, Bernadette's broth, just vegetables but with goat's cheese crumbled on yesterday's bread floating on top; truly delicious. She would rather have been concentrating on that than telling her tale, but the three other women were anxious for more.

Lottie rested her spoon against the pottery bowl. Her stomach gurgled again. "He came back, the teacher. He'd been roughed up pretty badly. Both his eyes were swollen, and his face was cut and bleeding. He said, if he'd been a Jew, he wouldn't have been allowed back at all. Apparently, the other teacher has already lost her job because she's Jewish. Everyone's ordered to register at the

Mairie, if they are Jewish. You'll have to register his birth, Françoise, when we go for our monthly ration cards."

Françoise gasped and squeezed her baby, waking him up. Startled, he began to wail. "Ssh, ssh," she crooned, rocking him gently.

Lottie took another spoonful of the rapidly cooling soup.

Bernadette looked pensive but remained silent.

It was Mireille who voiced her thoughts. "So, they are pursuing the Jews even here, just like in Paris. I can't say I like them either, but it does seem unfair. Is he handsome, this teacher?"

"Handsome? I can't say I noticed. He was certainly brave." Lottie scraped her empty bowl.

Bernadette snorted again. "Those who can, do. Those who can't, teach."

"But teaching is so important!" Lottie was genuinely shocked at Bernadette's attitude.

"Not as important as farming. It's times like these people finally realise who puts the food on the table. I'm charging twice as much for my cheese at the market these days. It's made a real difference. And people can't get enough of my honey. At the end of the day, it's food that counts." Bernadette, as if to make her point, ladled out more soup into Lottie's bowl, upending her saucepan to get the last dregs out. "Eat that and tell me I'm not right. You can't eat books."

Lottie, even though she was still hungry, pushed the bowl away. "No, but books can teach you how to grow things and how to milk a goat and more importantly, how to behave in a civilised way! Hitler's been burning books and look what he's doing. If you deny people access to learning, you deny democracy itself. You must excuse me. I'm tired and I'm going upstairs to rest. You can milk your own animals, for once, or maybe, Mireille, Françoise – one of *you* could do it!"

Lottie got up from the table without waiting for a reply to her outburst and made for the stairs. She climbed the ladder into her attic bedroom and collapsed on the bed, feeling as tired as she'd claimed. The morning had rattled her more than she'd cared to admit to the others. There had been so much admiration for the German soldiers' behaviour up to now. Restoring law and order, some had said, and others, Bernadette among them, "Better them than the Communists, at least they'll bring some money into the economy and they behave correctly."

Well they hadn't done that today. Lottie had been really shaken up by the sight of those German soldiers, some of whom didn't look much older than Jacques, pointing their rifles at innocent children. And the state of that teacher after they'd got their brutal hands on him!

No, there was nothing correct about their behaviour today, nothing.

The next morning, Bernadette cornered Françoise in the kitchen over breakfast. "She's right, you know." The old woman jerked her head towards Lottie.

Lottie laughed. "Well, that's a first."

Françoise scowled at her. "Right about what?"

"Registering the little one. You can't hide him forever." Bernadette scraped up the last of her breakfast milk with a crust of stale bread.

Françoise pouted. "No-one ever comes to the farm. Who's to know?"

Bernadette snorted. "For goodness sake, child. Face up to it. Your son exists. Short of smothering him, you must acknowledge him to the officials. It's ration card day on Thursday. We'll all have to go together to the Mairie."

"But I can't tell them who his father was! They'd take him from me." Françoise's voice caught on a suppressed sob.

Lottie stepped in. "Then we'll make something up. You're right, you can't give David as his father's name. In fact, I think you'd better not call him David at all."

"But I want to! I want to remember his father."

"Of course, you do," Lottie felt a stab of sympathy at Françoise's distress. "But can't you see how risky it would be to even hint at a Jewish connection?"

Françoise nodded her consent.

Bernadette swallowed her last morsel of food. "You must say you were married. You lost the marriage certificate on the journey. You must think who could have been the father. It must be someone they can trace, someone French."

"I have it!" Lottie reached out and gripped Françoise's arm. "Bertrand! He has the great advantage of being dead, don't you see?"

Françoise made a very French gesture of disgust. "That imbecile?

"I know, I know," Lottie smiled. "He was ugly and fat and belligerent as hell, but he was a real person, with real registered documents. He lived at your house so it's plausible he could have been associated with you, and he's dead. They don't need to know how unattractive he was."

Bernadette started collecting up the breakfast bowls. "Call the baby Bertrand. She's right. A real but dead person is ideal. Françoise, you have no choice. What was his last name?"

Lottie didn't know the answer to this. She'd only ever heard the Blanchards call their manservant by his Christian name.

"Paget." Françoise almost spat out the word.

"Good. A good solid French name." Bernadette looked at the baby, sleeping innocently in his mother's arms. "Bertrand Paget it is. Let none of us ever forget it."

Lottie, now confined to the farm for lack of documents of her own, stayed home when, a few days later, the three other women took the pony and trap to the village and duly entered Françoise's Jewish baby's name as Bertrand Paget. The name of David never appeared anywhere on the documents.

Françoise cried all the way home.

CHAPTER THIRTY FOUR
NORMANDY
CHRISTMAS EVE 1940

Lottie nestled her head into the goat's warm, smelly flank. The wind whistled underneath the rough door of the ancient barn, forcing snowflakes through the gaps.

Christmas Eve. Al's and Isobel's joint birthdays. How she longed to be with them instead of in this stinking barn with her face covered in goat hair and dirt. Would they be together back home in Wiltshire? Bound to be on their birthdays. They'd always shared it as children and she'd always felt left out. Al would be twenty this year. Twenty! Old enough to join up. Perhaps they wouldn't be together after all, if he had. Perhaps he was in danger. Which service would he choose? Lottie mused on the image of Al in uniform; she couldn't picture him as a sailor. Perhaps he was a soldier, like those German boys marching up and down the village square, following orders whether they agreed with them or not, even if it meant killing people. It didn't bear thinking about.

She pushed the images away from her mind and thought about her sister instead. Isobel would be sweet seventeen today. But then, Isobel had always been sweet, whatever her age. That was the problem, that and her beauty. Lottie had never stood a chance with Al, not romantically anyway.

The milk frothed into the metal pail, pressed tight between her knees, and steam rose up to her face in sharp contrast to the icy air eddying around her. The goat whinnied and shuffled, almost kicking the bucket over.

"Steady, old girl. Nearly done. Let's not waste your precious milk." Lottie hoped her voice would be enough to soothe the fidgeting animal, so she could carry on and get the job finished with the others. The sooner she was back by the farmhouse fire, the better. Her back ached but she didn't want to risk a spillage by releasing her knees. Suddenly, a knock at the door surprised her into letting go. The goat, equally startled, jumped away, kicking the nearly full pail over.

"Oh no!" Lottie sprang back from the flying hooves and watched the white liquid spill all over the straw-covered stone floor. Ignoring the knocking at the door, she leapt across to right the bucket. Barely an inch of milk was left inside.

Furious, she wrenched open the door. "Who is it? Don't you know I've lost all our milk because of you?"

A face loomed forward out of the darkness. "I'm sorry. I didn't realise."

"Too late for sorry now. Look at my empty bucket!" Lottie scrutinised her unexpected visitor. "Monsieur Thibault! What on earth are you doing here?"

"Aren't you going to let me in?"

Lottie stepped back. The young teacher entered the barn and shut the door quickly behind him. A swirl of snowflakes settled on his head and shoulders, but he seemed oblivious to the cold, despite his red nose.

He looked at the floor and then at Lottie's bucket. "I'm very sorry about the milk."

"So am I. Not only will we be hungry, but Bernadette will be furious. Is it her you've come to see? Why didn't you go to the house?"

"No, it's you I want. I watched you come into the barn and I followed you here once I saw you were alone." Monsieur Thibault removed his black beret, dislodging some snow which quickly melted into the gooey mess of straw and spilt milk at their feet.

"Me? Why me? And why did you sneak in here like a thief?" Lottie put the bucket down in the corner and grabbed some hay for the goat to eat. The animal snatched at the fragrant dried grass hungrily.

Lottie stroked the goat's face. "It's alright, old girl. Well, Monsieur Thibault? Explain yourself."

The young man ran his hand through his bright hair. "I want to make you a proposal."

Lottie burst out laughing. "Isn't that rather premature?"

Monsieur Thibault smiled back briefly. "Not that sort of proposal. You helped me a couple of weeks ago in the square, remember? When Jacques mocked the Germans."

"Of course, I remember. You came off rather worse than me from that encounter."

"Exactly. That's why I'm here. You showed courage that day and I was impressed by how calm you were. The Germans have kept a keen eye on me since then and I don't have the freedom of movement I would like. There are some things I need to do. I got the impression that you find this forced occupation as revolting as I do?"

"What are you suggesting?"

"I'm asking if you would be willing to help undermine their oppression of our people." He looked intense, his large black pupils obscuring the blueness of his irises behind their horn-rimmed spectacles.

"In what way? How can a solitary teacher, like you, take on an armed enemy?"

"There are many ways and I am not alone. All revolutions start with small actions. If we can get information to people, real information, not the lies the German papers put about, we can instigate change. They would have us believe that we are lucky to be invaded. That we should share our art and music with theirs. They think they are like us, that our two nations should join to form some new empire and lord it over the rest of the world. And our cowardly leader, Pétain, seems to agree. It makes me sick."

"I can see you feel strongly about it, but I can't imagine how I might help."

He came towards her, took her hand. "You must feel the same way, or you wouldn't have helped take the children back to school."

Lottie withdrew her hand. His was cool and dry, hers sticky with spilt goat's milk. "Monsieur Thibault, why don't you spare me the ideology and come out with it?"

"Call me Thierry."

"Alright, Thierry, tell me what you came all this way to say."

He ran his hand through his hair again and sat down on a hay bale against the wall. Lottie continued to stroke the long nose of the goat, who chomped contentedly, as if she was listening too.

"What I'm about to tell you is completely confidential, Mademoiselle Perrot – may I call you Charlotte?"

"You remembered my name."

"It was a memorable occasion. So, may I?"

"Can I stop you?"

"Very well, Charlotte, as you must realise by now, I detest this occupation of our beautiful country. I make it my business to remain informed and what I hear alarms me greatly. I cannot bear to passively allow these brutes to dominate us. Yesterday, a French civil servant, Jacques Bonsergent, was executed in cold blood by the Germans in Paris. The first civilian casualty. It's just the beginning. I can no longer sit idle and do nothing."

Lottie frowned. "What reason was given for this execution?"

"He was simply walking along the street with some friends. One of them had just got married and a German officer, drunk, molested his friend's new wife. Of course, the husband thumped him for taking liberties, but it didn't end there."

"What happened?"

"Bonsergent made his friends leave, before helping the German get up from the pavement. I suppose he was trying to calm things down, but some other German officers mistook him for the perpetrator, arrested him and put him in jail."

Lottie lifted her hand to her throat. "But surely, he was innocent and only trying to help?"

"Yes, he was, and not only innocent, but a true friend. They beat him up, and I know what that feels like, but he would not reveal the name of his friend. They tortured him for weeks, but he would not give way. So, they killed him by firing squad, up against a wall. Ah, these cowardly Boche! They call themselves civilized but they are barbaric! Now do you see why I must do something?"

"I see why *you* feel compelled to do something, but I do not see how it concerns me." Lottie dropped her hands to her sides.

"I have friends in Paris, many friends, from my teacher-training days there. They tell me the real news. I seem to remember you said you came from Paris. Is that correct?" Thierry's eyes had never left her face as he recounted the shocking story.

"That's right." Lottie broke his gaze by returning to petting the placid goat.

"But, forgive me, your accent is excellent, but I do not think you are related to Madame Perrot, or even French?"

"Why do you say that?"

"It was a little thing that gave you away."

"Oh?"

Thierry Thibault smiled. "It was the letter you began to write to the priest. You addressed him as 'Monseigneur' but a French man or woman would simply call him, 'Mon Pere'. The former title is reserved for bishops. A simple mistake, but easy for a teacher to spot."

Lottie stopped stroking the goat and sat down on the milking stool, perplexed as to how to answer this earnest, intelligent man.

Thierry stood up and paced up and down. "You can trust me, Charlotte, if I can trust you. What I am about to tell you is deeply secret and dangerous. No-one else has guessed you are not who you say you are, and I have not spoken of it to anyone. Everyone in the village is too concerned with their own safety to worry about the stranger in Madam Perrot's little smallholding. They seem to have accepted you are her granddaughter from Paris. If you have good identity papers, and are willing, this makes you a compelling candidate for what I have in mind."

Lottie folded her arms across her chest. She had started to shiver. "Why don't you just tell me exactly what that is and then I might tell you who I am."

"Very well. Let us both put our cards on the table. My friends in Paris know some brave academics who print an illegal paper called '*Resistance*'. They have managed to circulate it in the capital hoping to get this sleeping country to wake up and start defending itself against our German oppressors. They need couriers to deliver it in all regions. You have a bicycle and freedom of movement. I have neither and have already aroused suspicion. Will you join us?"

Lottie was silent. A part of her leapt at the chance to do something active, something other than shovelling goat shit and putting up with Bernadette's demands, Mireille's laziness and Françoise's complacency. Another, perhaps a larger part, resented this new imposition and the danger it brought.

"As you have said, I am not French; why should I risk my life?"

"Are you not equally constrained, perhaps more so, by these arrogant Germans? I suspect you are English, no? Are we not allies? Do you not wish to fight back? If not, I have misjudged you." It was Thierry's turn to frown.

Lottie got up from her low stool and paced the room. "And who do you think you are, passing judgement on me in the first place?"

He stopped his pacing and leant against the wall, watching her. "There you are, you have proved you have spirit, Charlotte Perrot – if that is your real name?"

Lottie stopped her pacing and looked at him. "What is involved?"

"Above all, secrecy, so perhaps you should not, after all, tell me who you are." Thierry grinned. It made him look ridiculously young, boyish even. "If you agree, you will await further instructions. I will go to Paris and bring back a batch of *'Resistance'* newspapers. No-one will notice me in the capital, I am unknown to the Boche there. It is here I must be careful. Once I return, I shall contact you and you will distribute them to the houses around here. You can use the pretext of selling Bernadette's produce. I'm sure she wouldn't mind spreading her wares around, plus, you have your bicycle. Then, I hope people will come forward and we can form a group."

"To do what?"

"I don't know yet, but we cannot just let them walk all over us."

Lottie fell silent again. She had much to consider. Thierry seemed to sense this and gave her time to think. He stood quietly, not fidgeting, his eyes resting on her face softly, without expression. Lottie found it strangely comforting. She took a deep breath to quell the thrill of fear that accompanied her decision.

She nodded. "Very well. I agree. However, it is on condition that I never tell you my true identity. Can you arrange for false identity cards, as Charlotte Perrot, to be made and given to me before I attempt any such deliveries?"

Thierry nodded back. "I think that is very wise. I know someone who might be able to do it. Have you a photo of yourself?"

"Only the one in my British passport."

"Ah, as I thought, you *are* English, but we can't use that, you might need it someday. I advise you to hide it very carefully in the meantime. The Germans have been conducting searches amongst the villagers. It is only a question of time for them to come out to the outlying farms, or you could be questioned when you come to the village for supplies. Leave it with me. I will make it my highest priority." He got up and came towards her, hand outstretched.

Taking her hand, he said, "Thank you, Charlotte. You have made a brave decision."

"Let's hope neither of us regrets it." Lottie shook his hand, no longer so cool but still dry, still relaxed. It would take a lot to make this man lose his composure. She opened the barn door. It had stopped snowing and a white layer of ice crystals covered the yard.

"Go that way across towards the farmhouse, till you get to the lane that leads to the road, and I will walk in your footsteps in the snow when I leave, so no-one knows you were here."

Thierry smiled that boyish grin again. "You have the natural instincts of a warrior. I'll be in touch soon. I'm going to Paris for the new year and will return before the school term starts, hopefully with a batch of leaflets. Watch for me then."

"Goodbye." Lottie shut the barn door behind him, having established he was walking in the right direction.

She turned to the nanny goat and whispered into her long, velvety ear. "God help me."

CHAPTER THIRTY FIVE
KATHERINE WHEEL GARAGE
CHRISTMAS 1940 – NEW YEAR 1941

Al waited until after Boxing Day to tell his parents about his decision. Isobel had remained cool after declining his proposal but said he must do what he felt was right. What would be right, would be for them to get married, but he was damned if he'd *beg* her to become his wife. Once she saw him in that smart blue RAF uniform, maybe she would change her mind. All the girls fancied a pilot, but they also probably liked rich, artistic types too.

It was still dark when the family had their breakfast early that morning, but Agnes had a fire roaring to keep the frost out. She didn't hold with electric fires and Al had to admit the real flames were a comfort.

"Back to work today, then, everybody." Jem put down his empty cup. "Holiday is over."

Lily put down her spoon into her empty porridge bowl. "I'm still on holiday, Dad. Can I go and play with Maggie? She said on the telephone last night that the snow in her garden is really deep - there's enough to make a snowman! She got a sledge for Christmas and she wants to test it on the hill next to her house." Lily never seemed to feel the cold.

"Alright, sounds like fun, Lily. Can you drive her over there, Al?" Katy buttered her toast.

"Of course, but, while everyone is here, I've something to say to you all." Al took a deep breath, aware of four pairs of eyes fixed on his face across the breakfast table.

There was a pause, an awkward one. "You know I'll get my call-up papers soon, don't you? Well, I thought I'd jump in first and try for the RAF. You have to volunteer for entry, so I'm going to give it a go before I get conscripted. After seeing those pilots in that dogfight

310

over the sea last summer, I've decided flying is for me. Can't be that different to driving a lorry."

The pause continued.

Eventually, Jem spoke. "Why not wait until you have to go?"

"Because, like I said, you have to volunteer for the RAF. They don't take just anybody, you know."

"But…" Katy swallowed her toast. She'd been chewing it for several minutes. "it might be better to wait, Al. Forgive me, but I've heard the RAF has the lowest survival rates, especially for pilots. Look how many got shot down in the Battle of Britain. I can see the attraction of wanting to fly, after all, I used to race cars, but look what happened to Douglas. Oh, Al, must you do this?"

"I made my mind up in the autumn, Mum, and I've waited all this time to tell you. I'll be careful, I promise."

Katy got up from the table, blinking her eyelids a little. "Have you really thought this through? Is there nothing we can say or do to make you reconsider?"

Al shook his head. "My mind is made up. I'm going to the recruitment centre today."

Katy covered her mouth with her hand. She nodded at her son and then ran out of the room without speaking.

Lily looked at her father, then back at Al. "What is so awful about joining the RAF? I'd love to have a go at flying a plane. I wish I was old enough to join up."

"Don't be so stupid, Lily." Jem's voice was harsh, gravelly. "You have no idea what you're saying." He turned to Al. "You could still apply for reserved occupation you know. It's no disgrace to serve your country at home."

"It would be for me. No, Dad, I understand your concern and I'm grateful for it, but this is what I want to do."

Perhaps unconsciously, Jem rubbed his shortened arm. "Alright, son. You must do what you feel is right, but it's a sad day, nonetheless."

"It's not a sad day, Dad. I don't even know if I'll get in! Come on, Lily. Get your coat on and I'll drop you off at Maggie's on the way."

Al had to drive slowly because of a fresh fall of lying snow. Lily's friend, Maggie Allsop, lived on the outskirts of Upper Cheadle in a detached house standing alone above a straggle of cottages on the main road to Woodbury.

Lily slipped on the ice when she got down from the lorry.

"Steady, Lily! Do you want me to walk with you?"

Lily got up from the slippery pavement, laughing. "I'm fine. Soft landing. Go and get kitted up in blue. I'm proud of you, Al, and even if Mum and Dad haven't said so, they are too."

"Thanks, Lil." Al revved the engine and drew away slowly, making sure the tyres had gripped the road before accelerating. He could see Lily's bobble hat in his rear-view mirror. She was waving both her arms. Bless her.

The recruitment office wasn't busy. Nowhere was. Al supposed it was the snow shrouding everywhere in white crystals. Beautiful, perhaps, but treacherous.

"Good morning, young man. Got your call-up papers?" A sergeant at the desk looked pleased to have something to do.

"No, not yet, but I'd like to volunteer for the RAF."

"Would you now? Got transport?"

Al nodded.

"Good. Get yourself off to their headquarters, then, sonny. Here's the address. We'll let them see what to do with you."

That didn't sound encouraging, but Al pocketed the address and climbed back in the lorry. He wasn't sure where St Edmund's House was, but he knew his way to Woodbury like the back of his hand. He drove to Baldwin Street and parked by St Edward's church. Sure enough, the RAF office was right next to the old stone church. Feeling nervous, he locked the lorry, crunched across the snowy pavement and opened the door of the plain, red-bricked building.

As he sat in the waiting room, he studied the poster on the wall. It's red title, splashed in big capitals across the top, read:

> 'VOLUNTEER FOR FLYING CREWS –
> Join the RAF.'

Underneath was a paragraph that sent butterflies cavorting through his insides.

> 'ONLY THE BEST ARE GOOD ENOUGH.'

He got up and stood in front of it, reading the small print. It continued in the same vein and a seed of doubt sowed itself amongst the butterflies.

> *'The RAF calls for men of the highest quality.*
> *Fitness, dash and initiative are essential, coupled with*
> *intelligence and a sense of responsibility.'*

Dash? What did they mean by that? The poster sounded pretty demanding. Was *he* 'one of the best'? Would Churchill think that so much was owed by so many to him? Could he really do this? Before he could answer the question so baldly posed by the poster, he was called in to the office and told to sit down.

Having given his name and address, he was asked for his educational qualifications. His answer was met with a frown. "I see. Well, you'll have to sit some exams to

313

prove you're up to scratch. You'll be tested on your academic ability – particularly mathematics - physical fitness, response speeds, that sort of thing."

Exams. His worst nightmare.

The official continued, "Of course, you'll have to go past the board as well."

"The board?"

"ACSB, don't you know?"

"Um, no I don't, I'm sorry."

"Hmm. Air Crew Selection Board. They'll tell you if you'll fit in."

The man coughed, implying more doubt. "Come back next Wednesday to this office, with your school certificates, and we'll see if you'll be eligible for an interview. If you get through that, you'll go on to the other tests but not everyone gets to be a pilot, you know. There's more ground crew than flyers."

"I see, thank you, sir. I'll be back first thing on Wednesday then."

"Right you are." The man closed his ledger.

Taking that as dismissal, Al returned to his lorry and drove back home. The weekend dragged by. He used the time to study lots of different aircraft, get his hair cut and polish his already shining shoes, instead of visiting Isobel like he normally did. She'd already telephoned and said she was busy sitting for Geraint's portrait of her. That made him even more nervous than the prospect of sitting the RAF exams.

He greeted the return to the working week with relief, glad to be distracted. His first delivery was to the RAF airfield in Southampton. A lucky break. He might pick up some useful hints from the chaps there.

Al loaded up the lorry in double-quick time.

Uncle Billy complained about his haste. "Oi, Al! You'll drop them boxes if you goes at it hell-for-leather like that, mate!"

"Sorry, just want to get going."

"What's the rush?"

But Al didn't want to confide in Billy Threadwell. His hopes of getting into the RAF were so slim, he didn't want egg on his face from all and sundry if he didn't make the grade.

He got to the depot in record time. He offloaded the boxes of components in the large hangar, same as usual. As he was getting the delivery signed off, a man in the coveted pilot's RAF uniform sauntered in, asking for an engineer to look at his Spitfire engine.

"I say, chaps. Take a look at the old girl, will you? I think there's air in the fuel pump, she's coughing and spluttering as if she's got influenza."

The foreman finished signing Al's form and turned to the young pilot. "Right you are, sir. I'll get an engineer over." The older man tucked his clipboard under his arm and went to the little office at the back of the hangar and picked up the telephone.

Al couldn't believe his second stroke of luck. This was exactly the opportunity he'd been waiting for.

He went up to the tall man in RAF blue. "Um, excuse me, but I'm thinking of volunteering for the RAF myself. Can you give me some pointers?"

The pilot turned to him and looked him up and down. "Think you've got what it takes, old man?"

"Well, I don't know until you tell me!"

"I suppose that's fair. Did you do well in school? You'll need your Higher Certificate to apply. The RAF is pretty keen on mathematics. What school did you go to?"

"Just the local one in Woodbury, that everyone goes to."

"Oh dear. And your father, what does he do?"

"He works at our factory and grows vegetables to sell in our garage."

"How delightfully rustic."

Without prompting, Al said, "And he fought in the last shout. Lost an arm, he did. My Mum was in the WAAC too. An engineer she was and a right good one. Started up her own garage and now she has a rubber factory. We make a lot of components for the army and for the planes in the RAF, you know."

The pilot tried to hide a smile behind his ginger moustache. "You might be better as ground crew, I'd have thought, with that sort of background. So, do you belong to any sports clubs? You know the sort of thing – tennis, rowing, cricket?"

Al shook his head. "Not clubs, no, sir. Played at school of course."

"Hmm, thought so." The officer spoke as if he had a plum in his mouth, posher than any of the Smythes. "Look, frankly, old bean, I don't think you stand a chance as a pilot." He yawned, signalling boredom. "Where's that bloody engineer?"

He turned away from Al towards the back of the hangar. "Ah, thank goodness, here's Smith."

The foreman came jogging back. "Engineer on his way, sir. Says to join him on the tarmac by the 'plane.

"Right, thanks. Cheerio, young man, and, if I were you, I wouldn't set my heights too high, you'd be doomed to disappointment." He gave a half-hearted salute and walked briskly away into the sunshine.

"Look, son, I couldn't help overhearing but he's probably right, you know. The RAF's not for the likes of us, not if you want to be a pilot, that is." Smith patted Al's shoulder in sympathy.

"But I'm desperate to fly."

"Have you thought about the ATA? They're recruiting and they train you up to be a pilot."

"The ATA? What's that?" Al was still struggling to hide his disappointment.

"Air Transport Auxiliary Service. The RAF couldn't manage without them, mate."

"How's that?"

"It's them that delivers the planes everywhere – yes, and pilots too. They're a vital piece of the supply chain. And I tell you something else – they're not so stuck up as that toffee-nosed lot in blue. If you volunteer for the

316

RAF, you'll just end up a grease monkey, like me. You'd never get off the ground. But the ATA takes all comers and they're a great bunch to work for – everyone says so. You'd still see plenty of action, son, and you'd stand a real chance of becoming a pilot with them.

"Not fighting action by the sound of it." Al pictured the dogfight in the air he'd witnessed.

"The Battle of Britain is over, son, but the war's just getting going. The ATA will be in the thick of it, you mark my words. Have a think about it, anyway. You've far more chance of success with them, I'm sure of it." Smith patted his shoulder again. "Right, got to get back to work. See you next time, Al."

Al watched him go. Deep in thought, he got into the cab of the lorry and thumped the steering wheel repeatedly, cursing his tongue, cursing his humble roots, cursing the service he now knew wouldn't want him to fly their planes. It took him a full ten minutes to regain command of himself enough to drive. The one person he needed right now was Isobel.

He drove directly to the manor house, skidding slightly on the glacial drive as he parked the lorry. He got down from the cab gingerly and stood before the side door, straightening his cap and tie.

He rang the bell. Eventually, old Andrews drew back the bolt.

"Hello, Andrews. Is Miss Isobel in?"

"I regret to inform you, young Phipps, that Miss Isobel is in bed with a heavy cold. She can't receive visitors today."

"But she'll see me, surely?"

Andrews opened his mouth to speak but, before he could do so, Cassandra appeared behind him carrying a bottle of medicine and a spoon.

"Who is it, Andrews?"

Al answered for him. "It's me. I was calling for Isobel."

317

"Oh, dear, I'm sorry, Al. She's in bed. Nasty bout of a cold. She's got a temperature today, so I don't think it would be a good idea. Sorry. If she's better, I'll get her to telephone you." Cassandra smiled thinly and turned away.

Al left before Andrews shut the door on him.

This was not turning out to be a good day at all.

Isobel lay in bed, shivering. She must have caught this chill when she'd sat for hours for Geraint while he painstakingly painted her portrait. Perhaps her choice of gown, the crushed blue velvet sleeveless one she'd worn to the solstice dinner party, hadn't been the best idea in the depths of winter.

Or perhaps she was suffering from shock. Had it been the difference in their ages that had prevented her from seeing how serious Geraint was about her?

When the portrait was finished and he'd nervously shown it to her, she had realised he truly loved her. It was the way he had painted her. His adoration shone through the painting like a golden thread, uniting every pore of her skin, every hair on her head, each eyelash framing her blue eyes. She was convinced she didn't look that good and said so.

"But you are, dearest Isobel, you are quite beautiful, but you are much more than that. You are one of the loveliest, kindest, gentlest, most resourceful people I have ever had the privilege to meet."

Geraint drew her away from the easel towards the chaise longue on which she'd posed for days on end. This time, he sat next to her, her hands in his paint-stained ones.

Isobel had always, from the first instant of meeting him on that sunny hill in Wales, felt very much at ease with him, but now she knew a moment of panic. She felt like a wild bird trapped in a cage, a pretty one made of gold and entwined with flowers, but a cage, nonetheless.

"Isobel, you must know how I feel about you, have felt from the moment I clapped eyes on you."

"Geraint, please…"

"No, hear me out. You probably think I'm a crusty old bachelor, but I can assure you I have remained

319

unmarried because I never met anyone before who inspired such love. You are very young, and doubtless think I am probably much too old for you, but you have made me feel as if I too am only seventeen."

Isobel didn't try and stop his outpouring. She could see he'd built himself up for this moment.

He carried on. "I could look after you, Isobel. I wouldn't curb your freedom in any way, but I could rescue Cheadle Manor. I'm very rich, you see, perhaps more so than you realise. I could easily pay off the bank loan your poor mother has had to burden the estate with. I know you love your mother very much, don't you? Wouldn't you like to erase all her worries and set her free too? I have an estate of my own up in Flintshire, and you would be the most marvellous mistress of it. We could live quietly or entertain lavishly, if you prefer. You could do just as you like, I wouldn't interfere. Just to see you every day, beautiful Isobel, would be my joy, and it would be enough, I know it."

He paused, waiting for her response, scanning her face.

She could think of nothing to say. This was enormous. There was no rush of joy, such as she felt when Al took her in his arms. This was solemn and serious. Grown-up. She thought of her mother and what a relief this would be to her. She remembered Granny's firm belief that she should find a rich husband and rescue the estate.

Her elderly grandmother's strident voice echoed in her head. "It is your *duty*, Isobel. We all have to do our duty."

While these thoughts raced through her head, Geraint remained silent. When she still didn't break it, he said, his voice dropping almost to a whisper. "I see the prospect doesn't fill you with unalloyed joy and I expected as much. I will return home with your painting. It will remind me of these tranquil days with you. I'll leave you to think about my offer. You can write to me at any time, or even telephone me if you prefer, once you have had time to reflect. I will say no more on this occasion but know this, Isobel, I will be watching and waiting, with all my heart, for your reply."

He kissed her hand and then her forehead. She dreaded more but he was sensitive enough to leave it at that. He got up and turned away from her. Isobel let out her breath and watched, as he packed up his easel and paints into the case he'd been carrying when she'd first met him, up on that Welsh hill in the sunshine. He rolled up the painting into a cylinder shape and packed it neatly into a matching tin.

"I'll leave now, I think. Please explain my departure to your mother. I'll leave you to decide how much to tell her, although I think she has probably guessed my intentions already. She is a very intelligent woman and loves you almost as much as I do."

Geraint hitched up the strap of his bag on his shoulder. "Goodbye, my dear. Remember, I'll be watching and waiting to hear from you. Please, don't make me wait too long, and yet, I suppose, hope will linger while I do."

With that, he left, shutting the door quietly behind him.

Isobel stared at the floor, where his easel had stood bearing them witness over the last week as the year turned from 1940 into 1941, but where would this new year take *her*?

She turned in the bed, restless and uncomfortably hot, despite the frost riming the windows. Granny's voice echoed around her bedroom, bouncing off the walls, hectoring her.

"Think of your mother. Save the estate. Marry a rich man. Use my diamonds. Catch a husband."

Isobel rammed a pillow over her ears, but she could not shut out the words circling round and round inside her aching head.

CHAPTER THIRTY SEVEN
NORMANDY
JANUARY 1941

Christmas came and went without celebration in Bernadette's snowbound farmhouse and the four women had no gifts to exchange. Their reluctant hostess had made an effort on the day itself by serving up the toughest chicken Lottie had ever eaten. A bird that no longer laid nice brown eggs was despatched into Bernadette's massive pot-au-feu and boiled there for several hours, stubbornly resisting tenderness.

A bit like its cook.

No-one felt festive anyway and the deep cold emphasised the short winter days. Even Bernadette acknowledged it was the coldest winter she'd experienced for many years. The only relief for Lottie was the knowledge that they had passed the nadir of the solstice and eventually the days would lengthen again. Her homesickness crippled her until the pain dulled to numbness, so even the routine chores of the smallholding became welcome distractions. The long nights had no such activity to break the monotony and the bitter cold reached out frosty fingers into every corner of her attic bedroom. Bernadette rationed the oil for the lamps as well as candles, so she couldn't even read in bed. She had to break the ice in her washing bowl and jug each morning and gave up the attempt when the new year bit even harder than the old.

New Year's Day fell on a Wednesday, and Mireille and Bernadette went off to sell goods from the farm at the market in Caen in high hopes of a good turn-out. Françoise went with them, unusually, with little David, now resolutely called Bertrand by them all, bundled up against the cold. Only Lottie remained behind. She dared not risk it without papers, there was bound to be a control post between here and Caen along the main road that separated them from the coast. Lottie watched the three other women set off in the bleak dark of the winter's morning. They seemed excited and happy, for once, united by their adventure and chattering away to each other. Lottie stood at the farm gate until the pony and trap disappeared around the corner and joined the main road.

She was alone at last. She couldn't remember the last time she'd enjoyed any solitude. There *was* a sort of bliss to it, although she had to milk the goats before she'd have any leisure.

Dawn broke while she was in the barn. She came out carrying two pails of warm milk and took them into the stone outbuilding that served as a dairy. She covered the milk with clean wooden boards and left it to cool. At these temperatures, that wouldn't take very long. She could see her breath in the frosty air, now it was light. The sun crept slowly over the horizon, looking sulky and reluctant to shine. Lottie shivered and hurried back to the farmhouse, delighting in its emptiness but dismayed to find the fire had gone out without Bernadette to tend it.

She had underestimated the amount of skill needed to get the thing to fire up again. By the time she had got some flames going, she was sleepy. She put some milk on to heat and stirred in some precious chocolate from a block in the larder. The bread was stale, but she crumbled some into her bowl of hot chocolate and drank greedily. Feeling deliciously full and enjoying prime position in Bernadette's fireside chair, Lottie fell asleep.

The cold woke her a few hours later. She had to go through the whole rigmarole of lighting the fire for the second time that day, but she didn't care. That warm fireside sleep had refreshed her more than any long night up in the chilly attic. She had truly relaxed for the first time in ages. She stayed by the fire all day, dozing and reminiscing about her life in Wiltshire, steadfastly ignoring her chores. She needed a day off.

Lottie pictured each one of her favourite people and wondered what they would be doing. Was it snowing there too? Would Isobel be with Al, perhaps having a snowball fight like they used to as children? Such happy memories. Would her mother and Katy be together, their friendship deepening now the ban on visiting Cheadle Manor had been lifted? She was sure they would. Her parents and Al's had been through so much together.

For the first time, she questioned her grandmother's decree. Granny had been wrong to condemn Al for that day at the river; to make a young child bear sole responsibility for their misadventure. She was glad that she and Isobel had defied her ban and seen Al at the garage whenever they could sneak away. And yet, no-one, absolutely no-one, had realised that she loved Al, including him. She felt so lonely here on this frozen patch of France, she would be happy to see Al and Isobel, even if they were together. She missed them all; missed the landscape around her ancestral home; missed the rhythm of her old life. She remembered her time with Mabs in Paris. Although it had not ended well, it had been splendid, and she wouldn't have missed *that* for the world.

It seemed unbelievable to Lottie that the Boche had upset everyone's lives, displaced thousands of people, disrupted and divided families and friends. There was a surreal madness to what was happening to her, trapped in this remote farmhouse with people who were almost strangers. She'd only met Françoise once before on that walking holiday in Switzerland. Then, they had been in a party of several girls, all giggling and carefree; another world.

Lottie looked at the flames in the fire. The warmth was such a comfort. She dozed off again and dreamt of that day on the river when they were innocent children, floating along the green water under the willows.

When she awoke, later that afternoon, she was sorry to hear the clip-clop of the pony's hooves on the lane. She rubbed the sleep from her eyes and stoked the fire ready for the influx.

Mireille and Françoise came into the kitchen first, having left their older relative to put the donkey in its shelter, speaking over each other.

"Oh, I'm freezing!"

"Is there any milk for David...um, Bertrand?"

Lottie gave up her fireside chair to Mireille, who flopped down into it. "I'm exhausted. It was such a busy day."

"Except for three o'clock." Françoise put the milk-pan on the hob to warm.

"Yes, wasn't that strange?" Mireille unknotted her headscarf.

Lottie looked at them. "What was strange?"

"We were at our stall; we hadn't got much left to sell but it was so busy, Mother decided to stay longer than usual. Then, at exactly a quarter to three, everyone disappeared! We got bundled into a nearby shop and they locked us in!" Mireille rubbed her manicured hands and held them to the blaze.

"Why?"

Françoise took up the story. "It was a protest against the Germans. For New Year's Day. A sort of self-imposed curfew by the local people. The butcher, whose shop we stayed in, said it was happening all over France!"

"What did the Boche do about it?" Lottie found this action decidedly cheering.

Mireille yawned. "Nothing they could do. We watched them from inside the shop. They were wandering about, looking confused and, I have to say, a little worried. They even started giving out potatoes to tempt people back outside!"

Françoise laughed. "Yes, it was good to see them on the back foot for once. Then, at four o'clock precisely, everyone poured out on to the streets, laughing and joking and wishing each other a happy new year. You should have seen the soldiers' faces!"

Lottie, heartened by this passive resistance, was desperate to mix with the local people again to talk about

325

the phenomenon. After the next market in Caen, Bernadette reported that the curfew on the first day of 1941 had indeed spread throughout France. It seemed that people were beginning to wonder what else they might do to signal their distaste at being occupied by a military force who had not been invited.

Another week passed and still she hadn't had a visit from Thierry Thibault. At first, she didn't worry, he'd said he wouldn't be back until the beginning of the new school term. After giving him a few days grace to settle into the new academic year, she cycled one morning into the village, ostensibly for bread. They had been making their own at the farm for the last couple of weeks, as bread was scarce in the shops and they were all sick of the hard sourdough Bernadette concocted, unleavened by yeast and laced with resentment. Lottie was glad of the excuse to go out.

For once, the late dawn was bright and clear. A tentative pale sun broke through the morning mist as Lottie pedalled along the lane towards the village. As she rounded a bend, she caught a glimpse of a roadblock with German soldiers standing next to it, fully armed and looking bored and cold enough to cause trouble.

The even colder realisation that she still didn't have any identity papers almost made her heart stop beating. Before they spotted her through the hedge that separated them, Lottie quietly turned her pushbike around, without pausing or putting a foot to the ground. Picking up speed, she bent her back over the handlebars and willed her legs to work harder. She didn't stop until she reached the farmhouse. Once inside, breathless with the effort, she collapsed on to the chair next to the range in the big kitchen.

"Why are you back so soon?" Bernadette was chopping onions for the regulation midday soup.

Lottie had to gasp out her answer. "Germans. Soldiers. Roadblock to village."

"So?"

"So, Bernadette, I don't have proper identity papers, do I? I'd be clamped in jail if they saw my British passport - or sent off to one of those camps." Lottie's breath was more even now but anger, mixed with real fear, lent urgency to her words.

"Well, you'd better stay at the farm from now on then. I'll get bread when I go to the market in Caen with the donkey and trap and get the ration cards on the way home. I'm making more profit these days. I suppose we could waste some on bread from town, if there is any to be had."

"Fine, but it's only a question of time before the Germans start looking in all the farmhouses for Jews and aliens. Technically I'm an enemy. I must sort out my papers, and soon." Lottie took the cup of coffee Bernadette offered. It contained very little coffee, consisting mostly of roasted chicory and barley, but it was hot.

Bernadette didn't return to her sizzling saucepan. Instead she removed it from the heat in the centre of the hob and disappeared upstairs, returning a few minutes later with an old cocoa tin.

"Here, these are the official documents for my son. It just so happens he shared the same name as you, almost." Bernadette prised the lid off the tin and took out some tattered papers. "Here's his birth certificate. He was called Charles – not so different from Charlotte – perhaps?"

Lottie took the yellowed paper, entitled "Acte de Naissance". It showed that Bernadette was twenty-five when she gave birth to Charles Jacques Perrot. She couldn't picture the dour old woman standing before her, her habitual frown deeper than ever, as a young woman - pregnant, beloved, giving life.

"Thank you for this, Bernadette. It's a good idea but I think it would be hard to fudge it. How would we change the word 'masculine' to 'feminine' without it showing? And the dates are all wrong. No, thank you, but I don't think it would work."

327

Bernadette snatched the document back, "I thought you might be glad of it."

Lottie looked up at the older woman. "I am, of course I am. Thank you for the kind thought, I wish I could use it. It's funny, I had an uncle called Charles and I'm named after him. He died in the Great War. What happened to your son, Bernadette, if you don't mind my asking?"

"Shooting accident. It's always guns with men, isn't it? And now we have another war. Charles died of pneumonia. Had weak lungs, like his father, and a night laying in a frosty ditch with a bullet in his side finished him off. He should never have gone hunting on his own. Stupid, stupid!" Suddenly Bernadette sat down. She looked deflated, all the normal anger that stiffened her spine and sharpened her tongue gone, leaving her looking even older and unusually vulnerable.

Lottie reached out her hand and placed it over Bernadette's careworn one. "It must have been hard without a man about the place."

Bernadette looked up at her, her flinty grey eyes glittering. "Yes. He was a good son. Always smiling, always joking. He'd do anything for me, worked hard to make sure I didn't. Unlike his father, who never did anything he didn't have to." Bernadette sighed, and her voice caught. "His father outlived him for fifteen years. Fifteen years of me having to do more and more of the work while he coughed his lungs out. Never stopped smoking. Never stopped drinking. Just did less and less and less. Mireille is just like him. But Charles, ah, he was my rock." Bernadette inhaled deeply. She folded the birth certificate into neat quarters and placed it back in the faded tin. She replaced the lid and pressed it down, stroking it gently as if it was a pet cat.

Then she took another deep breath and stood up, the tin tucked under her arm. "We haven't got all day, you know. That milk needs churning and the barn needs mucking out. Are you going to sit there till lunchtime or are you going to give me a hand?"

January slipped into February and there was still no sign of Thierry Thibault. Lottie got jumpier and jumpier as the days gradually lengthened. Every time she heard a vehicle along the road, which wasn't very often, her stomach, already flatter than it had ever been, tightened. With petrol severely rationed, the Blanchard's Citroën, parked up in the oldest barn with an empty petrol tank, was useless and provided no means of escaping the dreariness.

Bernadette returned from the market twice a week with the promised bread and a heavy purse, which would have made anyone else cheer up, but she seemed less pleased with bartering her unwanted milk coupons for real coffee or swapping eggs for chocolate, than ghoulishly re-telling tales of increased German brutality. The coffee and chocolate were welcome, but the dark rumours only made Lottie more anxious.

Mireille continued to smoke, despite her mother's request that she didn't, but increasingly the tobacco consisted of random herbs and smelt even worse than the French cigarettes she adored. So, she started going to the market every week with Bernadette, to try and barter for some better ones. Françoise, rapt at the progress of little Bertrand but tired from broken nights as he developed his milk teeth, wasn't interested in going to Caen for a change of scene and couldn't care less about Lottie's anxieties. No-one seemed to care about those. Increasingly, she felt truly alienated and was terrified this would become her official status. However tedious life on Bernadette's little farm was, Lottie had no doubt that prison camp would be more so, and with a lot less food.

She had to get a message somehow to Thierry. It was her only chance of getting forged papers.

When asked, Bernadette refused to go on an extra errand. "I'm busy enough with the market days without taking messages to damn schoolteachers. Hate the lot of them. No, I don't need another trip away from the farm. Now I must go and check on the bees."

Her daughter was equally, if more predictably, unhelpful. "I'm not going to ladder my last pair of stockings on cycling into that squalid little village. Fancy that schoolteacher, do you?" Mireille gave Lottie a smirk that she itched to slap away.

Bernadette snorted. "You should know all about that. You never thought the village squalid when you were after the mayor."

Lottie looked at the older woman.

"Oh, yes, this precious daughter of mine who gives herself such airs. Shamed us all, she did. I had to pack her off to Paris before it was too late. I don't go to the village at all now, if I can help it. People still point."

"Oh, Mother! That was years and years ago. I'm sure everyone has forgotten all about my little contretemps."

"What are you talking about?" Françoise came downstairs with a bucket of nappies to wash.

Bernadette opened her mouth to respond but Mireille got in first. "Nothing. Just a silly and very old story your grandmother likes to tell."

"Because it's the truth!"

"Oh, pah!" Mireille walked out and went upstairs.

Lottie could see that neither woman would ever accompany her to the village because of this old scandal. She didn't even bother asking Françoise.

The month of February opened with a false spring. For two whole days the sun shone, and the frost kept its icy fingers gloved.

"Take the goats for a walk in the orchard," Bernadette said. She still never used Lottie's name. "The sun will do them good and they can trim the hawthorn hedges for me. Stay with them, mind, or they'll wander off in search of other berries. Take them two at a time and tether them."

Lottie didn't bother to reply, just nodded. She threw a rope around the neck of the two youngest goats and lead them outside. Desperate for fresh fodder, they quickly became engrossed in foraging. Lottie let herself relax and lifted her face to the weak rays of the wintry sun. She leant against an apple tree, noting its buds of promise and wondered if this new year would bring any hope with it.

Her eyelids drooped, and she let them fall.

"Didn't think I'd catch you napping."

Lottie's eyes flew open. Over the hedge she saw a black beret and beneath it, a pair of spectacles and a smiling face.

"Monsieur Thibault!"

"Thought we'd agreed to use first names from now on?" Thierry leant on the fence that filled the break in the hedges.

Slightly stupefied from her doze and overcome with relief, Lottie greeted him with a kiss on either cheek, by leaning across the gap. "It's good to see you."

"Thanks for the warm welcome. Nice to see you too." New lines crinkled around his eyes.

"Thierry, I…I tried to get to the village but there are road-blocks now and, without ID papers, I didn't dare risk it."

"I guessed as much, that's why I'm here. Can you come with me to meet a friend? He has a camera and could take your picture for the identity papers. Once that's done, I can take it to the forger."

"You would do all that for me?"

"You won't be much help to me without papers."

Lottie felt absurdly disappointed with his reply. "Oh, I see."

"So, can you come now, or would you prefer to babysit these goats all day?" Thierry nodded in the direction of the munching goats.

"I can come. Give me five minutes."

Lottie gathered up the goats, hoping they'd be so full of food they'd comply.

"Come on you two, let's see if we can find some more for you."

She hoped they understood her lie. They trotted behind her willingly and she soon had them back in the barn, fobbing them off with more dry hay and leaving them before their mothers realised they'd been cheated of their foray into the orchard.

Lottie ran towards the farmhouse. She found Bernadette in the vegetable plot next to the kitchen, getting carrots from the clamp. "I'm going out for a bicycle ride, Bernadette. The youngest goats have had a good feed and they're back in the barn."

"It's the milkers who need feeding up! You can't go out now. And what about your papers?" Bernadette stood up, making her arthritic knees crack.

"Get Mireille to do it. I'm going to make the most of this gorgeous sunny day. I promise I'll be careful."

Before Bernadette could reply, Lottie went around the back of the house, retrieved the bicycle and jumped on it. She pedalled fast up the little lane and found Thierry waiting for her in the road on the other side of the orchard.

"That was quick!" That grin again. It transformed his face.

"Can you keep up if I cycle?" She was keen to put some distance between them and the farmhouse.

"I can try. It's this way." Thierry set off northwards.

"I hope we don't have to go through the road-block."

"No, I've arranged we meet by a disused barn. It's about a kilometre away, by the river."

Lottie eased back her speed and Thierry trotted alongside her. A rush of excitement flooded through her. She was free from the farm at last and, if she got some official papers, she could escape more often!

They soon reached the old limestone building. One wall had fallen in, dragging the corrugated tin roof down at the corner. A bare-branched sycamore tree growing inside disclosed the reason why.

Thierry slowed to a walking pace and said, breathlessly, "This is it. Pierre should be inside, waiting for us."

Lottie dismounted and walked alongside him. "It is very good of you and your friend to do this for me."

"I'm not doing it for you. You're needed for deliveries." Thierry opened the rickety gate, which announced their arrival with a loud creak of its warped wood.

"You mean I'm expendable."

An older man peered around the edge of the broken wall. He was tall and big-boned, white haired with a bushy moustache and, like Thierry, had a high forehead. He, too, wore a black beret and corduroy trousers.

"Salut, Pierre!" Thierry kissed the man's cheeks. "This is my young friend, Charlotte."

"Enchanté, Mam'selle." Pierre shook her hand. His was enormous and strong, despite his age.

Thierry nodded towards the barn. "Have you got your camera?"

"Of course. Come inside quickly."

They all went in. A white sheet hung against the far wall and before it stood a tripod supporting a box camera.

Without preamble, Pierre pointed at it. "Please, Charlotte, would you compose yourself and stand in front of the camera with the sheet behind you? Oh, and please remove your headscarf."

Lottie did as she was told and smoothed her hair down.

"No, don't smile. Look straight at me."

There was a flash of blinding light and then it was over.

Thierry looked at his older friend. "Got it?"

"I think so." Pierre nodded to Thierry.

Lottie felt invisible as the two men talked together in a low voice.

She cleared her throat noisily. "Can I move now?"

Pierre frowned at her. "Of course," and turned back to Thierry.

They resumed their conversation in tones too low for her to hear. Lottie tied her scarf back on and joined them.

Thierry looked cross and held up an autocratic finger. "A moment, please."

Annoyed, Lottie left the barn and went to stand outside. She wished she smoked, it would have given her something to do and an air that she didn't care about being ignored, which she did. She pumped up the tyre on her bicycle instead. It didn't need it really. Then, in the distance she heard the sound of a car, a rare thing these days with petrol severely rationed.

Immediately, Thierry came bounding out of the barn. "Quick! It's bound to be the Boche, they're the only ones with petrol. Come into the barn – and bring your bicycle!"

Lottie dropped her pump and wheeled the bike into the barn, struggling as she lifted it over the broken wall. They only just made it inside before a big Citroën drove past, the ubiquitous swastika flag on its bonnet signalling its allegiance. "I left my bicycle pump outside. I hope they won't see it."

"So do I." Thierry muttered, close to her ear.

They all crouched into the furthest corner of the broken building, listening to see if the vehicle stopped outside. They heard the gears of the big car change down. Lottie held her breath. Thierry looked at her with those intense blue eyes of his. She no longer noticed his spectacles. His gaze held until they heard the Citroën accelerate around a bend in the road and the drone of its engine faded away.

"We mustn't use this barn again, Pierre. Too close to the road." Thierry turned to look at his friend.

Pierre was already packing up his camera. Lottie unpinned the sheet and folded it neatly.

Pierre looked at her and nodded. "Thank you. That is helpful. Thierry? I must go. When I've developed the picture, I will take it to the forger and get him to send word when it's ready. Have you the payment?"

Lottie was shocked. Payment? Thierry had not asked for any money. "What is the cost?"

"Do not worry, Charlotte, I have it covered." Thierry passed over some notes to the older man.

Pierre took them, muttering that coupons would have been handier, and quickly disappeared with his kit in a leather satchel. For such a big man, he was surprisingly nimble over the broken pile of stones.

Furious, Lottie turned to Thierry. "You never told me this would have to be paid for!"

"It's not all for Pierre. It's for the forger too."

"I don't care who it's for! You have no right to assume responsibility and pay for something on my behalf without even telling me."

"You will pay, perhaps with your life."

"That's not the point! I won't be beholden to anyone. You will tell me how much and I will reimburse you."

"With what? I thought you were a refugee?" Thierry was walking away.

"Don't walk away when I'm talking to you!" Lottie followed him out of the barn.

Her bicycle jammed between two stones in the wall. Thierry turned back and effortlessly lifted it out.

It didn't help Lottie's temper. "I can manage, thank you, just as I can manage my own affairs."

"Suit yourself." Abruptly Thierry dropped the bike and it fell back against the limestone boulders.

"You oaf! You'll bend the wheels like that."

"Nonsense. These old bikes are tough as leather."

Lottie settled the bicycle against the pile of stones. "Now listen here, Monsieur Thibault, I insist you tell me how much this is costing, or I won't deliver a single one of your precious leaflets. And, for that matter, if you damage this bike, I won't be able to!"

Thierry burst out into laughter, which only made Lottie crosser than ever. "What's so funny?"

"You! With you on our side, the Germans don't stand a chance. I'm sorry, you are quite right about the bicycle. We'll need it and, if you're loaded, by all means pay for the forgery - or rather the bribes along the way. I'll need five hundred francs."

It was a lot more than she had bargained for. Thank God for Granny's jewellery.

"That's fine. I'll give it to you when you deliver the ID papers."

"Good." Thierry straightened his beret and held out his hand. "Goodbye for now, Mademoiselle Perrot. I have all the details of your so-called birth on French soil and your description." He tapped his pocket where he had put the note about her details. "I'll walk over one Sunday, after the deed is done, and then we'll see what we can achieve, yes?"

Lottie spurned his hand and reached instead for her bicycle. She got on it and cycled away, only realising, after she turned the first bend, that she'd left her pump behind. Gritting her teeth, she cycled back and, after rummaging around in the grass for a full ten minutes, found the wretched thing and attached it to the shaft of the bicycle.

Thierry Thibault was nowhere to be seen.

CHAPTER THIRTY EIGHT
CHEADLE MANOR
JANUARY 1941

Isobel felt rotten. Her cold had settled on her chest and taken most of her energy with it. She hadn't seen Al for days. She knew he was planning to volunteer for the RAF straight after Christmas, but he hadn't visited for a week. Neither had she heard from Geraint. He'd kept to his word of saying nothing more until he heard from her first. And she hadn't got in touch. She ought to send a card at least to say she was poorly, but even that had seemed too daunting a task. Now she felt more guilty than ever. She tossed and turned every night, her dreams filled with either Geraint's sad eyes looming over her or Granny's hectoring voice lecturing her. Between them both, her conscience was pricked sore and she knew no peace.

She came downstairs for the first time since she'd succumbed to illness and ventured into the big dining room. A waft of scrambled eggs from the huge buffet sideboard almost made her heave.

"Bella, darling!" Cassandra looked up from her newspaper. "How lovely to see you downstairs again. Tea?"

"Thanks." Isobel knees threatened to buckle under her, so she slid on to a dining-chair before they did.

"You know, I don't think that was just a cold you had. More like influenza. I think we should get Dr Benson to come and see you." Cassandra poured tea from the silver pot and passed her the cup and saucer.

Adding milk, Isobel shook her head. "Oh, don't bother the poor chap. I'm sure he's busy." She coughed and couldn't stop the spasms.

"Darling, you shouldn't be up. Go back to bed after breakfast."

Isobel put some sugar in her tea and stirred it. "I'm sick of being up in my bedroom, all alone. I'm sure I'm needed at Home Farm too."

"I doubt it. The ground is as hard as steel. They won't be able to do much."

"The cows will still need milking."

Cassandra looked back at her newspaper. "I suppose that's true."

"I'll give Farmer Stubbs a ring and see how he's doing." Isobel drank her tea. It wasn't quite hot enough.

"Good idea and, um, I didn't like to bother you before, but Al came round."

"Oh, Mummy, why didn't you tell me?" Isobel put her cup down with a clatter on its bone china saucer.

"Well, maybe I should have, but you still had a temperature and I was quite worried about you. I didn't think it right for Al to visit you in your bedroom." Cassandra gave up the pretence of reading the newspaper and folded it into neat quarters. She turned her face away on the pretext of pouring a second cup of Earl Grey tea. "I've been waiting to tell you, but I have had the official letter about the manor being requisitioned. The army officer responsible is visiting next week to look at the place."

"Really? Oh, my goodness. Will we be able to carry on living here?" Isobel coughed again. Her chest hurt.

"I don't know yet, maybe, but West Lodge is still empty. The Ponsonby's place has already been taken over and they've had to move into the west wing and camp there. Marion hates it. She says they are so noisy with their hobnailed boots on the stairs and it's ruining the wood panelling. Their house is even older than ours, you know. Elizabethan. I do hope the wainscoting survives all those soldiers. It's quite beautiful, don't you think?"

Isobel couldn't think of anything less important at that moment. Her headache was worsening by the minute. "I'm going to telephone Farmer Stubbs and see how he's getting on without me."

"Aren't you going to eat something?"

"Not hungry."

Farmer Stubbs, when pressed, insisted he could manage without her and she would be better at home till she was over her fluey cold. "I don't want you coming near my cows and sneezing all over them – or me for that matter. No, Miss Isobel, I'm managing fine on me own. 'Tis only milking, this time of year."

She put the telephone back on its cradle. She felt more relieved than she'd expected to. This bug had sucked the life out of her. She ought to telephone Geraint, she really should, but her head was pounding, and her sinuses ached from the catarrh clogging them up. She turned away from the receiver and mounted the grand staircase. When she reached her room, she sprawled on to her soft bed and fell fast asleep.

Cassandra called Dr Benson later that day and after he had examined Isobel, he declared she had pneumonia and mustn't get out of bed until her temperature had come down and her chest had cleared.

"Make sure she inhales steam with Friar's Balsam, Mrs Flintock-Smythe. Lots of fluids, only a little food, soups and such-like. Keep the room warm but aired. I'll be back in two days."

Isobel felt too weak to argue and collapsed back against the pillows in meek submission where she stayed for many days, sleeping and aching and worrying, with her mother and Mrs Andrews hovering over her whenever they could.

It was a full fortnight before she was up again, weak as a kitten, but finally with a ravenous appetite. Her mother, thinner and looking more worn-out than ever, greeted her once more over the breakfast table. This time, Isobel helped herself to kedgeree and wolfed it down.

Her mother laughed. "I wish I was young again. You look as hungry as a horse. No doubt you'll recuperate faster than me now you're on the mend and I wasn't even ill, only nursing you."

Isobel couldn't answer. Her mouth was too full of eggs and smoked haddock. After swallowing it down and before the next tasty morsel, she asked for coffee. "Can't face tea, somehow. I want a good strong cup of coffee."

"Hmm, that's hard to find, these days, darling. I'll call for Andrews and see what the kitchen can rustle up." Cassandra got up and pulled the bell sash.

Andrews appeared and, when asked for coffee, said doubtfully, "I'll see what we can do."

Having eaten nothing solid for days and days, Isobel felt suddenly full. Her plate only half empty, she laid down her knife and fork and sat back, replete. "So, Mummy, what's been happening while I've been in purdah?"

Cassandra smiled and returned to the dining table. She did look very tired. "Well, the army officer, a charming man, inspected our humble home and declared it just right for a hospital."

"So, it is going to be a hospital, after all?"

"That's right, darling. Seems we're to house wounded servicemen. Rather a lot of them."

"Where?"

Cassandra paused and gave her a hard look. "That's just it, Bella. It's as I feared. They want the whole house. They're going to set up an operating theatre in here, would you believe? And they say they need all the bedrooms for wards. The study will be an office and the drawing room a sort of recreation room for the patients to relax in."

"*What*? What about us? What about the staff?" Isobel now regretted the eggs. She felt rather nauseous.

"Mr and Mrs Andrews will remain in their cottage by the orchard and the other staff live out, anyway. The gardener, the youngest Phipps, has already taken over his father's cottage at East Lodge. As for us, darling, we're going to the West Lodge."

"You mean the Beagles' old house? Where Aunt Katy was born?"

"That's right. It's the only place that's currently empty."

340

Isobel gulped. "Good Lord, I thought that was a very remote possibility."

"Quite. Kate thinks it's hilarious." Cassandra looked out of the window. Her eyes looked glassy, not smiling at all.

Isobel didn't smile either. "So, we'll have no staff with us, then? Just you and me, fending for ourselves?"

Cassandra smiled at her daughter for the first time. "It'll be cosy, won't it? Yes, just you and me camping out together. It'll be such fun, darling."

"What will Al say about us living in his grandparents' old house?"

"Ah, now, he's been telephoning and calling most days. I think it's time you saw the dear boy. He has some news of his own."

"Oh?" Isobel's over-full stomach contracted painfully.

Cassandra got up from the table. "I'll leave him to explain it to you." She threaded her linen napkin through its solid-silver band, inscribed with her name. "Excuse me now, darling. You wouldn't believe how busy I am getting ready for this invasion. I promised I'd see Mrs Andrews about storing the linen this morning."

Her mother left the room and Andrews came in with the pot of coffee. It's fragrant steam consoled Isobel as the butler poured it out into her cup.

"Thank you." Isobel topped it up with some thin cream. "So, Andrews, seems we're to get shipped out."

"I believe so, Miss Isobel." Andrews, uncharacteristically, ran his gloved hand over his heavy brow. "I'm sure I don't know what the world is coming to."

CHAPTER THIRTY NINE
NORMANDY
MARCH 1941

By the time March blew the short month of February out with a blizzard, Lottie was so fed up with being stuck at the farm, she was seriously contemplating going to the village and braving the German controls, papers or no papers, and to hell with the consequences.

"Don't be stupid. You'd be clapped in jail in five minutes." Bernadette scoffed at her scheme.

"It's all very well for you but I'm trapped here. The best conversations I have are with your blasted goats."

"Well then, don't let me keep you from them." Bernadette turned her back and disappeared into the scullery at the back of the kitchen.

Lottie sighed and went out into the icy air, across the virgin snow transforming the dun-coloured cobbled yard into a white shroud, and into the relative warmth of the barn. At least it was light now when she milked the goats in the morning. She'd even got used to their smell and they had got used to her. Now, her fingers were no longer clumsy on their teats and they remained calm and still while she extracted their precious cargo. Despite the fresh fall of snow, the sun was shining brightly, and Lottie left the door of the barn ajar to give more light. She'd finished milking the oldest nanny and was shifting her stool to the next, when the door was pushed open wide. The blast of arctic air made her shiver, and she looked up, expecting Bernadette, but the blue shadow cast against the white mantel of snow was much taller.

"Thierry! At last! I had given up hope that you would ever come."

"Well, here I am."

"Have you got my papers?"

"I have." Thierry strode across the straw lying on the floor and held out an envelope in his gloved hand. He was grinning that transformational smile.

Lottie stood up and took the little packet he carried. Barely glancing at him, she tore open the envelope and stared at the picture of her face. She looked a lot older than when she'd left England, much thinner and very serious. She checked the details. Charlotte Perrot, daughter of Charles Perrot and Sylvie Merlin, both deceased. Her address was given as Bernadette's farm. She had given Mireille's housekeeper's house, the plump and loyal Sophie, as her previous address and claimed she was born in Paris. So, now she was officially French, female, with brown hair, brown eyes, a medium shaped mouth, clear skin. Such intimate details.

French. A new identity. Freedom. Escape.

She looked at Thierry. "Thank you, thank you, from the bottom of my heart."

Thierry mumbled something incoherent and shrugged. "You'd better sign it under your photograph."

Lottie nodded. She clutched the little booklet to her chest and let out her breath. She almost felt she hadn't done that properly since she left Paris.

"I must pay you Thierry."

"There is really no need."

"I don't believe that. You can use it to save someone else if it makes you feel better. Stay there."

She dashed back to the farmhouse and quietly slipped upstairs to her room. She had her money stashed away in her suitcase under the bed, with her precious books. She took out the five hundred francs and ran back to the barn with the wad of ten-franc notes.

Breathless with running, she went inside and handed over the cash. "Here you are."

Thierry took it, his face serious. "Thank you, this will be very useful. There is much need."

"I'm happy to pay you back. If you want to thank me, you could lend me a book or two to read? I've read the ones I brought with me so many times, I know each word by heart."

"I'd be glad to. Mine are all in French."

"All the better. So, now I'm official, what are my duties?"

"Before you undertake anything remotely dangerous, you should go into the village and pass through a control. Then we'll know if you'll be any use to us." Thierry removed his beret and ran his hands through his hair. He looked tired.

"Have you been doing dangerous things?" Lottie turned away and moved the full pail of milk to a safe place in the corner. She wasn't risking spilling it again.

"Perhaps."

"What happened to those *'Resistance'* newspapers you brought from Paris?"

"Oh, those got delivered alright. What we need now are coupons."

"Coupons?"

Thierry raised his eyebrows above the line of his spectacles. "Yes, food coupons. Stamps. Tickets. You know the sort of thing. Or maybe you don't understand. People are queuing in the shops for food. Trading cigarettes. They even trade themselves in Paris. You are cushioned here by Bernadette. She's a tough old bird."

"Cushioned! You should try it. It's true I've not left the farm for months and I'm keen to do so. There's no need to patronise my ignorance." Why did this man infuriate her so?

Thierry shrugged again and spread his hands wide. "Forgive me. It is hard to see people going hungry. I will tell you little of why we need these things. The less you know the better. We are developing a network of people who are willing to work underground against the Boche, and we have all agreed it's better if we know as little as possible about each other, or what we're up to. That way, if we get caught, we can't shop anyone else."

Lottie digested this before speaking. "I see. That makes sense. So, what do you want me to do?"

Thierry nodded at her acknowledgement. "Cycle into the village tomorrow. There's a control on this side at the moment. Usually it's on the zone interdit boundary by the main road, but they've moved it for some reason best known to themselves. You'll have to present your papers, of course. Buy bread, if you can, or something ordinary like that. Don't attempt to steal coupons this time, unless you get an opportunity you can't resist. Then, leave a message with Madame Leroy at the boulangerie. You may have to queue for a while." He gave a little smile. "Tell her, um, tell her the chickens are laying again at the Perrot farm."

It seemed too banal to Lottie. She'd imagined doing something far more daring than buying a baguette.

"I think I can manage that."

"Good. Don't worry. I'll keep you busy after we know you can get around." With that, he reached out and patted her shoulder. Before she could reply, he left, quietly shutting the barn door behind him.

Lottie peeped at her identity card again. How lucky that Bernadette's son had been called Charles, like her real dead uncle whom she had never met but was named after. How different was Charlotte Perrot's humble abode to Lottie Flintock-Smythe's privileged birthplace of Cheadle Manor. She wondered if she would ever see her real home again.

She finished milking the other nanny goat and, after depositing the buckets of milk in the outbuilding, went inside the farmhouse. Bernadette was peeling Jerusalem artichokes to make a gratin. Lottie hated the knobbly vegetables. They always made her insides growl, but potatoes were scarce.

She held out her little card to show her hostess. "I have my papers."

"How did you get those? Has someone been here?"

"You don't need to know, and I'm not allowed to say, I'm sorry, but it means I can go to the village now. I thought I'd go in the morning, try for some bread."

Bernadette shrugged. "I hope you haven't compromised our safety. You're not in with the blasted Communists, are you?"

Lottie shook her head.

Bernadette looked resigned, surprisingly. Lottie had expected more opposition.

"So, who are you?" Bernadette began to slice the tubers.

"I'm your granddaughter and your son, Charles, was my father."

Bernadette frowned. "You look nothing like him. Who was your alleged mother then?"

"Sylvie Merlin."

"Never heard of her." Bernadette started layering the slices into a gratin dish.

"That's probably because she never existed. I hope they don't try and trace her origins." Lottie was already very aware of this flaw in her plan.

Bernadette surprised her a second time. "You'd better make up some story. Say she was not from around here, that you resemble her, because you certainly don't look like my son. You'd better say she died recently. Say she came from Paris and that's where you grew up. That's a big enough place to be unknown."

"Thank you, Bernadette. That's a really good idea and I've already put that in as my place of birth. It's strange, I can almost imagine my pretend mother myself now." Lottie laughed.

Bernadette gave a grim smile. "I suppose you're not the worst granddaughter I could have had. Here, you'd better have some bread stamps."

Lottie slept fitfully that night and woke before dawn. Not waiting for the daylight to break, she got up and dressed carefully. The coat she'd brought from Paris was tailored and well cut. Too good for a peasant like Charlotte

346

Perrot. Despite the cold, she decided to leave it and wear an old one of her supposed father's. The rough tweed chafed her skin, but it fitted her new persona to a tee.

Bernadette was also up. "I'll milk the goats today. Bon courage." She passed her a bowl of real coffee and a less appetising chunk of her rock-hard home-made bread.

Lottie dipped it in the hot liquid until it softened and ate it quickly. She tipped the bowl up and drank from it. She was certainly adopting the ways of a peasant. Could she fool the German soldiers?

Frozen ruts had formed in the road near the village, making it hard to cycle straight. The tyres kept getting caught in them, making Lottie veer off. Very inelegant. But then, the last thing she wanted to appear was elegant. She supposed she should have a country accent. When the red and white barrier came into view, she desperately tried to mimic Bernadette's strong country burr in her head. The conversation with the guards ought to be short and straightforward. She ought to get away with it. Unless she didn't.

Would her schoolgirl French hold up? Could she adopt the local dialect?

"Halt!" The soldier held up his hand while keeping the other on his gun. Another soldier stood on the other side of the narrow road. His gun was pointing straight at her.

Lottie slowed her bike. It skidded on the ice as she braked. Before it stopped moving, she slid off and lost her footing on the slippery road. Neither of the young soldiers came to her aid. She just about managed not to fall over. Her body had gone inflexible with nerves and she almost dropped the bike.

"Papers, please." The soldier spoke in French with a strong German accent. He held out his hand, unsmiling.

Lottie fished in the pocket of her big man's coat. She should have roughed up the identity card, made it look used. She scuffed it under her frozen fingers.

"Schnell!"

Lottie jumped at the command. Slowly, despite his request to hurry, she drew the little booklet from her coat pocket and handed it over. She squared her shoulders and forced herself to look straight at him.

"I hope we don't get more snow today." She tried to look nonchalant by nodding her head skywards.

The soldier grunted. "It's worse than Germany here."

He scrutinised her face, then looked back down at her photograph. "Where do you live Mademoiselle Perrot?"

Lottie jerked her head back towards the farm. "Little farm back there. It's only a kilometre away."

"Why are you going to the village?"

"To buy bread, maybe some other things."

"You'll be lucky."

"I hope so." Lottie risked a smile, a big one.

The soldier's eyes widened fractionally, then he smiled back. "I hope you find what you want." He handed back her precious papers.

Miraculously, the barrier lifted. Lottie stuffed the ID card back in her pocket, making quite sure it was safely tucked away. She kept smiling as she clambered back on her pushbike, hoping her teeth wouldn't chatter and show her up. Then she was cycling freely, still wobbling on the ribbed road, still scared, but also elated. She'd made it!

Even though it was so early, a small queue had already formed outside the baker's shop. Lottie propped her bike against the wall and joined the group.

"Not too bad today," the woman in front of her said. "Haven't seen you for a while?"

"The snow kept me at home."

"Yes, terrible winter."

They kept to the safe topic of the weather until it was Lottie's turn. Madame Leroy, her kind face dusted with flour, screwed up her eyes when she saw Lottie.

"What can I get you?"

There was no choice. "Just a baguette, please. And Grandmère said to tell you that the hens are laying again at the Perrot farm."

Madame Leroy's stout arm paused in its reach for the fragrant loaf. She turned to Lottie and winked. "That's good to know."

Lottie sailed past the guards without being stopped on the way home. Much of the day still lay ahead. She felt triumphant when she reached the farmhouse, but it quickly evaporated into a state of anti-climax.

Bernadette had milked the goats. Françoise was helping her to decant some calvados into fresh bottles and Mireille was mending clothes – her own, naturally. In the course of the morning, the weather had changed. The freezing temperature had relented at last. Already the fresh snow was melting at the edges. Dull clouds obscured the sun and the evaporating snow misted the horizon, making the day darker and gloomier than ever.

Unable to find something to do with her new-found energy and freedom, Lottie grabbed the bicycle and jumped on it, heading towards the sea, hoping some exercise would force out the remaining wintry cobwebs fogging up her mind.

She pedalled fast, following the salty scent of the ocean by instinct, rather than by sight, as the hazy air parted only reluctantly around her and the edges of the lanes lay hidden under the bruised, melting snow. After a few kilometres, when the ground beneath her rose, she slowed her pace as she reached the main Route Nationale running from west to east, parallel with the coast. The big road was blocked. A wooden barrier barred her way and barbed wire barrelled across the entire road. Over it flapped the dreaded Swastika flag and beside that stood a sentry box painted with opposing diagonal stripes. Two soldiers paced up and down, guns at the ready, their gaze turned from her towards the sea.

Unwilling to risk interrogation, Lottie dismounted and walked her bike forwards, inch by inch. A westerly wind awoke and stirred the heavy, land-hugging clouds into motion. Lottie stood and watched as they shimmered, before splitting apart to reveal the grey tumbling sea far away in the distance. She gripped her handlebars and stared, not daring to move.

And that's when she'd seen the German officers. They stood on the grassy slopes to the west, where the clouds had now blown right away inland in a sudden gust of wind. She knew they were officers by their peaked caps, as opposed to those ugly metal helmets, like upside-down pudding basins, that the ordinary soldiers wore. The cluster of men wore tailored overcoats, the Nazi symbol emblazoned on their sleeves and collars and jodhpurs encased in long, highly polished black boots.

Lottie dismounted quietly and wheeled her pushbike as close as she dared, using the roadside hedge for cover. The German officers had left their cars parked on the smaller road on this side of the barrier and they stood, empty of life, between Lottie and the huddle of men in their smart greatcoats. She hid behind the nearest black car and tried to catch their words. It was useless. Even if she could understand their language, and her German had never been as good as her French, their earnest conversation drifted away on the brisk wind.

She could read their gestures though. They were pointing up and down from left to right and towards the storm barrelling in on the horizon beyond them. They nodded to each other as if in agreement. Harsh, male laughter floated across the tufts of rough grass between Lottie and the group of big men.

When the men turned back towards their vehicles, Lottie grabbed her bike and jumped on. She pedalled as fast as she could, ignoring the shouts to halt, praying none them would use the pistols she'd seen clamped to their belts.

When she got back to the farm, all thoughts of resenting Mireille's idle ways, Bernadette's unfair demands and Françoise's motherly complacency had been supplanted by the very real fear that she was truly trapped. She could see no possible avenue of escape while the Germans occupied this part of France. With hindsight, she now realised she might be physically nearer home than if they had joined the other refugees going south, but the reality was she might as well be on the moon for all the chance she'd get to sail back to England and her family.

Lottie remained restless and unsettled. Her new freedom of movement made her hungry for change. All week she waited for a message from Thierry. She hadn't known what to expect after her heady success in going to the village, but anything would be better than nothing. She felt keyed up, tense, and yet nothing changed. Except the weather. It continued to thaw the perma-frost of winter. Buds on the apple trees fattened up and rain washed away the last vestiges of muddy snow that hugged the hedge banks.

In the end, she decided to take matters into her own hands. The hens had started laying daily again and they had more eggs than the four of them could eat, or Bernadette could comfortably carry to the market in Caen.

"Shall I take some eggs into the village to sell, Bernadette? I'm sure Madame Leroy could use some at the bakery."

"That's not a bad idea. Make sure she pays full whack. She's always out for a bargain, that one." Bernadette handed Lottie the basket of eggs.

After such an easy victory, Lottie fully expected a confrontation with the German sentries, but that was straightforward too. The same two soldiers who checked her identity card were on duty again at the bridge into the village. What a boring life they led! She stopped at the bridge and lifted the lid of her wicker basket to show her eggs.

"Black market, eh?" Said the older man with a knowing wink.

"That's right, but you won't tell anyone, will you? My grandmother will be furious if I don't sell them for a profit." Lottie stood closer than necessary to the German.

He touched his nose on the side and jerked his head towards the village.

"Your secret is safe with me, Mademoiselle, in exchange for a couple of fresh eggs."

Lottie thought it a reasonable toll. She doled out the eggs into his massive palm. "There you are. I hope you enjoy them. They were laid this morning."

The soldier pocketed the eggs and jerked his head in the direction of the village.

"Heil Hitler!" The German saluted. Lottie got on her bike and pedalled away without reciprocating. Some things she would *not* do.

Outside the boulangerie, she elbowed her way past the queue.

"Hey, wait your turn like the rest of us!"

But Madame Leroy greeted her and her eggs like a long-lost friend. "Oh, Mon dieu, these eggs are magnificent. Quickly, put them under the counter. Take them out of your basket and put them in that wooden box. I shall make gateaux today."

While her head was under the counter, Lottie whispered. "Is there any message for me?"

Madame Leroy looked down at her and winked again. "Here, let me open the till and pay you. She counted out the coins and slipped them in some paper which she folded over the money. "Remember to thank Madame Perrot for the eggs. They look very fresh."

Lottie took the folded paper with its cache of coins and winked back.

"Thanks, I will."

"And take a baguette as part payment."

Complaints from the women in the queue who'd been passively waiting during the exchange of eggs and money now became vociferous.

"We've been waiting for half an hour for some bread. She just marches in and you give her a loaf straightaway!"

Madame Leroy held up her hands. "Ladies, please! Wouldn't you like some flan and patisseries for a change? Now I have some eggs, I can create wonders! Come back this afternoon with your coupons and see what delights there will be for you to buy."

The grumbles subsided into mutterings. Lottie took her chance and sidled past, ignoring the glares. Outside, she picked up her bike and wheeled it under the big trees in the centre of the square. Under their protection and hidden by their trunks, she unfurled the paper surrounding the coins. There was a message in a sort of code.

"Bicycle needed. Apply at the school."

Lottie folded the paper quickly and stuffed it in her pocket with the money. She clambered back on her bicycle and looked across at the soldiers guarding the Mairie's office, still draped with that dreadful Nazi flag. They didn't seem interested in her, but she still went the long way to the school, around the church in the opposite direction, through the graveyard and to the school beyond.

The children were playing in the yard, as children always do. Games of tag and skipping with lots of screams and shouts to go with them. They looked as if they hadn't a care in the world, though many of their fathers had been deported to work camps, and their mothers struggled to find enough to feed them.

Uplifted by their cheerful ordinariness, Lottie parked her bicycle and went inside the school. She found Thierry in the little kitchen, his hands warming on a cup of ersatz coffee as he watched the children play through the window.

"Mademoiselle Perrot, how nice to see you." He turned and smiled. A small, professional, polite smile rather than that wonderful grin. He still looked tired.

"Monsieur Thibault." Lottie inclined her head towards him. "Someone told me the school had need of a bicycle."

"That's correct, yes. Come with me. Did anyone see you enter the school?"

Lottie shook her head and followed the young teacher into the classroom. He fished about in the drawer of his big desk on the wooden dais and retrieved a brown envelope, similar to the one he'd given her not so long ago. He took out a book as well and slipped the envelope inside its covers.

"I hope you will enjoy *'La Gloire de mon Père'*, it's a good place to start your reading. Lots of dialogue and insights into the French way of life, at least for the last generation. Who knows what the future may hold for the next?"

Lottie took the book. "Thank you. I will enjoy something new to read."

Thierry smiled. "Good. When you have finished, I'll give you another. In the meantime, someone else has need of a new identity. I left a message at the boulangerie in hopes you might call there. My other contacts are, um, unavailable. Could you deliver it?"

"Who is it?"

"He's an escaped prisoner-of-war."

"Jewish?"

"You don't need to know." Thierry shut the drawer of his desk.

"But…" Lottie felt irritated at all the cloak and dagger stuff. Surely it wouldn't hurt to know a little about this unknown escapee?

"Really, Charlotte, it's better this way, trust me. Some friends of mine have already been caught and detained; otherwise I wouldn't be asking. These arrests, they have changed everything, don't you see? All those involved in *"The Resistance"* could be under suspicion now. They weren't told many names either. The less you know, the less you can reveal. Even so, my dear friends are in grave danger." He drew his hand through his hair, leaving some standing up like a cock's comb. "You need to take this packet to the next village to yours, the one with the watermill. Monsieur Bertholin, as described in his identity card, will be waiting for you in the flour store by the mill. If you have any spare eggs, he might be glad of those too, to pay for his keep at the mill. Perhaps you could do some bartering with the mill-owner at the same time – you know, eggs for flour? It would be good cover."

"Yes, I can do that. How will I get word to you when I've done it?"

"Just keep delivering the eggs to the boulangerie unless we have to change it. Madame Leroy will let me know when you've been. She may have something else for you to deliver."

"So, you won't need me to come here to the school, then?"

Thierry shook his blond head. "No, that won't be necessary. The fewer links in the chain, the better."

Lottie felt oddly disappointed at this. "I see." She put the book with the envelope inside in her basket. "I'll be off then."

Thierry picked up a handbell and stilled the gong within its brass barrel. "Yes, it's time to call the children back inside for their lessons. Good day to you."

He led the way out, leaving Lottie with no option but to follow.

CHAPTER FORTY
KATHERINE WHEEL GARAGE AND CHEADLE MANOR
MARCH 1941

Katy Phipps threw down her pencil. It rolled off the desk and on to the floor with a clatter. "You've done what?"

"I've joined the ATA." Al couldn't keep the grin from his face.

"What's that when it's at home?" Katy looked up from her desk.

She and Jem had been going through the accounts in the office when he barged in, unannounced, and blurted out his triumph.

"Air Transport Auxiliary service."

"What about the RAF? Thought you'd applied to them?" Jem sat back in his chair and looked at his son.

Al scuffed the dusty floor with the toe of his shoe. "Didn't think I'd get in."

Jem leaned forward on his chair. "What's that? Don't mutter, Al."

Al raised his head from studying the floor. "You have to sit some tough exams for the RAF including mathematics. I didn't think I'd pass anyway. Don't expect they'd want me – not clever or upper class enough."

His mother astonished him then. She got up, scraping her chair on the concrete floor. Katy Phipps stood in front of him and placed her strong hands on his shoulders. "I sympathise, Al. I went through something similar when I applied to join the VAD in the last shout. They didn't want me either, just because I wasn't posh enough."

"Really? You've never said."

"No, because joining the WAAC was the best thing I ever did."

"Thanks a bunch." His father shrugged.

"Apart from marrying your Dad, of course." Katy turned and gave her husband a weary smile. "That goes without saying."

"Wouldn't hurt to say it once in a while." Jem stood up and joined them. "Come on, then lad, spill the beans. What's this Transport thingy?"

Over a brew in the kitchen of the bungalow, account books abandoned, Al finally told them all about it, flooded with relief they hadn't criticised his failure to enter the hallowed ranks of the glamorous RAF. He hadn't expected his parents to be quite so sympathetic and understanding.

"It's only a driver's job to start with because the pilots have to be trained up unless they were already flying before the war, which a lot of them were - including women – you'll be glad to know, Mum."

"Excellent, and why not?" Katy poured out a second cup of tea.

"Where will you be based, son?" Jem held out his mug for a top-up.

"White Waltham aerodrome, I expect. That's their headquarters."

"Isn't that in Berkshire?" Katy stirred her tea.

"Yes, that's right, not far from London, but the main thing is I've a real chance of getting to fly with this outfit."

Jem sipped his tea. "How did you find out about this auxiliary service?"

Al stirred sugar into his mug. "Air Transport Auxiliary. Well, first off, I met an RAF pilot at the Southampton depot. He took a pretty dim view about me getting into the RAF as a pilot, but Smith, the foreman, he told me about the ATA and got me thinking. Then, next time I was delivering the parachute components to the depot, I bumped into a pilot from the ATA. He was delivering a Hurricane – that's what they do – deliver pilots and planes all over Britain."

Al's eyes shone at the memory. "You see, I realised then you don't always have to be in the RAF to fly. This ATA pilot told me they're recruiting on a massive scale. Apparently, the RAF training squadron have vacated White Waltham and the ATA is taking it over. He said Lord Londonderry, whoever he is, had been on the radio appealing for volunteers. That's how he'd heard about it."

"I never heard that on our wireless." Katy shook her head.

"No, Mum, me neither but there you go. Anyway, seems it's true. I'm only going to be ground crew to start with but, you never know, I might work my way up to pilot, if I watch my p's and q's."

"So that's what you were doing when you never made it back from Southampton last week. It wasn't a puncture after all." Katy smiled.

Al grinned back. "Didn't want to say anything until I was sure I'd get in, especially after the RAF chap put me off. I'd never be more than ground crew with them. This way I've got a real chance to fly."

"Sounds like a good job, Al. Not as dangerous as the RAF but just as useful. I'm sure you'll learn a lot. You already know your way around an engine and can drive well. Should be just the ticket." His Dad nodded his approval.

"Yes, good for you, my lovely. We'll miss you, no denying it, and we'll have to find a new driver, but I wish you well. Keep safe, won't you?" Katy leant over and kissed his cheek, his face held between her oil-stained hands and her dark blue eyes completely focussed on his.

Al felt his heart expand and thud with excitement.

"When do you start?"

"Next week, Dad. I can't wait."

Saying goodbye to Isobel was the hardest bit. Still pale after her illness, she seemed a little distracted and the whole thing was less emotional than he'd expected.

Disappointed, angry and hurt at her detachment, Al didn't prolong their parting.

"So, you start next week then?" Isobel said politely, as if to a stranger.

"That's right. No messing about."

"I'm going back to work at the farm next Monday too, so we'll both be busy." She gave a little smile, also polite.

"Do you feel up to it, Bella? You're still looking a bit peaky."

Isobel tossed her wayward hair back. "I'm fine."

"Still pretty cold of a morning." Honestly, it's as if he was talking to an acquaintance rather than the woman he adored.

"At least it's not wet weather. I'd rather have a frosty morning than a muddy one."

Al cleared his throat. He was stumped for something to say. He'd never felt awkward with Isobel before, not ever.

"Well, good luck then, Bella." He went to kiss her. She averted her face, so he missed her lips and caught her cheek instead.

"Goodbye, Al. Good luck. I'm sure you'll do a great job for the ATA. Stay out of trouble, won't you?" Isobel took a step back.

Was that it? He just about managed to say goodbye back without embarrassing himself further by blurting out his true feelings or losing his temper. He didn't want to part like that. Who knew when they'd see each other again?

He passed Aunt Cassandra in the hall as he left. "Are you off, Al? Best of luck in your new job. Flying, isn't it?"

"No, I'll just be a driver, same as ever."

"Oh, I see. Well, good luck to you anyway, my dear."

Cassandra went to give him a kiss, but he stopped her by saying. "Got to go. Train to catch. 'Bye!"

As he sat on the train, with the familiar landscape of home disappearing fast through the window, Al tried to figure out what on earth had happened between him and Isobel. They'd hardly seen each other, it was true, but that was due to her being ill and before that, he remembered with a flash of anger, she'd had that suave Welshman painting her for hours on end. No wonder she'd caught a chill, sitting still for too long in that draughty old house. Thoughtless bastard. He hadn't even shown anyone the painting. Couldn't be much good.

The train chugged into Paddington station and Al got out, having found no solution to the puzzle. He easily found the train to White Waltham and had a lucky connection without having to wait too long. He was glad the journey didn't give him more time to think things over. No matter how much his mind tried to solve the problem, his heart remained sore and bruised.

The aerodrome was bigger than he'd expected and, with the rainy weather that had followed the cold snap, quite muddy. All three runways were grassed, to his surprise, and the scruffy buildings near the car park looked functional rather than impressive.

Aeroplanes of different shapes and sizes littered the airfield and a new building was going up next to the main one. Everyone looked busy and purposeful. The smell of aviation fuel assaulted his nostrils. Al sniffed the polluted air, yes, this was where he was supposed to be, where he *wanted* to be.

He wandered across to the nearest landing strip and stood watching as a large aeroplane approached from the west. A man in greasy overalls came and stood beside him.

"Hello there," Al smiled at the man.

"Afternoon." The man looked at him briefly and then returned his gaze to the sky.

"Big plane, that."

"Yes, one of the new Lancaster bombers."

"Oh? How many engines?"

"Four. Made by Avro with a Rolls Royce Engine."

"Oh, yes I read about that. Based on the old Manchester isn't it? Blimey, no wonder it's big."

"That's right. Heavy aeroplane. Let's see how it lands. Could be tricky."

They both focussed on the noisy machine lumbering towards them against the setting sun. The sound was deafening as the Lancaster approached, banked and came into land in a perfect smooth swoop. The wheels opened out under the carriage at just the right time and the big bomber's tyres touched the ground with a soft kiss.

Al let out a long whistle. "Perfect landing!"

The other man laughed. "Yes, that'll have the Governor eating his words."

"What do you mean?"

"Just you wait and see who's flying her."

"Alright, I will. I'm Al Phipps, by the way. What's your name?"

"Pat McBride, at your service."

"What do you do here, Pat?"

"Ground crew engineer."

"Is it a good place to work, only I'm about to start as a driver for the ATA?"

"Mate, it's the bloody best. Oh, look here comes the pilot."

A petite woman, dressed in a pilot's uniform, emerged from the plane and walked nonchalantly towards them.

"Hello, Pat. What do think of this big bird, then?" The small woman took off her flying helmet and shook out her hair.

Pat McBride winked at her. "Not bad at all. Good landing, Flight-Captain Hughes."

The pretty woman laughed. "Thanks. Let's hope it got noticed. Who's this?"

Pat turned to Al. "It's Al, isn't it?"

Al tried to unknot his tongue. "That's...that's right, pleased to meet you, Miss, um Captain Hughes. I'm Al Phipps." He held out his hand.

"It's Miss but it's also Flight-Captain. Good to meet you, Al. Just visiting or planning to stick around awhile?"

"Oh, I'm sticking around alright."

"Excellent. Catch you later then." She walked off to one of the huts on the side of the main building.

"Did I really see that?" Al turned to Pat for confirmation.

"You'd better get used to it, son. Everyone's equal round here."

"But she only looked about my age."

Pat grinned. "Flight-Captain Hughes is twenty-two years old, five foot two and one of the best pilots and instructors we've ever had. Right, I'm back to work. You'd better go through that door there, marked 'Reception'. Someone will sort you out. See you around, Al."

Pat walked off towards the sheds.

Al picked up his bags, stunned by what he had seen. He opened the door Pat Hughes had indicated.

Another very pretty woman, also about his own age, greeted him with a dazzling smile. "Hello, there. How may I help you?"

CHAPTER FORTY ONE
NORMANDY
APRIL 1941

Lottie returned from her trip to the boulangerie with more than bread during the week after Easter. Not the chocolate treats she'd been used to in her previous soft life, but the treacherous identity card for the mysterious Monsieur Bertholin. She cycled past the sentries on the bridge, having paid her toll of a couple of eggs on the way in. Now she was returning with crusty bread covering the brown envelope in her basket, she desperately hoped the Germans wouldn't ask to share that too.

The two soldiers, their faces now familiar, waved her through. It was Bernadette's day for the market and only Françoise was home, out in the orchard, bouncing little Bertrand on her knee in the spring sunshine. The buds on the apple trees showed shy pink frills and dandelions reflected the yellow sun, their flat faces smiling through the grass, now green and lush with spring rain.

Lottie stopped her bicycle and put one foot to the ground to absorb the beauty of the little tableau. Françoise's pale lemon headscarf contrasted sharply with the black hair of her son. Françoise kissed his forehead then held him high up in the air. The baby squealed in delight as she brought him back to the safety of her lap.

Lottie forgot about her dangerous cargo in that moment of stillness. She drank in the domestic serenity before her, the gentle mother in the burgeoning orchard, the happy child safe in her arms and the promise of spring enfolding them both in a deceptive idyll.

Lottie got off her bike and leant it against the goats' barn. Carefully, she lifted the envelope out from under the loaf of bread and slipped it into her pocket. "Fancy a fresh crust, Françoise?"

"Hello, Lottie!"

"It's Charlotte, remember?"

"Oh, sorry, yes I forgot. Isn't it a lovely day? Bertrand's second front tooth has finally come through and he's very proud of it. I should be able to sleep tonight." Françoise scooped up her child and joined Lottie at the farmhouse door.

"Let's have some milky coffee and fresh bread before Bernadette comes home and rations it, shall we?" Lottie went inside. "I'll just take off my coat upstairs. Won't be a mo."

Françoise nodded and put a pan on the stove, one-handed, with Bertrand propped on her other arm. "Oh, you are getting heavy, young man."

Lottie laughed and trotted upstairs. She pondered where to hide the false papers. Under her pillow was too obvious. There was a squeaky floorboard under the rag rug in the centre of the room. She lifted the rug and then prised the loose board up with her metal comb. It gave easily, and she carefully lowered the envelope into the dusty recess. Even that wouldn't do. She had to cover it with something equally dusty.

Françoise called up the stairs. "Coffee's ready! I'm going to have some bread. I can't wait, I'm starving."

"You go ahead." Lottie called back.

She cast about the room and then she found it. A piece of ancient sacking stuffed around the windows to keep out the draught in the long icy winter. Already the long dreary days had receded in her memory, as if it was years ago, instead of weeks. The spring had brought energy and a sense of urgency with it. She felt alive, important, and with a sense of purpose at last. Lottie pulled the old sacking from its crevice around the window frame and stuffed it in the hole she'd made in the floor. Then she pulled back the floorboard and covered it with the rug. She sat back on her heels. It would do.

Downstairs, she drank her bowl of coffee straight down. Françoise giggled. "Do you think Bernadette would notice if we just cut a tiny piece of goat's butter from the slab?"

364

"I don't think she's gone as far as measuring it." Lottie salivated at the prospect of fresh bread and butter.

Françoise got the sharpest knife from the drawer and fetched the pale golden butter from the scullery. With precision, she sliced off the end from the primrose-yellow slab and cut it in half again. "There you are. I'm putting all of mine on one big piece of bread." Françoise bit into her feast. Bertrand put out his chubby fist to grab it before it went into her mouth. "Oh no, you don't, you little monster. This is all mine."

"Oh, Françoise. Why can't we be simple like this all the time? Why does life have to be so complicated? Why did that wretched Hitler have to be so greedy? Isn't it enough just to live and see the seasons change? Look at Bertrand. How can anyone want to harm a child?"

Françoise's face blanched. "What do you mean? Who's going to hurt him?"

"Forgive me. I was just thinking about those children separated from their mothers who are Jewish too. And those awful labour camps. I heard about them from…a, a friend."

"Don't ever, ever tell anyone that Bertrand has a Jewish father, Charlotte!" Françoise's eyes had hardened and narrowed. "Paget is a good solid French surname. I hope God will protect us because of it. What would my father say if he knew I named his grandchild after his boorish manservant! Poor Papa. I wish I'd shown him more affection. Having your own child makes you understand your parents better. He was only ever trying to protect me."

"And your mother? Are you closer now?" Lottie ate the last piece of buttered bread.

Françoise folded her lips, emphasising the resemblance to her grandmother. "Mama is different. You know she's seeing a German soldier in Caen?"

Lottie went cold and the milky coffee curdled in her stomach. "No, I didn't know that. I thought she was helping your grandmother on the stall?"

Françoise snorted. "You must be joking. Why do you think she has silk stockings again? No, she just uses Grandmother for a lift into town. Haven't you noticed it's German cigarettes she's smoking now? The traitor."

Lottie hadn't noticed either change. She paid Mireille little attention. "But how did she meet this German? Is he an officer?"

"Oh yes, quite high ranking, it seems. She was bartering for cigarettes and he came over and gave her a whole packet. She boasts about it when it's just the two of us in our bedroom. I'm just glad Bertrand isn't old enough to understand what she gets up to."

"Do you mean – is she - sleeping with him?"

"Not overnight in the traditional sense but certainly in the Biblical one. They use the hotel. Sordid, I call it. It's not love, not like I had with David. Oh, I wish I knew where he was now. I don't even know if he is still alive." Françoise leaned down and kissed the top of her baby's head.

Lottie remembered the illicit identity card under the floor of her attic bedroom. "Françoise, I have to go out again. I'm sorry about your David but I'm glad you have his child. I have to say, I'm shocked that your mother is seeing a German officer. Now, excuse me. I'll be back before the others return from Caen."

"But where are you going? What about the goats?"

"Take them in the orchard for some fresh grass and sunshine. They are very tame. Just let them out. There is so much to eat, they won't stray, and they won't need milking until I get back."

Lottie pounded up the stairs and retrieved the identity card. She counted out a dozen eggs, wrapped then in a cloth and put them in the wicker basket that fitted so neatly between the handlebars of her bike. Fuelled by her delicious late breakfast, she pedalled swiftly away from the farm in the direction of the river. Just before the tumble of limestone cottages huddled around the mill was another control post manned by soldiers she had never met or tried to charm.

She slowed her bicycle and tried to compose herself, plan her words.

"Halt!"

She stopped and lowered a foot to the road.

"Get off your bicycle!"

Lottie dismounted.

"Come here!" The soldier remained at his station. He was older than the other sentries she'd met on the bridge into the village and his French was much better. She'd been hoping that le Bessin would be too small to warrant a control at all. This one looked temporary. Unlike the one on the main road with their little wooden hut and big permanent barrier, this was just a barrel of barbed wire with wooden supports straddling the road. Just her luck.

"What is the purpose of your journey?"

Good question. Frantically, Lottie looked across at the mill, just visible in the distance. She could see the waterwheel plunging into the frothing river, propelled by its fast flow.

"Bartering eggs for flour." She didn't actually know if the mill was producing flour. Why hadn't Thierry told her more?

"Show me."

Lottie pulled back the check teacloth from her basket. There were a dozen hen's eggs cradled in its folds. Brown, speckled and white they sat serene and innocent, unaware of their role as camouflage.

The soldier nodded, then thrust out his left arm, his right held his rifle, and went to lift the edge of the cotton square.

"Hey! Don't do that, you'll break my eggs!" Lottie stayed his fat fist with her own hand.

The soldier scowled. "You cannot stop me searching your basket."

Lottie smiled and squeezed his cold fingers. "No, but, if I gave you enough eggs to make a sweet fluffy omelette, wouldn't you prefer to do that?"

For one second, they both froze, hands touching, minds deciding. Lottie held her breath.

To her disgust, the soldier upturned his hand and clasped her smaller one. "Eggs are a paltry payment for your liberty. How about a kiss to go with them?"

She tried not to recoil and forced a laugh to cover her reaction. "Oh, monsieur, that is a high price to pay for simply going about my business!"

"Not legitimate business, is it? Marché noir?"

"We must eat, you know."

"What else are you trading?"

There was nothing else for it. Lottie leaned over her bicycle and kissed his bristly cheek. The hairs on his face scratched her lips. "This!"

"Ach! Not enough!"

Lottie mounted her bike. "It's all you'll get today!"

To her intense relief the old soldier laughed. "You win, mademoiselle, show me your papers and you can go on your way. Germans do not take advantage of women."

"I'm glad to hear it," Lottie handed over her all-too-new identity card.

"I have a little sister your age," the soldier read her card, "but she wouldn't flirt with a stranger."

He looked severe again and looked at her with cold eyes. Had she played the wrong game? Lottie held out her hand and wiped the smile from her face. "Thank you," she said, returning his stare.

He shrugged and handed back her card. "On your way."

Lottie tucked the card into her pocket and pedalled away from him. She wanted to stand up on the pedals to make it go faster but controlled her speed to a slower pace, hoping she looked nonchalant. Only when she reached the first bend in the road, did she acknowledge the sheer terror she felt. She didn't stop to dwell on it, but sped down the incline, keeping the low-slung mill house firmly in her sights in the little valley below.

She arrived in five minutes, breathless with relief and effort. The waterwheel's wooden bars splashed their regular beats into the river and there was a hum from inside the stone building. Leaning her bike against the wall of the house, she lifted off the basket of eggs. Looking around to check no-one could see her, Lottie extracted the envelope and slid the precious papers under her coat. She glanced around again, then pushed open the big door. It was heavy, its iron bars adding weight to the thick, ancient wood.

Inside was noisy, with the huge millstone grinding away at the wheat berries, making great clouds of dust coil upwards from its incessant circulation.

A man, thick-set and middle-aged, saw her and left the other workers to join her at the door.

"Who are you?"

"Charlotte Perrot. The hens are laying again." Thierry had said to use the same code as at Madame Leroy's boulangerie.

The miller, his face white with flour, squinted his dark eyes. "I've been expecting you. Come this way." He turned to the three other mill workers. "Keep going, my friends. I won't be long."

"What is your name, monsieur?"

"Everard, Jean. You don't need to know more. Did you get through the control alright? They only set it up this morning. Ridiculous for a tiny hamlet like ours. You were unlucky it was today."

"I got through, but I had to pay a toll."

"Eh?"

"Just a little kiss."

Jean Everard guffawed and looked her over, his eyes dwelling on the curve of her breasts. He licked his full lips. "So, even the Germans are human. Be careful they don't ask for more than you want to give, understand?"

Lottie nodded. He was even more offensive, and a great deal smellier, than the German soldier. "Where is our friend?"

"In the barn." Jean glanced around his yard. "Come on." They entered a large barn, so old, Lottie guessed it must be medieval. Huge rafters soared up to the ceiling and sacks of flour stood in serried rows beneath it on raised decks.

Jean gave the sound of an owl and a dark head peeked over one of the sacks.

"You go on up. Better that he doesn't come down in the day, and better if I don't witness the transaction." He pointed up to the ladder leading to the loft.

Lottie mounted the wooden rungs. Crouched behind the sacks was an entire family. Three children, who all looked under eight years old, were huddled together with a woman in a smart coat and a hat with an incongruously jaunty feather. A man of about the same age, presumably their father, got up to meet her. Lottie drew out the papers from her inside coat pocket and handed them over.

"Thank you, mademoiselle. A million times, thank you." The man, his hook nose and black eyes giving away his Jewish background, shook her hand. A sob escaped his wife and their children stared at her.

The man's eyes filled up.

"Where will you go now?" Lottie couldn't bear to think of them holed up like rats amongst the sacks of wheat.

"Someone else is meeting us tonight to help us get to the unoccupied zone. It's best you don't know who that is. Now we have our papers, we have a chance. Go now, don't delay."

Lottie nodded, too choked with emotion to speak more. She smiled at the woman and the three kids, turned and descended the stairs.

"Here, take some flour, so you can show the guard at the control." Jean bundled her out into the spring sunshine.

"Oh, yes, and you must take the eggs from me. I said I was bartering them."

"Very good, my wife will be pleased with so many extra mouths to feed. The sooner *they* are out of here the better." Jean jerked his head back at the barn.

"So, why do you take the risk?"

"My wife is related to them. Go now. I won't say more, I shouldn't have told you that much."

They went to Lottie's bike and she transferred the eggs to a basket Jean provided.

He licked his lips again, leaving them wet and shiny. "Those eggs will make a good lunch." He strapped the sack of flour on to the back of her bicycle. Lottie said goodbye and started to pedal away. The heavy sack made the bike unsteady at first until she learnt to balance its weight. Already dreading another encounter with the guard, she didn't want anything slowing her down.

When she got to the control barrier, a different soldier was on guard. "Are you the girl with the eggs?" His French wasn't bad either.

Lottie nodded and handed over her papers.

"Made a nice omelette. On you go."

Was that it? Lottie gave him no time to chat further. She took back her identity card and shoved it in her basket. Within half an hour she was freewheeling the last sloping part of the lane to Bernadette's farm with her legs stuck out to the side in abandoned triumph.

CHAPTER FORTY TWO
NORMANDY
SUMMER 1941

Lottie found it increasingly frustrating that they had no radio at the farm, when news filtered out that Germany had declared war on Russia. What would it mean? Relying on Bernadette's terse reports from the market gossip was no substitute and Bernadette refused to 'waste her money on a newspaper'.

Bernadette did say the wholesale market for fruit and vegetables and cheeses had been forced out of the city and moved to the shipyard in Caen. "Damn the interfering Boche."

Lottie had hoped to see Thierry and talk to him - he would be bound to know more about the wider world, especially anything to do with Caen, as his parents lived there - but, although her illegal errands carrying papers and messages to Jean Everard increased, they had little contact. She saw more of Madame Leroy than anyone else outside the farm.

Madame Leroy took her to the back of the boulangerie one day leaving her assistant, a young village girl, to serve the customers. "You want to watch out for that aunt of yours."

Lottie had to think who she meant for a moment. The only aunts Lottie Flintock-Smythe had lived in America amongst the elite of Boston and she was sure Madame Leroy didn't mean her almost-aunt, Katy Phipps, owner of The Katherine Wheel Garage, either.

"People are talking about her and some Boche she's taken up with." Madame spoke in a low tone, so no-one in the boulangerie could hear.

Lottie knew a moment of dread. "You mean Mireille?" Of course, it was a different set up for Charlotte Perrot; she mentally kicked herself for not remembering that. It would be all too easy to slip up in a vulnerable moment under interrogation if she didn't believe in her new identity every minute of every day. "Yes, Françoise told me about it."

"Did she now? She should be ashamed of her mother. People don't forget what happened before she was married, you know. You are too young to have heard about it, I suppose?"

Lottie shook her head. Bernadette had only told her the bare bones that one time. She was curious to hear the whole tale.

Madame Leroy hitched up her ample bosom with her crossed arms. "Well, before she was Madame Blanchard, before she left for Paris in a hurry, young Mireille Perrot had an eye for the boys. None of the farm boys were good enough for her, though. Made a play for the Mayor, she did. Him engaged and all. Mind, she was beautiful then, I can't deny it. It was after her brother died in the Great War, you see. Her mother wouldn't go out; wouldn't see anyone, not even the priest. That's when her father took to the drink."

Madame Leroy shook her head, making her jowls wobble. "Everyone had sympathy with her until she took up with the Mayor, of course he wasn't the Mayor then.. Gave it to him on a plate, I heard. Well, anyone could see the way she was swaying her hips every time she saw him and wearing lipstick like a woman five years older. Young Voclain was besotted, until his fiancée, her who's his wife now, got wind of it. No-one knows how she stopped the affair, but one day, Mireille disappeared off to Paris. Never saw her till her father's funeral and never again after that till now." Madame Leroy sniffed. "Judging by her suits and jewellery, she got by."

Lottie tried to put the record straight. "She married Édouard Blanchard, but he was killed when they bombed the Citroën factory where he worked, last June."

"Oh, so that's what happened. Well, leopards don't change their spots, do they? I thought you ought to know, ought to tell Bernadette, that she's up to no good with a German officer. Same old tricks, I've heard."

Lottie waited for more.

"See, the point is, chérie, if we're doing a few things behind their backs and she's whispering in some Boche's ear, she might say a bit too much, know what I mean?"

"Are you saying I should stop my 'deliveries'?

"Might be wise for a while."

Lottie felt really angry as she cycled home. Helping Thierry and the other resistors, even if she didn't know who they were, had given her a sense of purpose, of belonging. Damn Mireille for plunging her back into a futile existence of non-action. She knew Madame Leroy was right. She couldn't risk the lives of the others.

Now summer had arrived, Françoise accompanied Bernadette to the market in Caen most weeks, taking little Bertrand with her.

Bernadette no longer wanted to go alone. "Crawling with Boche. I can't stand the sight of them."

Mireille went too but returned with them less and less. Lottie was left alone to manage the farm on market days, and she relished the peace. Tensions between the women had risen to such a pitch it had become impossible to relax when Mireille was in the house.

Gradually, Mireille was absent more and more of the time, and sheer boredom drove Lottie to tell Madame Leroy she was available again and to hell with the consequences. To her great surprise, there were no sentries at the bridge, and she saw no other German soldiers on the way. The baker looked relieved to see her but then, with some agitation, told her to bring her eggs to the back of the shop.

The plump woman looked anxious, even a little scared. "It's good news in one way, because now the Germans have invaded Russia, the local Communists have finally joined the resistance. They've dithered long enough with their comrades. With the Boche off on the eastern front, maybe now we'll see some action! It's started getting serious already because one of the Commies has managed to find a gun and we need it delivered urgently to the mill. Can you do that?"

Lottie didn't fully understand why Germany invading Russia should make the local Communist party start gun-running, but she jumped at the chance. Anything other than the constant tedious waiting. Maybe she'd never be bored again. Even Madame Leroy, no hysteric, looked excited, different.

"Of course."

"It will be more dangerous than delivering identity papers. You are sure?"

Lottie nodded.

Quickly, with deft movements of her fat fingers, Madame Leroy opened the drawer to her massive buffet and extracted a pile of tablecloths. "I shall be so relieved to get rid of the thing. Ah, but you are so young to carry such an ugly weapon. I shall worry for you, my little cabbage." She withdrew another cloth, which had an irregular object concealed within it.

She held it out to Lottie as if it was a live firework. "Take it then but, please, be very careful."

Another lumpy parcel followed. "Bullets."

Lottie took the two parcels, wrapped in their cotton shrouds, and shoved them down into the depths of her wicker basket.

"Here, take some more cloths to go over the top, so the bumps don't show. Oh, we shouldn't be doing this." Madame Leroy was gabbling now, and Lottie stopped listening. The big woman was making her nervous.

"I have some round loaves here which will cover it well." The fragrant bread, still hot from the oven, went on top, and Madame Leroy bound it up in another scrupulously clean cotton square. "Take two, so they make a tight fit." She jammed the two loaves into the basket, so they butted up together, sealing the contents underneath.

"Go now. Straight home. Don't keep it long but get to the mill as soon as you can. Jean will be expecting you but wait until he sends word. There's no mobile control near his village at the moment, his wife told me when she brought my flour. Let's hope it stays that way until you can get rid of the horrible thing. Like I said, a lot of the Germans have been mobilised to fight on the Russian Front. Now's our chance - before the bastards return."

Lottie nodded. Silently, she left by the back door. She didn't want to squeeze past the ever-present queue for bread.

She cycled home directly, as instructed. The others were still out, so she left the cooling loaves in the kitchen and pelted upstairs. She peeked under the teacloths at the weapon, hating its steel menace. Quickly, she pulled up the floorboard and buried the contraband inside, covering it with the old sacking. She was glad when the floorboard and the rug were back over her guilty secret. She could even persuade herself that there was nothing extraordinary beneath her feet. If only she felt as tranquil as the room looked.

Outside, she heard the weary clip-clop of the donkey. She looked out of her dormer window. Bernadette and Françoise were sitting on the cart, which was still half loaded. Bertrand was crying. She watched as Françoise hurried him indoors.

Lottie went to help Bernadette.

"Takings at the market are right down," Bernadette said, jerking her head back at the goods on the cart. She looked grumpier than ever.

Lottie looked at the half-full cart. "Why's that, Bernadette? I thought your goat's cheese was highly prized as everyone else round here only sells cow's cheese."

The old woman shrugged. "People don't want to buy off the mother of a whore. That daughter of mine might as well be in the brothel." Bernadette stomped off, tugging the donkey by its bridle.

Lottie carried two heavy baskets, one with cheese and the other still laden with jars of golden honey.

She looked at Françoise, who was changing Bertrand's nappy on the kitchen table, for an explanation. "It's mother. Everyone knows she's seeing that German officer. Another stallholder spat on Grandmère today."

They didn't see Mireille for a week after that. Lottie hardly noticed; she was far more worried about the gun hidden in her attic bedroom. By the end of the week she was tempted to go to the mill without Jean's signal. It was hard to sleep with her secret laying silently beneath her bed.

She was surprised when Mireille returned with the other two women from market the following week.

Françoise's pout, rarely seen since she became a mother, was very evident as they got down from the cart. Mireille was haranguing her in an unrelenting stream about the identity of Bertrand's father. Lottie heard her shrill voice above the sound of the pony's hooves even before they appeared around the bend in the little lane. She went downstairs to greet them.

"I don't want my new friends thinking I've got Jewish connections. It's bad enough you're not married. Thank goodness you've had the sense to make up a story about his father."

"Please don't tell them anything different, Mother. How could you jeopardise your own grandchild?"

"It's lucky for you I do have German friends. You'd get awkward questions at the control posts if I didn't." Mireille shuddered. "Oh, it makes me sick that you went with a dirty Jew."

"And it disgusts me that you're going with a filthy Boche!"

"Pah!" As Mireille dismounted from the little cart, she caught one of her high heels on the wooden wheel and cursed. Muttering about snagged stockings, she disappeared upstairs without even acknowledging Lottie. Bernadette came into the kitchen. She and Francoise both looked upset.

"What's going on?" Lottie looked from one to the other.

Françoise turned away and let out a sob.

"Bernadette? What's happened?" Lottie barred Bernadette's attempt to follow her daughter upstairs.

Françoise reeled round, her face blotchy with tears. "Tell her, Grandmère. Tell her before she finds out for herself in the village. Everyone already knows in Caen. I don't know how we'll show our faces there again."

Bernadette didn't flinch from Lottie's gaze. "My daughter is leaving. She's going back to Paris."

"Tell her who with, Grandmère!"

But Lottie could guess. "With her German boyfriend, is that it?"

Bernadette nodded silently, her mouth set in a grim line.

They could hear drawers being opened upstairs, then slammed shut, as if Mireille was either in a temper, or a hurry.

As one, the three women in the kitchen turned to the door, left open in the hot July sunshine, as they saw a big black car crunching up their private lane, trails of dust streaming behind its fat wheels, a Nazi flag fluttering on its shiny bonnet. It stopped short of the farmhouse, leaving its engine on, purring quietly.

Lottie's first thought was of the revolver she had hidden under the floorboards of her attic bedroom. Had they come for that? Had she been rumbled? The guards had increased in number all along the coast. You couldn't get near the sea anymore. Had one of the new German soldiers spotted her frequent bike rides? Guessed that it wasn't just eggs she was delivering? Did they know her connection to other resisters like Thierry and Madame Leroy? Had one of them been captured?

All these thoughts raced through her mind in a chaotic, rapid stream. Footsteps, heavy and booted, displaced the little pebbles in the yard as they approached.

Bernadette planted her feet wide; Françoise scooped up her sleeping baby and clutched him to her breast; Lottie's hand went involuntarily to her throat. She hoped no-one could hear the thump of her heartbeats as they drummed into her ears. She retreated into the corner of the kitchen, where it was darkest near the larder door, and placed herself carefully in its shadow.

Like frozen statues, the three women stood there. There was no rap on the door, no permission to enter requested. A tall, middle-aged man, wearing the peaked cap of a German officer, blocked out the sunshine, his thick-set outline casting the kitchen into shade as he entered the doorway unannounced and uninvited.

"This is the home of Madame Blanchard, yes?"

Bernadette cleared her throat.

"Well?" He tapped his foot impatiently.

"Mireille Blanchard is my daughter."

He raised cynical eyebrows. "Really? You do surprise me. You are not in the least alike."

Bernadette was silent.

The tall man frowned. "Is she here?"

Bernadette nodded.

"Show me to her." He came forward a step in a threatening movement.

"She's upstairs." Bernadette didn't move.

"So? I have legs, I can mount a staircase."

"I'm sorry, I don't allow strangers upstairs." Bernadette had two hectic spots of colour on her lined cheeks.

Lottie felt a swell of admiration for her hostess.

"Don't *allow*? Madame, you are under occupation. It is the German army who says what is allowed or not."

"Not in my house, you don't." Bernadette stepped forward, came between the man towering over her and Françoise.

379

Little Bertrand mewed his discomfort. Françoise clamped him tighter to her chest.

"Out of my way." The officer loomed over Bernadette's petite form.

Lottie feared he would hit the older woman, he looked so angry, but just then Mireille clattered down the stairs, dragging her enormous suitcase behind her and making a terrible din as it bumped down the wooden treads.

"Wilhelm! You're here, my darling."

The German officer whirled around at the sound of her voice. He no longer looked stern. His frown had gone, replaced by a charming smile, making his heavy jowls recede. "Are you ready, Liebling?"

"Completely, my dear." Mireille turned to her mother. "It is better this way. This farm life never did suit me. I'll get out of your hair. Let's not pretend you'll miss me. Make sure you send me some food parcels to my old Paris address, won't you, Mother dear?" She kissed Bernadette's withered cheeks.

The big German laughed. "You won't need food parcels! I shall treat you like a queen. We shall have the best Paris can provide! Now, let's get into the car." He gave a curt bow to Bernadette, barely glancing at Lottie or Françoise. "Guten Tag, Frau Perrot."

"Wilhem?" Mireille paused on the threshold.

"Yes?"

Mireille handed him some keys. "I have a car here. I'd like to take it back to Paris with me."

"Of course. It will be very useful. Where is it kept?"

Mireille told him.

The tall officer strode to his limousine and leaned in through the window to its driver. The driver got out and they exchanged words. The officer handed over the bunch of keys and pointed to the barn and the other man nodded and went to the boot of the car where he withdrew a large petrol can and walked off purposefully towards the barn.

Lottie looked at Mireille. She was smirking smugly. Lottie could have hit her.

Mireille turned to her mother. "You have no need of it, Maman. It's just sitting there, rusting up."

Bernadette looked at her daughter. "No, I do not want your stupid car. Are you sure you don't want the shirt from my back to go with it?"

Mireille didn't answer as Wilhem had come back for her. "I will drive my car. Are you ready?"

He stood back for Mireille to go before him and, with overt gallantry, took up her heavy case and followed her out to the big black limousine and put it in the boot. Mireille and the German officer climbed inside, and the luxurious car quickly accelerated away, leaving another cloud of dust from its wake to settle on the ruffled courtyard, shortly followed by the Blanchard's Citroën, now liberally splattered with owl droppings.

Soon, all that remained were tyre tracks in the dusty lane.

"She didn't even say goodbye to me. My own mother!" Françoise rocked baby Bertrand in her arms, tears silently tracking down her face, eyes staring at the open doorway through which her mother had departed with their enemy.

"Good riddance to bad rubbish. Don't go feeling sorry for yourself about your mother's departure. You're better off without her, my girl." Bernadette reached out and stroked Françoise's chin. "I'll look after you." Her voice and her expression softened.

Françoise nodded back, gave a tentative smile.

Bernadette turned to Lottie. "We'll cope, won't we?"

Lottie came out from the shadows, glad she'd received no attention from the formidable German officer. "Of course, we will."

Bernadette smiled at her for the first time. "It'll be easier for you to deliver your parcels without her spying on us now."

Shocked, Lottie was speechless. Had she been so transparent?

Bernadette grunted; Lottie wasn't sure if it was a chuckle, she'd never heard the older woman laugh.

Bernadette went out into the yard. "I'll fetch a pichet of cider to go with lunch."

CHAPTER FORTY THREE
NORMANDY
OCTOBER 1941

Lottie went around the back of the boulangerie, laden with a full basket of eggs and some little rounds of goat's cheeses, chalk-white and wrapped in bay leaves. Madame Leroy had said she could do with some for making quiches when Lottie had told her about Bernadette's sales being down at the market.

"Coucou!" She called, placing her heavy basket down on the scrubbed pine table. Madame Leroy came bustling in, dusting flour from her plump hands.

"Charlotte! It's good to see you. Have you got that last horrible package somewhere safe?"

Lottie nodded, hating to be reminded the gun was still lying like a traitor under her bed.

"Brave girl." Madame Leroy gave her a quick kiss on each cheek. She took a deep breath but only whispered. "I have a message for you."

"Oh? Is it about the…?"

Madame Leroy looked alarmed and raised a fat finger to her lips. "Ssh." She looked around her kitchen furtively and said in a loud voice, "But yes, Monsieur Thibault has asked for some eggs too." In a lower voice, she continued, "There have been developments with London, he said." She looked over her shoulder, back at the shop. "He said something about a disturbance in Nantes."

"What's that got to do with us?"

Madame Leroy shrugged, making her chins jostle each other.

"I'll go straight to the school." Lottie took back half a dozen eggs and nestled them in the bottom of her basket. "Anything to take?"

Madame Leroy shook her head. "Best not, if you are going across the square."

She laid three baguettes across Lottie's basket, wedging them against the wicker handle. "Go now, mon petit choux, but take good care."

Lottie was so relieved she carried nothing illegal, when she was stopped by a German soldier standing guard by the yellowing linden trees in the centre of the village square. He rifled through her basket and she wanted to laugh in his face when he found nothing.

"Where you going?" He pointed with his hands to help her understand his terrible French.

"To the school. Egg delivery." She didn't feel inclined to chat.

The soldier jerked his head in dismissal.

Feeling lightheaded with her narrow escape, Lottie hopped back on her bicycle and pedalled across the bumpy cobblestones. When she reached the stone passageway, she got off and wheeled her bike to the school door, before propping it against the limestone wall. She extracted the eggs in their cloth binding and pushed the school gate open.

The children were in the yard, playing. Thierry stood in the centre, holding a whistle and refereeing a fracas between two little girls. They were listening to him intently. In his other hand he held a rag doll.

"I shall give the doll to the toybox for everyone to play with if you can't share her."

He held it aloft. "Can you do that?"

The two little girls scowled at each other. "Toybox it is then."

"No, sir. We'll share!"

"As long as you do. Remember, I shall be watching you." He gave the doll to the smallest little girl who snatched it from him. "Do it nicely, Michelle. Now, give it to Eloise."

Lottie watched as the doll was passed over and the taller girl looked triumphant. She ran away, holding the doll to her chest and her friend chased her.

Thierry spotted Lottie and strolled over. "I don't think I handled that as well as I might have done!" He gave a rueful smile.

Lottie smiled back. "Madame Leroy said you needed eggs?"

"Yes, let me get the children settled and I will tell you why." He blew his whistle and the children fell into two lines, one of boys, the other girls. "Indoors now, children, and get out your reading books. Coats on hooks and hands washed first, please. Off you go, one at a time."

Dutifully, his young pupils trooped indoors.

"I have five minutes to explain." Thierry spoke in a low voice, glancing around the deserted schoolyard to see if anyone was listening.

Lottie moved closer to catch his whispered words.

"Have you heard of Jean Moulin?"

Lottie shook her head. "Is this about Nantes?"

"No, I'll tell you about that in a minute. Jean Moulin was the youngest sous-préfet in all France. Last year, he was imprisoned and tortured by the Boche. He tried to slit his own throat with broken glass rather than sign a statement blaming the massacre of civilians on some black Senegalese troops instead of the Nazis."

"My goodness!"

Thierry nodded at her sympathy and hurried on. "He shamed the Germans into releasing him, to save face, but he was sacked for it. I've just heard he's made his way through Spain to London and has reached De Gaulle." He put his hand on her arm. "Don't you see? This changes everything. If we can co-ordinate our efforts of resistance, we can really start to turn things around. His refusal to surrender was an inspiration to us all. He is a Frenchman we can be proud of, unlike our precious Maréchel Pétain."

"Fine words, Thierry, but what can we actually do?"

"There have already been assassinations in Paris but a few days ago, some Communists killed the

Feldkommandant in Nantes. He screamed like a stuck pig, by all accounts, the coward."

"You're not suggesting we kill a Boche?"

Thierry shook his head. "No, well, not yet anyway. Another German was shot in Bordeaux. The Boche have killed seventy-seven Frenchmen in reprisals, mostly in Bordeaux and mostly Communists. They are paying a high price for joining the resistance and because they are organised, they are easily traced."

"So many!"

"Now do you see? We must do more than distribute pamphlets, Charlotte. With Moulin in London, we must be ready for further instructions and become more organised. Are you ready to face further danger? I must know now, before I set things in motion."

Lottie thought for a moment. It was such a perfect autumn day. A sycamore leaf twirled lazily down on to the ground, joining its brothers in a golden carpet on to the school yard. Could she really do this?

She looked up and found Thierry's remarkable blue eyes boring into hers behind his lenses. There were so many emotions expressed in those eyes – compassion, understanding, but above all, a query.

"I'm ready."

He squeezed her arm. "I must go to the children. They will be making the most of my absence. He took the bundle of eggs from her by their knotted cloth handle. "Thanks for these." He fished in his coat pocket and brought out a food coupon. "Is this enough?"

"Thank you, yes."

"By the way, you know the Free French are calling for everyone to daub graffiti everywhere?"

"How do you mean?"

"You don't have a radio?"

"No, we don't even have a newspaper."

Thierry grunted his sympathy. "Pity. I have put mine in the basement in the school. I've hidden it behind the enormous boiler. No-one would ever look there, at least I hope not. The Boche have forbidden us to listen to anything from London and if you get caught you could be fined, or even imprisoned. I have a few friends who come every night to do just that."

"Really? But it's not illegal to own a radio, is it?"

"No, it's not. They want us to listen to Radio Paris all the time and be lulled into a false sense of security. They wanted to impose a death sentence for listening to De Gaulle on Radio Londres but, for once, Pétain opposed them, saying it was 'excessive'. Huh! Such a polite term for such a murderous intent. You can only trust the BBC now. The Germans have taken over Radio Paris and as for Radio Vichy, pah – pure propaganda for the Boche!" Thierry threw his hands in the air in a Gallic gesture of dismissal.

"Thank goodness the death sentence was lifted, but I can see why you'd want to hide it. Can you get the world news?"

He nodded. "The BBC let the Free French have five minutes every night. That's how I know they want everyone to daub 'V' for victory signs on the walls."

"What walls?"

"Any that can be seen by our French fellow countrymen, so they know we haven't given up."

"But what if a German sees it?"

"All the better! We don't want them thinking their jackboots have silenced us, do we?" Thierry passed Lottie a stub of white chalk.

She took it, wondering if she would ever be brave enough to use it, and slipped it in her coat pocket.

Before turning away, he nodded at her, his face still serious. "I'll be in touch soon. It's time to take the fight up a notch, no?" And then he grinned, and the sun burst through the clouds.

Lottie blinked. "Thierry, do you send messages through your radio?"

He shook his blonde head. "No, I can only receive transmission."

"So, you couldn't send a message to my mother?"

"No, and even if I could, I wouldn't use valuable airtime to send personal messages. I mean, they are *called* personal messages, but really, they are coded messages from the BBC about the movements of the Germans - you know, any changes or developments in various locations. They are not 'letters from Mummy'." His face looked stern and uncompromising.

Stung, Lottie retorted, "Perhaps a few genuine family messages might be just the thing to put the Boche off the scent."

Thierry spread out his hands in apology. "I'm sorry. I didn't mean to hurt your feelings, but some people are risking their lives doing transmissions. Some idiot sent a message last month signed as Alain Chartier, the sixteenth century poet from Bayeux. Haven't you seen the detector vans with their feelers out? They're crawling all over the area now, thanks to him."

"I see nothing at the farm. Nothing."

"Of course. Well, if they take more than ten minutes to send their message, the transmission can be detected by triangulation. They have to time it very carefully. But you've given me an idea. I'll be in touch. I have told you so much, there is no further harm in you getting more involved now. I'm afraid, mam'selle, you are now one of us. I hope you do not live to regret it. Good day."

A child shrieked from within the school and he left, breaking into a trot and quickly crossing the schoolyard before disappearing inside. His disappearance was so abrupt, Lottie stood for a moment staring after him. He perplexed her. He blew hot and cold and took such risks but, sometimes, he looked at her in a way that made her stomach churn. Was she frightened only of being discovered as a resister by the Boche, or was it something more personal?

Lottie retrieved her bicycle. As she pedalled home, she realised with a jolt that she had not thought of Al for weeks.

CHAPTER FORTY FOUR
CHEADLE MANOR
NOVEMBER 1941

"You get off home now, Miss Isobel. I'll do tonight's milking; we're not going to get much else done in this slashing rain." Farmer Stubbs stood inside the cowshed, the water dripping off his felt hat pooling around his wellington boots on the straw-covered floor.

"Are you sure, Mr Stubbs? I could look at those feed rations we talked about." Isobel forked the last bit of hay into the trough for the cows.

"Yes, I'm sure. Me and the missus are going into Woodbury. She's been planning it for weeks, so I can't get out of it."

Isobel laughed. Mrs Stubbs was not a woman to be denied but, like her husband, was warm hearted and generous. She liked them both and blessed the day she transferred to Home Farm from the dour Williams's miserable place. "Are you certain you wouldn't like me to be on hand in case something happens?"

"No, don't you fret. It'll give me just the excuse I'll need to come home early." Farmer Stubbs winked.

"Alright then, it'll be nice to put my feet up this afternoon. The days are so short now."

"You're right about that. Soon be Christmas and the turn of the year. Lord alone knows what the next one will bring." Farmer Stubbs had two sons fighting in the army. It couldn't be easy, waiting for news.

Isobel nodded silently, too troubled by her own worries to give an answer. They still had no news of Lottie and Al had been away for months now, working for the ATA. His letters were getting less and less frequent. He claimed he was too busy to write much and maybe that was true, but she was beginning to have her doubts.

She pulled on her overcoat and grabbed her umbrella. It was only a short walk home, but the rain was coming down like stair-rods. It was still strange not to take the shorter path to Cheadle Manor. She looked across at the big old house through the driving rain. It stood, as it always had, stalwart against the weather. The woodbine and ivy covering its base made it seem more a part of the landscape than ever, its grey, stone walls wet with rain, its slate roof slick and dripping, merging with the low clouds shrouding its chimneys.

Isobel shivered, turned away from her childhood home and headed downhill to West Lodge at the manor gates. She still couldn't believe that things had ended up this way, that she and her mother had been turfed out of their own manor. Her boots splashed mud up her legs as she tramped down the weedy path through the manor house grounds, an exile from the comforts within; comforts she had always taken for granted, assumed they were hers by rights; comforts now withdrawn. She and her mother had to fend for themselves. There would be no Mrs Andrews to cook her lunch, no Mr Andrews to bring it to her in the dining room under a polished silver dome, no Sarah to draw her a hot bath. In fact, there had been no bathroom at all at West Lodge when they'd moved in, only a tin bath hanging up in the porch. Cassandra had drawn the line at that and had had a bathroom installed with a proper flushing toilet within a couple of weeks.

"It's no good, darling," she'd said, "I can't bring myself to use an outside privy in all weathers at my age. Goodness knows, I lived in a tent in the last war, but I'm not prepared to put up with that at my time of life. We'll get a man in and have a proper bathroom added on." The small, functional bathroom was duly tacked on to the back of the little house. The plumbing worked well enough but the room that housed it was never warm enough, however long they left the paraffin stove alight before a bath. The only other concession to modern convenience was a telephone installed in the hallway, and it never stopped ringing.

Isobel hoped her mother was at home; she was more often out than in these days, as she was so taken up with supporting the work of the hospital, now housed in their ancestral home. Isobel pushed open the door of the glass porch covering the back entrance. It stood between the kitchen door and the garden and was a useful place to dump boots, coats, ripening apples and sprouting seed potatoes, depending on the season. There was never enough room inside the tiny cottage for anything extra. With two bedrooms, a small kitchen with a scullery and a tiny parlour, their new accommodation was cramped, to say the least. How Agnes Beagle had coped with all those children when Aunt Katy was growing up here, she couldn't imagine. Isobel had never even thought about it before she'd moved in.

Isobel peeled off her coat and the overalls underneath and hung them, with her gas mask, on a hook in the porch. Immediately, they drummed a steady metronome of drips on to the quarry tiles below. The sound made her more depressed than ever. She left the umbrella open beside them and it added its own melancholy rhythm to the tune.

She unlatched the wooden kitchen door. Inside, it was dark and gloomy. The kitchen seemed to have shrunk to an even smaller size in the dim light of the November day.

"Hello? Anyone home?"

Her mother called out a response. "Hello, darling, I'm in the parlour, hugging the fire."

Isobel ducked her head as she went through the tiny hall into the parlour. She'd bumped her head more than enough times already on the door frame.

"How lovely to see a cheery fire, Mummy."

"I know, it's a bit of an indulgence this early in the day but I couldn't resist, it's so dark today. Typical November, I'm afraid. Sit down, Isobel, you look whacked. How come you're home so early?"

392

Isobel explained about Mr and Mrs Stubbs's trip out to the local market town. She put her feet up on the little tapestry footstool and leaned back against the leather armchair. It creaked its protest.

Her mother got up from her armchair on the other side of the coal fire. "Would you like some hot cocoa?"

"That would be lovely, if you can be bothered."

"No bother, and by the way, there are two letters for you. I'll fetch them." Her mother went out into the hall and brought them back with her.

"Thanks, Mummy. Oh, looks like one from Al." She looked at the second envelope. "And one from Geraint."

"Ah. Then I'll leave you in peace to read them." Cassandra left the room quietly, shutting the door behind her.

Isobel held a letter in each hand, weighing them unconsciously. Al's was thin, the writing on the envelope rushed and uneven, but Geraint's missive was fatter and much larger, and he had obviously taken pains to write the address carefully. She opened the fat one first.

There was a small painting inside, wrapped in the finest tissue paper. Isobel pulled the wrapping off and took the painting to the window so the meagre November daylight could illuminate it.

"So beautiful." She spoke out loud, as if Geraint was actually present.

She held a summer scene in her hands. Geraint had captured perfectly the ephemeral multicolours of a wildflower meadow in its short prime. Each brush stroke meant something, not one was wasted or unnecessary. She knew a spasm of jealousy at his skill, having attempted the same thing in North Wales on a rare day off in June last year. Her efforts had not equalled this.

Blue cornflowers, butter-yellow marigolds, white horizontal plates of yarrow, frilly, pillar-box red poppies - all vied for attention amongst the curved sprays of paler vetch and plumes of grass seeds. She could sense the gentle breeze making the flowers sway, smell their delicate scents and feel the warmth of the summer sun they basked in. It was masterful.

Sleety rain hurled itself against the lattice window of the lodge house and Isobel shivered. June was a distant memory. She placed the painting on the stone sill of the deep-set mullioned window and put candlesticks on each side to flatten it, before returning to the comfort of her fireside armchair. She opened the folded letter. There were three sheets of neat prose to read. She settled back in the chair and tilted the paper to catch the firelight.

"Dearest Isobel,
How are you? I hope very much that you are well and not working too hard through these dark autumnal days."

It was funny how Geraint never called her Bella. It set him apart from everyone else in her life. She didn't know if she liked it, even though she knew it was a mark of his respect for her, but it maintained distance. The first part of the letter was all about his life in Liverpool, the devastating effect of the bombs on his factories and his workers. Geraint wrote well, describing people and places with wit and vivacity. It was interesting to hear about that other life, one she had never visited, however often he had invited her. Partly, she was genuinely too busy working at Home Farm, 'doing her bit', as everyone called it but, really, she knew it would signal too much of an interest and somehow she could never screw herself up to go and make that kind of commitment.

"I hope you like the painting. It reminded me of that time we strolled through the meadow by the river at Cheadle Manor in May when I visited you. The flowers were only in bud then, but I could picture you amongst them when the summer came. I hope someday

that I will see you in my wildflower meadow, pictured here. It's a fantasy I know, but I like to think of you picking a bunch of colourful blooms and bringing them into the house to arrange in a vase. I still want you here, Isobel. My love for you has deepened with your absence rather than lessened.

You'll have to forgive the ramblings of such an old man! But, in truth, I am not yet forty. You are so young. In some ways I wish you were older, or much better still, I were younger and we had met when we were both in the flush of youth.

I can tell from your letters that you are very busy on the farm and I admire you so much for the hard work you are doing. Everyone is under so much pressure these days and the end is not yet in sight in this dreadful war.

I look at your portrait every day, my dearest, and I would love to paint another. Would it be the most awful presumption on your mother to ask if I may visit again this Christmas? I know your beautiful home is now a military hospital and you are living in the lodge house, so I wouldn't presume to request accommodation but stay in a hotel nearby.

Or, you could visit me here in Flintshire! It would give me so much pleasure to welcome you and your dear mother into my home amongst the hills and waterfalls I love so much. I have ample room, in fact, I rattle around in the old place and it needs cheering up. I have plenty of staff, you would want for nothing and have all the luxury you so richly deserve. Please, dearest Isobel, do think about it, won't you? You've certainly earned a break and so has your mother and I would love nothing more than to provide it.

Isobel, it is now almost a year since I asked you to marry me. I promise I would not press you for *an answer to THAT question, unless you invited me to ask it again.*

> *God keep you safe, my dear.*
> *With my fondest love always,*
> *Geraint Lloyd."*

Isobel looked up from the page that had held her spellbound with its contrasting images of dockside industry and waterfalls and warm comfort and – love. She let the fine paper fall into her lap and stared at the flames dancing in the grate. Geraint offered all they needed – protection, comfort, security, freedom from debt, kindness, beauty, culture, travel – she could have all of this and more, anything she ever wanted. Didn't she owe it to her mother to accept? It's what Granny would have told her to do and in no uncertain terms. And Granny had made her promise she would before she died.

The door opened and Cassandra came in with a tray bearing two mugs. They had dispensed with bone china some time ago after several accidents washing them up by hand in the stone sink.

"Here you are, darling. Sorry I've been ages. Couldn't find the cocoa tin."

Isobel smiled at her mother's white lie. Cassandra had the kitchen laid out with military precision. "Thanks, Mummy. I could do with a hot drink."

"Yes, dismal day, isn't it?"

Isobel took the mug from the tray and curled her cold fingers around its white ceramic curves. She blew on the steam spiralling up from its brown surface, watching the vapour disappear in front of the bright flames in the fireplace.

"Penny for them?" Cassandra sat down in the fireside chair opposite Isobel's.

"Oh, nothing. I've had a letter from Geraint, that's all. There's a lovely painting of a wildflower meadow. Made me think about the glories of summer."

Isobel got up and fetched the painting from the windowsill. "Here, have a look. It's really very good."

Cassandra put her mug down carefully on the little table next to her. "Oh, my word, darling, it's beautiful! You can almost smell those flowers, can't you?"

"Yes, yes, you can." Isobel returned to her seat.

"I must say, Geraint is very talented. Such a nice man, too."

"Yes."

"What is his news? Has he been able to keep the factories going after that awful bombing?"

Isobel sipped her cocoa, measuring her reply. "Yes, I think so. Here, you can read the first page. He writes almost as well as he paints."

Cassandra took the elegant sheet from her. "Is there anything he can't do?"

Isobel tried to join in with her mother's laughter but failed miserably.

"Isobel, do you mind me asking...oh, bother! That ruddy telephone never stops." Cassandra got up and went to answer its shrill command. Isobel could hear her voice coming from the hall. "Yes, hello, doctor. No, it's no trouble. Always glad to help."

Isobel quietly got up and shut the door on the conversation. Left alone, she picked up the smaller envelope. It was a wonder it had reached West Lodge, her name and address had been scribbled in such haste.

"Hello gorgeous!"

Al certainly had a more informal style than Geraint. Isobel smiled and read on.

"Talk about hectic here in the ATA! The aerodrome is busier than ever with new raw recruits arriving every day and I'm proud to announce I'm now one of

them! Yes, I have finally been up in the air. It's the best feeling, Bella. I knew I'd love it and I do! There's never a dull moment, I can tell you. I'm still living out in the sticks in those same awful digs I was telling you about but once I get my wings, I'll be up and away and staying all over the place, delivering planes and pilots to other aerodromes.

I won't say it's not tough, the training, because it is. You have to really concentrate. In fact, I've just been 'gribbleised'. What's that you say? Well, Captain Gribbs teaches the three-week course in engines and technical aeronautics. He was in the BOAC before the war, you know, and really knows his stuff.

There's more than a hundred of us trainees taking off and landing at White Waltham every day, it's a wonder we don't bump into each other! Quite a few of the pilots are women and they get treated just the same as the men. Some of them are very glamorous, despite the hard work and the hours, and it's so impressive how they just get on with it, same as the blokes. You never hear anyone complain and there's always someone cracking a joke, even when things get a bit hairy. We have a fine old time in the pub when we get the chance, which isn't as often as I would like!

I'm hoping to pass out to a Class I pilot next week. That means I can fly light, single-engine aircraft and I'll get straight on to operational practice in a Ferry Pool somewhere. Real flying, Bella!

Oh, must go, Miriam is here and we're off to the pub.

How are you? Hope all's well.
Must dash, all my love,
Al. xxx

All his love? How much love was he giving this Miriam person? Isobel screwed up Al's letter and threw it in the fire.

CHAPTER FORTY FIVE
NORMANDY
DECEMBER 1941

Lottie nestled her head against the flank of the oldest goat and squeezed its tired udders. Poor old thing. Bernadette insisted the nanny-goat could withstand another pregnancy next year, but it seemed cruel to Lottie. The ancient animal stood patiently while Lottie milked her. They were both used to the routine. Lottie was glad of the evening quiet in the barn, the glow of the paraffin lamp and the soft, soothing patter of rain against the one window. Despite the calm hush, she didn't feel truly tranquil, she never did these days. How could she, living in a foreign country occupied by a malevolent army? How could anyone? At least that gun didn't reside under her floorboard anymore. She shuddered as she remembered her terror when she had taken the revolver to the mill last month.

Jean Everard had forgotten to flirt with her, he was so nervous. His flour-caked hands shook when she handed over the lumpy parcel, still wrapped in Madame Leroy's tea-towel, once pristine, now dusty from the attic floorboards.

Lottie had never been so glad to get rid of anything in her life.

"Did you have to go through a checkpoint this time?" Jean had said, his black eyes wide.

"Not this time, Jean. There seem to be less of them about nowadays."

Jean grunted. "All the young Boche have gone to Russia and bloody good riddance. God help them. Toughest place on earth. The Russian winter will kill most of them. Ah well, maybe it'll spare us more bloodshed."

"Ah! So that's why the few soldiers I do meet now are much older?"

Jean looked at her pityingly. "Of course!" He licked his lips. They looked very dry.

Lottie supposed it was all the dust from flour grinding. "Well, it gives us more of a chance, doesn't it, especially now the Communists have joined the resistance?"

"Hmm, I wouldn't trust those bastards any more than the Boche."

Lottie had no answer for this. She'd long since given up trying to understand the ins and outs of local politics. "I must go."

Jean nodded, his face serious. "Be careful, little one. Did you hear about the arrests in Caen?"

Lottie shook her head.

"Fifteen of our friends have been arrested and imprisoned. They await trial but it won't be conducted until May, I've heard."

"Fifteen?"

"Yes, it's destroyed the network."

"Did anyone get away?" Lottie didn't dare ask if Thierry was one of them, in case he wasn't.

"Some, I won't give their names."

"Of course." She had to know more. "But, Jean, no-one really local?"

To her intense relief he shook his head in denial. "Not as far as I know, but my God – fifteen! Pray they don't talk."

"I will."

A whole month had passed since then and no word from Thierry. After seeing him at the school that time when he'd given her the little piece of chalk – she'd still not found the courage to daub a 'V' sign anywhere – she'd expected him to march into the barn one day with a new dangerous mission for her.

But there had been nothing. In desperation, she'd cycled into the village, but she couldn't reach the school. The road to the village was swarming with soldiers on some huge exercise; she couldn't get past them and had to turn back.

A few days later, Bernadette brought back a newspaper from the market in Caen.

"I thought you should read this."

"But, Bernadette, you never buy a paper." Lottie took it from her, dreading what might be inside.

Lottie gasped out loud as she opened the pages and read the stark headline. Thirteen people had been executed on the fifteenth of December in Caen, including the journalist, Lucien Sempaix, who had written for "l'Humanité", the newspaper the communists illegally printed. Oh, if only she knew he was alright! If only she could have got to the village the other day. Lottie sat down on the chair by the fire and stared silently into the flames.

Bernadette gave her a hard stare. "I know, it's barbaric. You must be very careful."

Lottie returned her gaze, wondering if Bernadette knew everything she got up to. She opened her mouth to speak but Bernadette put her arthritic finger to her mouth and shook her head in warning.

"Not out loud, you know?"

Lottie nodded and folded up the newspaper. Much as she longed to get on her bicycle and pedal to the village for news, she knew she must sit tight and wait, however frustrating it was and however anxious she was to find out what might have happened.

Bernadette changed the subject. "We must prepare the farm for the coming winter and mend the barn roof. If we get another winter like last year, it'll not hold the weight of snow."

She and Lottie – mostly Lottie – had spent many a freezing hour up the ladder since then, resetting the slates that had slipped or replacing those that had cracked. The goats appreciated it and so did Lottie without the drip, drip of rain coming through.

The goat's udder ran dry. Lottie withdrew the bucket and put its wooden lid on top, carefully placing the tin pail against the wall by the door. She patted the goat. "Well done, old girl. Don't worry, I'll look out for you." The goat whinnied back.

Lottie pulled down the hay bundle so the goat could reach it. "Here you are."

The animal snatched at the fragrant hay and Lottie caught a whiff of summer, now past and gone. It was surprising how used she'd got to the rhythm of the farm and its seasons, how she felt more at home in France these days and thought less and less about her old home in Wiltshire. She tried to picture Cheadle Manor, shocked to find she couldn't remember little details anymore. Would she ever see it again? Would she even reach her twenty-fifth birthday and be able to claim her inheritance and go home? When would this war, this incarceration, this exile, end?

Isobel and Al must be involved in the fight by now. Where were they? Was Al up in the sky, dropping bombs on Germany, or a foot soldier, preparing to fight somewhere? Maybe he was on a boat in the Atlantic? And Isobel? What would she be doing? Her sister was young yet and would only just be finishing school this coming summer. At least that meant she would be safe, that's if she had stayed on for the sixth form. Lottie smiled, her gentle sister had never been academic, maybe she had left school already and was training to be a nurse or something? Oh, if only she knew.

She pulled her stool over to the next goat and wiped her udders clean before settling down to milk her. She was annoyed to hear the door scrape open, disturbing her peace. The light from the oil lamp flickered in the draught and a shadow cast darkness across her hands.

She looked up and saw Thierry Thibault standing in the doorway.

"Shut the door quickly!" Lottie frowned at him.

Thierry closed the door silently and came towards her, his expression inscrutable. Lottie swivelled round on her stool and stood up to greet him.

Thierry took off his beret and shook the raindrops from it. "I have a favour to ask."

"And good evening to you too."

Thierry gave a brief smile. "Excuse my lack of manners. I have something here which makes me a little nervous."

Lottie looked at him. "Have you more papers for me to deliver?"

"Not papers, something a little larger." Thierry turned around so she could see the big haversack on his back.

"What on earth is that? Thierry, I hope it's not another gun. I was terrified hoarding that revolver here."

"I'm afraid it's two guns and something less murderous that could also bring danger."

"Oh no. I hated hiding that revolver. What is the other thing?" Lottie watched as Thierry heaved the burden from his back and laid it down on the straw covered floor.

He opened the haversack and withdrew two rifles which he laid down on the floor with a pack of bullets for each.

Lottie felt a chill just looking at them. "Are they German? Did you kill a soldier to get them?"

Thierry shook his head. "No, things haven't gone that far – yet. These are left over from the last war, but they can still fire a bullet in a straight line. We have to take what we can."

The rifles looked convincingly lethal to Lottie. They were long and slim, made of wood and metal. She could see they were old and worn but had been well looked after. She hoped she'd never have to fire one.

Thierry undid the other straps of the haversack and pulled the fabric down to expose a radio.

"A radio?" Lottie hadn't expected that.

"Yes, it's mine. The Boche raided the school, they'd seen some, um, friends gathering at the time of the BBC broadcast and got suspicious. I've been really careful, so I think some collaborator must have betrayed me. You wouldn't believe how people will suck up to the Germans to get a few favours. It makes me sick. I have an idea who it is, but I can't prove it. I know if I carry on it's just a question of time before our little group is discovered, just like the network was, and it won't just be me that will be punished."

"Oh, Thierry, who told them?"

"I'm not going to say until I'm certain. Best not. It's the same with people on our side, the less you know, the better."

"I understand. You were lucky they didn't find the radio. You must have hidden it very well." Lottie looked at the square Bakelite box.

Thierry nodded. He stuffed his black beret in his pocket. "They turfed out everything in the school, inside and out. They even went in the basement but thank God, they didn't look behind the boiler."

"Were the children there?"

"No, which is another thing to be thankful for. It was in the evening – just when Radio Londres send their personal messages, of course - and the children had all gone home and thank God I wasn't listening in that night. I had marking to catch up on and was in my apartment upstairs."

"And they didn't beat you up this time?" Lottie looked at him more closely in the lamplight.

"No, not this time. They had nothing on me. I suppose they thought roughing up the school was enough."

"Were these guns at your place when they raided it?"

Thierry shook his head. "Thankfully, no. I picked them up from somebody on the way here tonight."

Lottie looked at the rifles on the floor and shivered. "What a horrible experience."

Thierry ran his hands through his hair. "War is horrible, didn't you know?

"My parents both fought in the last one. I have no illusions."

He frowned. "Just as well. You've heard about the executions and arrests in Caen? It's ruined our communications system. The network is decimated."

"Yes, it's shocking. I couldn't believe it at first when I read it in the papers. But we must carry on, mustn't we? Tell me, what am I to do with these things?"

He gave her a brief smile, acknowledging her acceptance. "The Free French are encouraging people to get together to listen to the Radio Londres broadcasts. Can you house the radio here? This farm is ideal. It is isolated and small. No-one would suspect anything."

"But who would come?"

"I will put the word out."

"Must I hide it?"

"That's for you to decide. Just stash it somewhere safe for now. It's not illegal to own one but it is vital no-one knows you're tuning in to Radio Londres. We need someone to listen every night and jot down any relevant messages. I will return and help you to set it up."

"But what about Bernadette?"

"I'm sure you can think of something." That smile again.

Listening to the radio was one thing and she was sure she could persuade the others to allow it in the house somehow. Lottie looked doubtfully at the guns. They were big items to sneak past her adopted grandmother and hiding them was not something she could persuade anyone was a good idea.

"Alright. I'll do it."

Thierry came over and grabbed her hands, squeezing them tight. "Thank you, thank you so much. I know what I am asking." He slipped the haversack off the radio and slung it on his back and replaced his hat.

"Goodbye, Charlotte. I am glad you are one of us. I will return as soon as I can."

Then he was gone.

Lottie finished milking the goat with shaking fingers, glancing at the door every few seconds to check no-one was going to come in and find the radio or the guns, now hidden under her coat behind the door. She'd rather be cold than caught.

As soon as she had put the milk away, she came back to the barn. She picked up the radio, it wasn't as heavy as she'd expected. Gripping it under one arm, she clambered up the ladder and nestled it under the hay, at the very back of the rafters, covered in some sacking. She replaced the hay, satisfied no-one would guess the radio was underneath and descended the ladder. But where to hide the guns? Rifles wouldn't fit under the floorboards of her attic bedroom. So, if not at the top of the house, why not at the bottom?

Lottie slipped off her jumper and put her coat back on over her shirt. She wrapped the rifles in the woollen pullover, but the barrels still showed below. Her coat was only just long enough to cover them. Feeling like a thief in the night, she crept into the farmhouse. Françoise was upstairs putting Bertrand to bed and Bernadette sat by the fire, knitting.

"Is that you?"

"Yes, Bernadette. I'm just popping down to the cellar for some more..." For a panicky moment Lottie couldn't think what she could possibly want from the store downstairs. "Um, more apples for the goats, they're looking hungry."

"Strange time to do it."

"I know, but the yield is down."

"Always is this time of year. A few apples won't make much difference." Bernadette looked up from her knitting needles. "Why are you holding your jumper like that?"

"I...I thought I could carry the apples in it."

407

Bernadette's sharp eyes narrowed as she studied Lottie's face across the narrow hallway. She looked at the bundle in Lottie's arms and then straight into her eyes. The old woman gave an infinitesimal nod and turned her gaze back to her knitting. Lottie didn't feel she could move until the needles clacked together again.

Letting out her breath, she lit a candle from the recess in the wall, kept there for the purpose as there was no electricity below, and descended the uneven stone steps to the cellar. The rifles were heavy for just one arm to hold and awkwardly banged against her thigh. Beads of perspiration broke out under her hairline and her heart began to beat uncomfortably fast.

The apples stood separately in lines along one wall in the cellar. No hiding place there. Lottie lifted the candle to see better. Shelves of cheeses gave off their pungent smell opposite the apples. That wouldn't do either.

Lottie jumped so high when Bernadette spoke behind her, she hit her head on the low ceiling. She hadn't heard her come down the stone stairs. "Here, child. I'll show you where to hide your secret."

"Bernadette!" Lottie clutched her uncomfortable burden to her chest, bruising her breasts as she did so.

"I may be old, but I'm not a fool. What is it?"

Lottie lifted the wool and revealed the rifles.

Bernadette drew in her breath sharply. "Who gave you these? No, don't tell me, I don't want to know. Come here, there's a hidden cache, where I keep the calvados. No-one but me knows it's there."

Bernadette went over to some barrels of cider in the corner. Using all her weight, she gripped the middle one and started to shift it, bit by bit, from its position.

"Here, let me help you." Lottie put down the guns and went to assist her.

Together, they rocked the barrel from side to side until it was in front of the other two. Lottie looked at the floor. She could just make out a faint crack in the dust.

Bernadette knelt down and felt around in the dirt. She flicked away the earth and revealed a circular handle inset into what Lottie could now see was a wooden trapdoor.

"Bring the candle closer." Bernadette lifted the hatch and Lottie held the candle aloft. To her astonishment, she could see a rough wooden ladder descending into what looked like another cellar, smaller than the one above but still a reasonable size.

"Are you going to go down, or do you want me to do it?" Bernadette squinted back up at her.

"I'll do it." Lottie lowered herself down the ladder and held out her arms.

Bernadette leaned in, holding the candle so that she could see, before placing it on the first step. She disappeared for a moment, then came back with the first rifle and gave it to Lottie. Lottie balanced it against her chest with one hand and gradually reached the bottom, another earth floor. She looked around. There were crates and bottles neatly stacked against the far wall.

"Where should I put it, Bernadette?"

"See that big crate?" Bernadette pointed to the farthest corner.

Lottie strained her eyes in the half light. "Yes, I can see it."

"Lift the lid."

Lottie put the gun down, went over to the crate and prised the heavy lid from its wooden base. It was full of kegs of brandy, all neatly labelled. The dates were very old, some from before the last war. Gingerly, she separated the line of kegs at the back, so as to make a space big enough.

"That's good. Now put the rifle in."

Lottie nestled the rifle in place. "I think we should cover it over with something. Is there an empty keg somewhere?"

"Good idea. I'll fetch one." The candle flickered as Bernadette turned away with a swish of her skirt. Lottie was terrified the little flame would go out and plunge her into absolute blackness. She could smell the earth all around her; it made her feel claustrophobic, trapped.

"Here, grab this." Bernadette leant over the ladder and held a wooden keg out to her, narrowly avoiding the naked flame of the candle.

Lottie reached out and took it, and quickly inverted the keg over the rifle, glad to disguise its alien shape amongst the stash of old alcohol. Bernadette passed down the second gun and Lottie placed it under the keg next to its twin. She pulled out the boxes of bullets from her coat pockets and shoved them down between the two guns, glad to be relieved of their weight. Then she lowered the lid of the crate and blew away her tell-tale fingerprints in the dust.

Lottie was at the foot of the ladder in two strides and climbed up it, grabbed the candle and regained the floor of the cellar with indecent haste.

She stood aside as Bernadette lowered the trap door back down. Silently, they pushed the barrel back over it.

Bernadette scuffed her shoes in the loose earth around the wooden barrels. "Good, no-one will know we've been down there."

Lottie didn't point out that Bernadette hadn't been down in that hellhole at all, only herself. All she could think about was getting up into the fresh air again. They carried a candle each up the stone staircase to the hall.

Françoise was in the kitchen, warming her hands on the fire. "Where have you two been?"

"To get this." Bernadette held up a bottle of calvados and cracked her lined face into a rare, wonderful smile.

The next morning, Lottie tried to talk to Bernadette about the guns in the cellar.

"Leave it. Best we don't discuss it. Just forget they're there, is my advice."

410

"But…" Lottie was desperate to at least say thank you to her grumpy hostess.

"I said, leave it!"

It was a whole week, each day filled with anxiety for Lottie, before Thierry finally came to relieve her fears. The short December days were quickly over and the hours of darkness had become unbearably long.

Lottie found it hard to sleep, knowing that her secret horde in the hidden cellar could send them all to a labour camp, knowing that Bernadette was also compromised. Every night she speculated on Bernadette's cooperation. Was she also part of the Resistance – perhaps in a different cell? Would she have helped if she'd known it was the hated schoolteacher – the disrupter of tradition, the man who opened children's minds so much they left her beloved countryside? Or did she, like Lottie, simply hate this German occupation? She knew the Boche never came near their isolated farm, but the thought of what would happen if they did was another reason she kept awake in the endless cold nights.

She was just picking up the pails of milk one evening, having settled the goats with more hay, when Thierry slipped inside the barn. He looked excited.

"I'm so glad to see you, Thierry! Have you come about the guns?"

He put his finger to his lips. "Don't say that out loud."

"Surely no-one can hear us here?"

"Can't be sure of anything anymore. Are they safe?" He looked around the barn as if expecting the guns to be where he had left them.

"They are well hidden."

"Good, and the radio?"

"I will get it for you. I've stashed it up in the rafters of the barn." She went to climb the ladder, but Thierry stayed her with his hand. He still looked excited.

"What is it?" Lottie couldn't understand his expression. He looked like Christmas had come early. "Thierry, what has happened?"

"Haven't you heard the news?"

Lottie turned around, her hand still on the rungs of the ladder. "The radio isn't working yet! What news?"

"The Americans are in!"

"In what?"

"This damn war. Japan has attacked their ships at Pearl Harbour and the United States has declared war against the Axis powers! Finally, we've got more allies, ones with great wealth and resources."

Lottie stood very still. "Thierry, do you think, can it really mean, that we might *win*? That this nightmare could soon be over?"

Thierry stared at her for a long moment. Slowly, a wide smile spread across his face. "It just might."

Before she had time to think, Lottie rushed over to him. Thierry held out his arms and wrapped them around her, crushing her face against his wet coat. The buttons pressed into her cheek, but she didn't notice. Lottie raised her head. Thierry bent his and kissed her. A flame spread throughout her cold, tired body and set it alight.

She kissed him back and all thoughts of war vanished.

TO BE CONTINUED...

The sixth and final book, *Ivy*, concludes The Katherine Wheel Series in the most satisfying and surprising way, bringing the characters from *Daffodils*, the first book in the series, full circle.

The Katherine Wheel Series

"Excellent novels with a well rounded and strong central female character. You do need to read all the books, but they are all good so go for it and enjoy."

Daffodils is also available as an AUDIOBOOK Narrated by the author

Book One of The Katherine Wheel Series

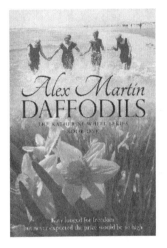

Katy dreams of a better life than just being a domestic servant at Cheadle Manor. Her one attempt to escape is thwarted when her flirtation with the manor's heir results in a scandal that shocks the local community.

Jem Beagle has always loved Katy. His offer of marriage rescues her, but personal tragedy divides them. Jem leaves his beloved Wiltshire to become a reluctant soldier on the battlefields of World War One. Katy is left behind, restless and alone.

Lionel White, just returned from being a missionary in India, brings a dash of colour to the small village, and offers Katy a window on the wider world.

Katy decides she has to play her part in the global struggle and joins the war effort as a WAAC girl.

She finally breaks free from the stifling Edwardian hierarchies that bind her but the brutality of global war brings home the price she has paid for her search.

"Impressively well-researched and vividly imagined."

"A fantastic story which was written beautifully. I have not read many books based around WW1 and this was just right. The characters have some hard times and I found myself in tears at times, but overall, the story was told in a way I could relate to and understand. Highly recommended for fans of historical fiction."

"Probably one of the best books I've read of this genre. Took me to the First World War as never before. Will certainly read the second with great anticipation. Only chose it because of the price and picture on the front but what a find and such a treat !!!"

"Daffodils is an extraordinary story of commitment and enduring hope which teaches us the power of resilience, integrity and true honor. This book was a deeply emotional experience that managed to reach the inner core of my being. This is such a powerful story! Highly recommended."

Daffodils is also available as an audio book, narrated by the author

Book Two of The Katherine Wheel Series

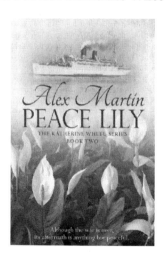

Although the war is over, its aftermath is anything but peaceful

After the appalling losses suffered during World War One, three of its survivors long for peace, unaware that its aftermath will bring different, but still daunting, challenges.

Katy trained as a mechanic during the war and cannot bear to return to the life of drudgery she left behind. A trip to America provides the dream ticket she has always craved and an opportunity to escape the straitjacket of her working-class roots. She jumps at the chance, little realising that it will change her life forever, but not in the way she'd hoped.

Jem lost not only an arm in the war, but also his livelihood, and with it, his self-esteem. How can he keep restless Katy at home and provide for his wife? He puts his life at risk a second time, attempting to secure their future and prove his love for her.

Cassandra has fallen deeply in love with Douglas Flintock, an American officer she met while driving ambulances at the Front. How can she persuade this modern American to adapt to her English country way of life, and all the duties that come with inheriting Cheadle Manor? When Douglas returns to Boston, unsure of his feelings, Cassandra crosses the ocean, determined to lure him back.

As they each try to carve out new lives, their struggles impact on each other in unforeseen ways.

"Daffodils' sequel Peace Lily is as enthralling and fresh as its predecessor."

"Great follow on book. Couldn't put down till finished."

Book Three of The Katherine Wheel Series

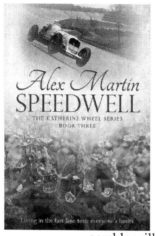

Living in the fast lane tests everyone's limits

Katy and Jem enter the 1920's with their future in the balance. How can they possibly make their new enterprise work? They must risk everything, including disaster, and trust their gamble will pay off. Cassandra, juggling the demands of a young family, aging parents and running Cheadle Manor, distrusts the speed of the modern age, but Douglas races to meet the new era, revelling in the freedom of the open road.

Can each marriage survive the strain the new dynamic decade imposes? Or will the love they share deepen and carry them through? They all arrive at destinies that surprise them in Speedwell, the third book in the Katherine Wheel Series.

"I really enjoyed the stories. Read all three books in the series while on holiday. Her writing style makes for comfortable reading. Her characters are credible and in the main her story lines are unpredictable and powerfully descriptive."

"A fascinating set of characters weave their magical story through a daring enterprise just after the end of the Great War. The story travels from humble but daring beginnings in a small Wiltshire village with Katy and Jem and takes us to Boston in the USA and back."

Book Four of The Katherine Wheel Series

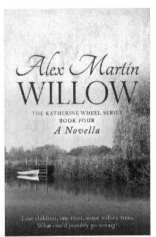

Willow is a short novella that bridges the generational gap. Book Four in The Katherine Wheel Series may be small, but it packs in many surprises for the children of Katy and Jem, and Douglas and Cassandra.

"This is a very well written and descriptive novella with the children and the idyllic countryside setting, well observed and portrayed. You feel you are there experiencing it first-hand. It draws you into a totally believable world, perfect material for a film or a Sunday evening drama series."

"This tale brings to life their distinctive well-rounded characters; the dialogue distinguishes each child's voice and fits exactly into the era it represents. The descriptive narrative sets the scene perfectly and moves the plot along in gripping speed."

The stifling heat of a midsummer's day lures four children to the cool green waters of the river that runs between Cheadle Manor and The Katherine Wheel Garage.
Al captains the little band of pirates as they blithely board the wooden dinghy. Headstrong Lottie vies with him to be in charge while Isobel tries to keep the peace and look after little Lily.

But it is the river that is really in control.

Lost and alone, the four children must face many dangers, but it is the unforeseen consequences of their innocent adventure that will shape their futures for years to come.

418

Book Five of The Katherine Wheel Series

*Two sisters, divided by love and war, must
each fight a different battle to survive*

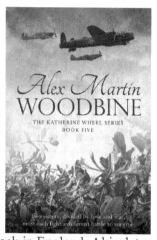

Lottie, her sister Isobel
and Al, the man they both
love, are on the brink of
adulthood and the Second
World War in Woodbine,
the fifth book in The
Katherine Wheel Series.
Trapped and alone in
occupied France, Lottie
must disguise her identity
and avoid capture if she is
to   return and heal the bitter
feud over the future of
Cheadle Manor.

Back in England, Al is determined to prove himself. He
joins the Air Transport Auxiliary service, flying
aeroplanes to RAF bases all over the country.
Isobel defies everyone's expectations by becoming a Land
Girl. Bound by a promise to a dying woman, she struggles
to break free and follow her heart.

"Great story - this is a real family saga through the important milestones of the 20th Century. It's all here. Love, hate, life, death, war and peace. Woodbine takes us through the second world war with real insight into people's lives. I especially enjoyed Lottie's time in France and the scenes in the Normandy farmhouse are very evocative. Looking forward to the next, and final, chapter to see how everything comes together."

"Woodbine is fifth book of the brilliant Katherine Wheel series and, having read and enjoyed all four of the previous books I was looking forward to this one. I was not disappointed; Alex Martin has once again brought to life the characters that I followed all that time and, I have to say, I've been riveted by the historic detail to the background of the stories. It is obvious that the author researches extensively to portray the atmosphere of each era – and succeeds again with Woodbine."

"This is Book 5 in the series and carries on with the next generation of Katy and Cassandra, both ladies from different spectrum of the social classes have a deep and abiding friendship. Now their children are grown and are now encountering WWII. Surprises of inheritance, a love triangle, and the turmoil of a world war. I've read all the previous books and would advise a reader to start with the first book so that they get the full impact of these two families. Well written, well researched."

IVY

Book Six in The Katherine Wheel Series

Two sisters, each caught in a trap in World War Two, must escape to find their true destiny

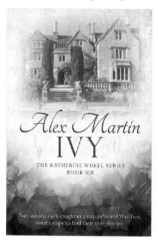

All the disparate threads of this epic saga are seamlessly woven together in Ivy, the sixth and final book in The Katherine Wheel Series.

Drawn into the Resistance in Occupied France, Lottie's strengths and endurance are tested to the limit.

Home-loving Isobel, torn between love and duty, must set herself free if she is ever to find happiness.

Flying planes for the Air Transport Auxiliary frequently puts Al in danger but securing the woman he loves proves much more challenging.

Cheadle Manor once lay at the heart of the lives of Lottie, Isobel and Al, but World War Two has broken every bond tying them to their safe haven. Can they ever come home and be together again?

"5.0 out of 5 stars A majestic Series finale: a perfectly paced drama, full of tension, mystery, I love this beautifully woven story of Ivy, the impressive conclusion of the Katherine Wheel Series. It is so easy to visualise how it could have felt being Lottie in wartime occupied France. She has to draw on her huge courage to face some very scary exploits, whilst her friends there also

risked their lives to help bring freedom to Europe. It's such a satisfying read, as the array of interesting characters pull us into into life from their perspective in France as well as rural England through their own adventures. Gripping at times, I really wanted to know how things would turn out for everyone - the families and friends in Wiltshire, her friends in France - and especially Lottie herself. The ending is excellent!
romance and compassion."

Alex Martin's debut book is based on her grape picking adventure in France in the 1980's. It's more of a mystery/ thriller than historical fiction but makes for great holiday reading with all the sensuous joys of that beautiful country.

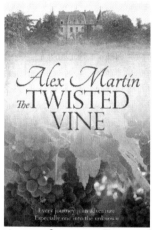

Every journey is an adventure. Especially one into the unknown.

The shocking discovery of her lover with someone else propels Roxanne into escaping to France and seeking work as a grape-picker. She's never been abroad before and certainly never travelled alone.

Opportunistic loner, Armand, exploits her vulnerability when they meet by chance. She didn't think she would see him again or be the one who exposes his terrible crime.

Join Roxanne on her journey of self-discovery, love and tragedy in rural France. Taste the wine, feel the sun, drive through the Provencal mountains with her, as her courage and resourcefulness are tested to the limit.

The Twisted Vine is set in the heart of France and is a deeply romantic but suspenseful tale. Roxanne Rudge escapes her cheating boyfriend by going grape picking in France. She feels vulnerable and alone in such a big country where she can't speak the language and is befriended by Armand le Clair, a handsome Frenchman. Armand is not all he seems, however, and she discovers a darker side to him before uncovering a dreadful secret. She is aided and abetted by three new friends she has made, charming posh Peter, a gifted linguist; the beautiful and vivacious Italian, Yvane; and clever Henry of the deep brown eyes with the voice to match. Together they unravel a mystery centred around a beautiful chateau and play a part in its future.

"The original setting of this novel and the beauty of colorful places that Roxanne visits really drew me in. This book was a lot more than I'd expected, because aside from the romantic aspect, there's a great deal of humor, fantastic friendship, and entertaining dialogue. I strongly recommend this book to anyone who likes women's fiction."

"This is a wonderful tale told with compassion, emotion, thrills and excitement and some unexpected turns along the way. Oh, and there may be the smattering of a romance in there as well! Absolutely superb."

The Rose Trail is a time slip story set in both the English Civil War and the present day woven together by a supernatural thread.

Is it chance that brings Fay and Persephone together? Or is it the restless and malevolent spirit who stalks them both? Once rivals, they must now unite if they are to survive the mysterious trail of roses they are forced to follow into a dangerous, war torn past.

"The past has been well researched although I don't know a lot about this period in history it all rings so true – the characters are fantastic with traits that you like and dislike which also applies to the 'present' characters who have their own issues to contend with as well as being able to connect with the past."

"A combination of love, tragedies, friendships, past and present, lashings of historical aspects, religious bias, controlling natures all combined with the supernatural give this novel a wonderful page-turning quality."

" I loved this book, the storyline greatly appealed to me and the history it contained. Fay has always been able to see spirits. The love of her life is Robin, whom she met when she was 11 at school. She trains to become an accountant and purely by chance meets up with an old school friend. The book develops into an enthralling adventure for them both as they slip back and forth in time."

All Alex Martin's stories are available as ebooks as well as paperbacks and make great gifts!

Alex writes about her work on her blog at
www.intheplottingshed.com
where you can get your FREE copy of Alex Martin's short story collection, 'Trio', by clicking on the picture of the shed.

Constructive reviews oil a writer's wheel like nothing else and are very much appreciated on Amazon or Goodreads or anywhere else!

Alex Martin, Author

Facebook page:
https://www.facebook.com/TheKatherineWheel/
Twitter handle: https://twitter.com/alex_martin8586
Email: alexxx8586@gmail.com